To Have and To Hold

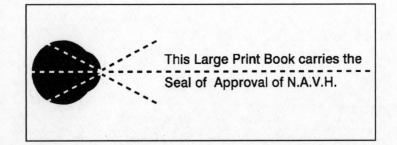

This Large Print Book carries the
Seal of Approval of N.A.V.H.

BRIDAL VEIL ISLAND, BOOK 1

To Have and To Hold

Tracie Peterson
and Judith Miller

THORNDIKE PRESS
A part of Gale, Cengage Learning

GALE
CENGAGE Learning

Detroit • New York • San Francisco • New Haven, Conn • Waterville, Maine • London

GALE
CENGAGE Learning™

LIBRARY OF CONGRESS CATALOGING-IN-PUBLICATION DATA

Peterson, Tracie.
    To have and to hold / by Tracie Peterson and Judith Miller.
        p. cm. — (Thorndike Press large print christian fiction)
    (Bridal Veil Island)
    ISBN-13: 978-1-4104-4062-4 (hardcover)
    ISBN-10: 1-4104-4062-1 (hardcover)
    1. Fathers and daughters—Fiction. 2. Islands—Georgia—Fiction. 3. Real estate development—Fiction. 4. Contractors—Fiction. 5. Large type books. I. Miller, Judith, 1944– II. Title.
    PS3566.E7717T625 2011b
    813'.54—dc23   2011033203

Published in 2011 by arrangement with Bethany House Publishers, a division of Baker Publishing Group.

Printed in the United States of America
1 2 3 4 5 6 7 15 14 13 12 11

To Lorna Seilstad

For your prayers, encouragement, and steadfast friendship during this difficult time. You have blessed my life.

With a grateful heart,

~Judy

CHAPTER 1

Bridal Veil Island, Georgia
Late August 1886

Audrey Cunningham knew that look. The wrinkled brow, the furrowed crevices around the lips, the eyebrows dropped low above gunmetal gray eyes — the look her father displayed when trouble loomed in their future.

She'd observed far too many of those worried expressions over the past months. And though she'd questioned her father on more than one occasion, he continually denied that anything was amiss. But not this morning. This morning, he motioned her toward the breakfast table and pointed to one of the spindle-back chairs. She settled on the cane seat and braced herself for the bad news that was sure to follow.

"We've got troubles." His shoulders hunched forward, and a thatch of dark hair that age and worry had peppered with strands of gray fell across his forehead. Even at fifty, his hair remained thick and unmanageable, much like Audrey's unruly coffee brown curls.

She pressed her spine against the hard wood of the hand-turned spindles, folded her hands into a tight knot, and waited.

Her father raked his fingers across his forehead and pushed the errant hair into place. "I've been keeping this from you for a while now. I thought I'd find a solution, but I guess the time has come that I've got to tell you."

When her father hesitated, Audrey leaned forward and reached for his hand. "What is it, Daddy?" Fear caused her to resort to the familiar moniker she'd used during her childhood.

Her father smiled and squeezed her hand. "Sounds strange to hear you call me Daddy. How long has it been since I've heard that word? Ten years?"

Audrey's thick curls bobbed against her pale cheeks. "Ten and a half." The day Audrey turned eighteen, she had declared the term far too childish. From that time forward, she'd addressed her father only as *Father* or *Dad.*

He stared at their entwined hands, and she feared he'd lost the courage to continue.

"Please, tell me what's happened. Together we can overcome any problem, can't we?" She forced a smile and hoped he wouldn't sense her fear. "We always have before."

After releasing her hand, he leaned back in the chair, his eyes clouded with defeat. "Not this time, Audrey. Even joining forces, we can't overcome this problem." He reached into the pocket of his blue chambray shirt and removed a folded envelope. After placing it on the table, he pressed the creases with his palm. "This is the delinquent tax statement on Bridal Fair and our remaining acreage." With a fleeting look of desperation, he pushed the envelope across the table and lifted his hand. "We don't have money enough to pay."

Audrey slipped her fingers inside the envelope and withdrew the contents. She rippled through the pieces of paper, carefully noting the amounts and dates on each of the pages. Her stomach tightened into a knot the size of a summer melon as she slowly grasped the truth. They'd been living there for only two years. These tax statements dated back to 1880. "Grandmother hadn't been paying the taxes? Did you know this before we left Pennsylvania?"

Moving to Bridal Veil Island hadn't been Audrey's idea. She'd been opposed to the return to Bridal Fair, the home her ancestors had constructed many years ago. She'd argued against the plan with great vigor. Remaining in Pittsburgh, where she could continue her work as a housekeeper's assistant and enjoy the company of her friends, had been her stated preference. Although her father hadn't articulated a plausible explanation for the move to the aging island home off the coast of Georgia, there had been no doubt he would not rest until Audrey agreed to his request. In the end, she'd been unable to deny his appeal. Now, faced with these tax statements, she silently wished she hadn't given in to his pleas.

"I won't lie to you, Audrey. I knew some money was owed. I just didn't know how much — not until after we'd already been here several months. I thought maybe we'd be able to —"

"Able to *what?*" All effort to remain calm vanished. "You've known for all this time, yet never said a word? How *could* you, Father?"

He bowed his head and cupped his face between his palms. "I thought it would all work out. Your grandmother was a close friend of the tax collector's wife. You know how things are in the South. Folks want to lend a helping hand."

Audrey shook her head. How did he expect her to know how things worked in Georgia? They'd left Bridal Veil Island when she was seven years old. She had a far better idea of how things worked in the North than in the South, but she doubted they'd be granted leniency on their taxes in either place.

"If so many folks want to lend a helping hand, why are you worried?" Though she didn't want to be unkind or disrespectful, Audrey's attempt to keep a civil tongue fell short. But her father's answer wasn't helpful in the least.

Lifting his head from between curved hands, her father met her eyes. "Not everyone is accommodating. Your grandmother's connection to the tax collector's wife helped keep a tax sale at bay — for her and for us. But the tax collector died a month ago, and a new fellow has taken over."

"And this new collector doesn't have any reason to be nice to us. Is that right?" Now she understood. Just like in Pittsburgh, it was *whom* one knew rather than *what* one knew. And whom one knew could maybe save one from having a tax-sale notice posted on the front door.

"That's pretty much the sum of it. I don't

11

even know a distant relative of the new fellow. We've been gone far too long to keep up with the necessary socializing. We're going to have to get to know folks over in Biscayne. Then maybe we can get this thing taken care of."

"Rather than socializing, maybe we need to figure out how we can pay the taxes. How long do we have?" Audrey's mind raced as she considered their options. Perhaps she could get a job in Biscayne. Leaving her father and Aunt Thora alone every day wouldn't be good, but right now there seemed to be no other choice. Given her father's physical condition, he couldn't take on construction work in Biscayne. It had been several months since he'd been able to work more than a day or two without having to recuperate for several days. Now the doctor said he shouldn't commit to any work — much less strenuous work. There weren't many options available. And over the past two years they'd depleted most of the funds from the sale of their home in Pittsburgh. This tax burden would be more than they could financially manage.

As if Audrey's thoughts had summoned Aunt Thora into the room, she plodded into the kitchen, her white hair askew.

She fanned herself with determined

strokes. "Land's sake, it's a warm one to-day."

"Good morning, Aunt Thora," Audrey and her father said in unison.

In truth, Thora wasn't related to the Cunninghams, nor was she aunt to anyone. She'd been Grandmother Cunningham's former companion and housekeeper of sorts. The housekeeping duties had fallen by the wayside as both of the women aged. When Lavinia Cunningham died two years earlier, there'd been no place for Thora to go, so Audrey's father invited the old woman to remain with them. Aunt Thora had appeared perplexed by the invitation.

In fact, she'd been quite clear in her response. "This here island is more my home than it is yours, Boyd Cunningham, and I don't have plans to go anywhere." Audrey's father didn't have a response for that.

Over the past two years, Aunt Thora had helped as much as possible, but she couldn't always be relied upon. Frequently her mind slipped into the past, and those lapses proved a challenge for both Audrey and her father. But when Thora was thinking clearly, she could be a fount of information. It was through her stories that Audrey came to know her grandmother and gained a better understanding of the Southern heart and mind.

Today Audrey wasn't certain if Aunt Thora was coherent or not. The old woman arched her thick white eyebrows and *tsk*ed. "You gonna get stuck paying them taxes, Boyd?"

"If we want to stay here, I don't see as I have much choice. 'Course figuring out how to pay them is the hard part."

Just like up North, the taxes on Bridal Fair and the surrounding acreage had continued to rise through the years. Though somewhat smaller than the plantation homes in Savannah, Bridal Fair was impressive enough to catch the eye of any tax collector eager to assess higher values on landholdings. The mansion hadn't been constructed to impress society, but its magnificent design couldn't be denied. Rather than brick, the mansion had been constructed of native wood with a row of pillars carved from local cypress to mimic the Classical Revival style preferred by her grandmother. When she'd been four years old, her grandparents had added a railing between the huge pillars to give the wraparound porch a more genteel appearance — at least that's what she'd been told several years later when she had questioned her grandmother. The structure remained an odd mixture of old and new, fancy and plain, yet, situated among the stand of live oaks, it appeared a perfect fit.

Aunt Thora eased onto one of the chairs and set her steely expression upon Audrey's father. "That was the hard part for your mother, too. She never did learn to manage this place after your father passed away. Would have been different if you'd been around to help her." The old woman shook her head. "Trying to keep things going by herself for all these years just didn't work." She leaned toward Audrey's father. "I know you did your best to help, Boyd, but your mother jest didn't know how to handle money. Instead of adding those newfangled bathing rooms and spending money like it was water, she should have been taking care to save what money was left from selling off the rest of the island afore your daddy died. 'Course, I know your mama done her best, God rest her soul. If it hadn't been for those Yankee soldiers, we'd still be fine and dandy."

Audrey cleared her throat. "The Yankees had nothing to do with Granny selling off most of the island, Aunt Thora."

The old woman pointed a gnarled finger at Audrey. "Them Yankees got everything to do with what's gone wrong in the South.

15

They came down here and tramped their boot prints of blood across our land." She shuddered. "The South will never be the same. Never!" Her pale blue eyes slowly glazed as she shook her head.

There was no doubt Aunt Thora's mind was slipping back in time. Hoping to hold her in the present, Audrey clapped her hands. "No need dwelling on the past. Father and I will worry about the taxes. You set your mind at ease, Aunt Thora."

The old woman stretched her hand across the table and patted the tax statement. "You need to summon up your Southern charm, Boyd. Go make friends with the tax collector. Ask him to come for a visit. I'll bake a jam cake." Her eyes sparkled as though she believed her jam cake could solve any problem.

Audrey's father grunted. "I don't think a jam cake is going to help. What I need is cash."

"Now, don't you go sounding like one of them Yankees who like nothing better than disregarding the importance of a cordial visit over a piece of jam cake and a cup of tea." Wisps of white hair fluttered as she shook her head. "Them Northerners grab hold of your heart while you were living up there among 'em? You need to remember your roots." She clucked her tongue and glanced back and forth between father and daughter. "Both of you!" She pushed up from the chair with a grunt. "You go ride yourself across the sound to Biscayne, and I'll start mixin' up the cake."

She seemed to think crossing the water to Biscayne was as simple as walking outside to sit on the front porch. Audrey might have commented had she not known it would do little good. Instead, she let her father calm the old woman.

"No need for a cake just yet, Thora. I sent a letter to the tax collector on the mail packet this morning and asked if I could have a couple more months. Let's wait until I hear back from him before you start heating up the oven."

Thora shook her head as if Father had just admitted to joining the Grand Ole Party. Aunt Thora would have just as soon shot members of the GOP as she would the Yankees. After all, most of the GOP *were* Yankees.

"That there is where you're makin' your mistake. Southerners like to talk face-to-face. Air out their differences in person. If you hadn't lived in Pittsburgh so long, you'd remember how we do business here. Land alive, but it's good you returned to your

17

roots afore you forgot everything your mama ever taught you."

Audrey's father grinned and folded the tax statement. "I'm sure I remember more than I've forgotten about living on this island. And it takes too much time and too much wood to fire up *Old Bessie*. Besides, that launch is on its last leg. Can't afford to fire her up for a trip that would probably prove useless. That tax collector is likely out pounding up tax-sale signs instead of sitting in his office."

"You got an answer for just about everything, don't ya? Well, you mark my words — there's nothing like a slice of jam cake and a cup of tea to convince a man." She tapped the gold band on her left finger with her fan. "I've got this here ring to prove it! Won over my Nathaniel with my jam cake — he liked it best with strawberry preserves." She leaned toward Audrey. "You need to be in the kitchen next time I make jam cake. Prob'ly why you're twenty-eight years old and never been married. You never learned to make jam cake, did ya?"

Audrey shook her head, amazed that the conversation had so quickly moved from delinquent taxes to jam cake and her marital status. "I've had my share of suitors. It's my own choice that I'm not wed." She'd unwittingly become defensive and was only adding fuel to Thora's burning embers.

"Ha! No woman wants to go through life without a helpmeet at her side. You need to read your Bible. Marriage is what God ordained. He said it weren't good for man to be alone, and He wasn't jest talkin' to hear himself. Man and woman working alongside each other to make it through the good and the bad times that be comin'. Just ask me. I don't know what I would have done without my Nathaniel to help me. Praise the Lord, your grandmother came to my aid a year after Nathaniel passed. But living without a husband ain't any kind of life for a woman your age. Why, you'll soon be too old to bear young'uns." She opened the fan again and looked away. "Although God didn't see fit to bless us with babies, He gave us each other, and that was enough."

A breeze carrying the scent of drying leaves fluttered through the open kitchen window, and Audrey peeked across the table at her father. Discussing childbearing years in front of him wasn't something she wanted to prolong. And from the heightened color in his cheeks, it didn't appear to be her father's favorite topic, either.

Trying to maintain her calm, Audrey

ignored the older woman. "Did the paper arrive with today's mail?" The launch that delivered mail to island dwellers came only three times a week, but no one complained. Most residents were simply pleased they didn't have to go to the mainland to pick up their mail. Besides, had they been required to make the trip, they likely would have gone only once a week, when they went to shop for groceries.

Her father looked up. "On the table in the hallway. Something special you're hoping to read?"

Audrey gave the old woman a sideways glance before she answered her father. "I thought I'd see if there were any advertisements for help wanted."

"I didn't have you quit your job in Pittsburgh to send you off to work for some family over in Biscayne. Where's the fairness in that?"

With a shrug, Audrey pushed up from her chair. "Life isn't always fair. If I recall, you told me that a long time ago. You and Aunt Thora can make do if I find work in town. I could come home on weekends if I found a position as a governess or housekeeper."

Even if she could find work in Biscayne, she'd need to work out an arrangement with the men who shuttled back and forth from the various nearby islands. Convincing them to let her ride might not be easy, either. The men took turns using their launches. They shared the burden of wear and tear on their boats and the cost of fuel to power them. To let her ride without using her father's launch would likely set a precedent the men wouldn't want, and using *Old Bessie* was out of the question — not that Audrey could man a launch.

"If them Yankees hadn't ravaged the soil when they come tromping through Georgia, things would be jest fine. I tell you, we're never gonna recover from what those uncivilized men did to us."

Audrey stepped back to the table and patted the old woman's shoulder. There was no reconciling Aunt Thora to the fact that not everything in life could be blamed on the War between the States.

"There were never any soldiers on Bridal Veil Island, but even if there had been, you need to remember that Father isn't a farmer. Good soil wouldn't be any more helpful than —" She stopped short. If she went ahead and said that good soil wouldn't be any more helpful than a jam cake, there'd be no end to Aunt Thora's ranting.

"I don't want my daughter going over and living in Biscayne. I want you here with me.

That was our plan from the start."

That much was certainly true. But those plans had been made when they thought they had amassed enough money to meet their needs. They'd sold their home in Pittsburgh and paid off the remaining balance on the bank loan, and her father said that with wise investing and a careful budget they could survive. But even with a frugal budget and her father's occasional work, there would never be enough to pay the back taxes.

Audrey returned to the chair opposite her father and sat down. She laced her fingers together and rested her hands in her lap. Finding a way to keep Bridal Fair wouldn't be easy. Though the Georgia coast was a mere two miles from their dock, it might as well have been two hundred miles. They were secluded from the rush and turmoil of life in a city, but their peace and quiet came at a very high price. A price Audrey feared they could no longer afford.

CHAPTER 2

Cup in hand, Boyd stared out the kitchen window at the beauty of his childhood home. He'd loved this island with its diverse terrain for all of his life. Whether he walked the beaches packed solid by the lapping waters of the Atlantic Ocean, the heavily thicketed woods filled with wildlife, the soft rolling hills along the eastern side of the island, or the marshes bordered by the Argosy River, he could feel the beauty of God's creation. Though visitors sometimes turned up their noses at the marshlands along the river side of the island, Boyd thought they possessed a special beauty all their own. He found pleasure standing on the dock as the lowering sun glistened on the sodden grasses that appeared during low tide.

When he was a boy, his parents had given him the freedom to explore all fifteen long miles of his homeland. While on foot or on horseback, he'd discovered the perils of encountering alligators or snakes, so he decided that he'd not be so accommodating with his daughter. During Audrey's youth, he'd been at her side during any ventures beyond the acreage surrounding their mansion. Though they had a good view of the river from the upper floor of Bridal Fair, the ocean remained hidden by an expanse of live oaks, as well as intermittent cypress, pine, and palmettos that struggled to inch their way toward sunlight from beneath the canopy of live oaks. At age six Audrey had begged to walk the mile-long width of the island to the ocean by herself, but Boyd had refused her plea. He'd been certain she possessed the ability, but he'd been unable to muster enough courage to grant her permission.

He smiled at the memory as he now watched his daughter stroll across the grassy expanse that surrounded their home. No doubt Audrey was slipping off to her favorite retreat beneath the wide-spreading branches of a live oak a short distance from the house. Audrey loved the ancient trees as much as he and their ancestors had before them. The draping moss that hung from the branches resembled gossamer veils and had been the inspiration for naming their island

Bridal Veil. Boyd thought the name continued to suit the island.

When he'd been a boy of five or six, his mother told him their four thousand acre island contained more live oaks than any other island along the Georgia coast. He wasn't certain that was true. No one ever took a count of live oaks on any of the islands. There were a few who had protested the claim, saying Bridal Veil was larger than the other islands and would naturally have more trees, but his ancestors had disagreed and insisted Bridal Veil had more trees per acre than any other island. Since no one had been able to prove otherwise, the story endured to this day.

His gaze locked on a red-throated wild turkey strutting in the distance. Holding its bluish head high, the bird spread a beautiful fan of iridescent plumage. The large turkey looked toward the window as if extending an invitation to enjoy the glories of early autumn, and Boyd could not resist. He downed the remains of his coffee, set the cup in the sink, and strode outside. A deer meandered from the thicket and lowered its head to forage in the undergrowth. Boyd wasn't certain what drew him more: the wooded landscape, the abundant wildlife that inhabited the island, or the ocean waves and river tides that sealed the island's tranquillity. In his youth, he'd pretended nothing could touch his family so long as they remained secluded on the island. As an adult, he learned that not even an island could provide complete seclusion. And since his return he'd learned that nothing remained the same.

In fact, most everything had changed a short time before his mother died. Now he couldn't imagine returning to Pittsburgh. Even more, he couldn't imagine how he had survived for all those years without Jesus. Plodding down the porch steps, Boyd decided he must clear the air with his daughter. His movement startled the deer, and with a graceful stride, the animal loped into the thicket out of sight.

Keeping to the path, he soon approached Audrey near one of the giant oaks. "I always loved these trees," he told her as he fell into step beside her. "When I was a little boy, I used to climb them to sit up high in the branches and pretend I was on the deck of a pirate ship looking out to sea."

She gave him a halfhearted smile.

"You're angry with me, aren't you?"

Her unruly locks tangled in the light breeze. "I think I'm more confused than angry. I can deal with Aunt Thora's comments. She doesn't understand that times have changed and many women earn a living these days."

He chuckled. "Just one more thing she'd blame on the war."

Audrey nodded. "I suppose you're right."

His shoulders ached almost as much as his heart. His daughter was willing to sacrifice and work on the mainland so that he could fulfill his dream of living on this island. Well, he wouldn't have it. Audrey had sacrificed far too much throughout her life — and all because of the choices he'd made. They reached Audrey's favorite tree and Boyd took hold of her hand.

"Let's sit for a bit." He helped her to the ground and then took a seat beside her. Easing back, Boyd rested against the thick, mossy trunk of the live oak.

"Before I'll let you spend your days working as a servant over in Biscayne, I'll sell this piece of land, and I'll hear no more of it."

When Audrey flinched at his comment, he realized his tone had been harsher than he'd intended. He hadn't wanted to hurt her, but he did want to make certain she understood his decision was final. Audrey had become accustomed to taking charge over the past years, and he wanted it clear that he'd made up his mind.

He reached for her hand. "You've already given up enough for me. I won't permit you to make any further sacrifices."

The mossy veil of the weathered oak lifted in the breeze, and Audrey squeezed his hand. "I thought we'd put the past behind us. You're a changed man. There's no need for this continued sorrow over the past."

"I know. I know. But when I think of all the time and money I wasted in taverns and the sorrow I caused you and your mother . . ." He looked into the distance, unable to complete his thought or push the memory from his mind. Clearing his throat, he straightened his shoulders. "You've been happier here than in Pittsburgh, haven't you? At least more content than you thought you might be?"

"I've been content. I continue to miss some of my friends, and I do miss the Morleys." She hesitated. "I'd grown to love their children very much."

Boyd tipped his head to one side. "I hope that one day you'll have a child of your own to enjoy." He grinned. "Maybe two or three?"

She tapped his arm. "Now you sound like Aunt Thora. If the Lord wants me to marry, He'll see that I meet the proper man. I'm not willing to settle for just anyone."

"And I don't want you to, either. The last thing I want is for you to end up with some useless fellow who will give you no better life than I gave your mother." Regret mingled with sorrow as he spoke. His years of drinking had created no end of pain for his wife and daughter, and he didn't want Audrey to bear any more heartache.

"I know you were trying to drown your sorrows after Mother died, but God was faithful and answered my prayers." A glint shone in her brown eyes when she looked up at him.

"I'm a fortunate man that you and your mother put up with me for all those years."

Both of the women in his life had done everything they could to put a stop to his drinking habit, but to no avail. Even when Catherine, his dear wife, had fallen ill, he'd refused her pleas to give up the bottle. In truth, during her illness and after her death six years ago, his dependence had only deepened. Each night he would soak his sadness in the muddled haze produced by alcohol.

He shook his head. "I created far too much heartache for both of you. Things might have been different if we'd have remained in the South. Maybe your mother would still be alive and you would have enjoyed getting to know your grandmother Cunningham."

"Please, Father. We can't live on what might have been. Things may have been much worse if we'd remained here. You had no choice but to move north. You needed to provide for us. It was a decision made for Mother and me — to give us a better life."

It was true he'd gone north to support his wife and child after the war, for the end of slavery meant the end of raising cotton and their comfortable life on Bridal Veil Island. He had hoped to earn enough money to save their land, but his wages hadn't proved sufficient to meet the demands. From the start, Catherine had been opposed to the move, fearful of how they'd be accepted in the North. He hadn't given her wishes or fears as much consideration as he had his own desire to save Bridal Veil. In fact, he'd not given her fears much thought at all. His hope of saving the island had superseded any other concerns. Well, that wouldn't happen again. His self-centered decisions had caused heartache and grief enough for two lifetimes. He'd see Bridal Fair sold to the highest bidder before he'd let his selfishness rule again.

"Neither your pleas nor your mother's

pleas for me to stop drinking got my attention. It took the death of a friend in a barroom brawl." He shook his head, disquieted by the images the event brought to mind. "I'll never forget that awful day."

Audrey picked up one of the small egg-shaped leaves that lay scattered beneath the tree and rolled it between her fingers. She didn't want to think about her father's drinking days — not now. "Remember that first big snow after we moved north? I couldn't believe my eyes. And the snowman we rolled out in the front yard? Mama was so cold she couldn't stay outside for more than a few minutes." A soft chuckle escaped her lips. "Mama never did get used to the cold. She said she thought I must have some Northern blood in me the way I took to playing in the snow."

Boyd smiled. "You're right. Your mama didn't like the cold weather. But she enjoyed watching us build that snowman from inside the front window." Boyd didn't remember taking part in much snowman building after that. The rest of the snowmen had been rolled by Audrey and her friends while he'd been at work — or sitting in a tavern.

And he'd been just as lax with his wife. He'd shown little compassion for Catherine when she'd complained about the cold.

What he had wanted was most important, and he had wanted to be in Pittsburgh, where he thought he could earn enough money to save Bridal Veil. Now that Catherine was dead, he knew better. He hadn't been able to send enough money to save the island, yet he wouldn't admit defeat. How selfish he'd been. How he wished he could change those decisions he'd made before coming to know the Lord. But things were different now. Now he had his priorities in order. First God. Then Audrey. Everything else followed.

"Somehow this will all work out for the best." Boyd could only hope his smile was enough reassurance to convince his daughter.

Audrey nodded. "In the past, God provided for us. We need to pray and trust that He'll provide again." She peeked up at him, the golden twinkle returning to her eyes. "Unless you'd like to believe that God is going to locate a job for me in Biscayne."

"Now, Audrey . . ."

"I know. You don't want to believe that would be His way of doing things, but you can't be certain. You should at least be open to the idea. Agree with me to pray about a position in Biscayne and see if God changes your heart on the matter."

He chuckled and shook his head. "You are one persistent young woman. Heaven help the man you marry."

"Then you agree? You'll truly seek God's answer and not your own wishes?"

The muscles along his shoulders tightened into knots. He wanted to tell her that was exactly what he'd been doing — pushing aside his own desires — attempting to right the wrongs of the past. For now, he held his tongue and gave his agreement.

She leaned toward him and placed a kiss on his cheek. "In my heart, I believe you're going to discover that my going to work will be the answer."

"I think I need your agreement that you are going to earnestly seek God's answer right along with me. I don't want you praying with the preconceived notion that He's already shown you what is best. We're going into this on a level playing ground. Otherwise, we need to discuss this agreement a little further."

Audrey brushed a loose curl behind her ear and sighed when it immediately sprung free. "I promise that I'll —" She glanced toward the house, fear glistening in her eyes. "What was that?"

Boyd jumped to his feet. "Sounded like a shotgun blast." Another report sounded, and he reached for Audrey's hand. "It is a shotgun! It sounded like the shots were coming from the direction of the house."

"I heard a boat a short time ago," Audrey hissed as they picked their way through the overgrowth. "You think it's the tax collector?"

Boyd continued to clutch her hand while he took the lead. "I don't think the tax collector would be armed." He glanced over his shoulder. "Then again, maybe he would. I imagine there are some folks who would take up a weapon to defend their land if a tax collector came calling."

They halted near one of the spreading live oaks not far from the rear of the house just as another gunshot blast erupted. "Sounds like it's around front. You stay here."

"I will not! You might need me."

"We'll be more easily spotted if there are two of us. Now, do as I —" Another blast erupted, and Boyd rushed toward the house with Audrey close on his heels. He waved her back, but she ignored the gesture.

His stomach tightened and, in spite of the breeze, perspiration dotted his forehead. There was a time when he'd possessed the physical ability to stave off anyone who might threaten his family, but not now. He didn't know what he'd do if his home and family required more protection than he could offer.

At the side of the house, Boyd stopped and took a deep breath. "Be our protector, almighty God. You know I don't have the strength to do this on my own." Once he'd uttered the prayer, he took another step forward and peered around the corner. He reared back and slapped his palm against his forehead.

Audrey grasped his arm. "What is it?"

"You're not going to believe your eyes." He pointed his thumb toward the front porch. "Take a look for yourself."

CHAPTER 3

Audrey stepped past her father and peered around the corner of the house. Aunt Thora was sitting in the rocking chair, reloading Grandfather Cunningham's shotgun. Before Audrey could speak, Aunt Thora slammed the gun shut and arched forward to study the surrounding landscape.

Lifting the shotgun from her lap, she rested it on the porch rail. "Come on out of there, you conniving Yankee, or you're gonna meet your Maker afore I stop shooting!"

"Aunt Thora! Put that —"

Another blast sounded and leaves on a nearby tree rustled and quivered as a shower of pellets scattered among the branches. Aunt Thora reared back in her chair from the impact. The old woman looked at Audrey with her mouth agape. "Mercy, child! You about scared the living daylights out of me."

When Thora waved the gun in Audrey's direction, both she and her father ducked.

"Put that gun down before you kill someone, Thora." Audrey's father raised his head a few inches. "At least turn it in some other direction, would you?"

Aunt Thora glowered and pointed the gun heavenward. Audrey hoped the old woman wouldn't blow a hole in the upper balcony. They didn't need the cost of additional repairs right now.

"You see here, Boyd Cunningham, don't you be telling me I shouldn't protect this land. There's a Yankee out there, and every time he sticks his head out from behind one of those trees, I try to get 'im." She dropped the barrel of the gun a few inches and pointed it toward the live oaks that dotted the front of the property. "He keeps moving on me, and I keep missing 'im."

She squinted and raised her voice. "But I got enough shells here to keep after him." She turned back to Audrey and Boyd. "My eyes ain't what they used to be. Think I'm gonna have to get me some practice shooting at moving targets."

"The war is over, Thora, and even if there is a Northerner out there somewhere, you're not supposed to shoot at him." With a determined look in his eye, Audrey's father rounded the porch, climbed the steps, and reached for the weapon.

"Hold on, Boyd! There he is." Aunt Thora yanked the gun from his grasp and took aim.

Before she could get off another shot, Audrey's father wrestled the weapon from her hands and took several backward steps. "Now, hear me out, Thora. No more shooting at anyone. Do you understand?"

Aunt Thora jumped to her feet and pointed in the distance. "There he is! Aim that gun or give it to me, Boyd!"

As Audrey neared the porch, she glimpsed a man waving a white handkerchief from behind one of the trees. "Boyd! Audrey! It's me — Victor Morley." He hesitated a moment. "Is it safe to come out?"

Audrey clapped a hand to her forehead. "You've been shooting at Mr. Morley, Aunt Thora. He's a dear friend and my former employer."

"He said he was a Northerner — that was all I needed to know. I put him on the run in no time." Thora pushed the sole of her shoe against the wooden slats of the porch floor and set her rocker into motion. Even after hearing Mr. Morley was a friend, the old woman exhibited no remorse. Instead, she appeared downright pleased with herself. "I told him to find his way off Bridal

Veil the same way he got here. When he didn't leave, I had no choice but to get the shotgun."

"You always have a choice, Thora, and as a general rule it shouldn't involve a shotgun." With his lips stretched as tight as a clothesline on washday, her father shook his head before he stepped off the porch and waved to Mr. Morley, peeking from behind the tree. "It's safe to come out now."

Mr. Morley took a cautious step from behind the giant oak. His face brightened when he noticed the weapon had been wrested from Aunt Thora's hands. He appeared relieved and thankful all rolled into one. "Good to see you — both of you." Though his words were directed at father and daughter, his focus remained fixed on the old woman.

Audrey's father extended his hand as he walked toward Mr. Morley. "This is quite a surprise." He glanced over his shoulder at Audrey, who continued to follow after him. "Unless Audrey has been keeping secrets. Did you know Mr. Morley was going to pay us a visit?"

"No, but it's truly wonderful. I hope your wife and the children are with you."

"Not this time, but perhaps they can come with me on a future visit." He grinned.

"Once I'm sure they won't be greeted with a shotgun."

The three of them approached the wraparound front porch, where Aunt Thora continued to rock her chair at a frantic pace. Audrey hurried to the woman's side. "This is Thora Lund. She was my grandmother's companion and housekeeper for many years. She elected to remain here on Bridal Veil after Grandmother's death."

Mr. Morley tipped his hat and nodded. "Pleased to make your acquaintance, ma'am."

Thora pursed her lips tightly and gave a throated growl of disagreement. Narrowing her eyes, she tried to look fierce. "I'll be watchin' your every move while you're on this island." She wagged her index finger between father and daughter. "These two may trust Yankees, but I know better."

Mr. Morley ascended the final step onto the porch. "I assure you I mean nothing but good, Mrs. Lund. I am quite fond of both Boyd and Audrey, and I hope my visit will prove that I am your friend, as well."

"Humph! If you think you can spout a few sweet words in my direction and I'm gonna trust you, then you don't know Thora Lund." Aunt Thora straightened her shoulders and shot a haughty look at Mr. Morley.

"Why don't we all go inside to the parlor? I'm sure you could use some refreshment after your journey, Mr. Morley." Audrey ushered him toward the front door. "I can't wait to hear how the children have been progressing. And how is your wife? And Mattie? I haven't had a letter from Mattie in a while." The men followed, but Aunt Thora remained in her rocking chair.

Audrey missed the Morley family, but she missed Mattie more than anyone else she'd left behind in Pittsburgh. Even though Mattie had been the head housekeeper and Audrey's supervisor at the Morley home, the two of them had become fast friends. Audrey cherished letters from Mattie. They were always filled with news and funny stories about the latest happenings.

"My wife sends her regards, and you'll be pleased to know Mattie sent a letter. She was excited when she learned I'd be visiting you and your father." Mr. Morley followed Audrey into the parlor and withdrew an envelope from his jacket pocket.

Her heart swelled at the sight of the familiar handwriting. Never had she had a friend as dear as Mattie. Someone she could confide in and trust, someone who'd stood

by her and wiped her tears when the problems with her father's drinking had been at
their worst. Mattie hadn't judged or tried to
solve Audrey's problems, but she'd listened
to Audrey's heartache and offered unyield-
ing friendship. When Audrey's father per-
suaded her to leave Pittsburgh, it had been
Mattie who had offered encouragement and
wisdom.

Audrey clasped the envelope to her bodice
before she slipped it into her skirt pocket.
"I'll save it for later so that I can savor each
word." The men smiled and nodded, but
she doubted they understood. "I'll prepare
some refreshments, but please don't exchange any news until I return."

Her father chuckled. "You don't want us
to sit here in complete silence, do you?
Perhaps you could ask Thora to prepare the
refreshments. It would keep her busy."

Audrey wasn't certain Aunt Thora would
be pleased to prepare food and drink for a
Northerner, but her father was correct. It
would keep her busy. Audrey opened the
parlor door leading to the porch. Aunt
Thora glanced up when she drew near.

"That Yankee still in there?"

"Of course he is. You would have seen him
if he'd departed."

"Humph! Never know about them Yankees. The way they sneak around, he could be anywhere by now."

There was no way she was going to win this conversation with Aunt Thora. "I'm going to serve some refreshments. Would you like to help prepare them?"

"You gonna serve that Yankee?"

"I am going to serve Mr. Morley, a friend and our guest, and I would appreciate your help."

The woman rested her weathered hands on the chair arms and pushed to a stand. "I suppose I can fix the refreshments, but I won't serve him. I'm dead set against that idea."

Audrey patted Aunt Thora's shoulder. "Thank you for your willingness to help me."

Thora pointed toward the south end of the porch. "I'm going around and let myself in through the solarium. You go on back and visit with your Yankee friend. I'll ring a bell when the tray's ready."

Audrey didn't argue, but she hoped Aunt Thora wouldn't think of some way to poison Mr. Morley. The thought sent Audrey scurrying after her. "What do you plan to serve, Aunt Thora?"

Her skirt wrapped around her legs as Thora came to an abrupt halt and made a quick turn. "Uninvited visitors can't be picky, Audrey. You can be sure I won't be serving him syllabub or ambrosia — those are for special guests. There's some leftover caramel cake, and I'll set a pot of coffee on to boil. Don't think he'll be wantin' tea — Northern folks don't take to tea like we do down here in the South."

Audrey clipped back a smile. Telling Aunt Thora that she knew many folks in Pittsburgh who enjoyed a cup of tea — and some Southerners, her own father included, who preferred coffee as much as a cup of tea — would only begin another long discussion. And Audrey didn't want to lose a minute of visiting with Mr. Morley. Her curiosity had continued to mount since she'd first set eyes on him. Why he would suddenly appear on Bridal Veil Island was beyond her imagination.

"The cake will be fine." Audrey headed back toward the parlor while Aunt Thora mumbled that uninvited Yankees should be more than satisfied with leftovers.

"I hope I haven't missed anything of importance," she said, settling on a chair across from her father.

Mr. Morley met her gaze. "Nothing of significance. You appear to be faring well since the move, Audrey. Are you content in

44

your new home?"

Audrey glanced at her father. "Yes. I am comfortable, and Father is quite happy. For his sake, I hope we'll be able to remain here. I can't tell you how surprised I am to see you appear. I didn't know you had interests in the South."

"Well, I hadn't until recently. And that's exactly why I'm here. I suppose you two are aware of the transformation taking place on Jekyl Island, the large resort and hunting club being constructed."

Audrey nodded. They would have to be completely isolated not to have heard of the plans. The island to the south of them had been sold to a group of New York investors, who had formed some sort of club and wanted to build a retreat where they could hunt, fish, boat, and escape the cold winters up north. "Jekyl is quite the talk among folks in Biscayne and in the local newspapers, as well, but I don't believe they've actually begun construction. Then again, I could be wrong." Suddenly it had all become clear to her. No wonder Mr. Morley had come for a visit. He wanted to see the island before he became a member. "So that's why you've come for a visit. You and your wife intend to join the Jekyl Island Club."

The idea sent Audrey's spirits soaring. If the Morleys belonged to the club, they would be making visits to the nearby island. And that would mean she would have an opportunity to see Mattie and the Morleys' children, June and Thomas. Before Mr. Morley could answer, Audrey was jarred from her thoughts by the unrelenting ringing of the bell.

Had the jangling been less insistent, she would have waited for Mr. Morley's response. Instead, she jumped to her feet. "Please excuse me. I'll fetch our refreshments, and then we can continue our conversation." She stopped in the doorway. "I do want to hear about your plans to join the Island Club." With a slight wave, she scurried to the kitchen.

Aunt Thora pointed to the trays. "You'll have to make two trips. Couldn't fit everything on one tray."

"Would you please bring the second tray? That way I can begin to serve without allowing the coffee to get cold." Audrey didn't want to beg, but she truly hoped the older woman would relent.

Thora curled her lip. "I s'pose, but I'm not serving your visitor."

Audrey sighed with relief. "Just carry the tray into the parlor and set it on the table,

46

and then you can go and take your after-noon nap." She pecked the woman on her cheek. "Thank you."

"*Humph.* So long as you remember that I'm doin' this for you and not for that Yankee."

With a grin, Audrey picked up the larger tray. The thought that Aunt Thora would do anything for a Yankee would never cross Audrey's mind, but she let the comment go unanswered. Any deeper discussion of the war or relations between the North and South would only delay Audrey's return to the parlor.

"Here we are. I hope you like caramel cake, Mr. Morley." Audrey placed the tray on a table to one side of the sitting area.

"I don't believe I've ever tasted caramel cake, but I'm always pleased to try a new dessert." He did his best to smile when Aunt Thora plunked her tray on the table.

"How could a man live to be your age and never eat caramel cake? I never heard the like!" Thora turned on her heel and stomped out of the room. "Yankees!"

Audrey's father shook his head. "Thora's a good woman, but she's still unwilling to accept the outcome of the war. She contin-ues to harbor a strong dislike for Northern-ers."

Mr. Morley chuckled. "After our encounter out front, I assumed we wouldn't become immediate friends." He tasted a bite of the cake. "This is excellent. Perhaps you could send the recipe to Mattie. I'm sure the children would enjoy it."

"I'll send it the next time I write." Audrey poured coffee into his cup. "You mentioned investing in Jekyl Island. I'm excited to hear you'll be spending part of the year nearby."

"I haven't thrown in with the men involved in the proposal. I spoke with several of them when I was last in Chicago — Marshall Field and Wirt Dexter both encouraged me to seek membership, but a few days later I was contacted by Thaddeus Baker, an investor from Syracuse who was visiting in Pittsburgh. He, too, had been asked to join the investors forming the club on Jekyl Island, but his wife wasn't in favor." Mr. Morley tipped his head to the side and glanced at my father. "You know how women can be when it comes to hunting and fishing and less than opulent living conditions. Most don't find it appealing. Mrs. Baker thought wives would be much more interested in spending their winters where the accommodations were more luxurious than those being planned for, where there were more options for enter-

tainment, and where individual accom-
modations would be available at the outset.
As I expected, my wife agreed with Mrs.
Baker's assessment."

Audrey's earlier excitement plummeted.
So she wouldn't have an opportunity to visit
with Mattie after all. Still, Audrey didn't
understand why her former employer had
traveled to Georgia if he didn't intend to
join the group. "Did you hope to change
Mrs. Morley's decision after visiting?"

"Not at all. As it turns out, I've helped to
gather another group of men, and we have
formed our own organization. An excellent
group of investors — and after one conces-
sion, I was even able to convince Thaddeus
Baker to join us. Our group has made
almost as much progress as the Jekyl group.
However, we have managed to keep our
activities less public — by choice, of course.
We have a few details that need to be
completed, and then we'll make a public
announcement."

Her father's brow furrowed. "So you're
going to set up some sort of resort on
another nearby island?"

"Indeed. I hope you will be pleased to
learn that our group has purchased Bridal
Veil Island from the heirs of Mrs. Lofton.
Except for your home and the twenty acres

you still own, our group now holds title to the entire island." Mr. Morley finished the last bite of his cake and picked up his coffee cup. "That's the reason for my visit."

"You've purchased Bridal Veil from the Loftons? When Mr. and Mrs. Lofton purchased most of the island, they assured my mother that their heirs would never sell the land." Her father dropped back in his chair, his eyes reflecting disbelief.

Audrey watched her father's look change from one of disbelief to disappointment and knew what he must be thinking. Her grandmother had been careful in her choice of buyer when she'd been forced to sell most of the island. She'd hoped to avoid anyone ever destroying the natural beauty of Bridal Veil. Yet, in spite of her caution, it seemed Grandmother had been unable to protect her beloved island forever.

Her father rubbed his jaw. "So the Lofton heirs have decided money is more important than the land their parents vowed to protect. I'm disappointed."

"I believe several of the Lofton children came upon hard times and decided selling was their only option. And that's what brings me here, Boyd. Our group would like to offer to purchase Bridal Fair and your remaining twenty acres of land so that we may have use of the entire island."

"No!" Her father's response exploded from his lips like one of Aunt Thora's shotgun blasts.

Mr. Morley recoiled at the abrupt reaction. "I didn't mean to offend in any way. It's just that the other investors asked that I come and speak with you, since we are already acquainted. They're willing to pay a substantial price, although they know the property is delinquent on tax payments."

"I'm not willing to sell to them. I don't want the entire island overrun and destroyed."

"But that's not our intent. We've hired a landscape architect who will help us maintain the natural beauty of the island, and we're in the process of employing a game-keeper who will work with us to preserve all of the wildlife. Some members will want to hunt, of course, but we don't intend for that aspect to be the primary focus of our club. I think you'd find all of the men are quite respectful of nature."

"I just can't do it, Mr. Morley. The taxes are a genuine concern, and if I can't find some way to pay them, then I guess you and your friends can purchase the land at the tax sale. But I don't think my mother would have ever agreed to such an arrangement."

"But your mother is dead, isn't she?"

"Yes. But I still feel obligated to honor her wishes regarding this island. At least the small portion that still remains in the family."

Mr. Morley arched forward and rested his arms across his legs. "Then let me loan you the money to pay the taxes. It's the least I can do."

"I don't want charity, and you don't owe me anything, Mr. Morley. I appreciate your kindness, but I'll figure out a way to pay the taxes on my own."

After he'd studied her father for a moment, Mr. Morley folded his hands together. "Then what about taking a job working as the primary foreman on our project? You're an excellent choice, and my partners have already approved moving forward to hire you." Their visitor straightened and awaited her father's response with an expectant gaze.

Her father shook his head with a slow determination. "I do thank you, but I'm going to have to reject your offer."

Audrey couldn't believe her ears. Her father had vowed to love this land more than life itself. He'd been determined to return to the place where he'd been born. And now, threatened with the loss of his family home, he refused a loan and then refused to take a job that suited him perfectly. Granted, his health had been unstable since shortly before they'd moved south, but supervising the project wouldn't be the same as performing manual labor. How could he so offhandedly refuse the help Mr. Morley offered?

Perhaps her father thought Mr. Morley's offers were made out of continuing feelings of thanks or obligation. All of their lives had intertwined three years ago, when Mr. Morley had been seeking an innovative and accomplished contractor to expand his mansion in Pittsburgh. A man who always aspired to being different and unique, Mr. Morley didn't want someone who would disagree with his plans — he wanted someone who would make his plans happen.

After searching for months, he had mentioned his difficulty in Audrey's presence. Her father had sworn off the bottle a year earlier and hadn't taken a drink since then. She knew he would be a perfect fit for the job, yet she'd waited a full month before mentioning his name to Mr. Morley. Even then, she made certain her father's future employment wouldn't be linked to her own. She couldn't afford to lose her job, nor did she have any desire to seek employment elsewhere. She'd been happy with the Morleys and wanted to remain even if things didn't work out with her father.

As it turned out, her father's work far exceeded Mr. Morley's expectations, and his words of praise to his wealthy friends brought any number of offers to her father. But it hadn't been her father's work that had won Mr. Morley's lasting allegiance. Rather, it had been the life of young Thomas Morley. The boy had climbed out a window and scaled the steep roof. Once he'd ascended to a ledge surrounding a turret on the west side of the house, Thomas had panicked, lost his footing, and slipped to a decorative projection several feet below. Had her father not interceded, the boy would have fallen to his death. Instead, his injuries had consisted of a broken arm and a few scrapes. After the Morleys' son had completely recovered from the incident, Mr. Morley had come to their home and promised to help her father if ever the need arose.

"I think you should reconsider, Boyd. This land obviously means a lot to you, and I don't want you to lose it." Mr. Morley's words rang with sincerity.

Still, her father shook his head. "No. I need to find my own way out of this problem. I don't want charity from you or anyone else."

Though Audrey sensed Mr. Morley's frustration, he remained calm. "Why don't we take a walk, Boyd? I have a proposition for you that I don't think you'll refuse."

Her father's reluctance was obvious, but he agreed to listen, and for that Audrey was grateful. "You two enjoy your visit, and I'll see to supper. We'd be pleased to have you join us, Mr. Morley."

"I'd be pleased to join you, if . . ." His acceptance hung in the air as he glanced toward the doorway, clearly uncertain if Aunt Thora would object to the idea.

"I don't think Aunt Thora will join us. Sometimes she takes her meals in her room."

He exhaled with obvious relief. "In that case, I'd be pleased to accept your invitation."

Once the men departed, Audrey gathered the tray and carried it to the kitchen, where Thora sat perched on a stool near the window. The older woman glanced over her shoulder when Audrey entered the room. "Where the two of them going?" Thora asked, indicating the two men, who were strolling toward the acreage at the rear of the house.

"To have a private talk. Mr. Morley is speaking to Father about the possible purchase of the house and acreage, and perhaps a position as foreman of a project here on the island."

Thora came off the stool in a startling leap, her mouth gaping as she approached the table. "You don't mean it!" She grasped Audrey's arm between her gnarly fingers. "Boyd wouldn't do such a thing. I know he loves this land every bit as much as his mother ever did. And if he sells this place, where will I go? Tell me he's gonna send that fella packing."

The old woman's fingers dug deeper into Audrey's arm, and she gently unclasped the woman's hold. "It's going to work out fine. There's no need for worry."

Aunt Thora's eyes clouded with tears. "That's easy to say when you're young and have the rest of your life spread before you. But I'm old. All my friends are gone."

Audrey patted the old woman's hand. "No matter what happens, you will always have a home with us."

A tear trickled down Thora's weathered face. "So many dear ones lost in the war, and now the Yankees are taking over the island. I've lived too long and seen too much. It's time for me to go home to the Lord." She dropped to a nearby chair and wiped her tears with the corner of her apron. "I do believe I feel one of my spells coming over me, Audrey."

When life didn't work quite the way Aunt Thora wanted, she had spells that required a long rest. Audrey didn't know if they were truly spells or simply Aunt Thora's way of coping with life. Either way, Aunt Thora wouldn't be joining them for supper that evening.

CHAPTER 4

After completing supper preparations, Audrey arranged a tray for Aunt Thora and carried it to her room. The old woman sat hunched forward reading her Bible by the waning light filtering through the filmy bedroom curtains.

"I thought you were going to rest, Aunt Thora."

The old woman nodded. "I did, and now I'm all rested up." She waved toward a table not far from her chair. "Just put it there." She closed her Bible and gave the tray a fleeting glance. "I thought I'd read the Bible and see if the good Lord would show me some answers. I just can't figure out what's goin' on in this world anymore. One minute life is running smooth as can be, and the next the Yankees are marching into the South and destroying everything in sight. And for years after, there's nothing but the devastation they left behind." She reached up and scratched her head. "So now life has settled down a little and what happens? The Yankees come back down here and start buyin' up all our land. There's something wrong with that, Audrey."

Audrey carried the table closer to the chair. "Did you find any answers in your reading?"

"None that suit me, but I plan to keep looking."

Audrey chuckled. Knowing Aunt Thora, she'd keep looking until she found a verse or two that would support her views, even if she had to twist them around a bit. "One day soon you're going to have to accept the fact that the war is over, that Northerners are not terrible people, and that God loves us all."

"I know God loves us all, but I don't share His opinion on that particular fact." She shook her head, picked up the napkin from her tray, and clutched it in one hand. "I know your daddy went north to earn a living and save Bridal Veil after the war, but after all he did to help the South during the war, I wouldn't think he'd want to keep company with Yankees unless he had to."

Audrey had heard the stories of her father's heroic efforts during the war. He hadn't served in a regular capacity. Instead, he'd been recruited to help smuggle goods to the Southern army, and the island proved the perfect location. With its irregular shoreline and numerous coves, boats could sneak in under cover of darkness undetected, offload needed supplies, and place them under her father's supervision for distribution. The danger had been great, but her father had used exceeding care, and their family had never been threatened. In fact, until she was an adult, Audrey hadn't known her father had participated in the covert activity. Even then, it had been difficult to believe, for he'd never been away from home for any length of time during the war.

Thora peered at the dinner tray. "You feed him fine food like this and he'll never leave. You should have fixed him some broiled robin on toast. That would have set his Yankee stomach to churning." She snapped the napkin and tucked it into the waistband of her brown serge skirt. "That's all some of our men had to eat while they were fighting those Yankees. And considered themselves blessed to have even a robin or woodpecker to eat."

"Now, Aunt Thora, it's not my objective to make Mr. Morley ill. He and his family were exceedingly kind to me. And to Father." At the familiar creak of the front door, Audrey glanced toward the hallway. "The men have returned. I'll come back for your tray after we've finished supper. No need to tire yourself coming downstairs."

The woman grinned. "You're not fooling me one smidgen. You don't want me around your Yankee friend. Well, you can set your mind at ease. I won't be back downstairs until he's gone."

Audrey clenched her jaw. Thora was set in her ways, and any further attempt to win her over would only meet with failure. Besides, Audrey needed to get back to the kitchen. Her father and Mr. Morley had been gone longer than she'd expected, and she worried the chicken would now be dry and the rice sticky. Lifting her skirts, she hurried downstairs to greet them.

"I'm pleased you've returned. I thought you'd be back a half hour ago."

"My apologies, Audrey. It is completely my fault. I needed more time than expected to plead my case to your father. He can be a difficult man to convince." Mr. Morley grinned. "But I suppose you already know that."

"I've experienced some of that behavior on several occasions." She smiled in return. "Once you've washed up, we can sit down

61

to supper."

While the men hurried off to do her bidding, Audrey scurried back to the kitchen and dished up the meal. If she'd known Mr. Morley would be there, she would have had Old Sam deliver fresh seafood. Throughout the years, Sam had steered his boat by the populated islands to see if the daily catch was desired for the following day. If Audrey wanted him to stop, she tied a big blue scarf to a pole on their dock. The next afternoon, the fish, turtle, crab, or other catch would be waiting on the dock, along with a note telling her how much money to leave the following morning. The system worked beautifully. But only if one had advance notice of intended company. In cases of extreme emergency, a red flag would be tied to the pole. Old Sam knew to keep a sharp eye for flags of any color, but especially the red one.

Tonight, Mr. Morley would have to settle for fried chicken, and she hoped he wouldn't mind the simple fare. Before she could give the menu further thought, the men returned.

Mr. Morley tipped his head back and sniffed. "Something smells wonderful."

Audrey offered a fleeting smile. "It won't compare to the food you're accustomed to eating at Temberly."

The Morleys had christened their Pittsburgh home *Temberly* shortly after they'd moved into the house. Mrs. Morley had insisted the edifice needed to be named something special and had chosen her grandmother's maiden name for the estate. Though Mattie thought naming a home ridiculous, Audrey thought it quite fitting. Mattie attributed Audrey's accord to her Southern childhood, where she'd become accustomed to the plantation homes bearing regal names. Whether it was located in the North or the South, Audrey believed a palatial home surrounded by beautiful acreage of well-manicured landscape deserved a name.

After helping Audrey with her chair, Mr. Morley sat down at the table opposite her father. "Not every meal need be served in luxurious surroundings to be considered fine fare."

Audrey didn't intend to apologize further. They didn't have servants to fill the bowls or keep the water glasses filled to the brim, but they did offer hospitality. And she was a good cook. She'd never utter such a thing herself, for it would be far too boastful. But she'd received enough compliments to instill her with an air of confidence in the kitchen.

Her father followed their normal custom and prayed before they passed the bowls and platters of food. Audrey didn't miss his words of thanks to God for providing a means to pay their taxes. By the time he finished the prayer, she thought she might explode of curiosity.

Instead of explaining, her father inquired about the construction he'd completed on the Morley home. "I just wondered how it worked out for you. I know you and your wife spent a great deal of time deciding exactly how the addition would best meet the needs of your family. I've been curious if after living in it for a while, you would change anything."

Audrey tapped her foot beneath the table and hoped Mr. Morley's response would be brief. If the two men had come upon some way to save the family home on Bridal Veil Island, Audrey wanted to know. Her mind raced while the men's talk about the Morleys' adjustment to the additional space added to Temberly swirled around her. She couldn't imagine what possible proposal Mr. Morley could make that would change her father's mind. After all, he'd quickly dismissed the idea of selling Bridal Fair and the twenty acres that surrounded the house, and he'd turned down with surprising haste the job offer of supervisor for the new project — something she hoped to discuss with him later.

Certainly Father's health wasn't the best right now, but she was convinced that with time, it would improve. Knowing there would be pressure from the investors and understanding the need to please a group of wealthy gentlemen rather than one property owner may have been the cause for her father's refusal. Still, they were in need of help if they were going to save Bridal Fair. And through the years, he'd learned how to deal with demanding clients, except for the two times he'd been drinking on the job.

On those occasions, the consequences had been swift and costly. After the second incident, her father had reserved his drinking to after working hours and on Sundays, when his friends would gather and spend the day drinking and acting as if they didn't have the sense God gave a goose. They'd met only one time at their home. It had been shortly after her mother's death, and Audrey had been shocked by the unseemly behavior of her father's friends and co-workers. When one of the men made an offensive comment to Audrey, that had been the end of that — and all future gatherings at the Cunningham home.

But even that incident hadn't been enough to keep her father away from the bottle. It wasn't until his best friend and fellow alcoholic, Wilbur Graham, died. Her father had relived that scene in the tavern over and over until he finally accepted that he wanted to seek a different life — a life that included forgiveness and God's grace. Since that time, he'd been a changed man — one she could depend upon, one who didn't shirk his duty, one who wanted the best for both of them. So what had Mr. Morley now proposed that had captured his interest?

"This is excellent chicken." Mr. Morley pointed his fork at the bones that lay scattered on his plate.

Audrey reached for the platter. "Have another piece. There are only the three of us. I've already taken a plate to Thora."

He patted his stomach. "I don't believe I could eat another bite."

"Don't even consider such an idea. I'm sure Audrey has some special dessert waiting in the kitchen." Her father's eyes shone with anticipation.

"I did prepare blackberry custard with hard sauce." She glanced at Mr. Morley. "But if you're full, we can wait until later."

Her father's smile disappeared. "Well, Mr.

Morley is welcome to wait for his, but I'd like to have some now and some later, as well."

"I might be able to make a spot for a small serving. Blackberry pudding sounds far too delightful to pass up."

Audrey pushed away from the table and began to clear the plates. "Once I've cleared away the dishes, we can have our dessert in the solarium, but the two of you must promise that as soon as we sit down, you will tell me what decisions you came to this afternoon. Otherwise, I plan to withhold your custard."

Her father chuckled. "I told you she'd be chomping at the bit to know what we decided. I'm surprised she didn't interrupt our dinner conversation."

Audrey rested one hand on her hip. "There's no call to talk about me as if I'm not here, Father. And it took every ounce of control I could muster to remember my manners and refrain from changing the discussion."

Her father picked up several plates. "Since you were such a dutiful hostess and daughter, I believe I should help you clear away these dishes. Especially since Thora isn't down here to help."

Audrey shook her head and insisted the

two men relax in the solarium while she cleared the table. She didn't take time to wash the dishes. Instead, she stacked them in the sink, prepared the dessert, and arranged the plates on a large serving tray.

The men jumped to their feet when she entered the room, and had she not been balancing the large tray, she would have motioned them to sit down. "No need to get up, gentlemen." She glanced toward the windows of the solarium. "The view from this room is beautiful in the morning. We have a glorious scene of the sunrise each day. It's one of my favorite rooms in the house."

"I can understand why," Mr. Morley said as he accepted his custard. "This looks every bit as delicious as our supper."

Audrey served her father before she settled into one of the cushioned wicker chairs. "Now then, who wants to begin? I'm eager to hear what transpired between the two of you."

Mr. Morley motioned to her father. "I think it's best you explain, Boyd. Besides, I want to eat my dessert."

Her father lifted a spoonful of custard to his mouth before he replied. "Mmm, this sure is good."

"Thank you. Now, please tell me what's

happened." Audrey gestured for him to quit eating.

"Since Mr. Morley and his investor friends are going forward with their resort, they're going to need living quarters for the men who will come to Bridal Veil to construct the buildings."

She nodded but assumed the workers would live on the mainland in Biscayne, where there were several boardinghouses and a small hotel. Granted, their workday would be governed by the boat schedule, but surely these wealthy men could arrange for one of the companies in Biscayne to haul the men back and forth on a schedule that suited their needs.

"Mr. Morley thinks it would be best if the men lived here on Bridal Veil during the construction period. Less opportunity for them to spend their nights in the taverns, and they could begin earlier in the day if they were already at the site."

"I see. And exactly where would they be living? In tents?"

Her father shook his head. "In the old slave quarters and the cabins occupied by the overseers and their families. Mr. Morley says the investors are willing to rent the buildings from us."

The slave quarters were situated on the

land still owned by her father. Not that she was proud of them. She had suggested they be torn down when they'd first returned to the island, but her father had refused, saying they were still in good condition and there was no need to destroy them. Now the buildings would be put to use and provide them with a source of income, though she wondered if they could accumulate enough to pay the back taxes.

"I see. Well, I suppose that will work." She wasn't convinced Thora would agree with the decision, and once the men arrived, Audrey wasn't certain the old woman could be trusted out of her sight. She might decide to improve her shooting skills by using the men for target practice.

"There's more."

Audrey arched her brows.

"With your consent, I've agreed that some of the supervisors could board with us here in the house. With four empty bedrooms upstairs, I thought it would provide a perfect home away from home for a few of the men." He looked at her with anticipation shining in his eyes. "What do you think?"

"I think it would be a perfect opportunity to make some additional money, and it would permit me to remain here at Bridal

Fair with you. Also, I believe we could make this solarium into two rooms that would be adequate for Aunt Thora and me, which would permit us to rent out two more rooms upstairs. Besides, I'll need to be in the kitchen early each morning so that I can see to breakfast preparations. And we have the additional bathroom down here that we can use." She leaned toward her father. "Do you think you feel well enough to make those changes?"

Her father hesitated and Mr. Morley immediately answered. "I can have a couple of workmen in here within the week. They can make any changes you'd like so that you'll be prepared when the men arrive."

"And you can supervise the work, Father."

At the sound of a gasp in the hallway, Audrey glanced over her shoulder and saw Aunt Thora leaning against the doorjamb, her fingers trembling, her eyes wild and glassy. "I heard every word of what you're planning." She pointed over her shoulder. "I've been listening from out there. I can't believe you would bring Yankees into Bridal Fair. It's one thing for them to be living over on the land that was sold, but you're gonna feed and sleep 'em right under this roof? Why, your granddaddy Cunningham must be spinning in his grave."

71

"Now, Aunt Thora, you don't want us to lose the house, do you?" Audrey strode toward the old woman.

She shook her head as if to ward off the very idea of agreeing. "You might as well take me over to the ocean side of the island, put me on a raft, and set me adrift. I've lived too long and seen too much. My heart can't take no more of these changes going on in the world. I'd be better off in a watery grave."

"Come with me and let's sit a spell in the other room." Placing a supporting arm around her aunt's waist, Audrey escorted her into the parlor and sat down beside her on the divan.

"I don't know how you can agree to this horrible arrangement. Don't you understand that the Yankees are taking everything from us?"

Audrey patted her hand. "No, Aunt Thora. I believe this is God's answer to prayer. A way to meet our needs — and it is Yankee money that will be used to save us. Don't you see the justice in such a provision?"

Thora initially appeared baffled by the explanation, but soon a light glimmered in her eyes. "You're right. Let's take those Yankees for every penny we can get from 'em."

CHAPTER 5

As the weeks passed, life changed on Bridal Veil. Slowly at first, and then the changes came more often and with greater speed. Audrey continued to embrace their new way of life, though the same couldn't be said for Aunt Thora. She considered visits from the new owners and the arrival of their architect, laborers, and supervisors no less than an invasion of Yankees come to take siege and destroy yet another beloved Southern jewel. As Audrey greeted Aunt Thora each morning, Audrey hoped she would see a flicker of tolerance or a smidgen of submission to this new way of life, but so far she'd seen neither.

Audrey looked up as the old woman trundled into the kitchen in early October, her Bible in hand. From the glint in her eyes, this would not be the day Aunt Thora would change her ways. "I saw two of the Yankees sneaking out last night. No telling what they're up to with their conniving ways." She plopped into a chair and placed her Bible on the table with a thump. "I think we need to do like Joshua and send out some spies to see exactly what those scallywags are up to. We need to know the enemy." When Audrey didn't immediately respond, Thora tapped the Bible. "Did you hear me?"

After a slight nod, Audrey turned back to the worktable. "Yes, ma'am, I did, but right now I think I need to concentrate on breakfast rather than recruiting spies to report on the construction workers. Besides, I have you to do that for me, Aunt Thora." She grinned as she started to cut the butter into the biscuit mixture.

"I can't see the half of what's going on by myself. Besides, I'm too old to be creeping around after dark. If it weren't for my rheumatiz, I'd get out there in the middle of the night and find out exactly what those Yankees are planning." She *tsk*ed and shook her head. "For the life of me, I can't believe how you're willing to open your arms to those traitorous vermin."

Audrey wheeled around and faced the old woman. "They are not traitorous vermin. They are citizens of these United States, just like we are. Not so long ago, you agreed that it would be a blessing if Yankee dollars would help save Bridal Fair. Do you recall that?" Audrey narrowed her eyes and rested one hand on her hip. "Well?"

"I vaguely remember something like that, but my mind isn't what it used to be." She pointed to her head and assumed what she obviously hoped would prove a pitiful expression. "Sometimes I think I have cobwebs for brains."

Audrey tightened her lips to a thin line. Aunt Thora was up to her old tricks. "You're not pulling that foolishness on me. When there's something you want to remember, your mind is sharp as a razor. You forget only when it's convenient. I notice you didn't mind talking to the Northerners when they were making changes to the solarium. You were ordering them around like a teacher on the first day of school."

"That's because those Northern boys don't know how to fix things right and proper. They needed someone to oversee their every move." Thora shot a look of defiance at Audrey. "Do you know what those bedrooms would look like if it weren't for me telling those boys how to wield a hammer and build a wall?"

Audrey couldn't restrain the giggle that started at the back of her throat. Aunt Thora wasn't about to give credit for a good job, no matter what. "I don't want to disappoint you, but I believe those rooms would look exactly the same. The men followed the architect's plans down to the last detail."

"Don't you believe it for a minute! I was here when Lavinia, God rest her soul, had the bathing rooms added. We had proper Southerners do the job."

"Yes, and had that money gone to pay taxes instead of to build indoor bathrooms, we might not be in this fix now."

"Don't you question your grandmother's decision. She was confident that the bathing rooms would bring you home, and they did."

Audrey stopped rolling out the dough. "Granny didn't build those rooms for us."

"She most certainly did. She and I was perfectly able to use a chamber pot and bathe in a copper tub as we always did, but she wanted your father to move back to the island. She figured if you had the same niceties that you two was spoiled with up north — then you'd return home where you belonged."

Audrey wondered if her father knew this. It would no doubt grieve him if he did. The money her grandmother gained by selling off pieces of the island should have gone to build her savings account — not bath chambers.

Thora seemed not to notice Audrey's thoughtful silence. She was already back to chattering about the changes to the solarium. "It was me what noticed those Northerners were trying to skimp on the nails in that wall that divides our bedrooms. I think they were hoping it would fall down and crush me in the middle of the night." She rubbed her arm as if she'd already suffered the blow.

"That is nonsense, and we're not going to take this kind of talk any further." Audrey waved toward the dining room. "Are you going to set the table or wait until the men come downstairs and see you sitting there in your nightclothes?"

Thora jumped up from the table, grabbed the Bible, and clutched her robe to her bosom. "I suppose if you're not willing to take God's advice, I'll take the Bible back to my bedroom."

"I thought you said God hadn't spoken to you yet — that you didn't find a proper verse," Audrey said with a raised brow. The woman immediately opened her mouth and then closed it again at the sound of footsteps on the upstairs floor.

There was no doubt that Aunt Thora

wanted to continue arguing about the "invasion of Yankees," which had become her favorite expression for the Northern workers who'd arrived at Bridal Veil, but no God-fearing Southern woman would be caught dead allowing gentlemen or Yankees to observe her in her nightclothes.

"I need to finish rolling out this dough. Those men are starting to stir, and they'll be half starved by the time they get down here."

"Wouldn't have to spend hours in the kitchen if it weren't for the Yankees," Aunt Thora called from her bedroom door.

"If it weren't for the Yankees, we'd be looking for a new home." Audrey silently chided herself for playing into her aunt's hands. Exchanging barbs had become Thora's favorite pastime, and it consumed far too much attention and energy. Audrey preferred to devote strength to her new duties as boardinghouse keeper rather than to defending the Yankees.

Thus far, only three men had moved into Bridal Fair, all of them hired by the investors and charged with the task of locating and hiring skilled workers. After one of her spying adventures, Aunt Thora had reported there must be hundreds of laborers who had moved into the old slave quarters, and they were a rowdy bunch with uncouth manners and foul mouths. But when one of the boarders commented they'd hired only twenty men and most of them were from Georgia, she quickly retracted her statement.

The current boarders occupied the three bedrooms located above the kitchen and dining room. Since they were the smallest of the bedrooms, Audrey had been surprised by the men's choice, but it hadn't taken long to discover that cost dictated their decisions. The smaller rooms were less expensive. Any money saved on room and board would mean extra coins in their pockets.

The overhead noises were increasing, and Audrey knew all the men were now up and would arrive downstairs before long. She cut the last biscuits and then slid the pan into the oven. While the biscuits baked, she turned the bacon and filled two jelly dishes, one with grapefruit marmalade, the other with scuppernong jelly. There would be grits, though the men would quickly pass them down the table to her father. None of them would touch the Southern staple, a behavior that served to reinforce Aunt Thora's dislike of them.

Wearing a worn cotton dress, Thora meandered back into the kitchen and tied an apron around her slim waist. "I don't know why you're making such a big pan of grits. You know those men aren't gonna eat them." Her aunt was still prepared to banter. "Never trust a man who doesn't love his grits. It's a sure sign."

"I'll remember that." Audrey knew her response wasn't what was wanted or expected. "Why don't you set the table while I finish scrambling the eggs? The men will be downstairs in a few minutes."

"If breakfast isn't on the table the minute their behinds hit the chairs, it won't hurt 'em to wait. You won't find Southerners rushin' a meal."

Mouth agape, Audrey swirled around. "Aunt Thora! What has gotten into you? And what has happened to your Southern hospitality? These men are paying for room and board, and they are required to arrive at work on time. Now, if you don't want to help me, that's your decision, but I have a schedule, and I plan to maintain it to the best of my ability."

"No need to get yourself in a pucker. I'll set the table, but just 'cause I'm helping doesn't mean I agree with harboring the enemy."

Had the men come downstairs early any other morning, Audrey would have been distracted, but today she was pleased to see them. Aunt Thora might not treat them with warmth, but she'd cease her insults once they entered the dining room. Audrey walked to the doorway between the kitchen and dining room.

"There's coffee on the sideboard," she told the men, "and breakfast will be ready in a few more minutes."

Audrey motioned to the old woman as she returned to the stove. "Would you fill these bowls? One with the grits and the other with the scrambled eggs. I'll get the biscuits and bacon."

"Sure are feeding them Yanks some fine food every day," Thora mumbled as she scooped the grits into the blue pottery bowl. Audrey wanted to counter that the men were paying for their meals, but she refrained.

Aunt Thora's grumbling finally ended when they were seated at the table. Audrey's father offered a prayer of thanks for the meal and asked God's blessing on the men as they continued to seek capable workers to oversee clearing of the land where the elaborate clubhouse would be erected. That prayerful request was followed by a grunt from Aunt Thora. Audrey's father didn't comment on her behavior, but he leveled a stern look in her direction once he'd completed his prayer.

Jim Parks, a burly man and the most experienced of the supervisors, took a drink of his coffee and gave a firm nod. "Good coffee as usual, Miss Audrey. And thank you for your prayer for our work, Boyd. This is going to be a full day, for sure. The three of us are going to Biscayne, where we'll be interviewing a group of men who've arrived in answer to ads the investors placed in several newspapers."

Aunt Thora shifted in her chair. "Northern or Southern newspapers?"

Mr. Parks hiked one shoulder as he slathered his biscuit with the scuppernong jelly. "Didn't ask. As long as they're qualified, I really don't care." He pointed to the bowl of jelly. "Sure do like this. Never heard of scuppernong jelly before. Tastes kind of like grape."

Aunt Thora curled her lip in disgust. " 'Course it tastes like grape. Any fool knows scuppernongs are grapes."

"What Aunt Thora meant to say is that scuppernongs are a white grape that is grown in the South, Mr. Parks. It's used much the same as darker grapes."

"Well, it sure is tasty." If Aunt Thora's remark offended him, he hid it well. "By the way, did you know the investors hired a doctor? Hear tell his two little girls will be coming, as well. We've made some adjustments to one of the overseer cottages where the family will be living."

Mr. Fenton nodded. "Yep, should be arriving today or tomorrow. Dr. Wahler from Atlanta." He arched his long neck and puffed his chest, obviously pleased to add an additional piece of gossip.

Audrey perked to attention at the news. A doctor's wife would prove a wonderful addition to the island. The company of another woman was always a welcome thought. Audrey loved Aunt Thora, but there were times when she longed to have someone closer to her own age, someone in whom she could confide. Still, Audrey was surprised that a doctor and his wife would want to leave Atlanta and move to Bridal Veil. The change would surely be difficult, but she'd do her best to see that they didn't find island life monotonous or dull.

"That is exciting news. I look forward to meeting them, especially Mrs. Wahler and the children." Had Audrey known they were arriving, she would have arranged to have basic supplies delivered to the cottage. Then again, perhaps Mrs. Wahler had the foresight to take care of that herself.

"Oh, ain't no Mrs. Wahler coming." Once again, Mr. Fenton's neck stretched until his beaklike nose overshot his plate, and Mr. Uptegrove, the third boarder, nodded his shiny bald head. "Word is, Mrs. Wahler's dead. Just gonna be the doctor, the two youngsters, and their housekeeper. If I understood correct, she's a colored woman." He lowered his voice to a whisper when he uttered the final two words.

Aunt Thora slid her napkin onto her lap. "There's no need to speak in whispers, Mr. Fenton. We know all about colored folk."

"Maybe. But this woman ain't a slave. He listed her as an *employee*."

A giant whoosh escaped Aunt Thora's lips. She directed a look of disgust at the man. "Nobody owns slaves anymore, Mr. Fenton. You may recall there was a war over slavery not so long ago." She'd sweetened her sarcastic words with enough honey to attract every bee in three counties. "That's back when you Northerners came down here and burned our —"

"That's enough, Thora. The war is over, and we'll have no more discussion of it at this table." Audrey's father slapped his knife onto the table with a decisive thud.

"As you wish, Boyd, but I'm just saying . . ."

Audrey's father held up his hand to silence her. "Does your trip into Biscayne this morning mean that we should expect additional boarders in the near future, Mr. Parks?"

"I think we'll have a houseful by week's end. I just hope they'll prove to be a good lot." Mr. Parks directed the final comment toward Audrey.

She hoped they would be a good lot, as well, but Mr. Parks's comment was enough to set her slightly on edge. There had been enough evidence in her past to prove construction workers could be a difficult group. Some were fine, upstanding men who offered a day's work for a day's wages, went home to their families, attended church on Sundays, and lived at peace with the world. Others, like her father in years past, enjoyed the taste of liquor, and though they performed their work, their families didn't see them — or their wages — on a regular basis.

Remembering the many days when her father stumbled into their house, his breath reeking of alcohol and his behavior as erratic and wild as a charging bull, Audrey decided she had best put some rules into effect prior to the arrival of the remaining boarders.

"Be sure you tell any of the men who will

be residing here at Bridal Fair that we have rules, and they will be strictly enforced. Those who don't adhere to the rules will be required to move to the workingmen's quarters."

Mr. Parks's eyes flashed with surprise, and his expression sobered. "Rules? I never heard about any rules before I moved in." He glanced at Mr. Fenton and Mr. Uptegrove. "Either of you hear about any rules?"

"Nope." They both shook their heads. Mr. Uptegrove leaned back in his chair. "What kind of rules are you referring to, Miss Audrey?"

Audrey could feel the heat climb up her neck. She'd spoken too soon. Telling the men her expectations in front of her father would cause them both discomfort. He'd think she didn't trust him. Still, she couldn't have men drinking or acting like ruffians in their home. She toyed with the edge of her napkin while she tried to sneak a look at her father. His focus was fastened on her like a starving dog eyeing a dish of food.

"I don't believe I've heard the rules, either. Why don't you run through them for us, Audrey?" Her father picked up his cup and took a deep swallow of coffee.

"I haven't posted the rules just yet because Mr. Morley personally vouched for the three of you. However, I don't want to have the order of our house disturbed by any unseemly behavior. It seems only sensible to post rules before the others arrive." She inhaled a deep breath.

"Audrey's right. I can only imagine what kind of roughnecks you're going to bring back to live under our roof." Aunt Thora blew a wisp of hair from her forehead. "Makes me shudder to think of it."

There was little doubt Thora was going to go off on one of her tangents if Audrey didn't interrupt. "First and foremost, there will be no drinking on the premises. Secondly, no man can return here if he is in an intoxicated state. No liquor can be brought into the house for any purpose. I don't want men buying alcohol and drinking it in their rooms," she explained.

Mr. Parks nodded. "Seems reasonable enough. Anything else?"

"Smoking is reserved for the porch only." Just yesterday she'd found evidence that Mr. Fenton had been smoking in his room. What if he fell asleep with a burning cigar or cigarette and set the house on fire? She wasn't about to take chances when it came to Bridal Fair. Besides, smoking indoors smelled up the entire house. "And every man must bathe on Saturday. Preferably more often, but I insist upon once a week."

"Whew! You sure got high standards. Hope there's nothing else." Mr. Fenton craned his neck and looked down his nose.

Audrey clenched her fingers until they started to lose all feeling. "There are a few other rules, but nothing I believe you'll find objectionable."

"Such as?" Mr. Fenton's eyebrows shot high on his forehead.

"I don't intend to keep food warm for stragglers. Meals will be served according to the work schedule. If someone dallies and isn't here, he'll have to wait until morning to eat. As you know, we pray before our meals. We expect the men to remain patient and quiet during prayers — even if it isn't their general practice." Audrey glanced back and forth among the men. "I will expect the men to strip their bedding on Monday morning so that I might have it washed and replaced by Monday evening. There may be a few other rules, but nothing beyond the normal expectations of mannerly conduct."

Mr. Parks shrugged his broad shoulders. "Well, I doubt you'll have any trouble from the three of us. We'll be sure to let the new hires know in advance. You'll be writing out these rules and posting them where the men can read them?"

"Yes, of course. I'll see to it this morning."

Once breakfast had been completed and the three men had departed for work, Audrey motioned to her father. "Were there any rules you wanted to add?"

He shook his head and grinned. "Still trying to protect me, even if I don't need it, right?" When she opened her mouth to object, he held up his hand. "No need to protest or apologize. If the rules make you feel better, then we'll have rules. I'm just glad you're willing to take on all this work so we can stay here." He pushed up from his chair and placed a fleeting kiss on her cheek. "I'm going to take a stroll and see what's happening at the work site."

Once her father departed, Audrey gathered the dishes and carried them to Aunt Thora, who'd taken up her position at the sink. She lifted a soapy hand from the water. "There's more rules you need to add to that list."

"Oh? And what would those be?"

The older woman wiped her hands on her apron. "This one is important. We need a rule that all of the men — especially the Yankees — need to pray nightly and ask God's forgiveness for their part in the War of Northern Aggression." Thora waved a crooked finger. "And they should seek forgiveness for their ancestors, too. Just being born into a family of Yankees is enough to put those fellas on the wrong side of the Lord's list, so they need to be doing a lot of praying." She pointed to a piece of paper. "Write that down before you forget it."

Audrey scraped the plates and placed them in the dishwater. "I don't think we want to try to force grown men to pray. I think it's best if they pray out of the conviction of their hearts, not because they're being compelled to recite what others want to hear."

Thora didn't appear convinced. One look at her eyes and Audrey could see she was formulating an argument. Finally, she simply muttered, "I'm not so sure."

There was no doubt that Thora's indecisive response was the most Audrey was going to get without further urging. "What if we agree to be faithful and pray for them instead?"

Thora clapped her hands together. "That's a perfect idea. We'll pray that they'll see the error of their Yankee ways and apologize once and for all for their ruinous deeds. And if they don't, we'll ask the good Lord to let 'em burn in —"

"Aunt Thora!" That hadn't been what Audrey had in mind, but she'd deal with the finer points of prayer later that evening. Right now, they needed to finish their chores.

After the dishes were done, Aunt Thora hung her apron beside the door. "I'm going to check on your father. He's been gone a while. I don't want him spending too much time amongst those Yankees. He's already too sympathetic. It was a sad day when he decided to let the enemy live on our fair soil." She clucked her tongue as she strode across the kitchen.

Audrey heaved a sigh of relief once the older woman departed. At least she'd be able to commit the regulations to paper without Aunt Thora's interference. Taking pen in hand, she carefully wrote out the list, pleased by the idea that if the men complied, these rules would provide protection and a peaceful household for all of them. She'd neared completion of the task when a knock sounded at the front door.

After pushing up from the desk, Audrey patted her hair and scurried to the front hallway. Pulling open the door, she was greeted by the delicious scent of the climbing asters that twined and bloomed along the front porch each fall. Normally, she would have taken a moment to inhale the

91

luscious fragrance, but the sight of a tall, muscular man on the other side of the threshold made any such idea flee from mind. She judged him to be no more than a few years her senior, but she couldn't be certain. The intensity of his dark brown eyes caused her to wonder if he might be somewhat older than he appeared.

Audrey took a step forward to block his entry. With her father away from the house, she didn't intend to invite a stranger inside. Offering only a slight smile, she nodded. "Good afternoon. If you're looking for the work site, you need to take the road that leads to the left at the end of the path."

"Thank you for the directions, but I'm searching for Boyd Cunningham, not a work site." He craned his neck and attempted to peer over her head. "This is his home, is it not?"

Audrey tipped her head to the side, hoping to obstruct his view. She was certain she'd never before seen this man. "Yes, but he isn't here right now."

The moment she'd uttered the words, Audrey wanted to stuff them back into her mouth. She shouldn't have told him she was alone. Then again, there was no reason to worry. He was a stranger who had no idea who else might be inside. For all he knew, there could be any number of men in the house — all of them prepared to come to her aid if needed.

"You must be his daughter, Audrey. Am I correct?"

Her mind raced as she attempted to place the tall, dark-eyed stranger. For the life of her, she couldn't connect him to anyone from their past. He didn't look familiar, and he didn't have a Southern accent.

Without giving him an answer, she jammed a fist on her hip and further blocked the doorway. "And you are?"

A slight twinkle sparked in his eyes as he dropped his traveling bag onto the porch. "I'm Marshall Graham, one of Wilbur Graham's sons. From Pittsburgh."

Feeling every ounce of strength drain from her body, Audrey slumped against the doorjamb for support. Her thoughts whirred at the memory of the Graham men. All of them in the construction business, all of them talented, and all of them rumored to be drunks, just like their father. She didn't have the vigor to deal with ghosts from the past — not now.

CHAPTER 6

Marshall stared in dismay as the young woman listed to one side and propped herself against the wooden framework. Surely it hadn't been his arrival that had caused such a reaction. He didn't even know Audrey Cunningham. Perhaps she was one of those timid women who fainted at every whipstitch. He mustered what he hoped was a friendly smile and reached forward to lend a hand. Before he could provide any assistance, she jerked away.

Surprised by her behavior, he retreated several steps. "I only wanted to help. I thought you were going to faint right there in the entrance." He remained at a slight distance. "You're quite pale. I'd be happy to help you inside, where you can rest."

The young woman brushed her fingertips along the sides of her face. From the defiant look in her eyes, he halfway expected her to pinch her cheeks just to prove him wrong. "When I need your help, Mr. Graham, I will ask for it."

Suddenly she'd regained her strength and assumed an air of authority that baffled him. "Well, excuse me. In the future, I'll remember that, Miss Cunningham. It is *Miss,* is it not?" If this woman thought she was the only one who could assume a prickly attitude, he'd set her straight right then.

She jutted her chin. "Indeed it is, though I don't believe my marital status should be of any importance to you, sir."

"Believe me, ma'am, your marital status is the furthest thing from my mind."

For the life of him, Marshall couldn't figure out what he'd done to offend this woman, but she wasn't the reason he was there. Doing his best to overlook her haughty behavior, he decided to begin anew. "I am here at your father's request. He asked that I pay him a visit at my earliest opportunity. Since I am currently between jobs, I decided this would be the perfect time to journey south."

He didn't miss the flash of surprise that crossed her face before she remembered to mask her emotions. This was one strange woman.

Her eyebrows knit tighter than the knots

in a fisherman's net. "You say my father wrote to you? And he asked you to come to Bridal Veil Island?"

"He did. And I must say that from the reports I'd heard about Southern hospitality, I'm more than a little disappointed." Marshall glanced toward one of the wicker chairs. "Since you're obviously not going to invite me inside, I'll just wait right here on the porch. I'm certain the chairs are comfortable." He turned, took two giant strides, and dropped into one of the nearby chairs. "I hope I can at least count on you to tell your father of my arrival. I wouldn't want to spend the night out here." He tipped his head and gave her a cocky grin.

Heat flooded Audrey's cheeks. "I told you my father isn't at home right now. You may await his return right where you are." She turned on her heel and scurried inside before he could question her further.

"Samson! Samson!" He heard the woman call from inside the house. "Samson, there's a man on the porch awaiting Father. Please keep an eye on him."

Marshall shook his head. Good grief. What a ruckus she was stirring up. He imagined a beefy servant standing guard at the door to bar him from any discourteous deeds.

"Sorry to disappoint," Marshall muttered.
Settling back, he pushed his hat forward to shade his eyes, stretched his legs, and rested his head against the back of the chair. He didn't know how long he'd been there before he was roused from his nap by someone grasping his shoulder. His hat slid to the ground, and he jumped to his feet.

Before he came fully awake, Boyd Cunningham grasped his hand and offered a smile as wide as the front porch. "Marshall! What a great surprise," he said as he took the chair next to him. "I was hoping you'd get down this way before winter set in up north." The older man glanced at the house. "Why didn't you go inside and have Audrey get you settled in one of the upstairs bedrooms?"

Marshall bent down and swooped up his hat. "From all appearances, she was none too happy to see me, though I'm not sure why. I've tried to recall if I did or said something that would have offended her, but for the life of me, I don't know what it would be." A fat gray tiger-striped cat rubbed against his trouser legs before jumping up to sit on his lap. "She even called for someone to keep watch over me in case I caused trouble."

"Truly? And who did she call on?"

Marshall gave the affectionate cat a scratch behind the ears. "Somebody named Samson. Said he was to keep watch over me."

Boyd laughed heartily. "Samson, eh? Well, meet your guardian." He pointed to the cat.

The cat gave a deep, throaty sound that came out more like a croak than a meow. Marshall looked at the animal and then to Boyd. "A guard cat?"

Boyd sighed and shook his head. "Don't worry about Audrey. She's a bit standoffish from time to time. I didn't tell her you were coming, so she's probably unhappy with me."

Marshall didn't believe that Audrey's lackluster welcome had anything to do with her father. There'd been something else, something about him that had set her on edge. Maybe once they became acquainted she would tell him. Then again, he wondered if he'd be around long enough to thaw that icy exterior of hers. Samson jumped off Marshall's lap, ambled off the porch, and plopped down by the steps in the shade as if completely bored with the conversation.

"Another Yankee! Heaven help us. They jest keep on comin'. Will there be no end to it?"

Marshall turned toward the spry old woman who was marching up the porch steps. She was eyeing him with obvious disdain as she approached.

"Thora, this man is a friend of mine, and I expect you to treat him with kindness." Boyd pinned the older lady with a meaningful stare before he nodded toward the door. "I'm sure Audrey could use some help with the noonday meal. And be sure to tell her that Samson approves of our new guest."

The woman's features pinched into an unswerving frown. "That cat has always been a good judge of character, but I'm not so sure this time."

Marshall trained his gaze upon her as she stomped into the house. What was it about him that had brought out the worst in these women? He hadn't wanted to come in the first place, but these women made him question his decision even further. If it hadn't been for Boyd's pleading letters, he would have simply continued on to Jekyl Island without stopping at Bridal Veil.

Boyd grinned at Marshall. "The ladies of the house think the cat is a good judge of character. Thought it might help if Audrey knew Samson had taken a liking to you." He pushed up from his chair and motioned toward the path leading away from the house. "Let's take a walk. I'd like to speak to you in private." They were only a short distance from Bridal Fair when Boyd looked at him. "What finally convinced you to come?"

"Maybe it had something to do with the fact that you wouldn't quit writing to me. I figured the only way to stop those letters was to come down here." Marshall grinned. "Besides, my work came to an end in Pittsburgh, and one of your earlier letters mentioned there would soon be construction work at Jekyl Island. Thought maybe I'd stand a chance of becoming one of the foremen if I got down here before they started to clear the land and build."

Boyd nodded. "There's some work going on over there. Not sure how much they've accomplished or if they're still hiring, but we can talk about that later. To be honest, I hoped the lure of work would bring you when my initial letters didn't seem to sway you."

"It isn't that you didn't write a convincing letter. Fact is, I was contracted for several jobs, and I couldn't just up and leave. I'd never be hired again if word got around that I'd walked off a job. You should know that better than anyone."

Marshall slowed his stride to allow Boyd to catch up. The older man's legs were a bit shorter than his own, but Boyd's step was heavy, as though he was having trouble putting one foot in front of the other. He wasn't the same man who had spent long hours performing construction work with Marshall's father years ago. But then, age had a way of stealing a man's vigor, and Boyd hadn't mentioned any health problems when he'd written.

"From what I hear, you're one of the best in the construction business nowadays. I think any of those contractors in Pittsburgh would give most anything to have you overseeing their projects."

"That's a nice thought, but a man is only as good as his last job. You may recall that word travels fast in the construction business." Marshall glanced at the older man.

There was little doubt Boyd remembered that architects and project managers would tolerate bad behavior only for a short time before they searched for a replacement. And though those in charge would never admit it, once a man was blackballed by one construction manager or architect, he'd have trouble getting hired by another — at least in the same city. And if one was somehow fortunate enough to find that second job and anything went amiss, he'd better be prepared to leave town and hope his reputation — or in this case his family's reputation — didn't follow.

Of course, back in his father's and Boyd's construction days in Pittsburgh, there had been project managers who enjoyed drinking and carousing as much as the men who worked for them. And it seemed both Boyd and Marshall's father had managed to work for those men during the greatest portions of their careers. Thoughts of his father and the mayhem his drinking had created for his family caused Marshall to shudder. That same demon had created pain and heartache for Boyd's family, as well.

"How are your brothers doing? Have they given up the bottle?"

Marshall shook his head. "I'd like to tell you they have, but I'm afraid not. All three of them live for the taste of liquor. Sad to watch them destroy their lives and follow in my father's footsteps. Quite a legacy the old man left for his sons."

Boyd pointed to a large flat rock. "Let's sit a spell. You know, Marshall, bitterness won't change things for you or for them." He lowered himself onto one corner and patted the spot beside him. "I call this my prayer rock. Reminds me of the solid rock I have in the Lord. When I can't figure things out, I come here and talk to Him. Thought it would be a good place to have a long overdue talk with you, too."

A stab of envy shot through Marshall as he dropped down beside the older man. He was glad Boyd had given up the bottle, but Marshall questioned why his own father hadn't done the same. Why hadn't he come to know the Lord and changed his ways before he died? If only he'd put down the bottle long enough to actually see the pain he was causing his wife and children, life could have been so different. Instead, he'd gone to his grave leaving a legacy of three sons who'd chosen to follow his bad example. Except for him, all of Wilbur Graham's sons had decided to travel the same path as their father. And for that, Marshall had paid dearly.

"You're right about the bitterness: It doesn't change things. But it's hard to tamp down that anger when trying to do your best. The pain remains." He rubbed his hand along his jaw.

Boyd tilted his head to one side and looked at Marshall. "I'm sorry for your pain. I know there was a deep divide between you and your father at the time of his death, but I hope that coming here to talk with me will help relieve some of that grief."

Marshall doubted Boyd could help. The problems ran much deeper than a father who had gone to his grave an out-and-out drunk. He'd lived through that heartache and so had his mother. And they'd endured the horror of having the head of their household die in a barroom brawl. But Marshall doubted there would ever be healing with his brothers, for they were just as set in their drinking habits as their father had ever been.

"I don't see how it can help much. My father would never take my advice to give up the bottle, and my brothers are determined to follow in his footsteps." Marshall leaned back and rested against the trunk of the tree that towered over the huge rock. "Since none of them will change their ways, I had to let them go from the last job, and I've refused to hire any of them. Now they won't speak to me." He glanced at Boyd. "Not one of them is dependable, and I just couldn't take any more chances with them."

Marshall didn't miss the look of understanding in Boyd's eyes. "They've put you in a hard place, for sure, but you had to meet your obligations to the men who hired you. I think the Lord expects a man to give an honest day's work for an honest day's pay. If your brothers weren't willing to do that, then they'll have to suffer the consequences — or find a contractor willing to tolerate their bad behavior."

"I know you're right, but they're married and have children to feed. The guilt has overwhelmed me at times." He kept his eyes fixed on the ground. "That's part of the reason I came down here. I figured if I left Pittsburgh, they'd realize they had to depend upon themselves and eventually see the error of their ways."

Boyd patted Marshall's shoulder. "I doubt the fact that you've left will have much effect on them. A man and his bottle are hard to separate. Probably the best thing we can do is ask God to look out for them and for their families."

Marshall agreed that God was the only one who could pull his brothers out of the revolting habit that had robbed them of their hopes, dreams, and dignity. But his prayers hadn't done much good for his father, and thus far, they hadn't helped his brothers, either. Maybe he hadn't been devout enough. Had it been Audrey's prayers that had saved Boyd from the demon in the bottle? If so, maybe he should enlist her help. Then again, one thought of her earlier greeting was enough to waylay such a plan. He doubted that even a hot Georgia sun could melt Audrey Cunningham's icy attitude.

"I know your pain runs deep where your father is concerned, but I need to pass along some things that may help." Boyd massaged his forehead. "I should have talked to you before now, but I couldn't get you to answer my letters."

That much was true. Marshall had wanted nothing to do with his father's old drinking buddy. On the day of the funeral, Marshall had attempted to bury his grief-stricken memories along with his father's coffin. But those memories continued to haunt him. Each of Boyd's letters had been a reminder of his father — a reminder he hadn't wanted. Yet as his relationship with his brothers continued to deteriorate, Marshall knew the time to put the past behind him had arrived. And putting the past behind him would be impossible until he let Boyd have his say.

"I don't know if you remember that I was at the hospital right before your father died."

Marshall bobbed his head. He remembered. At the time he figured Boyd had hidden a paper-wrapped bottle in his pocket and had come to offer Marshall's dying father one last drink before he passed on to his just reward.

"Your father asked me to tell you a few things that he couldn't say to you himself. I think he figured you wouldn't believe him." Boyd hesitated and looked Marshall in the eye. "Your father was proud of you — thankful that you have always been strong enough to avoid the lure of alcohol. He was truly sorry for the way he treated all of you, especially your mother."

"He should have been sorry. It was his drinking that sent my mother to an early grave. It was worry over him that killed her." The words left a bitter taste in his mouth as he recalled his mother's death.

"That may be true, but it can't be changed. The only thing that can be changed is you. If you're going to find any peace in this lifetime, you're going to have to forgive him and shed the past. 'Course, whether you choose to believe me or not is up to you. But I know he spoke the truth when he told me he was proud of you and all you'd accomplished, Marshall. A man doesn't speak lies on his deathbed." Boyd pushed to his feet. "You think about what I've said. It may take some time and prayer, but eventually I think you'll come to believe the truth of what I've told you."

Marshall wasn't certain he wanted to know that his father had spoken well of him. He'd harbored nothing but ill feelings toward the man. To think otherwise went against the grain. Still, he couldn't deny the twinge of pride he experienced upon hearing the words of praise. Perhaps Boyd was right — maybe in time he'd come to a place where he could set aside the past. But not now. First, he needed to digest what Boyd had told him.

"Come on and walk a ways with me. My bones ache if I sit too long, and there's something I want to show you." Motioning Marshall forward, Boyd turned to the left when they approached a fork in the path.

Marshall didn't know where they were headed, but he followed along, willing to explore the island before he departed. There was no denying the beauty of the area. The aged oaks with their festoons of moss provided the perfect place for birds to conceal their nests, and several winged creatures sang for them as they passed beneath the long, low branches. The beauty of Bridal Veil couldn't be denied, but not as a permanent home — at least not for him. Marshall preferred dramatic changes of season: leaves changing color on a fall day, the smell of damp grass and budding flowers in the spring, the warmth of sunshine on a summer day, and the sight of snowflakes in the moonlight on a cold winter night. He hoped to one day find all of those things in Colorado. Although these balmy winter days along the southern coast were a pleasant change, it wasn't a climate he'd want to embrace for a lifetime. Still, he wasn't unmindful of the advantages of a pleasant year-round climate, especially for a man in the construction trade. There'd be no delays because of snow or sleet, and no problems with frozen ground.

The sound of men's voices drifted toward them as they approached a large clearing. A few of the men picked up their tools when they arrived, but their appearance didn't cause much of a stir among the workers.

Boyd glanced over his shoulder before he pointed to an area where the men had been working. "This is where the clubhouse will be located. There will be a number of amenities on the main floor, including an elegant ballroom, and hotel rooms on the upper floors. I think this setting far out-shines what they've got planned over at Jekyl. Folks will have a much better view of the Argosy River from this site, and on a clear day guests will have a fine view of the mainland of Georgia from the clubhouse balconies." He chuckled. " 'Course some folks might say I'm a little biased in my opinion."

Marshall stepped forward and surveyed

the area. "Well, I'd say you're right about having an excellent view, but I can't compare it to Jekyl, since I've not yet been over there."

Boyd gave the younger man a pat on the shoulder. "And there's no need for you to go over there, either. I know Victor Morley and his investors would be more than pleased to have someone of your ability come to work for them. Mr. Morley is returning later today to check on the progress, and it would be an excellent opportunity for you to meet him. He and his partners can use a man with your experience, and I'm hoping you'll agree to stay here and work for them. There's no need for you to even consider the Jekyl project." Boyd pointed at several men who'd settled beneath a live oak in the distance. "Looks like these men need someone who can persuade them to keep moving, and I'm sure you're just the man to fit the bill."

"You may be sure, but I'm not. Personally, I prefer to hire workers who don't have to be watched over like young children."

"Exactly! And you can instill those values in these men. They just need a bit of guidance, and you'll have them on the straight and narrow in no time." Boyd leaned a bit closer and grinned. "Besides, I could use another man around the house to take my side when Audrey or Thora gets a bee in her bonnet."

Marshall doubted he'd be much help on that account. After the reception he'd received from Audrey, he imagined she would do her best to see that he was on the next boat to Jekyl Island. Thoughts of the young woman and the unruly brown locks that framed her delicate features caused his heart to quicken for a moment. He couldn't deny Audrey's appeal. Nor could he deny the aversion she'd exhibited toward him.

Boyd nudged him from his thoughts. "Say you'll at least give Victor a chance to argue his case and make an offer before you go looking for a job over on Jekyl Island."

Marshall nodded. "I suppose it wouldn't hurt me to hear him out. After receiving your last letter, I had planned to remain a night or two before going on to Jekyl."

Besides, staying a couple extra days would give Marshall an opportunity to figure out what he'd done to offend Miss Cunningham. Her hostility was truly a mystery. A mystery he'd like to unravel before he left the island.

"Thank you, Marshall. Once you talk to Mr. Morley, I think you'll be glad you decided on Bridal Veil."

"Whoa! I didn't say I'd decided to remain more than a night or two. Mr. Morley hasn't even offered me a job, so let's don't make this more than it is." As they continued to walk, Marshall waved toward the surrounding landscape. "Looks like there's plenty to be accomplished before this place will be prepared to welcome guests." Although the workers had begun grading roads, draining a nearby pond, and cutting a canal, all of those jobs would need to be completed before they began construction of a clubhouse and homes that would suit wealthy inhabitants. The project presented complex challenges, especially in light of the fact that promises had been made to ensure the preservation of the land. A fact Boyd had earlier indicated, and one that he didn't hesitate to mention.

The older man nodded. "Most of the island has been set aside for preservation, but there's no getting around some of the necessary changes that come with the construction of a clubhouse as well as many new houses. I've already accepted the fact that portions of the island will be changed, but I plan to hold Mr. Morley and his fellow investors to their word about the remainder of the island — I've got it in writing." His deep-set eyes glimmered with a spark of humor. "As for problems, we're not having near the troubles they're having over on Jekyl." A chuckle rumbled deep in his chest. "The investors over at Jekyl want to make the place into a hunting paradise, not just a place to relax with their families. To do that, they've first had to clear out the cattle and horses already on the island. They were able to sell the cattle, but rounding up some of those wild stallions proved to be more of a challenge than those fellows expected. And they still haven't gotten rid of all the wild boar."

"What?" Marshall glanced over his shoulder. "These islands are inhabited with wild boar?"

"Not here on Bridal Veil. But years ago the king of Italy presented a pair of wild boars to a friend of J. P. Morgan. When J.P.'s friend couldn't find a suitable home for the animals, J.P. offered Jekyl Island. Naturally, the boars mingled with the wild pigs that were already on the island. After a number of years, a herd of those wild, mean creatures was roaming the island. Read in the newspaper last week that a boar had killed some fine hunting dogs. Open season has been declared on the boar, and there's no telling how that will turn out. Just hope no one gets killed in the scuffle." Boyd removed

113

his hat and wiped the perspiration from his forehead.

Though dank, the temperature remained seasonably mild, and the older man's gesture surprised Marshall. After living in the South for the last several years, Boyd should be accustomed to these humid conditions. Then again, Marshall thought it would take him more than a few years to become used to the humidity. "You need to rest, Boyd?"

"No. I'm just feeling a little warm." He fanned his hat in front of his face. "As I was saying, you wouldn't have to contend with a wild boar population here on this island. Although we have enjoyed some of the fine meat. We have the benefits without the danger."

"Well, that's an argument in favor of Bridal Veil, for sure." Marshall nodded toward the path. "Maybe we should head back to the house." Although he would have enjoyed viewing more of the island, he noted that Boyd continued to perspire, and his complexion had turned a pasty hue. No doubt Miss Cunningham would take him to task if her father became ill while in his company. And that old woman they called Aunt Thora would likely agree.

Boyd didn't argue against returning home. "Maybe Mr. Morley will be there by the time we get back. I know you'll like him. He's a good, honest man. In fact, he was Audrey's employer back when we lived in Pittsburgh."

"Is that so?" Marshall didn't know what type of business Mr. Morley operated back in Pittsburgh. Although Boyd had mentioned having completed a construction project on his home, the older man hadn't mentioned Mr. Morley's line of business.

"What work did she perform for Mr. Morley?"

A hint of color had returned to Boyd's cheeks, and he picked up his step. "I guess I misspoke. She actually worked for both Mr. and Mrs. Morley. She was their assistant housekeeper and also helped with their children. She's missed the youngsters since moving down here." He tipped his head to one side and glanced up. "She enjoys children."

Marshall ignored the remark about children and moved on to more familiar ground. "So is Mr. Morley in the steel or coal business?"

"Neither one. He's strictly an investor and banker, but I'd guess he owns some interest in the steel and coal industry. Seems as though all of the money men in Pittsburgh have some kind of ownership in the steel mills, don't you think?"

Marshall shrugged. He assumed Boyd was correct, but Marshall's personal involvement with "money men" had been non-existent. Though he'd worked on projects for men such as Andrew Carnegie and Henry Frick, there had always been project managers and architects layered between Marshall and the wealthy men who signed the checks.

When they arrived back at the house, Boyd declared they should both rest until time for the noon meal. Though Marshall wasn't in need of rest, his options were limited. If he rejected the idea, Boyd would likely forgo a much needed nap, for he wouldn't want to be considered a poor host. And if anything happened to Boyd, Aunt Thora and Miss Cunningham would likely point a finger in Marshall's direction.

After brief consideration of his options, Marshall followed Boyd upstairs and settled into the room Boyd directed him to. Needed or not, he'd rest until time to eat.

When he descended the steps an hour later, Boyd appeared a bit sprightlier. The old woman walked into the dining room and was placing the dinnerware on the table as Boyd slapped Marshall on the shoulder. "You're in for a real treat — we're having shrimp and rice croquettes. They're one of Thora's specialties, aren't they, Thora."

There was a glint in the old woman's eyes as she turned and looked at Marshall. "That's what everyone tells me, so I got no choice but to believe it's true." A smile slowly spread across her lips. "You Northern boys like shrimp, Mr. Graham?"

Marshall hesitated. He didn't want to offend the woman, but shrimp wasn't one of his favorite foods. "We don't get much fresh seafood in Pittsburgh, but I'm sure I'll enjoy whatever you've prepared."

Thora cackled and meandered toward the kitchen with a slight wave of her hand. The woman's behavior had done little to enhance Marshall's appetite. For all he knew, she'd spent the morning dreaming up some way to poison him.

CHAPTER 7

Much had happened during the past forty-eight hours — some of it interesting, some of it perplexing, and some of it downright annoying. The day before, Dr. Wahler and his daughters arrived on the afternoon boat — at least that's what Audrey had been told. Thus far she'd not been introduced to the doctor or his children, an occurrence she had found most perplexing. Though she'd expected the doctor to stop at Bridal Fair before heading off to his own cottage, she surmised he had likely made a wise decision by settling the children into their new accommodations with as little fanfare as possible. A new home and strange surroundings could certainly overwhelm young children. If time permitted, she would visit the doctor's cottage this afternoon and offer a proper welcome. For now, she needed to complete breakfast preparations.

While she mixed cream into the eggs for a

satisfying Saturday morning breakfast, her thoughts skittered like bacon grease in a hot skillet. Last evening Mr. Morley and Stuart Griggs, his architect, had met in the parlor to discuss drainage problems on the island, and in the midst of their discussion, her father had interrupted them to introduce Marshall Graham to Mr. Morley. She'd been surprised when her father rattled off Marshall's credentials as a talented construction supervisor, but her surprise soon turned to annoyance. Her father had appeared as proud as a peacock. She'd briefly considered asking if Mr. Graham carried letters of recommendation to prove all the claims of his success, but she wouldn't embarrass her father. Yet, if Marshall possessed his father's penchant for alcohol — and she'd been told long ago that *all* of the Graham men enjoyed their liquor far too much — he had likely come south because he could no longer find work up north. Granted, he didn't appear to be a drinker, but he was still relatively young. In a few more years, it would catch up with him, and the physical effects would become apparent, just as they had with her father.

Last evening, the men had agreed to meet after breakfast, and Audrey now worried that her father's recommendation of Mr.

Graham could cause trouble. Truth be told, she'd been hard-pressed to hide her aggravation. She had hoped Marshall Graham would be boarding a boat and departing for Jekyl Island by now. She didn't need the worry of a probable drinker moving into their home. She could only hope that Mr. Morley would realize he had no need of another supervisor for his project. And if he didn't know it, she hoped the conversation during breakfast would prove her correct.

As soon as the men arrived in the dining room and settled at their places, her father offered thanks for breakfast and asked God's protection over the workers and a productive day for the men. His prayer gave Audrey the exact opening she wanted. While passing the biscuits, she directed her attention to Mr. Fenton, Mr. Uptegrove, and Mr. Parks. "You've been so busy that I haven't heard a progress report regarding your venture into Biscayne the other day. I do hope you were successful."

Mr. Fenton helped himself to a biscuit, broke it in half, and slathered it with butter. "We had more men show up than either of us expected. Most of them will start the first of the week." He peered down the table and met Audrey's gaze. "Mostly single fellas. The married ones aren't so keen on leaving their families behind all week, but I think we'll have those old slave quarters filled with a good crew of workers real soon. Best part is that I found a man who was a cook in the army, and he's already arrived to take over the cooking and laundry duties for the workers." Mr. Fenton grinned and spooned a dollop of jelly onto the other half of his biscuit. "Now I won't have to listen to any more bellyaching from the men we already got living in the slave quarters."

Audrey was pleased, as well, for there had been daily reports of discontent over the men having to cook their own food, while the supervisors enjoyed fine meals at Bridal Fair. Although she'd been willing to make grocery purchases for the workers when she did her weekly shopping in Biscayne, she didn't have the time or desire to take on cooking and laundry for all the men.

"Once we get all the workers we need, that cook is gonna need several assistants to help him, but it's a good start." Mr. Parks spooned up another helping of eggs. "It's gonna take a strong hand to keep those men in line, but once they understand the *rules,* they'll do fine."

Audrey didn't miss the supervisor's emphasis when he mentioned rules. She offered him a bright smile. "If you'd like, I'd be happy to help you compose a list that you can post in their quarters right away. I believe it's easier to have rules in place sooner rather than later, don't you?"

"Exactly!" They all turned toward Victor Morley as he added his agreement. "You do that, Audrey — help Jim get a list of regulations together and post them in several places where the men will be sure to see them. Wouldn't hurt to read them aloud as soon as the men are assigned to their sleeping quarters, too. If we're going to meet deadlines, the men need to know that they're here to work and we'll not tolerate bad behavior."

From the look in Mr. Parks's eyes, Audrey wasn't sure whether he was pleased with the idea of reading or posting rules, but she knew he wouldn't challenge Mr. Morley. "So all the positions are now filled?"

Strands of Mr. Parks's still damp hair drooped forward. "Oh, we're still gonna need more laborers as the work progresses, but you should have a full house here at Bridal Fair real soon." He grinned at Audrey.

His final comment set Audrey's teeth on edge. That wasn't what she'd expected or wanted to hear. "Having a bedroom or two available for visitors would be much preferred, Mr. Parks. We didn't plan to have all of the rooms filled with supervisors."

"We didn't?" Her father tipped his head to one side and stared at her as though she'd lost her senses. "You're the one who told me —"

"If we fill all the rooms, where will Mr. Morley and the other investors stay when they come down here to check on the progress?" She hoped the idea would give Mr. Morley pause before he hired Marshall Graham.

Mr. Parks picked up the cream pitcher and poured a dollop into his coffee. "That's not a problem, Miss Audrey. I'd be glad to go down to the other quarters when the investors come for a few days." Mr. Parks nudged Mr. Fenton. "You'd be glad to do the same, wouldn't you, Harry?"

Mr. Fenton's Adam's apple danced up and down as he swallowed a bite of buttered biscuit. "Wouldn't mind at all." He waved the remaining piece of biscuit in the air. "Just as long as I get to come back up here to the house for my meals. I doubt that fellow you hired to cook in the slave quarters will compare with Miss Audrey."

Audrey offered a feeble smile. Under normal circumstances, Mr. Fenton's praise would have pleased her, but not today. If she was going to prevent Marshall Graham's employment, she'd need another plan. Right now, she had no idea what that might be, but with the proper encouragement, perhaps Aunt Thora would come up with a scheme.

The minute the platter of biscuits emptied, she jumped to her feet and hurried to the kitchen. Aunt Thora was sitting at the small table by herself. Since "the invasion of Yankees," she'd refused to eat her meals at the dining room table. Audrey set the platter on the table and waited until the old woman looked up. "I think Mr. Morley is going to hire Marshall Graham, which means we'll have another Yankee moving into the house." Audrey hoped her reference to Marshall as a Yankee would win Thora to her side. "I think he's going to be one too many boarders for us. Maybe we should figure out a way to keep Mr. Morley from hiring him — or at least from having him move into Bridal Fair."

Thora hunched forward and reached for the jam. "Don't know how you 'spect me to help. You and your papa spread the welcome mat for those Yankee invaders, and now you want to yank it back?" She popped a piece of biscuit into her mouth and wiped her lips. "I say the best thing to do is shoot a round of buckshot into the dining room and clear them all out of there. I don't figure Mr. Graham's any worse than the rest of those Yankees sitting around your grandmother's table."

"Aunt Thora! How can you even suggest such a thing?"

The old woman looked up, her blue eyes as clear as a summer sky. "You asked for an idea. That's all I got to offer." She downed her tea and pushed up from the table. "You oughta give my suggestion a little more thought. Matter of fact, I'd be pleased to go and load the gun right now."

Audrey patted the woman's shoulder. "I appreciate your offer to help, but I think I'll need another plan. One that doesn't involve guns."

Aunt Thora looked up at Audrey. "There's a possibility we could overtake the Yankees with knives, but knives are risky, and we're not as strong as some of those men." She pointed a crooked finger at the dining room. "And we're outnumbered."

Audrey shivered at the suggestion. She'd made a dire mistake seeking advice from Aunt Thora. If she didn't redirect her, Thora would soon be gathering knives and attacking their boarders. "I believe we may need some additional biscuits, Aunt Thora. Would you mix up another batch?"

Thora's thick white eyebrows drooped low above her eyes, and her lips tightened into a thin line before she finally spoke. "One minute you're talking about wiping out the enemy, and the next minute, you're wanting me to feed 'em." Frustration shone in her eyes as she yanked off her apron and slapped it on the chair. "I'm not sure which one of us is crazy: you or me. I'm going down and sit by the river for a spell. Maybe by the time I get back, you'll decide what you want to do about the invaders."

For several minutes after Aunt Thora disappeared from sight, Audrey stared out the window. Her aunt was right: She didn't know what she wanted. While they needed the income from the workmen, she certainly didn't want the likes of Marshall Graham moving into their home and influencing her father to return to his old habits. Even though her father had given up drinking and grown in his faith throughout these past years, she didn't know if he had the strength to resist his old ways if lured by the appeal of a so-called friend offering liquor.

She couldn't guess how much sway Marshall might have over her father. Guilt still occasionally plagued him when he remembered the incident that had taken Wilbur

Graham's life. Her father had been the one who'd convinced Wilbur to stop for a drink after work the night he'd been killed. If Marshall should happen to dwell on that topic for long, Audrey couldn't be sure if her father would turn to prayer or down a bottle of liquor instead.

When she finally returned to the dining room, the men had completed their breakfast, and her father greeted her with a broad grin. "Marshall's going to be staying on with us, Audrey. Isn't that fine news?"

She turned an icy stare in Marshall's direction. "Be sure you read the rules, Mr. Graham. They apply to all of our boarders." Deciding whether Mr. Graham or her father had been more surprised by her remark was difficult to determine. They both appeared taken aback by her curt comment, but she didn't want Mr. Graham to plead ignorance to the rules. Not now. And not later, either.

"Yes, ma'am," Mr. Graham said with a hint of amusement. "Samson told me all about them when he was . . . um . . . keeping me company the other day."

Audrey felt her face redden. Her father stifled a choking laugh, while the other men appeared confused. Audrey looked at Mr. Graham and nodded.

"So long as you know."

■ ■ ■ ■

The late afternoon sun turned a shimmering golden hue that glistened as it shone through the kitchen windows, but before Audrey could begin supper, the dry laundry needed to be removed from the clotheslines. For a moment, she considered sending Aunt Thora to do the job, but four hands would be quicker than two. "We need to get that laundry off the lines, Aunt Thora."

The shuffle of the older woman's shoes announced her approach from the dining room. "Make up your mind. You want me to set the table or take down the sheets?"

Audrey glanced over her shoulder and shot the woman a warm smile. "Both." She waved toward the back door. "There will be plenty of time to set the table after we get back to the house. I haven't even started supper yet."

"You're the one who told me to set the table." Aunt Thora muttered her rebuke as they walked the path to the washhouse. "Sure would be easier if the clotheslines were closer to the house. Think I'll tell Boyd to move 'em between the trees in the backyard."

"I don't want the view blocked by laundry

flapping in the breeze. Besides, we'd have to carry the wet clothes all the way from the washhouse, and those baskets are heavy."

"I guess you got a point about carrying the baskets, but since the Yankees arrived, there's no time to enjoy the view anyway. We're too busy tending to the needs of the boarders you're inviting into the house at every turn."

Audrey sighed. Although Thora understood their plight, Audrey doubted she would ever accept the idea of boarders living in Bridal Fair, especially boarders that hailed from north of the Mason-Dixon Line.

When they arrived at the washhouse, Audrey proceeded inside and picked up two large wicker baskets. Outside, she plopped one of them on the grass near Aunt Thora's feet. "You begin with this line, and I'll go down and begin with the other."

The woman chuckled. "Trying to get as far away from me as possible? You just don't want to hear the truth. I tell you, this world has just turned upside down. If you would have ever told me that I'd be doing laundry for a bunch of Yankees, I would have said you were crazy as a goose."

Audrey waved and shook her head. "Just take down the clothes, Aunt Thora."

When her father had proposed the idea of

taking in boarders, Audrey hadn't considered the extra laundry. Not that it would have changed her decision. They were without many choices. Still, washing and ironing the clothes for the extra men, along with the additional linens, had already presented more work than she'd anticipated. Once they were on better financial footing, she'd speak to her father about hiring someone to help.

While still considering the possibility of another woman to assist with the chores, Audrey removed a clothes-peg from one of the sheets.

"Here, let me help you fold that."

Audrey startled and turned toward the man's voice. Marshall Graham! "What are you doing out here? Aren't you supposed to be off learning about your duties?"

He removed another wooden peg and continued walking toward her while folding the length of sheet. "We've finished for now, and I decided to take a better look at the property out here behind the house." He nodded toward the corner of sheet that she held in her right hand. "If you'll give that to me, I'll have it in a neat square in no time."

Audrey didn't move.

"During my younger years, I helped my mother with the laundry. If you'll just turn loose of that corner, I promise I'll fold this into a perfect square." He moved forward, and Audrey instinctively took a backward step and dropped the sheet from between her fingers. As the fabric started to fall, Marshall jumped forward and caught the corner. Aligning the edges, he snapped the fabric in the afternoon breeze and formed a perfect square. He held it at arm's length. "There, you see? My mother taught me the trick of folding sheets at an early age."

"And I'm sure that some years later your father taught you some of his tricks, as well."

Marshall tipped his head to one side and studied her for a moment. "I would say you're right on that account. Even his former supervisors would agree that my father was a capable tradesman."

Several sharp retorts came to mind, but Audrey held her tongue. She wouldn't speak ill of his deceased father, but she was certain Marshall's father had taught him about drinking as well as the construction business. Marshall dropped the neatly folded sheet into the basket and reached for another sheet. "I don't need your help, Mr. Graham. Aunt Thora and I have managed to do laundry without any assistance for many years."

He lowered his arm but kept his gaze fixed

on her. "Exactly what have I done to offend you, Miss Cunningham?"

He'd given her the perfect opening, but before she could open her mouth to reply, Aunt Thora stomped in their direction, her arms piled high with laundry. "You're a no-account Yankee, that's what!"

Marshall backed up a few steps as Thora continued toward him. A devilish grin played at his lips as he settled his hands on his hips. "Well, that's not entirely correct, Miss Thora. I'm actually only half Yankee. My mama was born and raised in Savannah."

Thora's eyes clouded with confusion as she stepped closer. "Savannah? As in Savannah, Georgia?"

Marshall chuckled. "Yes, ma'am. I don't believe I know of any other Savannah."

"And I don't know that I believe you." The lines in her weathered face deepened into a frown. "Whereabouts in Savannah?"

Samson sauntered over to Marshall and rubbed up against his leg. Marshall smiled and picked the cat up. "Over on Randolph Street, close to the river — at least that's what she used to tell me. Thought I might do a bit of looking for the place once I get settled in." He removed a clothes-peg from one of the shirts and dropped it into the basket. "Maybe you'd like to come along and help me."

Audrey wanted to yank the cat from Marshall's arms and declare him a traitor. *Goodness,* she thought, *I'm starting to sound like Aunt Thora.*

"Don't you be trying to win me over with your Yankee ways, young man. I can do some checking on you with my friends in Savannah, and I'll soon know if you're telling me the truth. Meantime, I'll be keeping a sharp eye on you."

Audrey grinned as she listened to the banter between the two. Mr. Graham had met his match with Aunt Thora. No doubt she'd be writing a letter to someone in Savannah and sending it with Old Sam in the morning.

"You're quite fetching when you smile, Miss Cunningham. You should try it more often." He put the cat down and gave Audrey a grin.

Thora took a step forward and waggled her finger beneath Marshall's nose. "How can I believe your mama was a true Southern woman when you exhibit the manners of a Yankee? No Southern gentleman would act in such a forward manner with a lady." She poked a gnarled finger at his chest and *tsk*ed. "It's clear your Yankee blood is stronger than your Southern heritage." Samson sauntered between the two of them. " 'Course maybe that's why Samson took a liking to you — he knows you're a Southerner at heart, even if you haven't entirely learned our ways."

Marshall chuckled and bowed from the waist. "Then I will rely upon you and Samson to help me improve my manners, Miss Thora."

CHAPTER 8

As the days passed, the work proved more exhausting than she'd imagined, and Audrey longed for help with both the cooking and laundry. In fact, if Marshall Graham would have made another appearance at the washhouse or the clotheslines, she would have gladly accepted his help — even though she hadn't yet learned to trust him. She still couldn't believe that Mr. Morley had hired Mr. Graham as project manager. Hopefully her father wouldn't regret his recommendation of the young man. And hopefully Marshall Graham wouldn't prove to be a bad influence on her father.

After their discussion with Marshall about his mother being raised in Savannah, Aunt Thora had immediately penned a letter to Delmar Ross, one of her few remaining friends there. Though Delmar's enlistment as a soldier in the Confederate Army had been refused due to a bad leg, his loyalty to the South had never been questioned. Especially when rumors surfaced that he'd acted as a spy for General Wheeler. Audrey doubted the claims, but Aunt Thora remained convinced and declared that her old friend could unearth the truth about anyone. Delmar had written back, acknowledging that Mr. Graham's assertion of his Southern roots was true. Aunt Thora had yet to decide if he possessed enough redeeming characteristics to qualify him as a true Southern gentleman, while Audrey remained skeptical of his sobriety.

He'd been the model of discretion since arriving at Bridal Fair, but that wasn't enough to convince Audrey. Even her father had been able to put aside the bottle for several weeks at a time when necessary to maintain a job or keep up appearances for outsiders.

She glanced up from the sink as her father entered the kitchen and neared her side. "You look to be deep in thought," he said.

"I'm trying to figure out how to keep ahead of all this work. Without some additional help, it's soon going to get the best of me. Thora tires quickly, and I can't expect her to work like a woman half her age."

"I feel terrible that it's come to this, Audrey." Her father massaged his forehead. "Maybe we should reconsider selling. This work is going to make an old woman out of you before your time." Sadness clouded his deep gray eyes. "My drinking ruined your mother's life, and now it's going to ruin yours, as well. If I'd saved my money instead of using it all for drink, we wouldn't be in this fix."

Audrey wished she could withdraw her complaint. She didn't want to burden her father with guilt. Smiling, she dipped a plate into the rinse water. "The past is behind us, Father, and we can't change anything that happened years ago. Don't pay any attention to my grumbling; I'm just a little tired today."

He picked up a dish towel and reached for one of the rinsed plates. "The least I can do is dry these breakfast dishes."

She laughed as he swiped the towel across the plate. He didn't have any more ability with a dish towel than she had pounding nails. A knock sounded at the door. "I believe you're going to be saved from your kitchen duties," she said. "Why don't you answer the door while I finish up here."

He grinned and dropped the towel onto the table. "You don't have to ask me twice."

Most folks didn't call at this time of morning. Audrey hoped the knock didn't mean more work for her. The door creaked. She quieted her dishwashing and listened as her father greeted their visitor. Dr. Wahler! Finally, he'd come calling. She had stopped at his cabin just after he and his daughters arrived at Bridal Veil, but one of the workers said the doctor had returned to Atlanta and wasn't expected back for several days. She'd thought his abrupt departure odd, but when she mentioned that fact to Mr. Morley, he'd appeared unconcerned. "Dr. Wahler has business matters that require his attention back in Atlanta. I knew that when I encouraged him to come here." Mr. Morley hadn't left the door open for further discussion, so she'd discovered nothing more about the doctor or his unexpected departure.

After swiping her hands down the front of her apron, Audrey untied and removed the protective garment. She gave her hair a slight pat of the hand before hurrying into the parlor to greet Dr. Wahler and his twin daughters. She smiled and nodded at the doctor as her father made a brief introduction, but Audrey's attention remained fixed on the two young girls. They peered up at her with eyes as blue and as bright as a summer sky.

"So you are Josephine and Julia. What lovely names you have." She stooped down between them. "I do believe I may have trouble telling the two of you apart."

The little girl on her left giggled and wrinkled her nose. "We don't like our names much, so we changed them to Josie and Julie. You can tell us apart because Julie has freckles on her nose." She pointed to her sister's nose. "See?"

"Ah, yes. You're right. That should help. At least when you are close enough for me to see them."

"We're both five," Julie piped up.

"Five! What a wonderful age," Audrey said. She stood and turned her attention to Dr. Wahler. "Please sit down. I've been eager to meet all of you."

The doctor arched his brows and tipped his head to the side, almost as though he didn't believe her. "We returned only yesterday, so I'm pleased we didn't keep you waiting for long."

"Several of our boarders mentioned your earlier arrival, and I stopped by the cottage to offer a welcome. However, I learned that you had returned to Atlanta."

"I see. I didn't realize word of our earlier visit had become common knowledge. When we first arrived, I still had a few patients in Atlanta who hadn't yet engaged another physician. I promised them one last visit before my final move." While the two girls examined several photographs on a table across the room, the doctor explained that his wife had died in childbirth two years ago. "It has been difficult for all three of us. And for Sadie — that's our housekeeper. She came to work for us when my wife and I first married and has been with us ever since. I wasn't sure she'd want to make the move, but she couldn't part with the girls." He glanced at his daughters. "Of course, I think Sadie was hoping the girls would decide they wanted to remain in Atlanta."

"You mean you would have left them in Atlanta with your housekeeper?"

"Separation from children isn't the most terrible of things, Miss Cunningham. Many are sent off to boarding school at a young age and survive quite well. However, I did promise them a look at the entire island, and they have now approved their new home."

Audrey swept a gaze between the two girls as they returned to the sofa. "Since you girls have decided to come here and live, I hope you'll permit me to show you some of my favorite places when I have some extra time."

"Oh yes." Their young voices chorused in perfect harmony.

Julie reached for Audrey's hand. "What are your favorite places? I can't swim, so I don't want to go near the water unless Papa comes with us."

"I promise to always ask your papa before we go anywhere, but you'll discover the river is quite peaceful."

"But the ocean has giant waves that can sweep you underneath and carry you away. Isn't that right, Papa?" Although Julie's question bore an expectant tone, fear pinched her tiny features into a frown.

"The girls have a young friend who has told them stories about the perils of the ocean. Once they learn to swim, I believe their fears will subside."

Josie's crown of dark curls bobbed about her head as she jumped up and dashed to her father's side. "I'm not afraid. Only Julie is."

"As I recall, you were clinging to my hand as tightly as your sister when we stepped off the boat yesterday."

"That was only because I saw a giant fish," Josie explained, "and I thought it would jump out of the water and knock me over."

Audrey clasped her palm against the

141

bodice of her dress. "Dear me! That would have given your father a terrible fright. We'll have to tell Old Sam to be on the lookout for that big fish, won't we?"

Josie quickly agreed, obviously thinking she'd managed to convince them of her story. She moved from her father's side and took a seat beside Audrey. "Have you ever been to Atlanta? That's where we used to live."

"Only once, and that was when I was a little girl."

Julie edged closer and settled on the other side of Audrey. "Then how did you grow up?"

The doctor chuckled. "My girls think everyone had to grow up in Atlanta."

"I see." Audrey turned her attention to the girls. "Instead of growing up in Atlanta, I grew up on this island until we moved away when I was seven years old." She leaned closer. "And do you know what that means?"

Julie's eyes opened wide, and she shook her head. "No. What?"

"It means that I know all the very best places to have picnics and to find butterflies and to play hide and seek."

"Why don't you take them out and show them the old tree swing, Audrey?" Boyd gestured toward the front door. "And you girls are welcome to come over here anytime and play on the swing or play in our gardens, just as long as your papa gives his permission."

Josie batted her eyes at Audrey. "You're too big for a swing."

Audrey chuckled. "Not for this one. It has a nice big wooden seat, and it's tied to the thick branches of a live oak tree. When I was a little younger than you girls, my father hung it for me. It's still one of my favorite places to sit and dream about the future." Audrey stooped down. "I think you'll like it very much."

Julie bounced up from the sofa and tugged on Audrey's hand. "Do you have a pretty garden? Sadie says our mama had lots of pretty flowers in her garden."

"My flowers aren't so lovely. And there aren't very many of them. I haven't had time to give them proper attention, so many of them have wilted." Audrey crooked her finger to resemble a drooping flower.

Dr. Wahler leaned forward and rested his arms across his legs. "Well, I know two little girls who are excellent helpers in the garden. They can water and weed better than almost anyone I know. Isn't that right, girls?"

The twins giggled and nodded their agreement. "Josie does better with the weeds. Sometimes I pick the flowers by mistake," Julie said.

"But you water better. Sadie said Julie is always careful to water the ground and not the tops of the plants, but the rain waters them from the top, so I think that's better. What do you think is the best way to water flowers, Miss Audrey?" Josie stared at Audrey with a glimmer of expectation in her eyes.

Audrey hesitated a moment. She didn't want to give an incorrect response, but she didn't want to dampen Josie's excitement over gardening, either. "I think most flowers and herbs like to be watered from the ground, but there may be a few that enjoy having water sprinkled on their blooms."

Josie clapped her hands. "I think we should come and help you with your gardens. Don't you think that would be a good idea, Papa?"

"Indeed, I think it would be a wonderful idea. You girls could plant some flowers and maybe a few herbs for Sadie and Miss Audrey to use when they cook. Perhaps Miss Audrey could help you from time to time." He flashed a smile in Audrey's direction. "What do you think, Miss Audrey? Do you think you'd be able to spare an occasional half hour to help supervise such a project?"

There was no denying the doctor's good looks and Southern charm — he possessed an abundant supply of both. How had such a man been able to resist the charms of Atlanta socialites for the past year? Audrey guessed the single ladies had admired him from afar for at least the first nine to twelve months after his wife's death, but she couldn't imagine why they hadn't descended in great number once the mourning period had passed. Then again, perhaps a doctor wouldn't bring enough status to the Atlanta social scene. Though her grandmother had moved in wealthy social circles during her lifetime, Audrey had never been privy to an ostentatious way of life. And though she had never longed for such frippery, her means assured she need not worry about a luxurious existence. While Audrey remained deep in thought, Samson strolled into the room. He purred and coiled himself in and out between the two little girls, who leaned down and stroked the cat's gray fur.

"Look, Daddy." Josie gathered Samson into her arms and plopped the cat onto her father's lap. The cat arched and let out a high-pitched meow before jumping to the floor. The irate animal remained only long enough to hiss at Dr. Wahler before running to the kitchen.

"Goodness, I don't know what's gotten into Samson. He's generally quite affectionate, and we've always thought him a good judge of character."

Dr. Wahler leaned back and shook his head. "I'm not fond of cats. I would guess that he senses my dislike of the species. I've been told animals are aware of those who aren't fond of them."

Audrey nodded. She'd heard similar comments, but she'd never before met anyone who seemed to have such a dislike for cats. "He really is a loving animal. Children can learn much from owning a pet."

"I think they will learn more from gardening or stitching than from having a pet," Dr. Wahler said.

Josie rushed to Audrey's side and pulled on her hand. "Oh please, Miss Audrey! Say you'll help us with a garden."

When Julie joined the plea, Audrey knew she'd be unable to resist, but she didn't know where she'd carve out the time for such a project. She continued to miss the Morley children, and having the twins around would be an absolute delight for her. How could she possibly deny such a request from the two bright-eyed girls — or their charming father?

CHAPTER 9

Marshall slowed his gait to keep step with Stuart Griggs's short-legged stride. During the past weeks he and the architect had become better acquainted, and although Marshall didn't consider himself an expert at land development, Stuart was a capable teacher. His architectural drawings were exacting, and each morning, the two of them met to go over plans for the clubhouse work site, where laborers continued to clear the land in preparation for the construction to begin. Then Stuart would head off to work on his drawings for homes that were to be built for several of the investors. He hoped two of the houses could be completed soon after the clubhouse was finished. Of course, much would depend upon finding additional skilled workers.

Stuart tucked several drawings beneath his arm as they headed toward Bridal Fair. "I hope this meeting won't take long. It seems like it would have been easier for Victor to meet us at the work site than for the two of us to walk over here."

Stuart was a loner of sorts and one of the few supervisors who had chosen to reside in an overseer's cabin rather than live in a room at Bridal Fair. He claimed to like the privacy of his own place as well as his own cooking, though Marshall thought the odors that drifted from the cabin were usually less than appealing.

Marshall hiked a shoulder. "Mr. Morley said there was another supervisor arriving this morning, and he wanted more privacy than the work site provided."

"Don't tell me Frank Baker has finally arrived." Stuart stopped in his tracks. "If it is Frank, you better prepare yourself for trouble — he's not the easiest fellow to deal with."

Marshall waved Stuart onward. "Keep moving or we're going to be late." He slowed only long enough to let Stuart catch up. "I pride myself on being able to get along with my men. If he's a seasoned construction supervisor, I don't think we'll have a problem finding common ground."

"You may not, but he will." Stuart's boots pounded on the hard dirt as he hurried to keep pace. "He's been around the construction business, but I'm not sure I'd consider him seasoned — more like lazy, annoying, and underhanded."

"If he's all that bad, why would Mr. Morley hire him?" Marshall stopped and trained his gaze on the architect as they stepped onto the front porch of Bridal Fair.

"Maybe you'd better ask Victor that question, because I can't imagine a good reason why anyone would hire Frank Baker." Stuart held the front door open, grinned, and waved his drawing in front of him with a flourish. "After you."

Marshall stepped into the foyer with Stuart close on his heels. The sound of the door had obviously alerted Mr. Morley, for he immediately called out to them. "We're in the dining room, gentlemen. Please join us." He stood as they entered. "Thought it would be easier if we could have the use of a table to spread out the plans." He waved toward the broad-shouldered, blond-haired man across the table. "Marshall, I'd like you to meet Frank Baker."

Marshall extended his hand to Baker while Mr. Morley nudged Stuart. "I believe you already know, Frank, don't you, Stuart?"

"Yes. How are you, Baker?" Stuart didn't attempt to shake hands with Mr. Baker.

Instead, he walked to the opposite side of the table, spread out his drawings, and turned his attention to Mr. Morley. "Did you want to review the changes on the drawings?"

"I do, but first I thought we should have a conversation about assignment of duties and bring Frank up to date on the progress." Mr. Morley motioned toward the chairs. "Please sit down, gentlemen. I do believe Miss Audrey is going to bring us some coffee as soon as she has a few extra moments."

Marshall didn't miss the irritation in Stuart's eyes. He was obviously eager to complete the meeting and get back to work. And though Marshall wouldn't say so, he'd much prefer to get back to work, as well. They were behind schedule, and these meetings usually went on far too long. Still, he needed another supervisor, and he couldn't expect the man to step into a position without some discussion of their plans, progress, and the assignment of duties.

Mr. Morley cleared his throat. "Frank has been working on a project in Charleston, but I believe he's now ready to devote his time to our project here on Bridal Veil. Isn't that right, Frank?" Mr. Morley's tone bore an undeniable sharpness.

Frank's detached look tightened into a

150

frown. "You knew I was going to be in Charleston, but I'm here and ready to take over. Just show me the plans, and let's get on with it."

Victor settled in the chair opposite Frank. "That's why I called this meeting, Frank. I wanted to tell you that you won't be taking charge as project manager. I've assigned Marshall to that position. His arrival has proved a boon to us, since he was able to begin work immediately. In fact, he's had the men excavating the construction site and soon should be able to begin laying the footings. You'll be working as Marshall's assistant."

Frank jumped up from the table and sent his chair crashing to the floor. "What do you mean, *assistant* project manager? I was hired to manage this entire project, and now you expect me to come in here as his underling?" He spat the comment in Marshall's direction.

"What's goin' on in here?" Rolling pin in hand, Thora rushed into the room as if prepared to do battle. Her eyes settled on the upended chair directly behind Frank Baker. Her eyes flashed with fire, and she pointed the tip of her rolling pin in his direction. "This ain't no barroom where you can brawl and tear up furniture. Pick up that chair and learn to act like a gentleman, or pack yer bags and get out of this house!" Still wielding the rolling pin, she pointed it toward the front door. "And don't slam the door on your way out of here, or I'll have to come after ya with my shotgun." She punched the rolling pin into the air. "Understand?"

Frank nodded before he leaned down to pick up the chair. "I apologize for letting my anger take hold of me, ma'am. I'd like to remain here at Bridal Fair."

He flashed a smile that Marshall figured any woman would consider charming, but the old woman didn't waver. "You can save that pretty smile for someone else. It don't mean a thing to me." She took a step closer and tapped his chest with the end of the rolling pin. "You jest remember that I'll be keeping my eye on you. If you can't follow the rules of the house, I'll jest send you packing." Before heading back to the kitchen, she turned to Mr. Morley. "Coffee will be ready in a few more minutes. I'll bring it out. Audrey's still busy upstairs."

Mr. Morley smiled and nodded. "Thank you, Thora. There's no rush. We have a number of matters to discuss."

"See that you do it quietly." After directing a stern look at Frank, Thora headed off to the kitchen.

Frank nudged Marshall once Thora was out of earshot. "She's one feisty old woman, isn't she?"

His disrespectful tone set Marshall on edge. "I think you'll find Miss Thora means every word she says. If I were you, I wouldn't test her."

Frank stiffened his shoulders and dropped to the chair. "I think the first thing we need to get straightened out is the project manager issue." He folded his fingers into his palm, pointed his thumb toward Marshall, and addressed Mr. Morley. "Do the other investors know you've given someone else my job?"

"I was able to contact a majority of the shareholders, and they all supported my decision. I don't anticipate any problems with the change. After all, I was the only investor willing to come down here and devote time to this project. And at no additional benefit to myself, I might add."

With a grunt, Frank shoved the drawings back a few inches. "If Marshall's in charge, I don't know why I need to go over the plans with Stuart."

Marshall didn't like the direction this was going. When Mr. Morley offered him the job, he hadn't mentioned the possibility that

Frank might object to the change. Instead, Marshall had been assured it wouldn't cause any problem at all. The last thing he wanted was a division of power on the construction site. He'd seen what that could do. None of it was positive — not for the workingmen, the supervisors, or the project. A division of the work force between a project manager and his assistant could cause the ruination of a job. And he didn't want that to happen.

Mr. Morley had enticed him to take this position with the promise of future work in Colorado — a huge project, constructing a new town in the foothills, that would permit him to test his abilities in a completely different environment. Long before he'd set foot in Georgia, Marshall had dreamed of traveling west to Colorado. If he did well on this project, his dream could come true. It had been the promise of helping develop a new town in Colorado that had spurred him to accept the job on Bridal Veil. Now he wished he'd asked more questions beforehand. If there were problems, it could prove to be more than he'd bargained for. He could end up losing his good name as well as the opportunity he'd been offered in Colorado.

"I plan to use your abilities a great deal,

Frank, and I want you involved in the project. In order to help, you're going to need to have a good understanding of the plans." Marshall hoped his words would encourage Frank to become a part of the team.

"What about my pay? You give that to him, too?" Frank snarled the question at Mr. Morley.

"Watch your tone with me, Frank. I'm not going to tolerate a bad attitude from you." Victor tapped his finger on the drawings. "Right now, we'll discuss the progress at the work site and your duties. We can talk about your wages when we're alone." Frank attempted to argue, but Mr. Morley held up his hand. "If what's going on here doesn't please you, feel free to look for work elsewhere."

"You know that isn't possible. I'm expected to be here." Jaw clenched, Frank slapped his hand on the drawings.

Coffeepot in hand, Thora stepped into the dining room. "You lose your temper again, Mr. Baker?" She lifted a cup from the sideboard, filled it with coffee, and handed it to Mr. Morley.

"No, ma'am. I was just pointing to a spot on this drawing and my hand slipped."

She set the pot on the sideboard and

rested a fist on her hip. "You expect me to believe that nonsense? First you show your temper, and now you're telling me a lie. Don't think you're gonna be with us for long if you keep on with your terrible behavior." She waved toward the coffeepot. "The rest of you can help yourself to coffee if you want it. I got other work to do."

Mr. Morley cleared his throat. "Why don't you give us a report, Marshall?"

Marshall nodded and, while pointing to the drawing, explained that almost all of the land had been cleared where the main complex would be constructed. "This first drawing shows how the Bridal Veil Clubhouse will appear when completed. As you can see, the first floor will contain the main dining room, kitchen, library, billiards room, two separate parlors, and a smaller tearoom, along with the grand ballroom."

Stuart reached around Marshall's shoulder. "Note that we're leaving plenty of room to build on to the club, should the investors decide they need additional facilities in the future."

"That dining room is much too large." From Frank's smug grin, it was obvious he thought he'd located an error in the drawings. "What were you thinking, Stuart — or should I say, were you thinking when you drew up these plans?"

Still holding his coffee cup, Mr. Morley disagreed. "You're wrong, Frank. The dimensions are correct. Even if some of the members build their own cottages, we will all take our meals together in the main dining room. We want to establish a feeling of camaraderie among all of the members. What better way than to take our meals together and visit or play cards afterward?"

Marshall didn't wait for a reply from Frank. "The main stairway is in the primary foyer. There's another stairway at the south side as well as a servants' stairway at the rear of the building. The upper floors will be divided into suites, each with a balcony, a bathing room, a large parlor, one large bedroom, and a fireplace."

"What if they have children? Did you think one bedroom would be adequate for all the guests, Stuart?"

Marshall didn't miss the fact that Frank had been directing his questions to either Victor Morley or Stuart Griggs — almost as if he could deny Marshall's existence by refusing to speak to him. "I can answer that, Frank. The rooms will be uniform in size, although they will have doors that can be locked or unlocked to the suite on either side. That way, those with larger families can rent additional rooms. The investors agreed that this was the best method to ensure good use of the rooms as well as a feeling of equality among the members. The four upper stories will all be quite similar."

Frank tipped his chair until it rested on the back two legs. "How you gonna make them equal when you get a view of the river only from one side of the structure? You know they're all gonna want a view of the water." His smug grin had returned.

Mr. Morley placed his coffee cup on the sideboard. "We've already considered that problem, Frank. It was agreed that the first guests to arrive on the island will have first choice of rooms for the season. However, none of this is of importance right now. The plans have been approved. What we need is to get the work completed." He waved at Marshall.

"As Mr. Morley told you earlier, we're about ready to lay the footings, and I'll be glad to have your help. Nothing better than having an experienced man like you helping to make sure the measurements are correct and the footings are properly placed." Marshall hoped the bit of flattery would ease the tension that permeated the room.

Frank dropped the chair to all four legs and stood. "Right now I think I'll go upstairs and unpack. I'll go down to the work site and speak to the other supervisors once I'm settled." He'd gone only a few steps when he glanced over his shoulder. "By the way, I saw Johnson Radliff in Biscayne. Has he decided to come in on this project, or is he throwing in with the group on Jekyl?"

Mr. Morley stiffened and paled. "I have no idea why he's in Biscayne, but he's not involved in this project, and he's not involved over at Jekyl, either."

"Just thought you'd be interested in knowing he's in the area," Frank said. He smirked before he continued up the stairs.

"If I'm not needed, I'm going to work on the plans for one of the investors' cottages." Stuart tapped the drawings. "I'll leave these with you, Marshall."

Marshall nodded. "Right. I'll talk to you later, Stuart." Once the architect had departed, Marshall turned to Mr. Morley. "I'm not certain this arrangement is going to work. Frank doesn't appear to be willing to work for me, and we're already behind schedule."

Mr. Morley leaned back in his chair. "He'll come around, Marshall. I have every confidence you'll complete our project on time. I know that job in Colorado means a lot to you."

Marshall nodded and wondered if the job in Colorado was going to be waved in front of him every time they were a day or two behind schedule. "I'm going to do my best for you, Mr. Morley, but we're going to need more laborers before long." He motioned toward the door. "I should be heading back to work."

"I'll walk along with you. There's something else I want to discuss."

Marshall inhaled a deep breath. He wasn't prepared for any more upheaval. The confrontation with Frank Baker had been enough conflict for one day. The two men headed down a winding path leading toward the work site. A group of male buntings vying for the attention of the female birds flew across the path. The birds' bright red bodies and purple heads flashed in the morning sunlight. No doubt each one hoped to be noticed by one of the shy females that remained hidden in the live oaks.

Marshall bent his head and passed under a low-hanging branch. "What was it you wanted to discuss? Something to do with the construction?"

Victor shook his head. "No, it's Boyd. I'm not certain how much you know about his condition, but I don't think he'll be with us by the time we've completed our building

ɔject. Alcohol has ruined his health, and ɛ doctors don't hold out much hope for im."

Marshall didn't interrupt, but he was surprised Boyd had taken Mr. Morley into his confidence. Although Marshall knew Boyd had worked at the Morley residence, there was obviously a closer friendship between the two men than Marshall had imagined.

"Boyd is very hopeful that you will remain here on the island after his death," he said as he sat on a wooden bench and indicated that Marshall should join him. "Audrey is going to need someone strong to rely upon, and he thinks you're the best choice. He worries about her being alone."

"Why me? He barely knows me."

"He believes you'll provide excellent help because you can provide the understanding she'll need."

It took only a moment of reflection before Marshall knew why Boyd wanted him to be present. Although Boyd's death and the death of Marshall's father would be completely different, the cause would be the same: excessive drinking. No doubt Audrey would experience some of the same anger that had surfaced when Marshall's father had died. For years now, Marshall had been

fighting to keep bitterness out of
but it had been an uphill battle.
didn't know that he had the strength
anyone else climb that mountain.

Before he could give voice to his thoug.
Boyd approached. "Hope you fellows don
mind if I join you." He drew near Marshall
and grasped his shoulder. "Victor told me
the two of you would have your talk down
here. I hope you don't think I'm a coward
for having him ask you to help me out, but
my emotions get the best of me nowadays,
and I didn't want to blubber."

Marshall stood and offered the bench to
Boyd. He couldn't fully comprehend how
Boyd must feel, but he did understand that
Audrey would have difficult times ahead as
she faced her father's death.

Boyd settled on the wooden bench. "It's
my hope that with the help of you two men,
Audrey will adjust to life without me. I
worry she'll grieve too much and blame
herself for things over which she's had no
control." He swiped away a tear that escaped
and trickled down his weathered cheek. "I
hope you know how much I appreciate both
of you. I know I'm asking a lot. It would be
different if we had some family. But Thora's
the closest thing we've got, and she needs
help herself."

Marshall couldn't deny a dying man's request, but he didn't think Audrey would accept his help — not that he had much to offer. Still, the woman held him at a distance, and he'd been unable to figure out why.

"Audrey will need someone to help her overcome losing me, but once she learns to lean on her heavenly Father, she'll be just fine." Boyd leaned forward and rested his hands on his cane. "You can show her the way, Marshall. I'm sure of that."

"I hope you're right, Boyd, but I've already told you that it's been only in recent months that I've realized my own need to trust God. Having had an unreliable father doesn't make it easy."

"I know. And that's exactly why I want you around. I've still got some time left, and I plan to help you all I can before I leave this earth."

Marshall nodded his agreement, but he doubted whether Boyd had enough time to teach him about trusting a father. And unless Audrey soon changed her attitude toward Marshall, he'd never be able to help her at all.

CHAPTER 10

Audrey couldn't be certain whether Mr. Morley had overheard her bemoan the need for help at Bridal Fair or if her father had privately spoken to him. However, she didn't care who or what had brought Irene Throckmorton to their front door several days previous. Audrey had simply been pleased to learn that she would have additional help. Of course, Thora hadn't been quite so thrilled by their new arrival.

Thora plopped her gardening basket on the front porch. "I say you can't trust her."

"And I say you need to remember that the war is over and a Northern girl can launder sheets and help with meals just as well as a Southern girl." Audrey had been defending Irene's competence and loyalty ever since the girl set off for the washhouse a short time ago, and she was growing weary of the battle. "I don't care if she's from Pennsylvania or Georgia. I'm just thankful for her help. Not only that, but she can milk a cow, and since Mr. Morley also sent along two of those for our use, I, for one, am quite grateful."

"It's that kind of attitude that caused us to lose the War of Northern Aggression," Thora said, her finger pointing at Audrey. "When you're willing to trust anyone who crosses your path, you're doomed for destruction."

"I don't think Irene has any intention of putting too much bluing in the wash water or adding poison to our milk. She came here because we needed help and because she needed a job."

"And because she's Mr. Morley's friend — yet another Northerner. The two of them are probably in cahoots." Thora traced her fingers through her thin white hair. "We'll probably all be dead by the end of the week. Then there won't be anyone to stop Mr. Morley from becoming the owner of Bridal Fair. I imagine that will make him mighty happy. 'Course we won't be alive to see his great pleasure."

Audrey stepped to the edge of the porch and waved to Dr. Wahler and his daughters as they rounded the bend in the road. "I think you must stay awake at night to dream up these farfetched ideas. I do hope you never mention any of this nonsense in front of the children. You'll frighten them out of their wits."

Thora shrugged. "The truth won't scare them any more than those fairy tales they hear before going to bed every night."

Audrey turned on her heel to face the old woman. "But what you've imagined is not the truth, Aunt Thora. You shouldn't spread fear with your outlandish tales, especially with young children." Before she could further expand upon her concerns, the two girls ran up the path and wrapped their arms around Audrey's legs. She bent forward to embrace their shoulders.

"We're going to help Aunt Thora pull weeds," Julie said.

"And I'm going to plant them in our yard," Josie added.

Thora shook her head and smiled at the girl. "We don't plant weeds. We throw them out. It's flowers and herbs we're going to plant down by your cabin."

"But some of the ones we pulled yesterday had pretty flowers on them. I think we should keep those," Josie argued.

"But those weeds choke out the really pretty flowers." Aunt Thora held her open hands a few inches apart and squeezed them in and out. "You don't want those weeds to strangle our pretty flowers, do you?"

Josie opened her eyes as wide as two china saucers. "Nooo."

"Then we better make sure we don't plant any weeds at your house." Thora extended her arm. "Come now. We've got lots of work to get done today. First we'll work in our garden. We'll dig up some special herbs that we can plant by your cabin. In the spot your papa dug for us."

Audrey listened as Aunt Thora told the girls about everything from lavender to dill weed. As she described each herb and its many uses, the girls became more and more excited. "And if you do good work, we'll come back and bake some cookies later on."

The girls clapped their hands, delighted by the possibility. Audrey wasn't certain Thora would have the energy for both garden work and baking cookies, but she didn't correct her. If she wasn't up to the task, they would reschedule the cookie baking for another time.

"Are you coming with us, Miss Audrey?" Julie offered her chubby hand.

Audrey patted the girl's curly locks. "Not today, but maybe I can help you another time." The answer seemed to suffice, for Julie skipped alongside Aunt Thora and offered to carry the gardening basket.

The three of them made a lovely picture as they walked down the path holding hands. Audrey smiled at the sight. She could tell from the set of her aunt's shoulders that the woman was in her glory. Of course, Aunt Thora was in her glory anytime she was in charge of a project.

Forcing her attention away from the threesome, Audrey turned toward the path leading to the washhouse. Unlike Thora, she was certain Irene would do a fine job, but she could likely use some help with the mounds of laundry. Besides, it would give her an opportunity to learn more about the girl. Except for the brief information Audrey had received from Mr. Morley, Audrey knew little about Irene. She had been employed by Mrs. Morley after Audrey's departure for Bridal Veil, and Mattie's letters seldom mentioned anyone other than the employees Audrey had worked with at Temberly.

How delightful it would have been if Mr. Morley had brought Mattie to help at Bridal Fair. Audrey smiled at the silly thought. Mrs. Morley would never turn loose of Mattie. She'd been with them far too long. Besides, Audrey was certain Mattie wouldn't want to leave Temberly and the Morley children any more than Mrs. Morley would want to lose her.

Audrey continued along the path but slowed her step and glanced toward an overgrowth of bushes to her right, certain she'd heard someone choking. Pushing aside the branches, she stepped through the underbrush and stopped in her tracks. Her father was leaning against the tree, gasping for air. As she approached, he leaned forward and retched. Her stomach knotted at the sight. For years, she'd come upon this exact scene after her father's nights of carousing and drinking with his friends. Lately, she had been so sure that he'd given up his old habits. What had changed? After all of his promises and his claims of turning to God, how could he pick up the bottle again?

She hurried to his side and reached into her skirt pocket. "Here — use this to wipe your mouth."

When he looked up she gasped at the sight of his pasty complexion. His hands trembled as he reached for the handkerchief she offered. He attempted a feeble smile. "Not feeling very well this morning. Don't know what's come over me."

She wanted to ask him how much he'd had to drink but quickly decided this wasn't the time for questions. After all, there was no alcohol in the house. She'd made it a rule when they moved to Bridal Fair. "Come on. I'll help you back to the house. I think you need to rest." Thankfully, he permitted her to guide him back to the house without argument. In the old days, he would have fought her attempts to help him into bed to sleep off the effects of his drinking.

As she pulled the sheet across his chest, her father motioned to her. "Tell Marshall I won't be able to go into Biscayne with him this afternoon."

Marshall! Her father had gone into Biscayne with him yesterday. So her father hadn't been drinking while at Bridal Fair. Instead, the two men had gone into Biscayne, and after they'd ordered supplies, they'd likely stopped at a local tavern — or two or three. How could Marshall entice her father to do such a thing? Her thoughts ran wild as she contemplated exactly what she'd like to say to Marshall Graham. The man was fortunate he wasn't within her reach at the moment, or he'd likely receive an earful that would be less than ladylike.

Late in the afternoon, Marshall stepped off *Old Bessie* and headed toward Bridal Fair. He'd been sorely disappointed when Irene had arrived at the dock earlier in the day and told him Boyd wouldn't be able to accompany him across the river to Biscayne. Though the girl told him Boyd had taken ill, she refused to give any additional details, saying she'd been advised by Miss Audrey to deliver the message and nothing more. Withholding information regarding Boyd's medical condition left Marshall perplexed, but Miss Audrey's behavior generally puzzled him. Today had been no different. He hoped the older man would be feeling better by now.

Glancing over his shoulder, he gave *Old Bessie* a final glance and wondered if Victor Morley and his associates would soon send money for a new launch. There was little doubt that *Old Bessie* couldn't make many more trips across the waters. He didn't know what a new boat would cost, but these were men who surely realized they'd need to replace the boat sooner rather than later. In fact, he'd been surprised the launch had managed to pull the barge carrying the two cows Mr. Morley sent a couple of weeks earlier. That event had likely done little to help the condition of the old boat.

Birds twittered and chirped overhead, and the scent of the river hung in the air as he sauntered along the path to Bridal Fair. No wonder Boyd loved this place. It had a peacefulness and beauty all its own — so different from the bustle of Biscayne. His excursion into the waterfront town, known for the fishermen who delivered abundant catches of shrimp and oysters, had buzzed with noise and activity, but Marshall had missed Boyd's company. Although today's trip had proved beneficial, it hadn't been nearly as pleasant as yesterday's joint venture with the older man.

Boyd had offered good advice regarding the construction, and they had collaborated about the many challenges of such a large project. They'd shared ideas they thought might prove helpful to complete the clubhouse early.

At first Marshall had been hesitant to leave Frank in charge, but Mr. Morley thought it might lessen some of the tension between them if Marshall occasionally granted his assistant oversight. And though Marshall had expected Frank to object to the idea, he had appeared pleased to take on the responsibility.

There was little doubt Frank still harbored resentment toward Marshall, but he had worked with men like Frank in the past, and eventually, he'd won most of them to his side. Now he hoped he could do the same with Frank. Truth be told, Marshall could understand the man's resentment. He'd arrived at the jobsite and been demoted from a promised position before he'd even begun work. Had the circumstances been reversed, Marshall knew he'd likely harbor some bitterness too. He probably would have turned down the job and found other work.

Though he'd attempted to sort out possibilities of why Frank had chosen to remain, he hadn't come to any reasonable conclusion. Perhaps it was the fact that he'd known and developed a kinship with the other supervisors, or because he feared he couldn't find immediate work elsewhere, though that idea didn't hold water. Frank could have secured a job at Jekyl Island or at the hotel construction site in Biscayne if he'd truly wanted other work. Then again, maybe he simply decided to remain in order to annoy Mr. Morley. Whatever the reason, Marshall hoped he and Frank could eventually forge a working relationship that would be beneficial to both of them.

After returning to his room and washing up for supper, he descended the stairs and glanced around the table. "Glad to see I'm not the last one to arrive."

Thora grunted. "You *are* the last one. Boyd isn't coming down for supper. He's still sick."

"I'm sorry to hear that. Anything I can do?"

Audrey flashed an angry look in his direction. "I believe you've done enough already." Before he could question her, she turned her attention to Frank Baker. "Would you care to lead the evening prayer for our meal?"

Frank traced his finger beneath his collar. "I'm not much of one for public praying. I'm sure one of the other men would be pleased to take over."

"If you have no objection, I will do it," Marshall offered. After her curt response earlier, he thought she might not accept his offer. Her only response was an abrupt nod. The men bowed their heads as Marshall thanked God for their food and asked that Boyd be granted a speedy return to health. He thought he heard Audrey murmur something when he prayed for her father, but he couldn't be certain, and she made herself scarce during the rest of the meal. Irene and Thora had taken over serving duties while Audrey remained in the kitchen.

It wasn't until an hour after supper that Marshall returned downstairs and found Audrey alone on the front porch.

A deep frown creased her face when she saw him approach. "Have I done something

174

to offend you, or are you simply worried about your father?"

After a quick glance toward the house, she motioned to him. "Why don't we take a walk? I'd like to speak to you in private."

They hadn't gone far when she stopped and folded her arms across her waist. "I want you to know that I'm more than a little angry with you, Mr. Graham."

"Me? What have I done?" Marshall stared down at her as the setting sun highlighted her unruly brown curls. There was no denying her beauty.

"I'd like to know what you were thinking when you took my father into town with you yesterday." Her dark eyes flashed with irritation.

The question caught him by surprise. He'd thought it was something serious that had caused her anger. Then again, perhaps there was some reason why she hadn't wanted her father to go into town. "I asked him because I enjoy his company. Besides, I knew he could tell me where to locate the best prices on supplies. I thought getting off the island for the day would provide a helpful diversion."

She took a backward step. "Ha! You expect me to believe that!" The look in her eyes changed from one of anger to disbelief.

"I don't know why you wouldn't — it's the truth."

"Is it? I'm not so sure." The words clipped off her tongue like deadly bullets.

What was wrong with this woman? She'd been contentious since the day he'd stepped foot on this island. It hadn't been his idea to come here, and he thought he'd made that fact quite clear. "Exactly what is it you've got against me, Miss Audrey?"

"What do I have against you? Well, let's start with the fact that you take my father into town and apparently convince him to return to his old drinking habits. Then you bring him back home and pretend that you have no idea why he's now ill. To make matters worse, I discover that you had plans to take him with you again today, and I'm sure you also planned to make stops at those same taverns." She paused only long enough to inhale a shallow breath. "I would think that you would understand the difficulties of living with a father who places liquor before his family. I'm shocked that you encouraged my father to take up the habit again. Is this some sort of retribution for your own father's death in that barroom brawl? Did you think it unfair that my father was finally able to give up his drinking? Did you want to prove he hadn't really succeeded?"

Marshall opened his mouth to answer, but she waved him into silence.

"Don't bother to answer. I know it will be more lies. That seems to be what drinking men do the best — tell lies." She turned to walk away, but Marshall grasped her by the arm.

"And it appears that you have a real gift for jumping to conclusions. I don't know why you believe I took your father into a tavern, but that has got to be the wildest idea I've heard in a long time." She tugged at her arm, and Marshall released his hold. "Is that why you've been shooting daggers at me ever since I got home this afternoon?"

"I have not been shooting daggers at you. It's your own guilt that's causing your discomfort." She pointed at him like a mother correcting a naughty child. "My father can't be permitted to slip back into his old ways — his drinking nearly killed him, and I'll not permit you or anyone else to lead him back into a life of alcohol."

"Obviously you're not listening to me, Miss Cunningham. I would never encourage your father or anyone else —"

Audrey stomped her foot. "I don't expect you to own up to your reprehensible behavior, Mr. Graham." She arched her neck and glared at him. "But you had best remember that Mr. Morley is an old friend of our family. He cares about me, and he cares about my father. If you don't stay away from my father, I'll see that you're fired."

Marshall couldn't believe his ears. This woman had no business making such threats, yet he admired her tenacity and desire to protect her father. He wanted to tell her it was her father's urging that had brought him to this island and her father was the one who had encouraged him to remain. Marshall's first choice had been Jekyl Island, not Bridal Veil. At the moment, it took everything he had to not pack his belongings and head over to Jekyl, where he wouldn't have to deal with Audrey Cunningham.

CHAPTER 11

Over the next two weeks, as October gave way to November, Marshall maintained a safe distance from Audrey. It wasn't difficult, for he and the others were working overtime in an attempt to repair the footings along the west side of the clubhouse. Marshall had double-checked measurements on all of the wooden forms that had been prepared and laid out for the foundation. It wasn't until after the footings had been poured and the laborers had begun to set the beams that he'd discovered the measurements were off. He'd done his best to remain calm, but the loss of time weighed heavily on his shoulders. No one seemed to know what had occurred, but when he went back to closely examine the area, it appeared the forms had been moved at least two inches. In the end, he was the one responsible for mistakes and would need to answer for the delay.

Rather than taking time to make amends with Audrey regarding her father, he'd devoted most of his time to correcting the mishap at the clubhouse. He had tried to speak with her after dinner on a couple of occasions, but she'd been unreceptive. At one point he had considered telling her the truth about her father but had stopped himself. He'd promised Boyd to keep his secret, and he didn't want to break his word — at least not as long as he could abide Audrey's haughty attitude — though he wasn't certain how much longer he'd last. Marshall soon decided that Boyd Cunningham's daughter was as bullheaded as she was beautiful. For the time being he waited, hoping Audrey's icy exterior would begin to melt.

With each passing day, he wondered if he'd made a mistake coming to the island. At first the laborers had been an industrious group, but they'd now become lazy. Without constant supervision, they would sit idle until ordered back to work, for they realized there was a lack of available workers in the area. Dealing with the men as well as being faced with Audrey's cold stares and Thora's barbs about Yankees made him long for life somewhere else. Even arguing with his brothers seemed more bearable than dealing with the issues he now faced each day. And the worrisome delays at the work site haunted him at night.

Except for brief visits with Boyd, it seemed he could find little respite on this island. And if Audrey had her way, he'd be banned from keeping company with her father. However, today he wanted to speak with Frank Baker and see if together they could encourage the men to move with greater speed.

As soon as they finished breakfast and departed for the site, he hurried to catch up with him. "I was hoping to talk with you about the foundation. We've got to keep the men moving or we're going to get so far behind we'll never get back on schedule."

Frank clenched his jaw. "So I'm not supervising the men to your satisfaction, is that what you're trying to tell me?"

Marshall arched his brows, surprised by Baker's tone. "I didn't say you were to blame or that you lacked the ability to oversee the men, but you'll have to agree that things are falling behind and something needs to be done."

"You're the one in charge. Maybe you need to look at yourself for answers instead of everyone else." His lips curled in an angry frown. "If the men aren't working to your standards, maybe it's because they don't respect you. This is the first time I've ever had a problem like this."

Marshall sighed. "But you do agree there's a problem?"

"You'd have to be a fool not to see the men aren't puttin' in a full day's work unless there's someone watching over them."

"Well, I'd like to know who was watching over them when they moved the forms and poured those footings on the west side of the building."

"So now you're accusing me of having the men move the forms, are ya?" Frank slapped a branch away from the path. "You best be careful who you're pointing a finger at, Marshall. If I up and quit, you won't be left with much of a crew. Most of these men would follow me."

Marshall held his tongue. What he had hoped would be a productive discussion was creating a wedge that could spell even further disaster. Somehow, he needed to smooth the waters. "I trust you and I trust your judgment, Frank. It's because you know these men that I'm asking for your advice. My intent isn't to accuse you, but to ask for your guidance."

Frank snorted. "Well, since I'm not the project manager, I don't think I'll be giving you any free advice. Mr. Morley decided you're the one who's qualified to hold the title, so you're the one who's going to have to figure things out. Without my help."

Marshall's frustration reached new heights, and though he didn't want to lose more ground in this battle, he was finding it difficult to hold his temper in check. It was obvious Frank didn't plan to lend him any help with the men. "You're right, Frank. I am the project manager. And you're my assistant. I placed you in charge of the laborers on this job, so here's the situation: Either you get those men moving on this project, or I'll have to consider someone else for the position."

Frank stopped and folded his arms across his chest. "Maybe you better check with Victor before you make too many threats about what you will or won't do about replacing me."

His comment carried a challenge that irritated Marshall, but he did his best to remain calm. It would only make matters worse if Frank realized he'd managed to get under his skin. As they entered the work area, Marshall caught sight of several of the men sitting idle.

He waved toward the construction site as he approached them. "I'm only going to tell

183

you men one more time: Either you work during working hours or you catch the next boat to the mainland and look for work somewhere else. No need for us to pay you if you're not going to work."

A couple of the men nudged each other and snickered. "You ain't gonna find replacements for us over in Biscayne. We're the best you're gonna get."

Marshall shook his head. "If you're the best I can get, then I can do without you. Either get to work or pack your bags. Those are the only two options I'm giving you."

The men turned their attention to Frank, who stood only a short distance away. They obviously were waiting for him to give them a sign as to what they should do. When he didn't reply, one of the men stood. "What you got to say 'bout that, Frank? You think we should be packing our bags, or you think we should get back to work?"

Frank removed a pouch of tobacco from his pocket and started to roll a cigarette. "Guess it depends on how bad you need to earn some money. I'm not the one in charge of this construction, and I'm not the one who hands out your pay. You're gonna have to decide for yourself."

The men appeared baffled by Frank's response and mumbled among themselves before picking up their tools and returning to their duties. Marshall didn't know how long his threat would keep them productive, but at least his warning had gotten them moving. If he had to fire two or three to keep the rest working, so be it. One way or another, he was going to get this project back on schedule.

For the rest of the morning, Frank and all of the laborers remained hard at work. When Marshall headed toward the house several hours later, he held out hope he'd gained the respect of the men and they would continue to perform their assigned duties. Victor had mentioned the possibility of a future putting green, and Marshall wanted to gauge the distance from the construction site to the area the investors had discussed. Though it would be some time before the putting green would come to fruition, it gave Marshall an excuse for a walk before the noonday meal. He needed to assess what the future would hold if he couldn't keep the men motivated and whether he wanted to visit with Mr. Morley or wait to see what would occur over the next few weeks.

He strode down one of the paths leading to the ocean side of the island. During his first week on Bridal Veil, he'd begun taking walks to the coastline and watching the ocean lap onto the shore. The peacefulness had calmed his spirit like nothing else. Perhaps he'd find that same tranquillity today.

He hadn't gone far when he spotted a lone figure walking toward the shoreline. A single gull swooped overhead, landed, and strutted in the sand. Marshall cupped his hand over his eyes and squinted against the bright sun. Once certain the solitary man in the distance was Boyd, he broke into a run.

"Boyd! Hold up." With nothing but the lapping water to break the stillness, his voice echoed like a ringing church bell.

The older man stopped and turned. He stared for a moment before removing his floppy-brimmed hat and waving it overhead. Panting by the time he reached Boyd's side, Marshall bent forward, rested his palms on his knees, and inhaled several deep breaths.

"What are you doing down here? Something wrong?"

Marshall tipped his head back and detected a hint of panic in Boyd's eyes. He shook his head. "No." He gulped another breath of air and pushed himself to his full height. "Maybe I should qualify that answer. There's no immediate emergency, but things at the construction site sure aren't what I'd like."

"More trouble with those footings?" Boyd motioned toward a piece of driftwood not far off. "Think I better sit down for a few minutes. I'm feeling a little weak."

While Boyd settled himself on the decaying piece of wood, Marshall dropped to the sand. "No more than what I've already told you, but the setback has caused me to fall off schedule."

Boyd nodded. "I don't doubt that one bit. Any time you have to tear up part of the foundation and start over, you're looking at delays. You're just going to have to keep those men working extra hours if you need to."

"The workers are the other part of my problem. I can't figure out exactly what's happened with them. They'd been doing good work, but lately I can't depend on them to keep working unless there's a supervisor watching them. And even then, I'm not sure they're working as hard as they should be." Marshall raked his fingers through his wind-blown hair. "I don't want to sound like I'm pointing a finger, but it seems like ever since Frank took over as assistant, they've been slacking."

"Have you tried talking to Frank?"

"I've tried, but he's no help. Says I'm the

project manager and I need to figure it out on my own."

Boyd listened while Marshall continued to recount his earlier conversation with Frank. "Sounds like Frank has hard feelings and he's going to undermine you if he gets the chance." The older man stretched his legs in front of him. "He's probably already swayed the opinion of the men, and that doesn't surprise me. He knows a lot of them, and they'll side with him over a stranger. He figures that if you get too far behind, Victor will fire you and take him on to manage the project. Maybe you ought to have a talk with Victor. Let him know what's going on and see if he's willing to set Frank straight. Might help keep Frank in line if Victor knows he's stirring things up with the men."

"The thing is, I can't prove he's said anything to the men, and you know both Frank and the men will deny any wrongdoing. For now, I think it might be best to keep Victor out of it. But I plan to keep a sharp eye on how things are going."

"Better keep a sharp ear on it, too. Those workmen are likely talking among themselves, and you might overhear something that will help you find out if Frank's set his sights on becoming the manager." Boyd rested his palms on his thighs and pushed to a stand. "You should pray on the matter, as well. The best way to get your answer is through prayer."

Marshall wasn't certain prayer was needed as much as a new assistant manager, but he didn't express that thought to Boyd. He'd take the older man's suggestion and give prayer a try. He'd be pleased to receive an answer to his dilemma. In the meantime, he'd keep his mouth shut and his ears open.

"Something else on your mind besides the construction?" Boyd took a few steps and motioned him to come along.

Marshall nodded, surprised by Boyd's awareness. "As a matter of fact, there is. Audrey lit into me after we'd been to Biscayne a couple weeks ago. She thinks I'm leading you down the path to destruction."

Boyd arched his brows. "What? I think I'm going to need a clearer picture of this path you're supposedly leading me down. Exactly what did Audrey say?"

Marshall quickly repeated what he remembered of Audrey's tongue-lashing — which was just about every word she'd said. He'd been mulling her angry statements over and over in his head each night when he tried to go to sleep. "She was like a dog fighting over a bone. Every time I tried to say something, she growled at me. I finally backed off, but it sure bothers me that she thinks I'm resorting to some sort of revenge against you because of my father's death."

"To tell you the truth, I'm more than a little surprised she'd have that kind of an idea, but she's mighty protective. And frightened. Even though it's been a long time since I've tasted liquor, she still lives in fear that I'll start up again."

Marshall sighed. "I understand her desire to shield you, but I'm not the enemy."

"You're right. And it's not fair to you," Boyd said, massaging his forehead. "She's trying to save me from the bottle, and I'm trying to shelter her from the truth about my physical condition. I think I need to have a long talk with my daughter."

Marshall hadn't intended to burden the older man by divulging his conversation with Audrey. Revealing the truth to his daughter would surely cause Boyd distress. And it wouldn't help Audrey's attitude, either.

Throughout the day, Boyd contemplated how he could ease into a conversation with Audrey. It would be no simple task to tell her the truth about his condition. She still believed that with rest, a good climate, and a proper diet, his health would improve. He didn't know how much of his daughter's conviction had developed because he'd hidden his weakening condition from her by remaining somewhat involved in the island development or how much had been pure conjecture on her part. Either way, he'd never said or done anything to sway her from the belief that he would regain his health. Thinking to protect her, he'd intentionally withheld the truth. Now he wondered if he'd been trying to shield himself rather than his daughter. In his mind, putting voice to the doctor's diagnosis of cirrhosis made it official — as if there was no turning back.

His increasing weakness had already proved there was no turning back, but repeating the doctor's death sentence to his daughter would be more difficult than accepting the frailty of his body. Knowing he'd soon be with the Lord was assurance enough for Boyd. He'd accepted the doctor's assessment without fear. But leaving his daughter to fend for herself — now that was another matter, one he wanted to resolve before he drew his final breath. Besides, telling Audrey would mean she'd hover over him like a mother caring for a newborn babe. Between Audrey and Thora, he'd be relegated to bed while the two of them decided upon a treatment they thought would save him.

Still, for Marshall's sake, he needed to tell her. "And for her own sake," he muttered, knowing it would be better if his daughter had time to accept his impending death. He pushed up from his chair and walked into the kitchen, where Audrey and Irene were cleaning up. "I know it's getting late, but when you've finished your supper chores, I'd like to visit with you for a few minutes."

Irene dipped her hands into the dishwater. "You go on with your father. I can finish up these dishes."

Audrey hesitated, but when Irene gave her a slight nudge, she untied her apron and hung it on the hook beside the kitchen door. "If you're certain you don't mind. There are pots and pans that still need scrubbing."

Wisps of dark hair had escaped from Irene's thick braid, and she lifted a damp hand to push them behind one ear. "I can manage just fine. Go have your visit." Her plump cheeks dimpled as she shot Audrey a bright smile. "I'm happy to be of help."

Boyd didn't miss the warmth of their exchange. He was pleased Mr. Morley had chosen a helper who was close in age to his daughter. The two were obviously becoming fast friends — and Audrey had missed having a companion near her own age since leaving Pittsburgh. Spending all of her time around Thora and their boarders wasn't good for her. Of course, she'd taken an immediate liking to Dr. Wahler's daughters, but they were too young to be the friends that she needed. She needed someone with whom she could share her concerns, and from all appearances, Irene was a perfect fit.

While still considering how he would broach the topic of his illness, Boyd motioned Audrey toward the front porch. "I don't think it's too cool for us to sit outside, but you might want to bring along your shawl just in case."

Audrey shook her head and stopped in the parlor. "Why not sit in here? I'm not concerned about myself, but you might catch cold in the damp evening air."

"I'd prefer a little more privacy," he said as he picked up his lightweight jacket. "I promise to keep this buttoned clear to my throat if it will make you feel better." When she arched her brows, he started buttoning his jacket and then handed her the shawl.

"I'll wait until you have it buttoned — all the way." She pointed to his neck before tossing her shawl around her shoulders.

They walked outside and Boyd waited while she settled in the chair beside him. "There are a few things I want to discuss with you."

She leaned toward him. "Has something gone amiss with Mr. Morley or with the construction?"

"No. This is about us. Well, mostly about me."

She folded her hands in her lap. "You have some deep dark secret that you've never before told me. Is that it?"

Boyd caught the sparkle in her eyes. Unfortunately, she didn't know how close she'd come to the truth. "I'm sorry to say that I have withheld something from you."

Concern replaced the sparkle that had shone in her eyes only a moment ago. "After learning about the taxes, I thought you vowed you wouldn't keep any more secrets from me. Do we owe more money?"

He shook his head. "I wish money were the issue, but it's something more serious. It's my medical condition we need to talk about."

"I believe you've made some progress. Granted, you've had your bad days, but —"

"Please listen before I lose my courage, Audrey." He leaned forward and grasped her hands between his own. "First of all, I

194

want you to understand that my faith in God is strong. I know you've questioned whether I'm drinking again; you can set aside that concern. I no longer have any desire for liquor." After inhaling a deep breath, he squeezed her hands. "The truth is, I'm dying. I have cirrhosis of the liver, and I don't have much longer — the doctor told me before we left Pittsburgh."

She reeled back in her chair. "Dying? But that can't be. You told me . . ."

"I know. Back then I . . ." He looked down at his hands. "I hadn't digested the news myself, and I couldn't bring myself to tell you. But our lives have changed, and I don't want you to accuse others of wrongdoing. You have every right to be angry with me, but I can't change it now." He lifted her chin with his index finger. "I'm telling you the truth, Audrey. The doctor told me my liver is failing."

"This can't be true."

"I know this isn't news you want to hear, but the doctor was certain — and so am I. The years of drinking have taken their toll. I wanted to protect you for as long as possible, but you have a right to know." His heart ached as her face contorted into a mixture of fear, anger, and sorrow. "I'm sorry to cause you more pain." His words sounded hollow to his ears. Only he and the Lord knew the true depth of his sorrow. The last thing Boyd wanted was to cause his daughter more pain.

Audrey yanked away and jumped to her feet. "There has to be something or someone who can help. We'll find a doctor who has more experience treating disorders caused by alcohol. Surely in a city the size of Atlanta we can locate someone. Perhaps Dr. Wahler can advise us. I'll go and ask him first thing in the morning." Her words tumbled forth in fitful bursts. "Better yet, I'll go to his cabin right now."

With Audrey's additional duties at Bridal Veil, it had been easy enough for Boyd to mask his weakening condition. During the past weeks, he had worried she might take notice of his yellowing complexion, the jaundice the doctors had warned him to anticipate. But if Audrey had observed any changes, she'd kept it to herself. Before she could step off the porch, Boyd stood and reached for her arm. "No, Audrey. Neither Dr. Wahler nor any other doctor is going to have any words of encouragement. I visited more than one doctor in Pittsburgh. They all agreed that my time is short for this world." He motioned to the wicker chair. "Please sit down."

Tears glistened in her eyes as Audrey dropped to the chair. Slipping her hand inside her skirt pocket, she withdrew a white handkerchief and dabbed her eyes. When her tears continued to flow, Boyd leaned forward and embraced her. How did a father soothe his child? What could he say that might lessen her pain? He thought his heart would break as he held her in his arms.

"I want you always to remember that even when I'm gone from this earth, our separation isn't permanent. We'll have a reunion in heaven, but until that time, you must learn to lean on the Lord. I want you to call upon God when you're lonely or sad. He will be your strength and comfort. You're going to discover that the Lord will comfort you more than you can ever imagine." Boyd wiped away one of his daughter's tears. "Will you promise to do that for me?"

"I'll do my best, but it won't be the same. I don't know how I can bear being without both you and Mama. Somehow this doesn't seem fair."

Boyd couldn't agree more. His daughter had suffered a great deal of loss and pain during her short lifetime. "It's a fact that God's plans don't always make sense to us, but that's when we learn to trust." Stroking her hand, he considered the depth of that simple word. Trust wasn't an easy thing, especially during the hard times. Before he died, Boyd wanted Audrey to grasp the importance of trusting God during demanding circumstances, as well as during the easy, untroubled times. "I know it's hard to set aside fear and place all your trust in God — even when you're my age, it can be difficult. But believe me, the reward is worth pushing yourself to trust Him." He pulled her close. "I have faith that you're going to be just fine, Audrey. I'm trusting God to make certain of that — and I pray you'll do the same."

CHAPTER 12

Long after she'd slipped into bed, Audrey attempted to push aside her fears, but her father's words continued to haunt her. For hours, she wrestled the covers as sleep eluded her. Turning on her side, she yanked the quilt beneath her chin and recalled her father's comment regarding false accusations against others. There was little doubt he'd been referring to the remarks she'd made to Marshall. Little wonder Marshall continued to shy away from her. He knew the truth about her father's illness yet hadn't divulged the secret to her. Audrey didn't know whether to admire his behavior or find it offensive. On the one hand, she thought Marshall commendable for maintaining a confidence, but on the other hand, she believed he should have told her. In the midst of planning how to approach Marshall the following morning, she drifted into a restless sleep.

When morning arrived, Audrey trudged to the kitchen, still exhausted. She would have to rely on Irene to help her with breakfast. Otherwise, the men would likely be served underbaked biscuits and over-cooked eggs. Thankfully, Irene had already made a pot of coffee and set the water to boil for tea.

"From the look of those dark circles under your eyes, I'm going to guess that you didn't sleep well." Irene lifted a cup from the shelf and filled it to the brim with dark stout coffee. "Try this. It should help keep you awake until midmorning."

Audrey took a sip and sputtered. The coffee would need at least half a cup of cream before she could down any more. "It's a wonder the boarders don't all have a good case of indigestion." She touched her fingers to her neckline. Already, she could feel the strong brew working its way back up her throat. "I believe I'll have tea instead." Audrey didn't miss the wounded look in Irene's eyes. "I'm sorry, Irene. I've never learned to drink strong coffee, but I'm sure the men enjoy it. I've not had any complaints since you began making it."

The girl offered a timid smile as she retrieved a clean cup and set it on the table. "For your tea. Shall I start the biscuits?"

"That would be a great help. Has Aunt Thora already gone to the henhouse?" The old woman usually arose early and made a daily trek to collect the eggs. For some reason, the hens didn't peck Aunt Thora — probably because they feared the consequences. If one of them dared peck her, it would likely end up in the stewpot.

"She left a little while ago. I expect she'll be back any minute." Irene peered out the window. "She's coming down the path right now."

Audrey lifted a large pottery bowl to the table. "Good. I can begin the scrambled eggs once the biscuits are in the oven."

Muffled sounds of the men moving overhead helped to keep her on task. Otherwise, she might have settled in one of the chairs and fallen asleep. Moments later, Thora burst through the door with her basket. "Either the hens have quit laying or a poacher was in the henhouse." She removed four eggs and placed them on the table. "Better plan to fix something other than scrambled eggs this morning."

"Irene has the biscuits ready for the oven. I can make sausage gravy, and with those four eggs, I can make enough pancakes to help fill their plates."

"Maybe some fried potatoes?" Irene continued to dip the rim of a drinking glass in flour and cut the biscuits.

"I say give 'em grits. If they're gonna work in Georgia, they need to eat grits and drink tea."

The pan of biscuits slipped from Irene's hand and landed on the top of the stove with a clang. "Oh, I do hope that isn't a rule, because I'm fond of coffee and I can't abide grits. They have no flavor."

Aunt Thora shook her head. "The way you're throwing that pan of biscuits around, they're gonna be flatter than Audrey's pancakes. If that happens, those men will have no choice but to fill up on grits." She grinned as if she hoped that's exactly what would happen.

"Why don't you finish frying the sausage while I mix the pancake batter, Aunt Thora." Audrey handed the old woman a wooden spoon. "And you may as well give up on forcing the men to eat grits. No matter how little food I put on the table, they won't touch them."

"*Hmph!* If a man gets hungry enough, he'll eat the bark off a tree. I remember during the War of Northern Aggression how our men were starving and —"

Audrey rapped a metal spoon on the worktable. "Not now, Aunt Thora. There's work to be done, and I'm too weary to cook and argue at the same time."

"Looks like someone got up on the wrong side of the bed this morning." Thora's lips tightened into a frown as she turned her back to Audrey.

Audrey sighed. She'd apologize to Aunt Thora later. If she attempted to do so now, it would only lead to further talk of grits or Union soldiers, and neither was a topic she cared to prolong. Besides, she needed to decide how and when she should approach Marshall. The sooner the better. She didn't want to spend the entire day worrying over how he would react to her apology. He'd been careful to avoid her since their last conversation, so gaining his attention would likely prove difficult.

"You want me to make the gravy, or you think you can do better?"

Audrey ignored the challenge in her aunt's question. "You go ahead, Aunt Thora. I'm certain the men would prefer yours over mine." Although Audrey didn't remember if the men had ever commented on Aunt Thora's gravy, the remark had a soothing effect upon the woman, who immediately set to work spooning flour into the skillet.

In order to settle upon a plan to speak with Marshall, Audrey needed peace and quiet. If paying Aunt Thora a compliment or two would keep the woman occupied and silent, Audrey was more than willing to offer a few flattering words. While the three women completed the breakfast preparations, her mind swirled with possibilities. She wanted to speak with Marshall in a place where she was certain no one would overhear their conversation. But determining such a place and escaping the house without drawing attention remained a dilemma until after the men had eaten their breakfast.

She waited until Marshall pushed away from the table, thankful he was the last of the men preparing to depart. While he stopped for a brief exchange with her father, she returned to the kitchen. She did appreciate the fact that Marshall provided her father with some much needed company. Although he'd continued to become less vibrant, her father's interest in construction on the island remained steadfast. He wanted to know all the details, details she couldn't provide.

"I'm going out to the henhouse to see if I can discover if there was a prowler on the property last night."

Aunt Thora turned from the sink and shook her head. "No need. I'll take care of finding the culprit."

"I prefer to go and check for myself, Aunt Thora." Without giving the woman time to argue, Audrey yanked the apron from around her neck, flung it on the hook, and exited the back door.

She'd gone only a few steps when Thora called out to her. "No need to slam the door. I know your grandmother taught you better manners when you were just a toddler."

Audrey waved an acknowledgment but continued down the path without a backward glance. She didn't want to miss this opportunity to speak with Marshall. Once certain she was out of Thora's sight, Audrey circled away from the henhouse and back toward the path leading to the work site, where she remained by one of the large oaks until she heard the thud of footfalls on the hardened dirt.

Edging around the tree, she peeked around the thick trunk to make certain her father hadn't accompanied Marshall. If so, her plan would be thwarted. Discovering he was alone, relief flooded over her and she stepped into the path. She looked into his eyes, and her relief immediately vanished.

"I'm pleased to see you're alone. I wanted to speak to you." She could barely hear her voice above the crescendo of her pounding heart. "I owe you an apology." Though Marshall made no attempt to elude her, he remained silent — waiting . . . watching . . . obviously uncertain what to expect. "I don't know if my father mentioned that we had a talk yesterday."

Marshall shook his head and then squared his shoulders as if prepared to do battle. There was no doubt he was at odds with her. And little wonder, after the way she'd spoken to him.

"I've come to ask your forgiveness." She blurted the simple apology with the hope it would set him at ease.

"Have you? Would you care to elaborate just a bit?"

"For the accusations I made against you regarding my father." Marshall obviously didn't want to assume anything. Even now, she was certain he wanted to safeguard her father's confidence. "I wanted to protect my father. I know my response was ir-rational, but I permitted fear, rather than good sense, to guide me. My father has confided that he is dying and hasn't much longer to live." She choked out the final words as tears slipped down her cheeks.

Marshall reached toward her but then took a hesitant backward step. "I'm very sorry, Miss Audrey. I know you and your father have a special bond." He withdrew a handkerchief from his pocket and offered it. "Why don't you sit down?" Stepping closer, he grasped her elbow and guided her to one of the low thick branches of the live oak.

Her tears created an awkward silence that hung between them like the veils of moss clinging to the tree. "Please." She nodded toward the space beside her.

For a moment, Marshall looked as though he wanted to disappear, but he dropped down beside her. "I do appreciate your apology. I know the kind of fear that sets in when a father drinks too much. I also know what the love of alcohol can do to a man's family. I hope you now believe that I would never influence any man to partake — especially a man like your father. I admire what he has done over these past years — his ability to overcome the habit and create a better life for both of you. He told me how God has helped him through these changes. I only wish my father would have experienced the same before he died."

Audrey wanted to find solace in what he said, but words did little to relieve her pain. Kind words wouldn't help her accept the news that her father would soon die. And her father's faith in God didn't help, either.

More than anything, she wanted her father to live — she wanted their lives to continue without change.

The morning sun saturated the mossy veils and cast delicate patterns of light beneath the low-hanging branches. Marshall leaned forward and retrieved a twig from the ground. With methodical precision, he stripped away the budding leaves and continued to speak of the heartache he'd experienced while growing up with a drunken father, all of it a mirror image of her own past — all except the portion about his brothers. She'd had no siblings with whom to share her childhood or adult years. But after listening to Marshall describe the difficulties he'd experienced with his brothers, she wasn't certain she'd missed out on much — except additional pain. If either of them had been blessed with sisters, perhaps their lives would have been different. While Audrey had heard stories of women whose lives had been ruined by overindulging, those tales were few and far between.

She wanted to offer sympathy to Marshall, but she remained speechless, unable to think of anything that might lessen his pain. Though well-meaning, his words didn't help her, and she didn't believe such platitudes would be of use to him, either. She knew she would be with her father in heaven someday, but that knowledge didn't fill the void she would feel while she remained behind.

She pulled a loose thread on her skirt and twisted it around her finger. "I remember when I was a little girl and my father would be gone for days at a time. I would miss him terribly. After my mother died, he would go on drinking binges and stay away from home for long periods. I was always thankful that he was gone during those times. Truth be told, I didn't miss him at all then. In fact, there were occasions I wished he would never come home."

She glanced at Marshall, who nodded his understanding. "You shouldn't be embarrassed by those thoughts. I experienced the same feelings about my pa on more than one occasion."

Now that she'd revealed some of her secrets, Audrey couldn't stop. It was as if a cork had been removed from a bottle and she couldn't quit until she'd emptied herself of every dark thought. "Now that my father has become the man God intended — one who knows and worships Him as Lord and Savior, one who has given up his dependence upon liquor, and one who has become a wonderful father — it seems he is to be snatched away from me. And knowing I'll see him in heaven doesn't fill the hole in my heart. Instead, it makes me angry."

Marshall's eyebrows rose high on his forehead. "Angry at God?"

Audrey gave a firm nod. "Yes, at God. I know it sounds terrible to say such a thing, but I need my father here with me. Sometimes I think God is selfish and unfair rather than good and just."

He scooted a short distance down the tree limb. When Audrey frowned, he motioned toward the sky and grinned. "I thought I'd get a little distance between us — just in case lightning strikes."

She knew his actions were an attempt to lift her spirits, but she'd wanted him to remain serious, to say something that would help her understand. "You don't need to be afraid. There won't be any lightning. God knew what I was thinking before I ever spoke. Thus far, He hasn't inflicted any further harm." She leaned forward and rested her chin in her palm. "Don't you ever question what happens around you and wonder why?"

"Of course. But everyone experiences difficult times. It's part of life. That's why we need God — to help us get through the rough times. Your father is the one who's been telling me that I need to place my trust in God and lean on Him."

Audrey smiled. "He said the very same thing to me."

"Your father knows that the two of us have experienced many of the same losses. He's a wise man, and I think he knows that we both need to place our trust in God." Marshall cleared his throat. "For me, that's not an easy thing, either. Maybe we can help each other. I could use a friend to talk to — one I can trust. Other than your father and Mr. Morley, I've found friends to be in short supply around here. What do you think?"

His tentative question surprised her. Certainly their lives had many similarities. Each had watched a mother suffer, each had experienced the financial difficulties wrought by an alcoholic father, each had endured embarrassment and social shame, and neither of them wished to go through any of those experiences again. There was much that could bring them together, but could she trust him? If she couldn't trust God, how could she trust Marshall Graham?

She wasn't certain she could trust either one, but she needed someone who understood her plight — and Marshall was the likely candidate. In addition, her father hadn't hidden the fact that he thought Marshall an upstanding young man. And since giving up his drinking habit, Audrey's father had proved he was an excellent judge of character.

Still, she didn't want to commit and then discover Marshall an untrustworthy friend. It could prove difficult to rid herself of him should that occur. "I suppose we could give it a try, but if either of us should have a change of heart and want to dissolve the friendship, the other must agree without protest. And we must respect each other's needs — there will be times when neither of us will wish to talk to the other. Oh, and our conversations must remain between us." She met his steadfast gaze. "Agreed?"

He chuckled. "Agreed. I must say that you drive a hard bargain, Miss Audrey. Rather than using a lawyer, perhaps Mr. Morley should hire you to enter into negotiations for his future business contracts." His eyes twinkled and he held out his hand. "Friends?"

She grasped his hand and gave a firm shake. "Friends. At least until I decide otherwise."

"Or I," he said. "Don't forget we both have the same right to forfeit the arrangement." His quick response caused a smile, and she nodded. "For the moment, I think we can agree that other than our duties, your father and his health should be our priority. I hope you'll permit me to help in any way that I can."

His generous offer brought tears to her eyes. She hadn't expected such kindness — especially after the way she had treated him during their previous encounter. "Thank you . . . Marshall." She swiped away the tears and handed him his handkerchief. "I suppose we both should get to work. The men will wonder what has happened to you, and Aunt Thora will soon come looking for me. I promised to check the henhouse and see if I could discover evidence of a poacher. There were only a few eggs when she went to collect them this morning. She thought there might be a few hens missing, but she wasn't certain."

"Probably a fox or some other wild animal. Do you want me to go along with you?"

"No. I'm simply hoping to find a clue that will give me an idea whether it's man or beast that's taken a liking to the eggs. You best get off to work, but thank you again for all of your kindness." She stood. "And since we're to be friends, you can address me as Audrey."

He turned and smiled. "Thank you, Audrey."

She was pleased their exchange had gone well. Knowing she could depend upon Marshall would provide the sense of ease Audrey would need when her father's condition worsened. At least she hoped it would. Despite her father's illness and the darker days to come, Audrey already felt that her burden was no longer quite so heavy.

She'd nearly reached the henhouse when a gunshot rang out. With little thought for her safety, Audrey hiked her skirts and ran toward the wooden structure. Before she rounded the bend, another shot sounded. She stopped in her tracks and cupped her hands to her mouth. "Hold your fire!"

"Is that you, Audrey?"

Audrey moved her hands away from her lips. "Yes, it's me, Aunt Thora. Please don't shoot me."

"I've got a bead on the henhouse, so don't cross in front of me. If that varmint in there shows his face, he's gonna get a scatter of buckshot he won't soon forget."

Shading her eyes against the morning sun, Audrey spotted the old woman behind a tree, her shotgun resting on one of the branches and aimed directly at the door of the henhouse. Audrey picked her way through the undergrowth and came alongside the woman. "Are you certain there's someone in there?"

"Saw 'em with my own eyes."

That reply didn't set Audrey's mind at ease. The woman's eyesight couldn't be trusted. "Exactly *what* did you see?"

"There's someone inside. I saw shadows moving around." She turned long enough to direct a frown at Audrey. "And where have you been? You said you were coming down here to take a look for yourself, but when I got here, you were nowhere to be found."

"And how did you know it wasn't me inside that you were shooting at?"

"Because I called your name and you didn't answer. I gave that scoundrel a second chance — told him I had a shotgun and intended to use it if he didn't come out with his hands over his head." She hiked one shoulder. "When he didn't come out, I shot. Had to let him know I meant what I said."

Audrey wondered how Thora had once again gotten her hands on the shotgun. After the incident with Mr. Morley, Audrey's father had hidden the weapon, but obviously not very well. "I thought Father told you —"

"Look! There he is." Thora leaned in close and settled the weapon against her shoulder.

"That's nothing more than an old tarpaulin hanging from the tree. It's casting a shadow when the wind blows." Audrey pointed to the tattered canvas as the wind blew through the trees. "See? I'm going down there and make certain no one is in the chicken coop, but I'm sure I won't see a soul down there." She started to stride off but glanced over her shoulder before descending further. "Don't shoot me, Aunt Thora!"

"I won't shoot, but you just remember you told me to hold my fire when man or beast takes hold of you inside that henhouse."

Thora's warning rang loud and clear, and though Audrey didn't expect to find anyone, she would have preferred a more secretive approach. She could hear her aunt muttering in the background as she walked inside. As expected, she discovered nothing but the agitated hens. After being disturbed by Thora and her shotgun, there'd likely be no eggs tomorrow, either.

She walked to the doorway and waved at Thora. "Nothing here. I think we both should go home."

Moments later, Thora joined her on the

path leading back to the house. "You never did tell me where you were this morning."

"And you didn't tell me how you found the shotgun," Audrey said.

The older woman clung to the weapon as though she feared Audrey might snatch it away. "I s'pose we've reached what General Lee would have called an impasse."

"I suppose we have," Audrey said.

"Still doesn't explain the eggs. Think I may set up again tonight and see if someone comes prowling around." Thora pursed her lips into a tight knot.

"You will do no such thing. If necessary, I'll post one of the men outside your door to make certain you don't leave the house." Audrey waved Aunt Thora forward. "Come along, and keep that gun pointed at the ground."

Her aunt's grumbling didn't cease until they neared home and she caught sight of Josie and Julie Wahler sitting on the front porch with Sadie pacing back and forth in front of them. When she spotted Audrey, she hurried down the steps to meet her.

"The girls and I come to apologize and bring back your eggs." She waved to the girls. "Get on down here and tell Miss Audrey you's sorry for takin' her eggs."

"We're sorry," the two girls said in unison.

Audrey stooped down in front of the twins. "You two went to the henhouse by yourselves and gathered these eggs?"

They nodded their heads. "It was Josie's idea. She wants to have some baby chicks, so we got up before the sun, tiptoed out of the house, and went down there." Julie shivered. "I was scared 'cause it was dark, but Josie said the moon was real big and bright so we'd be able to see."

"And we could," Josie said. "There wasn't anything to be scared of until Papa found out we took your eggs."

Julie's curls bobbed up and down. "He was so mad and said we had to bring your eggs back to you." She glanced at her sister. "Josie cried because she wanted to wait until they turned into chicks."

"Doctor said to tell you that he sends his apologies, too, and he hopes it didn't cause you any problems what with fixing breakfast and all. Wish we woulda found them earlier, but the girls had them hid in their bedroom. If I hadn't gone in there to clean their closet, I don't know when I mighta found them eggs." Sadie pinched her nose between her thumb and forefinger. "I can jest imagine the smell. Ew-whee."

Audrey chuckled. "Well, I'm glad the mystery of the missing eggs has been solved." She glanced at Thora. The old woman was still clutching the shotgun in her hand.

Thora shrugged her shoulders and grinned. "Guess that takes care of my shotgun practice — at least for now."

Chapter 13

On a beautiful Sunday, after the noonday meal, Audrey poured Marshall a cup of coffee and joined him at the small table in the kitchen. Irene and Thora had gone to visit the Wahler children. No doubt the twin girls would convince Thora to bring them back to Bridal Fair for the remainder of the afternoon. The other men had wandered off to their rooms or decided upon a stroll through the woods or along the beach. Only Audrey and Marshall remained behind — and, of course, her father.

"My father was asking about your progress on the clubhouse. He said you hadn't been in to visit with him for a couple of days, and he was concerned that maybe there'd been another problem. I told him you'd been busy." Like her father, Audrey had wondered about Marshall's absence at the house. He'd been rushing out as soon as he gulped down his breakfast, and he hadn't been returning for the noonday meal of late. When she'd inquired, he said he had been eating with the men at the cookhouse near the slave quarters — it saved him time and allowed him to more closely oversee the men.

"I keep hoping we're going to get back on schedule, but each time I get my hopes up, something else goes wrong. Yesterday I discovered a major support beam for the main dining room had been compromised." He shook his head. "I don't know how it happened. There was a huge cut in the beam, and it had been placed in such a way that it wasn't clearly noticeable. Although it would have likely withstood the weight of the flooring, in time and with added weight the whole thing would eventually come crashing down. Can you imagine a roomful of guests gathered to enjoy a meal and having the floor collapse beneath them?" He shuddered as he looked up and met her gaze. "I spoke to every one of the workers individually and asked what they knew about the beam. Of course, nobody admitted to knowing anything about how it could have happened. I couldn't even discover who had placed the beam." He dropped his head into his hands. "I get so angry at the lack of progress. Each time we near getting back on schedule, there's another problem."

"Do you think the men are intentionally causing damage to slow the project?"

He shrugged. "I don't know. I think Frank may be encouraging them to disrupt the work so I'll be fired, but there's no way to prove it. I feel like I need to be down at the site night and day to make certain nothing goes wrong."

She forced a smile. "Yet even staying there so much of the time, things continue to go amiss. Maybe you should send a letter to Mr. Morley and ask his advice."

"I don't want him to think I can't solve my own problems. I keep hoping to find the answer." He took a final sip of coffee. "Your father doing any better today?"

"I'm afraid not. It doesn't seem possible that only a few weeks ago he was up and about each morning and required only an afternoon nap." Her voice caught and she looked away. "Now he's up in his chair only long enough to read his Bible for a short time before he must return to bed." She could feel tears forming in her eyes. "I fear his time is very close."

Marshall touched her hand. "I know how difficult this is for you, Audrey, and I want to help both of you in any way that I can. No matter how busy I am with the construc-

Each evening he insisted Audrey eat her supper and rest while he sat at Boyd's bedside. At first she had protested, but as days became weeks and weariness set in, her objections ceased and she would hurry from the room as soon as Marshall arrived. There was little doubt that watching her father's life slip away had taken its toll on Audrey. Dark circles rimmed her dark brown eyes, and the beautiful golden glint had disappeared weeks ago. She'd lost weight, and even her curls had lost their sheen.

Although it sometimes proved difficult, Marshall did his best to push construction concerns from his thoughts when he sat with Boyd. He'd sit at the bedside and read aloud from the Bible. Often during those evening readings, John Nichols, a pastor from Biscayne, would pay a visit. Boyd had mentioned the preacher shortly after Marshall arrived at Bridal Fair, and on one of his trips to the mainland, Marshall had stopped to visit with the man.

Since then, Pastor Nichols had taken it upon himself to visit Boyd whenever possible, sometimes even remaining overnight. Like Marshall, a couple of the boarders enjoyed the preacher's visits and were encouraged by his willingness to share

226

tion, I want you to feel free to tell me when you need my help. I know Mr. Morley will understand."

She nodded, but she didn't want to think about her father's death. She wanted a miracle — she wanted her father to once again be whole and free of pain.

"I can't imagine a single day without him here." She felt her chest tighten and found it hard to breathe. "I didn't want to come here in the first place, but he talked me into it. I don't know how I can go on if he isn't here."

"It won't be easy," Marshall told her. "The wise thing is to just bide your time. Don't mourn him before he's gone. He looks forward to your visits and likes sharing stories of his boyhood. Think on those pleasant things. There will be plenty of time to mourn him when he's gone."

Audrey shook her head. "It's too hard. This is too much for anyone to bear. I think God is cruel. If He truly knew what it was to experience this kind of pain, He wouldn't allow it."

Marshall gave her a sympathetic shrug. "God let His own Son go to the cross. I think He understands your pain."

His words wormed their way into her heart. Audrey didn't want to think of God

223

understanding. If He understood, why didn't He do something? It was easier to imagine Him without a clue than to think He knew and did nothing.

Marshall squeezed her hand again. "Trust Him, Audrey. He knows what you're going through, and He will see you through."

By the middle of November, Audrey could no longer deny that her father's days were drawing to an end. Dr. Wahler said it could be weeks or perhaps a month, but the doctor had quickly followed up by saying one could never tell about these things, and it might be only days.

Though Audrey was loath to believe him, she saw the gray cast to her father's skin and ached each time he refused to eat even his favorite foods. That morning she'd offered him a sip of coffee with cream and sugar — the way he had always enjoyed it — but he only gave a shake of his head. When she'd returned with it to the kitchen, Audrey had thrown the contents into the sink, not even caring that the cup broke into pieces.

"Oh, Miss Audrey, are you all right?" Irene asked, coming upon the scene. "Let me clean that up for you."

Audrey wanted to scream. "It was my fault. I'll clean it up." She grabbed pieces out of the mess, cutting her finger the process. She winced but said nothing. Dropping the broken cup into the dustbin, she examined her finger. The cut wasn't bad, but it did need attention.

Irene brought a dish towel and wrapped around Audrey's finger. "I'll get some bandages and iodine."

"No need," Audrey said. "It isn't that bad."

Irene patted Audrey's arm. "I'm so sorry for your pain, Miss Audrey."

Audrey knew the young woman was referring to more than just the injury on her hand. Biting her lower lip, Audrey exited the room before she burst into tears. Her life was like a nightmare that she wanted to end, but one she clung to all at the same time.

Marshall did what he could to lend a hand whenever possible. He knew that Audrey had placed a protective wall between herself and most people. Generally, he could push aside the barrier she'd constructed and get her to open up to him, but she was so wrapped in pain that Marshall often came away feeling he'd done more harm than good.

God's Word. However, Frank Baker didn't share their enthusiasm. He'd taken Marshall aside and suggested the preacher save his sermons for Sunday mornings.

It had given Marshall great pleasure to tell Frank that Bridal Fair belonged to the Cunningham family, and unless they made such a request — which he knew they wouldn't — Reverend Nichols would be free to share his beliefs with anyone in the house. The response hadn't set well with Baker, but he hadn't argued further. Instead, he made himself scarce whenever the preacher visited.

The pastor's unexpected appearance today had surprised both Audrey and Marshall. He quickly explained that Old Sam had made a special trip to bring him over to Bridal Veil and would return for him in the morning. Frank had been less than welcoming when he noted the preacher's appearance at the supper table, but if the pastor noticed, he didn't let on.

"You gentlemen care if I join you for a while?" The pastor stood in Boyd's doorway with his worn Bible in one hand. "I planned to come up here earlier, but once I started visiting with Audrey, time got away from me."

Boyd lifted his hand and waved the

preacher forward. "Good to see you, Pastor. No need for apologies. I'm glad to hear you and Audrey had some time to visit. She's having a hard time accepting my illness. I've been trying to set her mind at ease, but maybe she'll take more stock in what you have to say. More than anything, I think she needs to be assured of God's love."

The preacher nodded and took a chair near Boyd's bedside. "And what about you, Boyd? What do you need?"

Tears welled in the older man's eyes. "I need to know that Audrey is going to be all right when the good Lord decides to take me home. So far, I don't think she's willing to accept the fact that I'm going to die."

"Death is a part of life. In her heart, she knows we all will die, and in time she'll grow to accept that your death isn't a punishment. It may take her time, Boyd, but Audrey is a strong girl who believes God's Word. She'll be fine. You've got good friends to make sure of it. Right, Marshall?"

The pastor arched his brows in expectation, and Marshall offered a slight nod.

Pastor Nichols patted Boyd's hand. "You see? You have friends committed to help Audrey, so you can set your mind at ease." After they'd visited for some time, the preacher opened his Bible. "I'm going to read a few verses of Scripture and pray before I leave you to get some sleep. I don't want you getting overtired."

Boyd chuckled a short, raspy laugh. "I wouldn't worry too much about that, Pastor. I get more than my share of sleep. Besides, I enjoy listening to your words of wisdom."

"Thank you, Boyd, but the wisdom I've given you isn't mine — it's directly from God's Word." He tapped his index finger on the pages of his open Bible. "This is where we find all the answers to help us navigate through this world."

Both Marshall and Audrey had noticed the positive effect the preacher's visits had on Boyd. The pastor's appearances lifted Boyd's spirits and provided comfort. And the visits provided strength and insight for Marshall, as well.

"He's a fine man," Boyd murmured as the pastor departed the bedroom. "And a wise one, too."

Marshall nodded. "I hope Audrey heeds his words, for he's surely given me much to think about. He's made me understand that nothing will change the past and that I have a choice. I can use the painful experiences from my past as an excuse for failure, or I can learn from them and create a fresh start in life."

"Like I said, John is a wise man. We can't remake the past, but God holds our future in His hand, and there's always a place to begin anew." Boyd shifted in the bed until he was facing Marshall. "I've been praying that this island will be your new start. And that Audrey might also become a part of your future plans. I know that you care for her — I can see it in your eyes each time you look at her."

Marshall glanced at the floor as the heat climbed up the back of his neck. "I didn't realize my feelings were obvious." He rested his arms across his legs and leaned forward. "Unfortunately, I don't believe she shares my feelings."

Boyd reached forward and patted Marshall's shoulder. "Don't you worry. I believe that in time she'll come to care for you very much. Already I've seen changes — her attitude about you has softened." After a glimpse toward the door, he continued. "I want you to make a promise to me, Marshall."

"Of course. Anything." He met the older man's steady gaze.

"I want you to promise to take care of Audrey once I'm gone."

Marshall dropped back against the chair's wooden spindles and swiped his palm down his jaw. "I don't know about that, Boyd. Don't misunderstand — I'd be pleased to take care of Audrey, but I'm not sure she'd welcome such an arrangement. Have you talked to her about this?"

"No. 'Course not. She'd be mad as a wet hen if she knew I was suggesting such a thing. What she doesn't know won't hurt her, and I know it will help her — a lot. She needs a good man in her life — someone she can depend on. I've spent a lot of time praying about this, and I know you're the man. Do I have your word you'll take care of her?"

Marshall didn't want to argue with Boyd's supposition, but he'd feel a lot better if Audrey thought he was the man for her rather than her father. "I don't know whether Audrey would agree that I'm the man for her, but you have my word that when you die, I'll look after her and do everything I can to help her. I can't say if that will include a wedding. I think your daughter will need to share your conviction before that will happen."

Boyd grinned and gave a weak nod. "I think she cares for you more than you think. She's just careful to guard her emotions — doesn't want to get hurt."

Marshall knew about guarded feelings.

For most of his life, he'd done the same thing, remaining a loner rather than taking chances with people who might disappoint. It was clear Audrey had been careful with her feelings, as well. After all, he'd met great resistance when he'd tried to befriend her. How in the world could he woo her?

Granted, they'd now become friends, but he'd seen nothing that indicated she had feelings for him — nothing beyond friendship. And he didn't want to do or say anything that would harm their fragile alliance. Should he say anything unexpected or unwelcome, it could halt all progress he'd made thus far, and he didn't want to chance that possibility. Still, he wanted to assure Boyd that he would give Audrey as much love and assistance as she would permit.

"So we're agreed?" Boyd attempted to wink but failed in the effort.

"We're agreed that I'll do everything in my power to take care of Audrey — unless she finds someone else who can do a better job."

"Don't know where she'd find such a fellow."

Boyd's eyes drifted closed, and Marshall remained silent. When he'd first arrived at Bridal Fair, Marshall might have agreed with Boyd. But things had changed on

Bridal Veil Island. Now there were plenty of men on the island, and most of them would be pleased to court Audrey Cunningham, particularly Dr. Wahler. At least that's what Marshall had decided as he'd watched events unfold in Bridal Fair.

CHAPTER 14

As the days drifted by, Boyd's request continued to haunt Marshall. Each evening he considered speaking to Audrey — not to tell her about the conversation, but rather to gain a better understanding of her feelings for him. No matter what he attempted, Marshall met with little success.

Although Boyd hadn't requested additional medical treatment, the doctor's house calls had become more and more frequent. Almost every evening after supper, he would arrive at the front door. Boyd said the doctor was likely bored with little to do since his arrival, but Marshall hadn't missed the glances he and Audrey exchanged from time to time. And if the doctor had no interest in Audrey, why did he remain after completing his examination of Boyd? Soon after leaving Boyd's bedside, Audrey would slip from her father's room and join Dr. Wahler in the parlor. And, as if to make the situation more difficult, Frank Baker had been finding various reasons to take Audrey aside and speak privately with her. Putting up with Dr. Wahler was difficult enough, but Frank Baker — well, that was altogether unthinkable.

As if Marshall's thoughts had summoned the man, Dr. Wahler appeared at the bedroom door. After a quick glance into the room, he came in and settled his black case on the table beside the bed. Nodding in Marshall's direction, he turned toward the older man. "How are you feeling this evening, Boyd?"

"About the same as yesterday. I keep telling you, there's no need to stop here every evening. We both know I'm not going to get any better, and I'm sure you've got your hands full taking care of injured workers and those two little girls of yours." Boyd croaked the last words and fell back against his pillows.

Doctor Wahler placed his index finger against his lips. "No need to strain yourself talking, Boyd. And don't concern yourself about my visits. Coming to Bridal Fair is the highlight of my day."

Marshall arched his brows and gave Boyd a see-what-I-was-telling-you look, but the old man's eyelids drooped and closed before

Marshall could gain his attention. After taking Boyd's pulse and listening to his heart and lungs, the doctor grunted and returned the stethoscope to his black bag. "You go ahead and rest, Boyd." The doctor closed his bag and crossed the room in three long strides. "I'm going downstairs and visit with Audrey." He looked to Marshall. "She's invited me for coffee and pie." He smiled rather smugly, as if he'd just won first place in a turkey shoot. "But I'll be back tomorrow, Boyd. Never you fear."

"I'm not . . . gonna promise to be here," Boyd said weakly, "but I'll see what I can do."

"I figure you'll be here, and I'm the doctor, so you must do as I say."

Dr. Wahler didn't wait for a response before hurrying down the hallway. From his hasty departure, Marshall decided the good doctor didn't want to be detained. Marshall didn't know what annoyed him more: the doctor's eagerness to visit with Audrey or Audrey's willingness to stop her work and sit with him.

As the evening progressed, Marshall's irritation ascended to new heights. Audrey almost always returned to sit with her father by eight o'clock. Now it was nearly nine, and she still hadn't appeared. No doubt Dr.

Wahler was the reason.

For weeks the doctor had been sharing more and more time with Audrey. Marshall didn't want to admit that he'd eavesdropped enough to know their conversations weren't focused on Boyd's health or medical treatment. Rather than talking about her father, the doctor seemed to be regaling Audrey with humorous stories of his children and their latest antics.

This evening apparently was no different. Instead of giving Sadie a reprieve from her duties and caring for his children on a Sunday evening, the doctor chose to remain at Bridal Fair for an extended visit with Audrey. The man was no doubt doing his level best to court Audrey in a roundabout manner, and from the sounds of it he was making progress. She delighted in his girls, and whenever Dr. Wahler brought up their need for a mother, Audrey was always sympathetic and agreeable.

A short time later, the bedroom door opened. He was prepared to comment on Audrey's tardiness, but it was Irene rather than Audrey who greeted him.

"You haven't had supper yet. I saved you a plate in the warmer," she told him. "Go on now, and I'll sit with Mr. Cunningham."

"Thank you," he muttered and headed out

of the room. When he topped the stairs, Marshall could hear Dr. Wahler bidding Audrey good-night.

"I'll come again tomorrow, just as I told your father."

"I appreciate your concerns. I can't begin to thank you enough."

He looks like a lovesick schoolboy, Marshall thought as the doctor bent over Audrey's hand and murmured farewell.

As soon as the door was closed, Audrey shot past the stairs without even looking up. Marshall was starting to follow her as she made her way back to the parlor when he heard Frank Baker bid her good evening. Apparently he'd come in the side door after his evening smoke.

"Goodness, Mr. Baker, you startled me," Audrey declared.

Marshall made his way into the parlor and spotted Frank watching Audrey's backside as she bent to gather teacups. The man suddenly realized Marshall had caught him and leered a grin. Marshall wanted to punch him in the mouth and see just how funny the man thought it was then, but he held his temper in check.

Audrey placed the pieces on a tray, and when she straightened she saw Marshall. "Is Father all right?" Her voice trembled.

"He's fine. Irene is with him so that I could have supper. It's getting rather late."

She put her hand to her mouth and then pulled it away just as quickly. "Oh, Marshall, I am sorry. I'm afraid I forgot you hadn't eaten. Please forgive me."

"It's all right," he assured her before looking at Frank. "Don't let us keep you."

"Oh, you aren't. I have plenty of time," Frank said and took a seat.

Audrey reached for the teapot. "I should get these things washed up and go relieve Irene. Would you care to speak to me in the kitchen while you eat?" she asked Marshall.

Unable to keep from sneering at Frank, Marshall replied, "That would suit me just fine."

"Miss Audrey, I was hoping I could speak to you in private." Frank's words yanked Marshall from his thoughts. The assistant supervisor was smiling at Audrey as though he would devour her.

"Audrey is going upstairs to sit with her father once she's finished with her duties." Marshall blurted the response before Audrey could open her mouth.

Audrey turned toward Marshall, her face pinched in an angry frown. "I believe I'm capable of answering for myself." With a tilt of her head, she directed a lovely smile at

Frank. "I'll meet you on the front porch once I've returned these dishes to the kitchen, Mr. Baker."

The moment Audrey stepped out of earshot, Frank leaned forward. "Guess she told you. Maybe now you'll keep your nose out of my private business."

"Don't count on it." For a fleeting moment, Marshall considered going into the kitchen and asking Audrey if she'd taken leave of her senses. Why would she take up with a man who didn't have her best interests at heart? Couldn't she see that the supervisor planned to take advantage of her? Anyone with an ounce of good judgment could peg Frank Baker as a shallow cad. Marshall's anger soared as he left the room. He'd lost his appetite. If Audrey was going to sit on the porch and swoon over Frank Baker, he didn't want to see it.

He tromped up the stairs with the image of Frank Baker's smug grin taunting him. If Audrey wanted to surround herself with the likes of Frank Baker and Dr. Wahler, then so be it. After all, he'd only been attempting to look out for her, trying to do her father's bidding, hoping to provide assistance. And what had that gained him? Obviously, she thought his good deeds obtrusive rather than helpful.

Irene stopped him before he passed Boyd's room. "He's asking for you."

The fact that he'd been out of the room only a few minutes and Boyd was asking for him caused Marshall's fear to mount. Was it Boyd's time? He entered the room, noting the single candle that was burning by the bed.

"That you, Marshall?"

The younger man would have preferred to nurse his wounded spirit in the privacy of his own room, but he stepped closer to the bed and offered a halfhearted wave. "It's me. Something wrong, Boyd?" Instead of sitting, Marshall remained standing by his bedside.

"Nothin' wrong that hasn't been wrong for a long time. You have a good supper?" Boyd shifted in the bed and grimaced from the effort.

Marshall did his best to smile. He didn't want to worry Boyd by admitting that he hadn't eaten. "There's never anything but good food that comes out of the kitchen here at Bridal Fair. You know that, Boyd."

The old man studied him. "Something troubling you? Problems downstairs? Audrey's all right, isn't she?"

"No problems that I've been told about. As for how Audrey's doing, you'd do better to ask Frank Baker or Dr. Wahler. They'd know better than me." The minute he'd spoken, Marshall wanted to take back the curt remark. Boyd lay dying. He didn't need to hear trivial nonsense.

A surprising twinkle shone in Boyd's eyes. "You're jealous. You care for my Audrey, and you're jealous 'cause those men are showing her attention. Am I right?"

Marshall clenched his jaw. "I'm not jealous. I'm only trying to do what you asked of me. You said you wanted me to look out for her, but if she wants to spend her time with the likes of Frank Baker, there's nothing I can do about it. She's a grown woman who wants to make her own decisions."

"Sure enough, she's a grown woman — and you're a grown man — and a jealous one, at that." His soft chuckle soon ended, but a slight grin remained on his lips. "I can see you're unwilling to own up to your feelings for Audrey, but you'll admit them to yourself and to her in time. Of that, I'm certain." Boyd inhaled a ragged breath. "Don't push her too hard. She can get headstrong when she's pushed. Let her think she's making the choices. That's the secret."

Marshall couldn't help but remember the way she'd snapped at him when he'd answered Baker just moments earlier. "She's definitely headstrong."

"Don't let your jealousy get out of hand. It won't serve you well."

Although he wanted to deny he was jealous, Marshall wouldn't argue with a sick man. "Think I'll head off to my room. I'm feeling a little tired this evening."

"Don't spend your time brooding, Marshall. Life's too short for that sort of thing. If you want to be alone, I understand. But use the time wisely — maybe a little Bible reading would be in order. Try taking a look at Proverbs."

Marshall agreed, but only so he could escape to the privacy of his room. Besides, it was Audrey who needed to get her head out of the clouds every time Frank Baker or Dr. Wahler stepped through the doorway. She was the one who needed to read the Bible.

Marshall hadn't intended to heed Boyd's suggestion. The evening was late, and he would need to get up early. However, his restless spirit told him going to bed would only result in rumpled bedcovers. Lifting his Bible from the small bedside table, he tucked his thumb at the upper right-hand corner and watched the chapter headings flash by in rapid succession. Before he could shove his hand between the pages, he'd flipped ahead to the book of Isaiah. Mumbling to himself, he turned the pages back until he arrived at Proverbs. It took only a cursory read to understand Boyd's intent: The book of Proverbs contained excellent instructions on how to live a good life. After a more detailed reading of Proverbs 16, Marshall made a decision. He wanted to commit some of these verses to memory.

He followed the verses down to Proverbs 16:32. *He that is slow to anger is better than the mighty; and he that ruleth his spirit than he that taketh a city.* If he could bring it to mind, that verse would serve him well the next time Dr. Wahler or Frank Baker annoyed him. Once in bed, Marshall repeated the verse. Over and over he recited it until his lips would no longer move or his eyelids remain open.

When his feet hit the floor early the next morning, Marshall once again repeated the verse, pleased when he remembered all of the words. He snapped his suspenders over the shoulders of his blue chambray shirt. Marshall preferred to wear clothes that allowed him to get into the midst of the workers without worry, while Mr. Baker donned a white shirt and remained at a distance.

They were as opposite as two men could be, finding little upon which they could agree.

"Today, I will remember to be slow to anger," Marshall murmured as he descended the stairs and took his place at the breakfast table. Even when Frank attempted to gain Audrey's attention, he held his tongue in check. *Slow to anger, slow to anger.* He cast his gaze downward and didn't lift his head until he'd finished eating.

Instead of waiting until the others prepared to depart, Marshall stood and nodded to the other men. "I'm going down to the dock to meet the boat. Mr. Morley's due in this morning. We'll be over to the work site shortly." Marshall kept his eyes fixed on Harry Fenton rather than Frank Baker. "Make certain the men keep to their assigned tasks. We're getting closer to being on schedule again, and I want it to remain that way."

Marshall grabbed his hat from the hall tree and headed out the front door. For once, he was looking forward to Mr. Morley's visit. In spite of earlier delays, he'd finally been able to prod the men into giving a full day's work for their pay. If they continued at this pace, the resort would be completed for the grand opening. January of 1888 seemed like a long time off, and indeed it was just over a year away. Even so, if they were going to finish on schedule, they'd need good weather and good workmen. He was praying they'd have both.

Achieving the anticipated deadline would provide him with ample time to arrange for his move to Colorado in the early spring of 1888. He smiled as he considered his plan. *What about Audrey?* The question invaded his thoughts with such force that he stopped and looked over his shoulder to see if someone had spoken the words.

He looked upward and surveyed the cloudless blue sky. "What about Audrey? I can't help someone who won't accept my offers." Using the toe of his boot, he kicked a stone and watched it skip and tumble from the path. The idea of delaying his departure now seemed a foolish agreement. Audrey wouldn't appreciate his sacrifice, of that he was becoming more and more certain. And if things continued as they had in recent days, it would be Dr. Wahler or Frank Baker providing her with comfort when her father died.

Marshall was a man of his word, but if Audrey looked to either of those two men for consolation, surely he could consider his obligation fulfilled. Couldn't he? And what if she wanted to remain on Bridal Veil Island? She'd told him it had been her father who'd wanted to leave Pittsburgh, but women could be as changeable as the weather. She now seemed to enjoy living on the island, and maybe she'd decide to remain there forever. Then what would he do? His stomach clenched as his frustration mounted. None of this was making any sense. He cared for Audrey. He didn't want to go to Colorado without her, but he didn't want to remain on Bridal Veil. And he certainly didn't want Dr. Wahler or Frank Baker to win her heart.

His thoughts were still in turmoil when Victor Morley stepped out of the boat and onto the dock a short time later. "You look rather glum. Things not going well with the clubhouse?" His eyebrows dipped low on his forehead.

"We've made enough progress that I think you'll be pleased. Right now, we're only a few days off schedule. Barring any unexpected problems, I think we'll be right on schedule by the time you leave the island."

A smile spread across the investor's face. "Now, that is good news! I'm proud of you, my boy." He patted Marshall's shoulder as he offered his congratulations.

"Thank you, sir. I won't deny it's been a

challenge, but I think the men now understand that I'm in charge."

"You look as though you've lost your best
friend." The two men matched their stride
as they continued toward Bridal Fair.

Though he hadn't planned to confide in
Victor, Marshall soon found himself divulging his hopes, fears, and concerns.

By the time Marshall had finished his
explanation, they had neared the front
porch of Bridal Fair. Mr. Morley grasped
his arm. "So you believe your commitment
to Boyd may ruin your plans to move on to
Colorado. Is that right?"

Marshall nodded. "I know it sounds selfish, but —"

"Do you love Audrey?"

"I . . . I . . . I care for her, but I can't say
for certain that I love her. Not yet. There
never seems enough time for us to be alone.
And when there is, she's with Dr. Wahler or
Frank Baker."

Mr. Morley chuckled. "The jealousy I hear
in your voice sure makes you sound like a
man in love, but I won't argue with you. I
will tell you that it's best to follow your
heart when it comes to love."

Marshall arched his brows. If Audrey
decided to remain on Bridal Veil, that would
mean giving up the Colorado project. Surely

Mr. Morley didn't think he could so easily push aside such an opportunity.

Before there was time to question Mr. Morley further, the front door opened and Audrey stepped outside. "Mr. Morley! I didn't know you'd arrived. Father's been asking when you might come for a visit."

"I was just going to come inside. I want to change clothes before going to take a look at the construction site." He glanced at Marshall. "I'll take a minute to say hello to Boyd, and then we can be on our way."

"I'll wait out here. Care to join me, Audrey? It's a beautiful day."

She hesitated a moment. "It is a beautiful day, but I need to go help with the laundry while Father is resting."

"I don't think Irene would mind if you took a few minutes for yourself."

Audrey shook her head. "Irene's already had to take over too many of my duties. I can't sit idle while she's working. It wouldn't be fair."

Marshall shrugged a shoulder. "Seems you're willing to take time to visit with Dr. Wahler when he comes calling."

She whirled around, her lips pressed in a tight thin line and the golden fleck in her eyes dancing with fire. "What is that supposed to mean?"

"N-n-nothing. Forget I mentioned it. You have a right to spend your time however you please."

"You're absolutely correct on that account!"

Audrey yanked open the door and let it slam behind her. The sound of heavy footsteps clapping down the hallway emphasized what he already knew: He'd spoken without thinking. He dropped back into a chair and rubbed his forehead. Would he ever understand how to talk to a woman?

CHAPTER 15

When Mr. Morley returned to the front porch a short time later, Marshall was still confused about Audrey as well as his future. He jumped to his feet, glad to get away from the house and have something other than Audrey to fill his thoughts. "I think you're going to be surprised to see how much has been accomplished since your last visit. The bricklayers and stonemasons you hired in Pittsburgh have been a real help. They've even been training some of the other men."

Mr. Morley clapped him on the shoulder. "Glad to hear that. I imagine those fellows will want to return to Pittsburgh to visit their families from time to time, and we'll want the work to continue at a regular pace."

As they neared the clearing and the construction site came into view, Marshall cupped his hand above his eyes. Leaving Mr. Morley to keep up with him, Marshall picked up his pace. "What's going on?" he shouted, now at a full run.

Except for the workers who had arrived from Pittsburgh and a few of the other workers, most of the men were lounging beneath trees that bordered one side of the clubhouse. Frank Baker sat among them, his laughter ringing out louder than the rest. Although Frank glanced in his direction, he didn't answer, and he didn't get up. None of the workers appeared worried that he'd discovered them lounging about instead of working.

Marshall bent from the waist and panted for air. When he'd finally regained his ability to breathe at a somewhat normal rate, he pointed at the men. "Why aren't you working? We've finally gotten back on schedule, and now I find you lounging around as if the building is already completed." He turned an angry glare at Frank. "And why have you allowed this to happen?" Before Frank could answer, Marshall waved at the men. "All of you! Get back to work, right now!"

His shouted command echoed in the crisp autumn air, but the men didn't move an inch. He clenched his jaw, his frustration mounting as Mr. Morley approached the group. The older man frowned at the men.

"I've been told you're making good progress on the construction." He studied the completed foundation for a moment. "And I can see that's true, but I don't understand why none of you men are working." He looked directly at Frank. "Care to explain?"

Moving ever so slowly, Frank pushed to his feet and extended his hand to Mr. Morley. "Truth of the matter is, these men aren't feeling real comfortable working here right now. Not after what one of them discovered earlier this morning."

Marshall moved closer. "And exactly what was that?"

Ignoring Marshall's question, Frank stepped closer to Mr. Morley. "Don't know if you realize it, but lots of Southerners can be mighty superstitious, and I'm afraid we got the superstitious type working here at the clubhouse. I think it's gonna take a whole lot of convincing to get 'em back to work."

Mr. Morley motioned Frank and Marshall away from the group of men. "Why don't you tell us exactly what caused this sudden behavior, Frank."

Turning his back to Marshall, Frank motioned toward the clubhouse. "One of the men went inside this morning and discovered some bones."

Mr. Morley stiffened. "Human bones?"

"Can't say for sure, but they look like they could be. Soon as Joe — that's the fella that found the bones — soon as he came upon those bones, a bird flew overhead and then landed beside the bones."

Marshall sighed. Such nonsense. "And what's that supposed to mean?"

"A sure sign of death if they continue working. They're not about to go back until something's done."

"Like what?" Marshall hadn't meant to shout, but he was having trouble controlling his anger. He didn't know what annoyed him more — the men sitting around or Frank ignoring him.

Frank shrugged as he finally turned to look at Marshall. "Guess that would be your problem to solve. You're the project manager." He smirked and folded his arms across his chest. Marshall didn't miss the evil gleam in his eyes.

Mr. Morley strode across the dirt and rubble and tipped his hat at the workers. "Good morning, men. I hear there's some concern about returning to your duties. Care to tell me how we can solve this problem?"

After murmuring among themselves, one of the men stood. "We're thinkin' you're gonna have to find someone to break the spell 'fore any of us is gonna commence to working agin."

Marshall didn't know if he should be thankful for the older man's help or resent the fact that he hadn't given him the opportunity to solve the dilemma on his own. If the men looked to someone else to solve their problems, Marshall would never gain their respect. He'd already had enough difficulty trying to convince them he was in charge rather than Frank.

He drew closer to the men. "Why don't all of you gather around and we'll pray. I'll ask for God's protection over all of you while you continue working here on the island." He hoped his enthusiastic offer would result in their agreement.

One of the workers leaning against a tree trunk shook his head. "You go ahead and pray if you want, but it's gonna take more than a prayer to get us back to work." He nudged one of the other men. "Right, fellas?"

They looked like chickens pecking the ground as they bobbed their heads in unison. Marshall couldn't decide whether to laugh or to bellow at the men. He doubted either would be effective. He strode toward them and came to a halt beside Joe.

"I can't help if you don't tell me what needs to be done." He waved his arm in a wide circle that encompassed all of the men. "I'm pretty certain all of you need to earn money, especially those of you with families. I'd say it's best for all of us to get this taken care of as soon as possible."

He hoped mention of pay would prove persuasive with some of the men. Finally, one of the laborers stood and ambled toward him. "You gotta find someone with the power to remove the curse."

Marshall waited for further explanation, but none was forthcoming. He sighed. "Exactly where would I find such a person?"

"Only one I know of is Ole Blue Lightnin'. 'Course I don't know how you'd go 'bout finding him."

Marshall didn't know if Ole Blue Lightnin' was man or beast, but if that's what it was going to take to get the men back to work, he knew he'd better find out — and fast. "You must have some idea. Otherwise, how do you know this Blue Lightning even exists?"

A chorus of gasps erupted, and Marshall took a backward step as the men jumped to their feet and shouted at him.

Frank tipped his hat to the back of his head and grinned. "Now you really got 'em riled up with your disbelieving ways."

Marshall ignored Frank. "Settle down and let's try to reason together. I need you back at work, and you need your pay. Right?" He didn't wait for an answer. "So for all of us to get what we need, I'm giving you the rest of the day off to try to find Ole Blue and bring him back here to take care of this curse. Are we agreed?"

The men looked at each other and nodded as Joe stepped forward. "We'll see what we can do, but ain't no guarantees."

"There's no guarantee on your pay, either, so keep that in mind while you're looking. And if you decide prayer might work better than Ole Blue, just let me know. I think the power of God will do more for you than Ole Blue."

The men walked off, obviously unaffected by his final comment. Mr. Morley's visit wasn't going as he'd planned. Not by a long shot.

With a smirk as wide as the Argosy River spread across his face, Frank leaned against one of the trees. "Looks like you're gonna fall behind schedule again, Marshall." He shoved a piece of dry marsh grass between his teeth. "Too bad."

Marshall glowered at him. "Instead of standing around doing nothing, I think you better get over to the clubhouse and lend a hand. After all, you've got plenty of experience. Or did that curse include you, too?"

"Come, Marshall," Morley said. "Show me what's been completed and then you'd better see what you can do about locating this Ole Blue fellow." Mr. Morley strode past Frank and called over his shoulder. "If that curse included you, Frank, you can pack your bags and head back home. Otherwise, I suggest you do as your project manager ordered."

From the scowl on Frank's face, Marshall thought maybe he would decide to leave. Would the assistant manager's departure halt the problems that gave rise at every turn? Marshall pushed the thought aside, and though he did his best to point out all of the progress and give a positive report to Mr. Morley, the idea of locating Ole Blue Lightning wasn't far from his mind. "The foundation is in good shape and I had hoped we would begin work on the first floor tomorrow."

"It is looking quite —"

Shouts of alarm came from the rear of the building site, and several men raced toward them, shouting for the doctor. Marshall grabbed one of the men by the arm. "What's happened?"

Fear shone in the man's eyes. "One of the men fell off the foundation wall into the basement. He's hurt bad. Landed hard and hit his head on one of the stone walls. He needs a doctor."

Marshall raced to a far oak tree where an emergency bell had been tied to one of the upper branches. He grabbed the heavy rope and yanked with all his might. Waving to the worker who had delivered the news, he motioned toward the path. "You watch for the doctor. If you don't see him coming in a couple minutes, ring that bell again. I'm going back to see how . . ." He hesitated. "What's the man's name who's been injured?"

"Jonas. Jonas Fuller."

"I'm going back to see if I can lend a hand with Jonas. Keep your eye peeled for the doctor. You hear me?" Terror strained his voice as he attempted to remain calm. Panic wouldn't help.

Dr. Wahler declared the injured worker would eventually heal. He'd suffered a blow to the head and a broken leg that would mend over time, but the doctor ordered that Jonas be transported to a hospital in Savannah for further treatment of the injuries. He also suggested someone accompany the young man to the hospital.

Since work had all but come to a standstill, Mr. Morley announced that he would accompany the young man as far as Savannah and then return home to tend to his investment business. "Get out there and locate that Blue Lightning fellow. I'll expect to hear as soon as work has commenced at full force," he'd told Marshall before he boarded the launch.

Marshall hadn't needed the instruction. The accident had reinforced the workers' opinion that the curse was real. Wages or not, they wouldn't return to work until the curse had been lifted. Marshall had no choice: He had to locate Ole Blue Lightning.

CHAPTER 16

Audrey's life now consisted of watching and waiting. She watched her father's health decline, and she waited for Marshall to find Ole Blue Lightning. She felt powerless to help either of them. In spite of reports that several men were spending each day searching for the man who could remove the dreaded curse, no one could report any success, and Marshall said he doubted the men were truly looking.

Audrey's father continued to assure her that he was prepared to die. Yet she wasn't so sure. He seemed to be holding on for some reason beyond her understanding. Though Dr. Wahler expressed surprise that her father continued to cling to life, Audrey was thankful for each extra hour with him.

The late afternoon sun glistened on the windowsill as Audrey drew a chair close to her father's bedside and grasped his hand. In spite of the warm, glowing embers in the fireplace, a cool clamminess pervaded his body. Bones left bare of muscle and fat protruded from beneath the pale skin that once stretched across broad shoulders. Shoulders that had balanced her high in the air as a little girl. Shoulders that had supported the weight of lumber and brick at construction sites. Shoulders that had sagged low with grief when her mother died.

Placing his hand beneath the covers, she brushed strands of hair from his forehead. His eyelids flickered, but instead of revealing his familiar sparkling gray eyes, she was met with a rheumy, glazed stare.

Her heart heaved with sorrow at the sight of him — a once strong and virile man brought to this low state. *Why, Lord? Why must he suffer so?* In spite of her best efforts to remain brave, a single tear rolled down her cheek.

"Don't cry for me, Audrey. I'm going to be just fine."

She startled at the sound of his voice, surprised at his unexpected burst of strength. Did he truly believe he was going to be fine? Perhaps he was having one of those delusional episodes Dr. Wahler had mentioned several days ago. The ones that sometimes occurred shortly before death.

Audrey wasn't certain how to respond.

She didn't want to destroy her father's will to live, but she was opposed to giving him false hope. Dr. Wahler had been honest with her: There was no cure for her father.

"I'm pleased to know that you're going to get well, Father, but . . ."

Wisps of hair fanned across her father's forehead as he moved his head back and forth. "I understand I'm not going to get well, Audrey. I was trying to tell you that I'm ready for death to come — ready to see your mother again, ready for heaven." He wheezed as he inhaled a lungful of air.

"Don't try to talk, Father. It's too difficult."

"I must talk. There are a few things I want to tell you before I die, so listen carefully." His eyes fluttered at half-mast before he managed to once again hold them open.

"If it's easier, you can whisper." She scooted to the edge of her chair and leaned close.

"I want you to marry and enjoy life. I don't want to die thinking you're going to turn into a withered old prune that lives the rest of her life alone, dressed in black, because she won't turn loose her heart."

"I must say that you haven't lost your way with words. If that statement doesn't convince me to seek a husband, I don't know what will." Audrey grinned at him and shook her head.

"I'm serious about this, Audrey. I want you to promise me that you'll open your heart to the love of a good man." With a trembling hand, he clasped her arm.

She placed her hand atop his and looked into his eyes. "If a good man can be found, then you have my word that I will open my heart to love."

Her father shifted beneath the covers, grimacing against the pain. "Don't be foolish, Audrey. You've been surrounded by good men. Open your eyes, along with your heart, and you'll see the love that waits for you." He panted and gave soft moaning sounds as he exhaled. "Don't live . . . without love."

Her father's eyes drifted closed, and he slipped into a restless sleep. She touched his cheek then leaned back against the chair and closed her eyes.

"God, I hate to see him suffer. . . . Please ease his pain."

Audrey didn't know how long she'd been sleeping when Dr. Wahler tapped her on the shoulder. "You should go and get some rest. I've examined him, and it appears he's slipped into what may be a permanent state of unconsciousness. Although he may awaken. I've seen it before, and he's already lived much longer than I'd expected." He helped her to her feet. "I'll stay with your father for a while."

Her gaze settled on her father, his complexion almost as white as the sheet that covered him. "No. I want to —"

"I'm the doctor, Audrey. You need your rest, or you'll be no good to yourself or to your father. Please go and rest. I promise to come and get you if there's any change in his condition."

She hesitated for only a moment. "If you promise."

Dr. Wahler's reassurance was all she needed. After kissing her father on the cheek, Audrey took halting steps toward the stairway. She'd gone only a short distance when she turned around. "You promise to send for me if there's any change?"

He waved her onward. "I've already given you my promise. Please. Get some rest."

She trudged down the steps and into her room, Dr. Wahler's promise fresh in her thoughts. While she loosened the collar of her dress and removed her shoes, she recalled the promise she'd made to her father a short time ago. What men had he been speaking of? Had he meant Marshall or perhaps Dr. Wahler? Certainly the doctor was a good man — one who was capable of love. He demonstrated love to his children every day, and from all accounts, the doctor had loved his wife. And she knew her father admired Marshall. Was he thinking of him? The house was filled with men — had he been referring to one of them? She wanted to consider the matter, perhaps even question him further when she returned upstairs. But for now, even the clatter of pots and pans in the nearby kitchen couldn't keep her awake.

"Audrey, wake up." Irene leaned close to her ear. "Doc says to hurry."

Not even bothering with her shoes, Audrey jumped from the bed and dashed to the stairs. She came to her father's room and spied the doctor and Marshall standing near the bedside. Not a word was spoken, but one look told her she was too late. Her father was dead.

Dr. Wahler extended his hand. "I'm sorry, my dear. He was stable, and then his breathing grew shallow and his heart slowed. I sent Irene as quickly as I could."

"Did he . . . did he wake up?" she asked, afraid of the answer.

"No. He passed quite easily."

"I should have been here," Audrey said,

reaching out to touch her father's peaceful face. She had wanted to be with him at the end, to hold his hand, smooth his brow, and express her love for him one last time. Grief assailed her, both for the loss of her father and for the lost opportunity to be with him in his final hour.

An invisible band wrapped around her chest and cut off her breath. A strangled cry escaped her lips and tears rolled down her cheeks. Gasping, she turned and met Marshall's eyes. He stepped toward her just as her knees gave way and the room went dark.

Waking up some time later, Audrey heard Thora issuing instructions. "Bring the smelling salts — she's been too long in this faint. It will cause her brain fever if we're not careful."

"I assure you, Miss Audrey will not get brain fever. She's simply had a shock," Dr. Wahler explained. "It's best to let her recover gradually. When she awakens —"

"I'm awake," Audrey said, attempting to sit up. Someone had placed her in bed. Marshall, no doubt. He had been the one nearest to her when she'd collapsed.

"You oughten to be sitting," Thora declared, pushing her back against the pillows. "Too much strain on your heart."

"My heart is broken at the loss of my

father," Audrey said and scooted to the edge of the bed. "Otherwise it continues to beat just fine." She wasn't about to add that perhaps it would be better had it stopped along with her father's. Such talk would be misinterpreted, and before she knew it, Thora would have her drinking healing concoctions and tied to the bedpost.

"I'm sorry for making a scene," she said, looking at Dr. Wahler. "I've never been one given to fainting spells."

"Never had this many Yankees at Bridal Fair, either," Thora said in a huff.

Audrey ignored her. "I need to ready Father's body for burial."

"Don't you worry about that," Thora declared. "Irene and me, we can manage."

It was the first time Thora had suggested she could work at ease with the younger girl. Audrey was too tired to argue. "He'll wear his blue suit. I'll brush it —"

Thora held up her hand. "Already bein' done." She put a hand to her back and shuffled to the door. "I've done my share of burial preparations. I can do this for all of you."

Audrey looked at Dr. Wahler and then around the room. The doctor smiled. "Mr. Graham is helping Irene. I believe he felt a . . . brotherly . . . responsibility. Mr.

Cunningham was quite dear to him, it would seem."

Nodding, Audrey thought of Marshall's kindness to her father — to all of them. "He's a good man," she murmured, her eyes widening as the words spilled out. "A good man."

As they prepared for her father's funeral, Audrey couldn't help but take note of the many good men in her company. The kind words and deeds of the men — both their boarders and the ones who lived in the old slave quarters — were clear proof of their attributes.

One of the carpenters constructed her father's coffin, and she was amazed by his dogged determination to create something beautiful as a final tribute. Men came to the house with bouquets of fall flowers that continued to bloom in spite of Audrey's sorrow. They dug the grave and placed some of Aunt Thora's toad lilies, colorful pansies, and some of her beloved rockets of yellow ligularia near the gravesite. And there wasn't one complaint from Aunt Thora.

Pastor Nichols arrived from Biscayne to conduct the funeral. Audrey stood stock-still, Marshall on one side of her and Aunt Thora on the other, while Pastor Nichols offered the final prayer.

"And to you, Father in heaven, we give honor and praise. We thank you and celebrate the life of this man, Boyd Cunningham. We ask your blessing on his beloved daughter and on the friends who have gathered here today. Let us go now in your grace. Amen."

"Amen," the crowd murmured.

The word stuck in Audrey's throat. It was too final. Like reading *The End* on the last page of a book. She looked at her father's closed coffin, knowing he was inside, but also knowing it wasn't really him at all. His spirit — the very heart and soul of this man whom she loved — was gone. Life would never be the same.

While Audrey was thankful for the preacher's eulogy, it was his kindness afterward that spoke to her heart. He remained for several hours and spoke of his conversations with her father. "He loved you very much, Audrey. More than anything, I know your father wanted you to find a good husband and be happy. Even more, you have the assurance of knowing that you'll be together again one day. For those who know the Lord, there is great comfort." He patted her hand. "You're going to be just fine, Audrey." He tapped his fingers against his chest. "I can feel it right here."

She forced a feeble smile. Maybe one day she would feel the same way. Right now, she wasn't so sure.

When they returned to Bridal Fair a short time later, Mr. Morley drew Audrey aside. His eyes mirrored Audrey's pain. "I wish there was something I could do to ease your grief, but I find words inadequate at this time." He pressed an envelope into her hand. "This is the deed to Bridal Fair. I've paid the back taxes, and . . ."

Audrey gasped. "Oh no, I couldn't. My father was opposed to taking charity, and I plan to continue working so that I can pay off the debt."

Mr. Morley gently patted her hand. "Please, Audrey. Let me do this." His lips curved in a slight grin. "Heaven knows I need you to continue your boardinghouse duties here at Bridal Fair until we've completed the construction. The supervisors would never forgive me if you quit. But I want to release you from the tax burden." When she didn't reply, he tipped his head and met her gaze. "Please. I truly want you to accept."

His generosity and kindness caused a lump to rise in her throat. She knew if she tried to answer, she'd begin to cry and might never be able to stop. She nodded her head as tears ran down her cheeks, unchecked. God was providing for her security. Now, if He could only mend her heart, as well.

Two days later, the twins accompanied Sadie to Bridal Fair, each of the girls bearing a handful of flowers while Sadie carried two large baskets of food.

"She thinks I'm too old to keep up with the cooking around here." Thora hissed the remark in Audrey's ear while Sadie coaxed one of the twins from beneath the settee in the parlor.

"Of course not, Aunt Thora. She's extending a kindness, and you need to quit thinking that the goodness of other people is intended as an insult to you."

"I do not. This is the first time —"

Audrey held up her hand. "No, ma'am. This isn't the first time. The day Father died, you thought the boarders' offer to take their meals in the dining hall down near the slave quarters was an insult. And yesterday, when Old Sam tried to give us all those shrimp, you accused him of trying to sell off his extra catch on our doorstep. Today, you think Sadie has prepared this food because she thinks you're incapable of keeping up with your duties." Audrey sighed and lifted the cloth from one of the baskets. "People want to extend help and sympathy. Let them do it without your thinking it has something to do with your ability or that someone is trying to take advantage of us. After all, this is the way of the South — just as you've always told me."

Thora's expression softened. It was her only sign of agreement. She pulled back the cloth on the other basket and removed warm loaves of nut bread, a pan of pecan squares, and three jars of preserves. "She must think we all have a sweet tooth."

Irene peered over the old woman's shoulder. "Well, I know I do. I'll be more than happy to eat your share."

When Irene inched forward and reached for one of the pecan squares, Thora slapped her hand. "Don't think you can just help yourself whenever you please. If I recollect, I told you to pare those sweet potatoes."

Irene pointed to the pan sitting near the kitchen window. "I finished five minutes ago." Turning her attention to Audrey, the younger woman motioned toward the doorway. "Why don't you go and rest. We can manage just fine. You have other things to attend to."

While grasping a hand of each of the

twins, Sadie returned to the kitchen. "If there's any way I can help, you jest let me know, Miss Audrey." She glanced at the young girls. " 'Course, I got the young'uns to look after, but I'll do my best to lend a hand wherever you need me."

Josie wrapped her free arm around Audrey's skirt and gave a tug. "Wanna come outside and play with us so Sadie can help Miss Thora with her cooking?"

Audrey stooped down and looked into the child's eyes. "Not today, Josie, but if Sadie brings you over next week, we can spend some time together. How would that be?"

Julie nodded at her sister. "We'd like that. Papa says you're sad because your papa died. I was sad when our mama died, too."

"I'm sure you were, Julie."

Josie shook her head. "She doesn't really remember. We were only three when Mama died."

Julie stomped her leather-clad foot. "I do too remember!"

"Time for us to go home, girls." Sadie offered a sympathetic smile. "I'm sorry for your loss, Miss Audrey. I'm sorry the girls aren't better behaved. Our little talk before we came over didn't help much." She directed a stern look at each of them. "Come along. We're going home."

Though the girls protested, Sadie marched them toward home. Audrey watched as the three of them headed down the path. "I believe I'll go for a walk if you're certain you don't need my help."

"You go on, Miss Audrey. We're just fine," Irene said.

"Since when did *you* take charge of this kitchen? Never had a Yankee in charge of anything at Bridal Fair that I recollect." Thora stomped to the kitchen doorway. "You put the Yankee girl in charge, Audrey?"

"I told you I'm not a Yankee or a Confederate; I'm an American, and so are you." Irene rested a fist on each hip and gave the older woman a look that dared defiance.

Audrey stepped toward the kitchen. "Neither of you is in charge — I am. And I'm ordering you to get along while I'm gone." That said, she hastened out the front door before another argument ensued.

Learning to deal with Aunt Thora was a survival tool Irene had begun to hone the day she arrived. She had quickly discovered that the best way to deal with Thora was to meet her head on. Audrey hadn't stopped the girl when she'd voiced her objections to being called a Yankee, and after a few weeks, Thora had ceased such activity. With the recent stressful events, Thora had reverted

275

to her old ways, but Irene held her ground.

"Smart girl. She's not going to let Thora get the best of her," Audrey whispered as she descended the front steps.

At the end of the path, she turned left, away from the narrow path leading to the small family cemetery. She passed the wash-house and continued on toward the beach. Birds fluttered overhead, disturbed by the invasion of any species other than their own. A branch cracked in the underbrush, and she turned, expecting to spot a rabbit or perhaps a deer — praying it wouldn't be Frank Baker.

Instead, Marshall stepped into sight. He seemed to drink her in — his dark eyes sweeping her from head to toe. "I was hop-ing to find you. Irene said you'd gone for a walk." He came alongside and slowed his step to match hers. "How are you feeling?"

"I do not plan to faint again, if you were concerned." She tried to sound lighthearted, but it fell flat. "I'm fine."

He nodded toward a piece of driftwood. "Why don't we sit down." He held her hand as she lowered herself and then sat beside her. "I know this is difficult for you, and I'm worried about how you're doing."

Her lips curved in a faint smile. "I'm not sure. Mostly, I feel as though I'm in a dream

— that none of this is real. Yet I know it is, and I know that life must go on. There are people depending upon me, and I can't let them down."

"You need to take care of yourself, Audrey. There's nothing that can't wait until later. Besides, you have Irene and Thora. Between their arguments, they're going to manage just fine."

"I know you're right, and I'm trying to get my proper rest, but there are decisions I need to make about my future and the future of Bridal Fair."

A curl fluttered across her face, and he reached forward, tucking it behind her ear. Her skin tingled at the sensation. He leaned toward her until their lips were no more than a hairsbreadth apart. She held her breath and wondered if he would kiss her. Her heart pounded beneath the bodice of her black mourning dress. Did she want him to kiss her, or were these emotions surfacing because she'd lost her father? Perhaps she simply wanted to fill the hole that had taken up residence in her heart since his death.

"Audrey, I —"

"Miss Audrey, Miss Audrey, we've come looking for shells!" Josie Wahler shouted with delight as she and her sister came running toward them, their father close behind.

Audrey couldn't be certain who scooted backward first, Marshall or herself. Either way, it didn't matter. Marshall managed to maintain his balance, but she slipped off the piece of driftwood and, dress askew, landed on her backside.

The doctor stared down at the two of them. "I do hope we didn't interrupt anything."

Audrey attempted to maintain a modicum of dignity, which proved difficult. "No, of course not. I'm afraid I lost my balance." With arms and legs akimbo, she likely resembled a turtle that had fallen off a log and landed upside down on its shell. Marshall leaned down and extended his hand while the twins giggled in the background. Their gazes locked as Marshall pulled her to her feet and into his arms. For the briefest of moments she held his embrace before he stepped aside. She had the strangest urge to reach up and touch his lips with her fingertips.

What *would* it be like to kiss him? She didn't want to admit it — not even to herself — but she wished Dr. Wahler and the twins hadn't appeared.

CHAPTER 17

Christmas arrived without much fanfare. Old Blue Lightning hadn't been located, and Mr. Morley had declared there wasn't much reason for the men to remain on the island during the holidays. Although the women served an exceptional dinner of baked ham, candied yams, and Aunt Thora's traditional pecan pie, the day passed quietly. Most of the workers had traveled home for the holidays, and even Marshall had been absent. The only visitor on Christmas Day was Old Sam, who stopped by to leave a basket of fresh shrimp. He mentioned that one of his felines had given birth recently and if they wanted a kitten or two, they were surely welcome to them.

"They won't be as fine a cat as old Samson," he said with a wink. "Seems to me ain't hardly any cat as fine as that ol' gentleman. But they's sure to be a passable one or two in the litter."

Audrey thought it might be a nice surprise for the twins but then remembered Dr. Wahler's comment about animals. He'd likely be opposed to such a surprise. "I can ask Dr. Wahler if he'll permit his daughters to have one of them, but I doubt he'll agree."

"Too bad. I'm guessing those little gals would be mighty happy to have a pet. Let me know if the doctor gives in to the idea." He waved and strode off, whistling as though he hadn't a care in the world.

Other than this, the holidays were rather somber and lonely. Dr. Wahler, Sadie, and the twins returned to Atlanta for a two-week visit, and the investors, including Mr. Morley, enjoyed the holiday with their families at their respective homes in various cities. Irene returned to Pittsburgh with Mr. Morley, and Marshall departed for a short visit to Savannah. Audrey tried to put the quiet time to good use. She caught up on some much-needed mending and sewing and took more time for Bible reading, but she found herself quite happy to see the workers return after New Year's Day — especially Marshall and Irene. Thora seemed happy to have the younger woman back, as well. She didn't even seem to mind that Irene had been visiting folks up north and listened intently to Irene's stories.

"I have a surprise for you," Irene told Aunt Thora.

The old woman seemed indignant. "I don't much like surprises."

But Audrey knew better. Aunt Thora was just embarrassed. Irene withdrew a small handkerchief-wrapped object from her pocket.

"I know it's a little late for Christmas gifts, so we'll just call this a New Year's novelty."

Aunt Thora unwrapped the present and stared at it for a moment. Enclosed was a small carved-shell cameo brooch. Audrey was first to comment. "That is lovely."

"Thora was telling me how she'd lost hers during the War of Northern Aggression," Irene supplied. "When I mentioned it to my mother, she suggested such an item would make a perfect gift."

"Isn't it beautiful, Aunt Thora?" Audrey asked.

Her aunt fingered the piece with great gentleness. She clearly didn't know what to say. It was the first time anyone had been able to render the old woman speechless. Seeming to sense she was in danger of appearing too pleased, Aunt Thora gave a curt nod.

"Can't wear it until my mourning for

Boyd is past."

Audrey would have argued that the woman was not under any kind of obligation to wear black on behalf of Boyd Cunningham but knew it would only serve to hurt her feelings. Instead, Audrey decided to agree.

"Your mourning ends in March. Three months is long enough. I promised Father I wouldn't sit around wearing black and being sad."

To her surprise, Aunt Thora only nodded, while Irene beamed a smile.

Marshall was glad to be back on the island and ready for the start of a new year. After a short trip of exploration in Savannah, he found that the formalities of Southern customs didn't appeal to him. Traditions on Bridal Veil Island were enough to keep him constantly fretting over his manners, but in Savannah it was an entirely different matter. Perhaps, however, the best thing about being in Savannah was that it constantly reminded him of how much he missed Audrey's company.

Seeing her again was confirmation that something had happened in his heart. Even though Boyd had tried to persuade him to see it months ago, he'd resisted. After all, he'd come south in search of a job — not a wife. With Audrey in the picture, that possibility no longer seemed so strange.

"But she may not feel the same way," he reminded himself.

With Boyd gone, who could say what Audrey might do. He might just have to wiggle himself right into whatever plans she made for herself. The thought made him grin.

"You look mighty pleased with yourself," Thora declared, making her way to where Marshall sat on the porch polishing his good boots.

Marshall popped to his feet. "No, ma'am. I'm pleased with this day God has given us. Pleased, as well, to be back here at Bridal Fair."

She looked at him for a moment and nodded. "I can tell just what pleases you to be back."

Marshall gave her a quizzical look. The old woman seemed to pin him in place with her stare. Waggling her crooked finger, she narrowed her eyes. "You'd just best mind your ways, Marshall Graham. You've got just enough Southern blood in you to be dangerous."

He couldn't help but grin, which was entirely the wrong thing to do. Aunt Thora straightened as if he'd slapped her. Marshall was completely perplexed.

"Don't you think to try any of that charm on me," she declared. "I'm immune to it. My mama, God rest her soul, taught me early on to spot a lovesick suitor. You've gone and gotten yourself in a pretty pickle, haven't you?"

He quickly decided perhaps it would be best to make her his confidante and coconspirator. Perhaps with the old woman on his side, he would be able to woo Audrey.

"You're a wise one, Mrs. Lund. I'm not at all surprised that you were able to deduce my predicament."

She nodded knowingly and arched a brow. "You may be more Southern than I give you credit for."

"I don't suppose you would consider helping me, would you? I mean, you know Miss Audrey better than anyone here."

The older woman considered his question for a moment. "Audrey's papa, God bless his newly departed soul, was fond of you. I can't deny that." She drew a deep breath. "Let me ponder this for a while. I'll give you my answer after I spend some time in the Scriptures."

Marshall nodded. "Of course. I would be honored to wait."

"Pshaw." She gave him a wave of her hand

284

and toddled off into the house.

After she'd departed, Marshall sat back down and picked up his supplies. Samson meandered over, as if to check on the outcome of Marshall's polishing, and stopped just short of sticking his nose into the polish when Marshall placed the can back on the porch floor.

"You'll help me, too, won't you?" Marshall asked the cat.

Samson looked up and gave a garbled kind of meow. Marshall laughed. "I was hoping you would say that. With you on my side, I'm sure to make progress."

For the next several weeks work at the site continued at a snail's pace. Except for the men who'd come from up north and didn't believe in the curse, most of the men had returned to their homes on the mainland with a promise to return once Ole Blue could be located. The few who remained had continually refused to work until Marshall declared that the cook would stop feeding them if they weren't going to work. They finally conceded, though they begged for work beyond the perimeter of the clubhouse — preferably at least ten feet away. Marshall's patience had reached new heights, yet he tried to remain thankful for any progress at all.

That afternoon Frank had delivered news that some of the workers had gone to work on Jekyl Island. Marshall's spirits plummeted at the announcement. "And exactly how did you come by this information? Have you been over to Jekyl Island yourself?"

Frank shook his head. "No. I went into Biscayne to purchase a few personal items and thought I'd see if I could convince some of the men to return, since we've had no further signs of a curse. 'Course I didn't meet with any success. These folks don't budge from the old superstitions." He shrugged his shoulders. "Anyway, one of the fellows told me that about forty of our workers had gone to Jekyl."

"Any word about whether they'll leave Jekyl and come back here once I find Ole Blue?"

Frank chuckled. "You mean *if* you find Ole Blue, don't ya?" He didn't wait for an answer. "Living conditions are better over here, and the pay is five cents an hour more — they'll come back." He began to walk off, then stopped and turned.

"Did you ask about the whereabouts of Ole Blue?" Marshall asked.

"You know, I didn't even think to ask."

Marshall bristled at the smug response. Frank was enjoying the fact that the project was falling further and further behind. He strode back to Bridal Fair, his anger rising with each step he took. He entered the house and slammed the door behind him with a bang that brought Thora around the corner at a quick clip.

"Didn't your mother teach you better manners? We don't slam the doors in this house."

Marshall dropped into one of the chairs. He didn't need Thora blathering at him. "I apologize." Samson wound his way around the furniture and jumped onto Marshall's lap.

"What's got you so riled up?"

"Same thing that's had me riled up since before Boyd died. I can't find Old Blue, and until I do, we're at a near standstill. You don't have any ideas, do you?"

The old woman glanced over her shoulder before she leaned close and whispered, "I s'pose I could get on out and see if I can find him."

Marshall jumped to his feet and sent Samson leaping to the floor. "You know where he is?"

She arched her brows. "I might know a few places to look for him. Can't promise

287

anything, and you can't come with me. He'd never forgive me if I was to give up one of his hiding spots. He's got a small skiff — comes and goes among some of the islands, but mostly he stays here on Bridal Veil. He helped Boyd some during the War of Northern —" She stopped short. "During the war."

Marshall couldn't believe his ears. Why hadn't Thora stepped in to help before now? He wanted to scream the question at her, but that would never do. She would stomp off and leave him without an answer and without Old Blue. "Any reason you didn't mention you might know his whereabouts before now?"

She shrugged one shoulder. "You didn't ask. I've never been one to interfere where I'm not wanted."

He almost laughed aloud. Thora had her nose in everything that happened at Bridal Fair — on the entire island, for that matter. "Well, I'm asking you now, Thora. I would be most grateful for any help you could give. And when you find Old Blue, will you tell him I need a curse removed from the construction site and I'm willing to pay whatever he charges for his curse-removing services."

She cackled. "He don't charge money. It's

friendship and loyalty that's important to Ole Blue. Like I said, he was a big help to Boyd during the war — and to me, too. If Audrey comes looking for me, you tell her I went to meditate and don't want to be bothered." She poked his chest with her index finger. "And don't follow me! Think you can remember all that?"

"I believe I can. Thank you, Mrs. Lund."

"Don't thank me yet. You best wait and see if I find him."

Marshall had gone to the work site three times and returned to Bridal Fair in between. He didn't know where or when Thora might reappear, but he didn't want to miss her. As he once again neared Bridal Fair, he caught sight of the old woman's white hair rounding the house. "Mrs. Lund!" He waved and ran toward her, his hopes swelling when he saw her grin and wave in return.

"Did you find him?" He gulped a breath of air and stared into her eyes.

"Yep. He'll be over to the construction site tomorrow mornin'. I suggest you get on that boat and go tell them workers to get on over here if they want to see him get rid of that curse. The more that see he was here, the better. Then there's no way of denying he come and took care of things for 'em." She shook her head. "Bunch of nonsense, but there ain't no talking good sense to them what believes in such things."

Marshall couldn't believe she'd so easily located the man. He'd spent weeks looking — even left messages nailed onto trees in the hope of locating the man. "You're certain he'll show up?"

She shook her head and *tsk*ed at him. "He'll be here, but I got me another idea, and I want you to help."

Marshall followed Thora's instructions and went to Biscayne. Many of the men returned with him that evening. Others agreed to return the following morning and promised to send word to the workers on Jekyl Island. Now Marshall hoped that Old Blue would appear as promised.

The next morning the men were gathered around the construction site, and if all went well, they'd be hard at work within a short time. There were gasps of anticipation when a bedraggled white-haired man appeared from the thicket at the rear of the site. Leaning heavily on a walking stick, he approached the building and peered inside. He reached into his pocket, withdrew a substance, tossed it into the doorway of the structure, and then began to chant.

Thora nudged Marshall. "Start praying." With their arms lifted toward heaven, Marshall and Thora prayed for God to release the men from their pagan beliefs. The men's attention darted back and forth between Ole Blue and his chanting and the two of them and their prayers. When Ole Blue quit chanting and tossed something from his other pocket into the work area, the men inched forward.

"I think they were more impressed with Ole Blue's chanting than with our prayers."

"Thing is, they can't be sure if it was his chants or our prayers that's gonna have the most power over their lives. If God decides to have His way with 'em, they'll quit believing that gibberish and turn to Him when they're in trouble. In the meantime, you can get back to work."

Marshall leaned down and embraced the old woman. "You do have a way about you, Thora."

"Go on with ya," she said, patting his chest. "Get those men to working, and I'll go have a talk with Ole Blue afore he takes off."

Life at Bridal Fair returned to the regular routine. For two weeks the men had been working from daybreak until dark, but they still remained far behind schedule. When Marshall received a letter that Mr. Morley would be arriving to inspect the progress, he doubted Mr. Morley would be impressed with the amount of work accomplished. In a previous letter Marshall had suggested hiring more workers from further north, but Mr. Morley said they'd go too far over their allocated budget by doing so. It seemed there was little else he could do to hurry the process.

To make matters worse, it seemed they were suffering minor setbacks at every turn. Though Frank blamed the men for their inexperience, Marshall wasn't certain the entire blame could be placed upon their shoulders. During Marshall's observations, he'd seen nothing to indicate the men lacked proper skills. He'd begun to think it was a lack of direction rather than lack of ability.

Marshall motioned to Frank and waited until he drew near. "I want to inspect the second floor. We'll begin framing the third floor tomorrow. Make sure all the scaffolding is in place. I don't want any accidents."

"Hoping to impress Mr. Morley, are you?"

"I'm not trying to impress anyone. I just want to get this clubhouse up and running.

I'm going up to check out the second floor."

Weaving among the workers, Marshall trudged up the stairway. Once it was properly finished and the decorative railings and posts were installed, it would be beautiful. Right now, it was no more than rough steps. Marshall stopped at the top of the stairs and shook his head. "This isn't correct." He continued onward, unable to believe his eyes. "Frank! Get up here! Now!"

Moments later Frank joined him on the upper floor. "Yeah?"

"These rooms aren't laid properly. Where are the drawings?"

Frank walked to the top of the stairway. "Joe! Bring me those plans for the second floor, would ya?"

A few minutes later, Frank handed the plans to Marshall. After unrolling the sheet, he spread it across the floor and glanced at the framework. "Look at this and then check the position of the framework." He tapped the drawing. "It's all wrong."

Frank scratched his head. "It does look like it's off, but I followed these plans."

"If you think you followed these directions, you don't know how to read an architect's drawing." He rolled up the drawings. "We'll have to start over on this tomorrow."

Frank rubbed his jaw. "It doesn't look like Mr. Morley's gonna be too happy with the job you're doing."

Marshall clenched his jaw. "Or you, Frank." He turned and stormed down the steps before he lost his temper in front of all the workers.

He'd supervised other building projects that had been plagued by problems, but this one was testing his limits. And he didn't need a reminder from Frank that Mr. Morley would be disappointed with their progress.

As Marshall suspected, Mr. Morley was not happy. The following morning he pulled Marshall aside and voiced his frustration. "I wanted to give the setbacks some thought before speaking to you, but there is no doubt that something must be done to avoid these continual delays."

Marshall nodded. "I agree, and I've given it a great deal of thought, as well. My suggestion is that we dismiss Frank Baker and hire another assistant. I can't be everywhere at once, and I need a man I can depend upon. Frank simply doesn't have the necessary skills for the job. I didn't want to let him go until I spoke to you."

Mr. Morley shook his head. "I'm afraid

he's one person you can't fire, Marshall."

Marshall shoved his hat to the back of his head and arched his brows. "Why not? I heard you tell him he could pack his bags and get off the island several months ago."

"An idle threat. Frank knows I can't fire him. He's related to Thaddeus Baker, our largest investor. Thaddeus refused to throw in with us until we agreed to use his nephew. To be honest, I took a huge risk when I demoted him to assistant project manager. I can't chance anything more drastic." Mr. Morley shoved his hand into his pocket. "You understand?"

"I can understand your dilemma, but you can't expect me to meet deadlines when I have an incompetent assistant. Sometimes I feel Frank is directly responsible for some of the things that have caused our delays."

Mr. Morley chuckled. "I really doubt that Frank would bite the hand that feeds him. He wouldn't want to anger his uncle."

Even though Mr. Morley agreed to remain on the island for several months, the decision left Marshall feeling stranded and alone in his attempts to meet the deadlines. He'd counted on the man's support. Obviously that wasn't going to happen — at least where Frank Baker was concerned.

CHAPTER 18

Audrey gazed out the window, where the late summer flowers vied for attention, their blooms providing a beautiful array of color as they perfumed the air. Over the past weeks Josie and Julie had been sharing their abundance of herbs with Thora, Irene, and Audrey. Upon each visit, the girls proudly presented herbs from their garden, along with some of the flowers they picked along the paths near their cabin.

Today was no exception. They bounded into Bridal Fair, their plump hands grasping baskets filled with herbs and flowers. Julie thrust her basket toward Thora while Josie handed hers to Irene. "We gave Papa some of our flowers to give you, too," Josie said, pointing behind her father's back.

Julie grinned. "We told him to hide them and surprise you."

Samson padded into the room, stopped beside the doctor, and arched his back. Dr.

Wahler glared at the cat and then kicked him aside with his foot. He hiked a shoulder when Audrey frowned. "That cat doesn't seem to like me for some reason." He forced a smile. "I'm usually quite good with animals."

Julie looked up at her father. "You said you didn't like animals, and that's why we couldn't have a puppy or kitty."

He appeared befuddled by the little girl's remark. "We'll talk about this later, Julie." Turning toward Audrey, he shrugged. "Children. You never know what they're going to say." He brought his hand from behind his back and offered Audrey a lovely bouquet.

"They are absolutely beautiful. My thanks to all three of you. I'll get a vase."

"Not much of a surprise, but I'm pleased you like them." He followed her across the room with Josie close on his heels.

"Papa was going to pick some weeds. He doesn't know the good flowers like we do, so we had to help. It's good we're smarter than him."

Brow furrowed, Julie nudged her sister aside. "We're only smarter about flowers, and that's because Aunt Thora and Miss Audrey taught us." She grasped Audrey's hand. "You need to take Papa on a long walk and teach him about flowers, too."

While Audrey placed the flowers in a vase, Thora plopped the basket of herbs on the table. "We can take your papa with us tomorrow while Miss Audrey is helping Irene with the laundry."

Josie clapped her small hands together. She offered a wide smile that revealed dimples in her plump cheeks. "Oh yes. That will be great fun."

The hopeful gleam in Dr. Wahler's eyes faded. "I would be delighted to have Miss Thora give me lessons on the flora and fauna of Bridal Veil."

Julie wrinkled her nose. "What's that?"

Audrey brushed her finger against the wrinkles in Julie's nose. "Flora means plants and fauna means animals."

The little girl turned on her heel and looked at Thora. "Ohh. Are we going to see any wolves, Aunt Thora?"

Thora placed her palm along the side of her cheek. "Land alive, I hope not. Miss Audrey took my shotgun, and without it we'd be defenseless." She winked at Julie. "Maybe you should tell her to give it back to me."

Julie's dark curls bobbed up and down as she agreed. "Aunt Thora needs her gun so she can save us from the wolves."

Dr. Wahler directed a warning look at the

old woman. "I don't think you need to worry about wolves, children. I'm sure we won't find any wild animals roaming the island during the daytime. Isn't that right, Thora?"

She hitched her shoulders in an exaggerated shrug. "You may be right. Seems like only the two-legged wolves are out during the daylight hours."

The doctor attempted a smile, but his features didn't mask his annoyance. "If you have time, I'd like to speak with you about the girls and their future education, Audrey." He glanced toward Thora and Irene. "Unless this is a bad time."

"Not at all. I'm certain Irene would be pleased to put the teakettle on to boil, wouldn't you, Irene?"

Irene bobbed in a mock curtsy. "Of course, Miss Audrey. I'll bake a batch of cookies, too, if you like. Shall I start the cookies before or after the laundry?"

Audrey sighed. It seemed that both Thora and Irene were in poor humor today. "I won't be long, I promise."

"You girls go out on the front porch and play until I finish talking to Miss Audrey. Both Miss Irene and Miss Thora are busy with their chores," Dr. Wahler said.

"I'd rather help Miss Irene bake cookies,"

Josie replied as she gazed longingly toward the kitchen.

Irene hesitated, obviously aware of the mistake she'd made. "I was only teasing about making cookies, Josie. I don't have time to bake today, but if you come back tomorrow, you can help me bake cookies."

Josie's lips tightened into a pout. "You shouldn't tease about cookies, Miss Irene. That isn't nice."

"You're correct. I shouldn't tease about cookies, but I hope you'll return and help me tomorrow." Irene lifted an expectant brow as she awaited the child's response.

"We'll see. Tomorrow I might want to see the flora and fauna instead."

Thora chuckled and nudged Irene. "Josie don't take too well to being teased."

Once the girls were outdoors, Audrey and Dr. Wahler settled in the parlor. "Now then, what is it you wished to discuss?"

"As you know, the girls will soon be turning six, and it's time for them to receive a more formal education. I was hoping you might consider taking them on as pupils. I know you are already busy here at Bridal Fair, but I can think of no other solution." He hesitated. "Our cabin is far too small to bring someone to live with us. And although I will likely send them away to boarding school next year, they're in need of preparation."

"The girls are delightful, but I'm not certain I can devote time to their lessons." At any other time, she would have been delighted to accept the position.

"Without the training they would have received from their mother, the girls are going to lag behind other children their age." When she didn't immediately respond, he continued. "They truly need to learn how to become proper young ladies. Along with providing them with book learning, I know you would be the very best person to instruct them in proper etiquette."

Audrey realized he was hoping to convince with his praise — and it was working. Though she disliked admitting it, his flattery pleased her. "I would enjoy nothing more, but my duties here at Bridal Fair must come first. As you see, it is difficult for me to slip away for even a brief conversation. There simply aren't enough hours in the day."

"But I know you are the perfect choice."

"That may be true, but I must decline."

Dr. Wahler leaned forward until they were only inches apart. "I'm not a man who normally begs, but I implore you to reconsider. The girls are quite fond of you, and I believe you have feelings for them, as well."

Marshall stood on the other side of the parlor door listening to Dr. Wahler's plea. He'd seen the twins playing at one end of the wraparound porch when he'd come home to retrieve an old pair of work shoes for one of the men. Hearing Dr. Wahler's voice in the parlor, he became inquisitive. He'd heard only snatches of the conversation but enough to realize the good doctor was trying to entice Audrey. His stomach clenched into a knot the size of his fist. He didn't know which was worse: the fact that Dr. Wahler would use his children to lure an innocent woman or that Audrey would sit still long enough to entertain the man's suggestion. Why didn't she get up and walk out?

"I know the girls care for me, Edmond. And I care for them — very much."

Edmond? When had Audrey begun to call the doctor by his first name? Marshall took another step closer and strained to hear what she was saying.

"That's exactly why I was drawn to you. The girls need someone like you. Someone who will show them all of the things their mother would have. I know you're that person, Audrey."

"Even if that's true, I would never want the girls to think that I was making any attempt to take the place of their dear mother."

Marshall silently chided himself. He'd been too busy at work. Rather than taking time to reveal his true feelings to Audrey, he'd spent long hours at the construction site. Obviously, she didn't understand the depth of his desire or his intent. How could she? Though his thoughts were constantly about her, he'd never made them known. Now the doctor was sitting in the other room practically proposing to Audrey. And from what he'd heard, she was bordering on acceptance. Well, he'd have none of that. At least not without putting up a fight for the woman he wanted.

Pushing aside any thought of proper manners, he burst into the room. "I arrived home a short time ago and need to speak with you, Audrey."

Audrey looked at him and blinked, clearly surprised by his sudden appearance. "I'm sorry — I'm busy at the moment, Marshall." She glanced at the doctor as he pushed up from his chair.

"I've taken too much of your time, Audrey. I'm certain the girls are eager for some attention, so I'll be on my way." He took hold of her hand, and Marshall thought for a moment he would kiss her fingers. Instead, he merely bowed over her hand. "Do promise that you'll consider my proposal."

Proposal? Marshall's irritation rose to new heights as the word slid from Dr. Wahler's lips. Had the doctor's young daughters not been playing on the front porch, Marshall would have escorted him outdoors and settled any further talk of the good doctor's marriage proposal. How dare that man ask for Audrey's hand! And in front of him! The blatant audacity of Dr. Wahler infuriated him.

Marshall stared at Audrey, amazed by her calm and unruffled appearance. Why had she been willing to overlook the doctor's ill-mannered conduct? Perhaps the two of them had been secretly courting while Marshall worked overtime at the clubhouse. Now he wondered if he'd made a mistake by allowing his work to become his only priority. He should have taken more time to court Audrey, for now it appeared he'd lost his opportunity. And Dr. Wahler had quickly stepped in.

Not that the doctor hadn't shown interest in Audrey from the outset. Even during Boyd's illness, the doctor had sometimes appeared less interested in caring for his patient than in gaining Audrey's attention. It seemed he always wanted advice about his daughters or had some silly question that could have been answered by Irene or Thora. Instead, he would seek out Audrey. And if she wasn't available, he'd return rather than ask someone else. Well, he hadn't fooled Marshall. The man had been after a wife and mother for his daughters from the first day he'd laid eyes on Audrey Cunningham. There was no doubt in Marshall's mind.

Audrey tucked a wisp of hair behind one ear and uttered a charming good-bye to the doctor. In fact, it sounded downright alluring to Marshall. He wanted to step between the two of them and block the doctor's view of her.

Once Wahler disappeared out the front door, Audrey turned toward Marshall. "After such an abrupt entrance, I assume there is something urgent you wished to discuss?" The charm had disappeared from her voice.

Suddenly, Marshall couldn't put two words together. At least not two words that made any sense. "Well, I thought . . ." He shuffled his weight to his left foot. "I mean, I wanted to . . ." Embarrassment got the best of him, and he swatted the air. "Seems

I've forgotten what I wanted to ask. I need to get a pair of work boots from upstairs and return to the work site." He could see the confusion in her eyes, but it was no match for the confusion in his heart. He dared not talk to her right then, for he'd surely make a fool of himself.

CHAPTER 19

Audrey stopped Marshall as he came down the stairs the next morning. "Aunt Thora isn't feeling well, but she mentioned she'd like a word with you in her sitting room before you leave."

"I'm sorry to hear she isn't well, but I'll take a minute to visit with her." He wondered if the old woman had decided to become a help or a hindrance where his courtship of Audrey was concerned. Way back in January she'd said she would study the Scriptures and then get back with him, but she never had. By now she'd taken enough time to read the entire Bible, and he didn't hold out much hope.

He tapped on the door and waited until she signaled for him to enter. "I heard you wanted to see me." Thora Lund must be quite the actress to fool Audrey, Marshall thought. The woman didn't appear sick at all. She pointed to the door.

"Close it. I don't want no one to over-hear."

Marshall nodded and closed the door. "Am I to guess that the Lord has finally spoken to you through the Scriptures regarding my request for your help?"

She studied him a moment, pointed to the chair beside her, and took up her large, worn Bible. "You're impatient, but the Lord moves at His own pace — just like me. Now, sit down, and I'll tell you what He told me."

Marshall did as instructed. Thora turned to where she'd marked a passage. She looked up. "This is from the forty-first chapter of Isaiah. Are you familiar with it?"

"With Isaiah? Yes. The forty-first chapter — not so much."

"Well, this is what it says. 'Keep silence before me, O islands; and let the people renew their strength: let them come near; then let them speak: let us come near together to judgment.' "

She paused and looked over the Bible at him. "I've been silent, and now I've called you to come near. That means the Lord is ready for me to talk to you and to judge the situation."

Marshall nodded. "All right. Let's talk."

"But there's more." Her tone of voice sounded rather ominous. She bent down over the book. " 'Behold, all they that were incensed against thee shall be ashamed and confounded: they shall be as nothing; and they that strive with thee shall perish. Thou shalt seek them, and shalt not find them, even them that contended with thee: they that war against thee shall be as nothing, and as a thing of nought. For I the Lord thy God will hold thy right hand, saying unto thee, Fear not; I will help thee.' " She stopped and looked at Marshall once again. "Do you understand? That's the Lord sayin' He's taking a stand against them that warred against us. He's gonna restore the South."

It puzzled Marshall how the old woman had pulled that from the passage, but he said nothing.

She seemed to sense this as his approval and continued to read. "Here's the part where God spoke to me about you. 'I have raised up one from the north, and he shall come: from the rising of the sun shall he call upon my name: and he shall come upon princes as upon mortar, and as the potter treadeth clay.' " She looked up with brows raised. "Makes it all perty clear if you ask me."

"I'm . . . not sure I understand."

The old woman frowned. "God has taken

pity on us here, but in order to help us, He raised up one from the north. At first I thought maybe it was that Mr. Morley who the Scriptures spoke of, but it weren't. It's you."

"And how do you figure that, Mrs. Lund?"

"Because you're the one workin' with mortar — with the tabby. Only seein's how Isaiah's folk didn't have tabby, they had to write about mortar, and you're the prince of mortar."

Marshall was completely baffled. "Mrs. Lund, I don't mean any disrespect, but I'm not clear as to how that verse could possibly be about me."

She sighed in exasperation, as one might when working with a child. "God's tellin' me here that He's raised up one from the north who calls upon His name. You profess to be a God-fearin' man who prays, and you're the one God is gonna use to help us against the Yankees takin' advantage of us. It's as plain as that."

"All right." Marshall decided to take another direction. "How does that pertain to my asking for your assistance in getting Audrey's agreement to let me court her?"

The older woman smiled and slammed the Bible closed. "If the good Lord has sent you to help us, then He would want me to help you."

Marshall shook his head, but smiled. "Mrs. Lund, you are a wonder, indeed."

"You can call me Aunt Thora."

Later that night as Marshall prepared for bed, he pulled out his Bible and pored over the forty-first chapter of Isaiah. Somehow he just couldn't seem to fit the pieces together in the same way Thora had. He couldn't help but marvel nevertheless. The old woman was adamant that she had interpreted this passage to be a personal message from God. How many other people made the Bible twist and turn at their convenience?

As he neared the end of the chapter, however, the last verse caught his eye. Murmuring the words aloud, Marshall read, " 'Behold, they are all vanity; their works are nothing: their molten images are wind and confusion.' "

A shudder ran through him. Was it a prophecy of their labors on the island? Maybe Thora understood more than he realized.

The following morning, Marshall, Mr. Morley, and the other foremen were still gathered around the breakfast table when a thunderous explosion reverberated in the distance. Moments later, the alarm bell clanged until it peaked in a frenzied crescendo. Several chairs fell backward as the men jumped to their feet and raced for the front door. That bell meant only one thing: injury or death at the work site. The words of Scripture echoed in his mind as he ran toward the clubhouse.

Mayhem. That was the only word to describe the scene. Workers scurried in all directions, each shouting to be heard above the other. Marshall came to a sudden halt, unable to fully grasp the disastrous sight that greeted him. Screams of injured men, the pealing bell, groans of weakening joists and beams all mixed together in a discordant composition that wailed tragedy. He needed to move. Somehow, he needed to make sense out of chaos.

Marshall grasped Frank Baker's arm. "The third floor has collapsed. You take control of the east side of the building. I'll see to the west side. Get the men calmed down and make certain there's no one trapped in that debris." He saw Dr. Wahler running toward them. "Once the doctor assesses the situation, we'll have a better idea of how to proceed. Until he gives us the order, we don't want to move anyone and risk causing further injury."

One of the young workers balled his fingers into tight fists as he approached Marshall. "My brother is in there, and I aim to go and get him out — with or without instructions from any doctor. We don't need no doctor tellin' us how to move a heavy beam off a man's chest."

Another laborer stepped alongside the younger man. "He's right. If they're underneath heavy rubble, their injuries will only get worse. I say we go down and begin looking for them that's hurt. Ain't right to leave 'em down there suffering. Who can say how long it's gonna take the doctor to get 'round to all those men?" The man's eyes shone with disdain. "Is this your best plan of how to handle a disaster, *Mister* Graham?"

The worker's eyes shone with a mixture of anger and hatred. Even now the men preferred to take their orders from his assistant. These men were not easily won over. They trusted no one they didn't know, especially a man from up north. Their allegiance was to Frank Baker.

Marshall gritted his teeth and stepped forward. Trust him or not, they were going to follow his orders this time. "If the rest of you promise to keep your distance, I'll see if I can work my way upstairs. If I find some-

thing, I'll call from one of the windows."
The men weren't happy, but they mumbled
their agreement.

All appeared safe enough as he climbed
the stairway. He could only pray that the
damage had been contained to the second
and third floors — and that none of the men
had been seriously injured in the collapse.
"Please, Father," he murmured as he continued the upward climb, "keep the men
safe."

As he approached the second floor, it appeared that at least a quarter of the third
floor had collapsed onto the second floor.
Floor joists had snapped like twigs while
others swayed overhead like broken tree
limbs after a storm. The sound of groaning
timbers told a story of their own: Further
damage could occur at any moment. Anyone
on the second floor was in danger. A couple
of the injured called out to him while others simply groaned in pain.

The sights and sounds tore at Marshall's
heart. "Help will be here soon, men. Just
hold on." He stooped down to speak to one
or two as he edged along the perimeter
toward the window openings.

When he finally reached the first opening,
he caught sight of Mr. Morley approaching
and waved to him. "The steps are still

intact. Once the doctor gives the okay, I'll need some help moving the men. From the looks of things, more beams could fall at any moment." He'd no more than spoken the words when another beam crashed to the floor and missed him by only inches.

Mr. Morley cupped his hands to his mouth and called toward the window. "The doctor's on his way up. The men and I will await your direction, Marshall."

For once, Marshall was glad to have the doctor around. Wahler quickly assessed the men and passed his orders on to Marshall. Obviously, his experience as a physician during the war was serving Dr. Wahler well. He didn't seem disturbed by the pain and suffering. Instead, he appeared quite detached.

Marshall assigned seven laborers to assist him. He would have preferred to swarm the place with men to help carry out the injured, but the weight and activity could do more harm than good. They worked feverishly and without further incident until all the injured men were safely outside the building.

Irene and a couple of the cooks assigned to the kitchen in the old slave quarters delivered sandwiches and coffee while Audrey instructed and helped some of the workers tear and roll strips of bedsheets for dressings. She'd even gone and hoisted the red flag to signal passing boats of their emergency situation. Marshall hoped someone would take heed and stop at Bridal Veil or at least deliver a message of disaster to the authorities in Biscayne.

Marshall's body ached as he continued to move among the injured men. Two fishing boats heading back to Biscayne noticed their flag that evening and docked at the pier. The captains were willing to take the injured into Biscayne and promised Marshall their crew members would transport the men to the hospital.

In total there were only ten needing transport — most of them for broken limbs. Dr. Wahler declared the rest of the injuries to be only cuts and bruises. Before striding off to wrap another cut, he told Mr. Morley they should be able to return to work within a few days.

The shoulder seam of Marshall's shirt had given way, and the pocket was hanging by a slender thread. He turned toward Mr. Morley, his face and hands smeared with a mixture of dirt and blood. Swiping his hands down his pant legs, he shook his head. "The men may be able to return to work in a day or two, but this damage won't be repaired so quickly." Marshall approached the uninjured men. "I'd appreciate it if the rest of you would help the doctor as needed and then get to bed. There's much that will need our attention come morning." Marshall pointed to four of the workers who were standing huddled together. "You four stand watch. If any more of those joists drop, or anything else goes wrong during the night, ring the bell."

Mr. Morley's lips drooped into a heavy frown while deep creases cut across his brow, aging the dapper gentleman by at least ten years. He cast a weary gaze upon Marshall and then pointed to Frank Baker. "I want to talk to both of you back at the house."

When they arrived at Bridal Fair a short time later, Mr. Morley led them into the parlor. "I'm going to want a full explanation as to what caused this disaster."

Marshall nodded. "An inspection is needed, but from what I could see during the time I was up there, it appears there may have been some sort of explosive involved." He looked at the other two men. "You heard that blast before the first beams collapsed, didn't you?"

Frank shook his head. "The only crash I heard was that lumber falling and the men screaming." He pointed a thumb in Marshall's direction. "You just ask around, Mr. Morley. I think you'll find it's your project manager that's the problem. Word is that he's been ordering inferior lumber and materials in Biscayne and forcing the men to use them in the construction. My men can vouch for the problems they've had trying to work with the likes of him. You just ask 'em. They'll speak the truth." Frank's lips curled in an evil grin.

Marshall's jaw went slack, but it would serve no purpose to deny Frank's claims — at least not now. The foreman would parade his men in front of Mr. Morley, and the workers would repeat whatever they'd been instructed to say. Besides, his nerves were on edge, and they were all exhausted from the day's events. He would wait until he could speak to Mr. Morley in private.

When Marshall didn't protest, Frank nudged Mr. Morley in a surprisingly familiar way. The investor shot a warning look in Frank's direction and took a backward step.

"Sorry, sir. I didn't mean any disrespect."

Mr. Morley motioned toward the stairs. "I think we'll all do better after a good night of sleep."

Marshall had hoped to speak to Mr. Morley before retiring, but the older man immediately headed for the stairs, obviously intent upon getting some rest before morning. Would Mr. Morley interpret his silence as guilt? Marshall chided himself. He should have spoken up when he had the opportunity. He glanced into the kitchen. With a bit of good fortune, he might be able to locate Audrey.

His hopes plummeted when he spotted Thora sitting alone at the small worktable. She looked up as he entered the room. "Sorry to see me, are you?"

Marshall stiffened at her astute observation. "Did I say I was unhappy to see you?"

She cackled and tapped her index finger alongside her right eye. "No, but any fool could see it in your eyes. Is it Audrey or Irene you was hoping to find?"

He did his best to appear indifferent. "I wanted to borrow a bottle of ink. I used the last of mine and would like to write a note this evening."

"Likely story," Thora muttered, pushing up from the table. "Audrey tells me things is a mess down there at the clubhouse. I'm mighty sorry about the injured men, but not so much about that monstrosity of a place. Gonna be an eyesore, for sure. You think the investors might change their mind and move somewhere else?" Marshall shook

319

his head as she made a wide circle around him and headed toward the parlor. "More's the pity. We'd be better off without it," she muttered. After a glance over her shoulder, she stopped and perched her fist on one hip. "Well, you coming or not? Thought you wanted some ink." He stammered his response and followed close on her heels. "Don't need to get so close. If I stop, you're gonna plow me over."

Marshall raked his fingers through his hair. There was no pleasing the woman. The moment she handed him the bottle of ink, he thanked her, exited the room, and marched upstairs, glad to be away from her watchful eye. He penned a quick note, telling Mr. Morley he would like to speak to him privately after breakfast. Careful to avoid any creaking floorboards, Marshall tiptoed down the hall and slipped the note under the investor's door. Come morning, he hoped this matter would be resolved in his favor. If not, he'd have to break his promise to Boyd. Though he'd made a promise, remaining on the island would be impossible if Mr. Morley considered him an inadequate project manager.

After a restless night, Marshall was relieved when the sun began its ascent in the eastern sky. He wanted to state his case and clear the air with Mr. Morley. Weariness and worry etched the faces of all the men surrounding the breakfast table — all except Frank Baker, who appeared curiously relaxed. A fact that caused Marshall no small amount of unease. Was Frank already confident Mr. Morley believed what he'd told him the previous evening? Marshall shoved a final bite of biscuit and jelly into his mouth. He hoped Mr. Morley hadn't prejudged him.

When the men departed for the work site, Mr. Morley motioned for Marshall to wait a few minutes. "If you want some privacy while we talk, we best follow at a distance." As they walked, Marshall explained that he was certain some sort of explosive had been used to cause the disaster.

The older man shook his head. "I can't imagine anyone doing such a thing, Marshall. You really believe this?"

"Unfortunately, I do. Even worse, I'm thinking Frank may have played a part in this."

Mr. Morley stopped in his tracks. "I can't believe Frank would do such a thing. Besides, I don't think he's smart enough to think up such a complex plan." Mr. Morley's eyebrows dipped low on his forehead.

"Both you and Frank are pointing the finger at each other. You think Frank set some sort of explosive, and Frank thinks your choice of inferior lumber is the cause."

"I don't like to call anyone a liar, but I won't take the blame for what happened. I've never used inferior products on any construction job. I wouldn't consider such a thing." Marshall glanced at the older man. "I know many of the workers are friends with Frank and will likely take his side, but I've done nothing to compromise that structure. I hope I can find something in the rubble to convince you of that."

Mr. Morley took long strides as they continued down the path. "Frank has been known to be difficult to work with from time to time. I don't doubt your word, Marshall. I understand that he has caused you problems in the past. Still, if we can prove you weren't at fault, it will make this much easier to explain — especially to Frank's uncle. Before blame is placed on anyone, we must be certain of the facts." He rested a fist on each hip and stared at the clubhouse. "Let's see what we find in all of that rubble."

Marshall headed up to the third floor, still worried he hadn't won the older man's confidence. It didn't take long for him to locate the place where some sort of explosive had been lodged into trusses beneath the floorboards of the third floor. Why the person had chosen one of the upper floors remained a mystery. To avoid being seen was Marshall's best guess. He also surmised that either the person who'd set the charge was inexperienced or the powder had somehow gotten wet. Otherwise, the explosion would have caused a fire and further damage. Pushing aside the rubble for a better view into the corner, he caught sight of a metal object. After rubbing it on his pant leg, he held it toward the daylight for closer inspection. What once had been a filigreed silver money clip was now a blackened and twisted piece of metal. Marshall stared at the object and tried to make out the initial at the center. It appeared to be a scripted *P* or perhaps an *R:* he couldn't be certain. Other than Mr. Morley, he didn't know anyone who carried a money clip.

"Find anything up there, Marshall?" Mr. Morley's question drifted up the stairs.

"I believe I did. I'll be right down."

Moments later the two of them weighed the importance of Marshall's find. Mr. Morley paced back and forth as he stared at the item in his palm. "This looks like something that would be owned by a man of wealth, not a laborer. I think there's more to this than meets the eye. I'm beginning to think it's going to take some cautious investigating to unearth the truth."

Marshall wasn't as convinced. "I'm not sure I'm following you on this. Care to give me a hint?"

"I may be grasping at air, but we now know this wasn't an accident, and we also know someone who carried an expensive money clip is somehow involved. I don't like to think the investors on Jekyl would sabotage us." He gazed into the distance. "I always want to think the best of my fellow-man, especially those with whom I socialize and do business. However, there's something malicious about this building collapse." He held up the money clip, as if to reinforce his idea.

Marshall thought Frank might have had some assistance, but what he thought didn't matter. Not unless he had some sort of proof.

Several days passed, but no further clues were discovered in the rubble or around the building. Marshall's aggravation reached new levels as he calculated the time that would be lost rebuilding the destroyed portions of the clubhouse. He pushed away from the table after breakfast and walked to the parlor with Mr. Morley. "I'm going into Biscayne this afternoon for some building supplies. Anything you need?"

"Not that I can think of, but I'll keep an eye on things down at the construction site. You've told Frank you'll be gone?"

"I mentioned it to him yesterday and told him I wanted the men to concentrate on rebuilding the third floor before anyone starts trim work on the lower floors."

Mr. Morley nodded. "Have a good trip." He tipped his head closer. "I understand Audrey is going over to Biscayne to complete some shopping, as well."

"I'll be sure to lend her a hand," he said. He'd been hoping for an opportunity to speak to her about Dr. Wahler's proposal. With all of the chaos over the past days, he'd had no chance to question her about it.

Audrey arched her brows when Marshall announced that he would be accompanying her to Biscayne. "I assumed you would be far too busy to accompany me on a shopping excursion, but I'm pleased you'll be coming along."

Her comment surprised him. "Really?"

She reached forward and rested her hand

atop his sleeve. "Surely you know that since my father's death, I've come to trust you more than anyone. I know I can depend upon your advice and help."

The moment Marshall glanced at his arm, Audrey lifted her hand. He missed the warmth and longed for the return of her touch. "You have a strange way of showing your trust."

"I thought you understood that I'd come to trust you," she said softly. "After all, I know Mr. Morley esteems you, and my father had nothing but good to say whenever he spoke of you. And though the men make it difficult, I've watched as you've attempted to keep peace among them." She sighed. "I would be honored to have you at my side when I go to Biscayne."

His shoulders relaxed at her soft and convincing tone. "It will be my great pleasure." He longed to hear her say she would be honored to have him by her side for the rest of her life. Perhaps that would come in time. For now, he would escort her to Biscayne and hope to convince her she shouldn't make any quick decisions — at least none that included Dr. Wahler.

Marshall was happy to be seated inside as they crossed the choppy waters of Bridal

Veil Sound and the Argosy River with Captain Holloway at the helm. Though the investors had finally purchased a new boat and hired a captain to man the helm, crossing to the mainland during windy days still remained a challenge. Yet *Bessie II,* as the new launch had been christened in honor of her older namesake, provided much safer transportation for both cargo and passengers.

When Marshall attempted to bring up Dr. Wahler, Audrey quickly changed the subject. "He's very intelligent and I do love his daughters. They're truly delightful." She went on at length about the girls. So much so that when she finally stopped, he feared to make any further mention of the doctor or his daughters.

Marshall instinctively glanced over his shoulder toward the island. "You or Irene haven't heard any talk about the collapse at the clubhouse, have you?"

"No, but Mr. Morley asked me to let him know if I saw or heard anything that might indicate some sort of foul play." She straightened her shoulders a bit. "I was pleased that he took me into his confidence. He said if he was gone, I should report to you. Otherwise, I wouldn't have mentioned my conversation with him."

A short time later they docked in Biscayne. Audrey slapped one hand atop her hat and grabbed her skirt with the other. "This wind is going to make shopping difficult."

Marshall chuckled and pointed to the fabric Audrey held tight around her legs. "It's going to be impossible to walk unless you loosen the hold on your skirt."

"I suppose you're right." She released the fabric and took Marshall's arm. "If the wind turns my garment into a sail, don't let me fly away."

"I promise to hold on." Marshall glanced at a flag whipping in the breeze. "The way the wind is blowing today, we may end up in the middle of the Atlantic Ocean."

She smiled at his amused tone. "If that happens, I'll depend upon you to hoist me back to land."

He gave a brief salute. "I shall endeavor to keep you grounded, ma'am."

Audrey straightened just a bit and pointed. "Let's make our way to Reinhart's, and I'll place my order for groceries first."

Keeping his head bowed against the wind, Marshall carefully led Audrey around the mud puddles and far from the unsavory men who frequented the docks. His step was brisk, yet he was mindful of her inability to keep pace with his stride. At the end of the dock, they crossed Merchant Street, but as they prepared to turn down Washington Avenue, Marshall circled her waist with one arm and pushed her into a dark alleyway.

The heel of her shoe caught in her skirt hem, and she gasped as she attempted to free herself from his tightening hold. "What are you doing?" Her voice quivered with fear.

"Quiet! Look! Over there!" He cradled her chin between his thumb and fingers and forced her head to the right. "Do you see?" He hissed the question into her ear.

"See what?" Barely able to speak, she tried to wrench free of his hold on her chin.

"Ted Uptegrove." He released her chin and grasped her shoulders between his hands and turned her. "Ted Uptegrove is over there, and it doesn't appear he's up to anything good."

Audrey frowned. "It looks like he's visiting with that man. What's wrong with that?"

"First off, he should be over on the island working. Second, I've seen that man before — when I came over here to hire men to work at Bridal Veil. He had a surly attitude, and I refused to hire him." Marshall squinted into the sunlight, hoping for a better view of the two men.

Audrey brushed a streak of dirt from her skirt. "Why are we hiding? If you want to know why Mr. Uptegrove is talking to that man, I can wave my handkerchief and gain his attention."

"No!"

She startled at his angry reply.

"I'm sorry. I didn't mean to frighten you, but I don't want him to see us. In fact, I'd like to get closer and try to hear their conversation."

"I'm not certain snooping in their business is a good idea."

"Maybe not, but I need to know if he's involved in the problems we've been having at the work site. He's supposed to be overseeing the men, so why isn't he over on Bridal Veil?"

She shrugged and tipped her head. "Someone could ask the same about you, couldn't they?"

"Maybe, but it wouldn't take long for them to realize I'm here to order construction supplies. Why don't you go ahead with your shopping. I'll meet you back at Reinhart's in an hour. If I'm not back, wait for me there. We're not due back to the wharf until five o'clock"

Audrey didn't think any of this was a good

330

idea, but she'd learned long ago that arguing with a determined man wouldn't end in a good result. "I repeat that I believe this is foolish, but if you insist, I won't argue further. I'll meet with the cobbler first and order the groceries last. However, if you're not back at Reinhart's shortly before five, I'll have my purchases delivered to the dock. I doubt Captain Holloway will want to wait. He likes to keep to his schedule."

Marshall pulled two lists from his inside pocket. "Could you leave this list at the lumberyard, and this one with the blacksmith? Just in case I run short of time. And don't worry, I'll be fine." He didn't give her time to object.

Pulling his hat low on his forehead, Marshall stepped from between the buildings and hurried down the street. Audrey wanted to call after him that she didn't intend to worry, but she feared such an outburst would draw Mr. Uptegrove's attention. Marshall might never forgive her if that should occur. She straightened her shoulders and stepped from the alleyway. With her thoughts racing in all directions, Audrey headed toward the shoe repair shop. She'd like to meet the person who said women were the dramatic members of humanity.

That person certainly hadn't met Marshall
Graham!

CHAPTER 20

After she'd completed her errands, Audrey
returned to Reinhart's. Much to her surprise, she spied Marshall pacing in front of
the store. She considered waving to him,
but decided against it. Marshall might accuse her of signaling his whereabouts to Ted
Uptegrove or to some unknown stranger.
She snickered at the idea. In truth, she
hadn't expected this strange behavior from
Marshall. He seemed such a sensible fellow,
but today he'd been acting more like Aunt
Thora than the normal young man she'd
been quietly observing over the past months.

The minute Marshall spotted Audrey, he
loped toward her, his eyes alight with excitement. "I was right! Ted is up to something."

Audrey arched her brows. "Such as what?"

"I'm not exactly certain, but it isn't
anything good. I couldn't make out exactly
what they were saying, but that fellow
handed Ted an envelope of some sort." He

shifted and looked over his shoulder, as if he expected to see someone lurking around the corner. "I tried to follow, but I lost them in the crowd down at the wharf."

"Maybe you're permitting your imagination to get the best of you. They could be old friends or acquaintances from years ago." Audrey didn't want Marshall jumping to conclusions. On the other hand, perhaps this was the type of information Mr. Morley desired.

Marshall shook his head. "No. This has nothing to do with old friendships. Ted Uptegrove isn't a friend of that man. There's something fishy going on between the two of them." Marshall nodded toward the door. "Let's get your order down to the dock. I want to return and report this to Mr. Morley. No one needs to know we've seen Ted. Agreed?"

She offered a firm nod. "Agreed."

By the time they boarded the launch to return to Bridal Veil, the waters had calmed. Audrey and Marshall once again settled near the windows inside. Audrey leaned sideways and peeked out the window. "I do wish we could sit outside. There would be a better view of the setting sun."

"The water makes it a little chilly outside. I'll ask Captain Holloway if he has any blankets onboard. If so, we could go out once we're underway." Marshall picked his way toward the captain, careful to maintain his balance as the boat moved away from its mooring and slowly gained a little speed.

The captain didn't appear overly eager to accommodate them, but Marshall nodded in Audrey's direction and continued to plead his case. Even if he failed, she would give Marshall credit for a valiant effort.

A short time later, he returned and dropped down beside her. "Once we're clear of the shrimpers returning to the harbor, the captain will try to locate some blankets he keeps stored for emergencies."

"Thank you, Marshall."

Shrimp boats of every size and description dotted the waters, each vying for position, each captain eager to moor his trawler, each crew member impatient to return home before sunset. Their own launch was one of few attempting to head out in the opposite direction, and Captain Holloway maintained a keen eye on the watery landscape.

"Mr. Morley was fortunate to hire Captain Holloway, don't you think?" Audrey glanced over her shoulder, surprised to see Marshall looking at her rather than the picturesque scene before them.

Marshall grinned and nodded. "I'd say they were both fortunate. The captain is experienced and seems a good fit for the position. I'm sure he appreciates being free of the pressure and anxiety endured by the captains of those shrimping trawlers."

Not long after wending their way through the maze of boats, Captain Holloway appeared with an armful of blankets. "Seems this young fellow doesn't know how to keep a lady warm, so I brought you some blankets." Deep creases fanned the outer corners of the captain's sparkling blue eyes as he smiled down at them and handed the blankets to Marshall. "Enjoy the view."

Marshall unfolded two of the woolen covers and wrapped them around Audrey's shoulders before they walked to the deck. A light breeze tugged at the blankets, and Audrey clamped her fingers into a tight hold. "I don't dare let loose or the wind will carry Captain Holloway's blankets into the river and out to sea. I doubt he'd be too forgiving."

"I think I can solve the problem." Marshall placed his arm across Audrey's shoulders and grasped her upper arm in a snug hold. "Between the two of us, we shouldn't have any trouble holding the blankets in place."

Audrey looked up into his eyes, her heart

quickening at the warmth of his touch. Her voice failed her, and she cleared her throat. She needed to regain her composure or Marshall would think her a complete ninny. "Thank you very much. You are most kind."

He chuckled. "You are welcome. And you are most kind, as well."

She giggled at his mimicked response. "I did sound rather dull and stiff, didn't I?"

He rested his free hand on the railing and grinned. "Your reply could have passed for the proper response listed in an etiquette book."

"Oh, it wasn't as bad as that!" Her laughter faded, and while the sun continued its slow descent, her gaze settled on the horizon. In spite of the cool wind, she longed to remain at the railing and commit the sight to memory. Her father had loved everything about this place, and though she initially hadn't longed to return with him, she was glad they'd come back. Tears pricked her eyes at the memory of his excitement the day they'd returned. She pictured him standing near the edge of the boat as they'd docked at Bridal Veil. He'd jumped to the aging pier and held out his arms to her. "Welcome home, Audie!" he'd called out, using the familiar childhood nickname he hadn't spoken since they'd left the South.

"A penny for your thoughts."

Surprised by Marshall's comment, she swiped at her tears. "I was thinking about my father and how he loved the beauty of this place. 'One of God's greatest achievements,' he'd tell me each morning."

Marshall smiled. "There's no denying the beauty that surrounds this entire area. That's one of the many reasons it's been chosen as a retreat for the wealthy." He removed a handkerchief from his pocket and daubed the tears that continued to trickle down her cheeks. "Your laughter has turned to tears. I'm told that's common for those who are grieving."

"I'm not sure it's common for everyone, but it has proved true enough for me." She smiled faintly. "Father envisioned my marriage taking place on Bridal Veil. He said it was the perfect place for a wedding." Her tears started to flow unchecked. "But now he will never walk me down the aisle." She hesitated and tightened the blanket around her neck. "My tears begin to flow at the most unexpected times, which can prove quite embarrassing."

Marshall looked down at her as if committing her features to memory. "Please don't ever be embarrassed in my presence, Audrey. When I'm with you, I want you to feel free to laugh or cry, to shout your anger or sing out your praises — whatever makes you feel better at the moment."

"I don't think you'd want to hear me sing. Aunt Thora says I can't carry a tune in a bucket. I'm not certain what that means, for I've never heard anyone attempt to sing in a bucket, have you?"

He chuckled and shook his head. "Do you stand in the bucket while you sing or stick your head in there? I think either would be mighty uncomfortable."

Audrey laughed. "When we get home, I should stand in a bucket and sing to Aunt Thora." Tears of laughter rolled down Audrey cheeks. "She'll think I've gone mad." At the moment, she wasn't sure she was completely sane. She'd gone from laughter to tears and back to laughter. Now she felt as though she might begin to cry again. "I believe I need a few moments to compose myself before we arrive home. I think I'll return inside."

She was thankful Marshall didn't follow, for she couldn't understand the swirl of emotions his closeness brought forth. She'd enjoyed the warmth of his arm around her, and when he touched his handkerchief to her cheek, she thought he might kiss her. Thoughts of their earlier encounter on the beach came to mind, and she once again wondered about the feel of his lips upon her own. Heat suffused her cheeks at the thought of his embrace, his kiss. She dropped the blankets from her shoulders, no longer needing the warmth they provided.

Marshall leaned on the railing and turned his face into the breeze. The cool air felt good against his cheeks. He closed his eyes and recalled Audrey's every feature. How desirable she was with the glint of gold in her mahogany eyes and the dark curls that refused to be tamed. Standing with his arm around her shoulder, so close to her that he had longed to bend his head and kiss away her tears, to capture her lips with his own. Had she guessed his thoughts and hurried inside to prevent such an event? He didn't want to think so.

She'd spoken of her father's desire for her to wed, and she hadn't pulled away when he wiped her tears. Still, that didn't mean she desired his romantic attention. After all, there was Dr. Wahler to consider. Audrey had developed an obvious affection for his daughters. And probably for him, as well. With the doctor's recent proposal still awaiting her response, Marshall dared not linger with his own decision. He wanted to be respectful of how little time had passed since her father's death, even if that hadn't delayed Dr. Wahler's proposal.

The launch cut through the water, leaving a trail of white foam in its wake. When they drew near the dock a short time later, only a narrow crescent of deep orange remained on the horizon. No doubt Captain Holloway was pleased to be back at the Bridal Veil dock before nightfall.

Marshall glanced over his shoulder. He had hoped for a few more minutes alone with Audrey. If the captain didn't request his assistance tying off the boat, he'd have a little more time to visit with her as they walked from the dock to Bridal Fair. He'd need to make good use of those precious minutes.

While the captain skillfully maneuvered the launch alongside the dock, Marshall contemplated several choices of how to best use his remaining time with Audrey. He'd taken hold of her arm to assist her off the boat when the sound of children's laughter captured his attention. Peering toward the far end of the dock, Marshall caught sight of Dr. Wahler and his twin daughters. Arms akimbo and hair flying in their wake, the two girls raced toward Audrey with the unbridled enthusiasm reserved for young children. At the sight of them, Audrey's subdued expression changed to one of unrestrained delight.

She leaned forward, extended her arms in a wide arc, and with a smile that could light up a darkening sky, she welcomed them into her embrace. "I'm so pleased that you've come to greet me."

At the sight of Dr. Wahler and the girls, Marshall's hopes flagged. How could Marshall compete with all three of them? The doctor could provide Audrey with a comfortable life, one free of financial worry, and she'd already developed a love for his daughters, and they for her. He should walk away and leave them to their joyful reunion. Was he such a coward that he feared rejection? Would he give up without even stating his case? He wavered for a moment, but jerked to attention when Audrey greeted the doctor.

"I'm so glad that you've come to the dock. I was going to send word that I would like to speak with you this evening if you have time." Audrey hesitated for only a moment. "In regard to your earlier request." The doctor smiled, obviously pleased that she'd come to a decision. "And I've brought a treat for you girls." Audrey patted the sack she carried in her hand. "Come along and I'll show you."

He who hesitates is lost. The thought pummeled Marshall like two fists to the midsection. He should have spoken of his feelings for Audrey while they were on the launch. Why had he waited? His indecisiveness was his downfall — and Dr. Wahler's good fortune.

The four of them gathered together — a living picture of the perfect family. Audrey glanced over her shoulder. "Are you coming, Marshall?"

He shook his head. "You go on. I'll help unload." As soon as he'd uttered the words, he wanted to snatch them back. He was giving the doctor yet another opportunity with her. But to run after them now would appear foolish. No doubt the doctor would make some embarrassing comment. If that happened, Marshall wasn't certain he'd be able to hold his temper in check.

His anger, at himself and the doctor, continued to mount while he helped unload the goods. By the time he arrived at Bridal Fair, he was thankful he didn't have to sit down and eat supper with the other men. Irene had saved him a plate, but his appetite had disappeared long before she placed the plate of chicken and dumplings in front of him. He attempted several bites but finally pushed away from the table, his mind clear about what he must do.

There was no longer any doubt in his mind that he loved Audrey, and if he was going to have a chance to prove his love, he'd have to do everything possible to stop her from accepting Dr. Wahler's proposal. Granted, he might make a fool of himself, but that would be better than losing the woman, he now realized he loved, to another man.

When Irene returned to the dining room, Marshall handed her his plate. "Any idea where I might find Audrey?"

"She's in the parlor with Dr. Wahler." Irene looked at the plate. "Something wrong with your dinner?"

"No, it's very good, but I'm not hungry." While offering his clipped reply, Marshall hurried toward the parlor and came to abrupt stop in the doorway.

Audrey and the doctor were seated on the divan facing each other. The doctor was leaning toward her, obviously making an earnest plea. *He who hesitates is lost.* This time he wouldn't let his head rule his heart. This time he wouldn't let Dr. Wahler circumvent his plans. This time he would tell Audrey of his love.

Marshall stepped across the threshold. "Stop!" He hadn't meant to shout, but his emotions had gotten the best of him. "This can't go any further, Audrey. You can't accept Dr. Wahler's proposal. I object."

With their mouths gaping and eyes opened to huge proportions, they both turned and stared at him. They obviously thought he'd lost his mind. In fact, he felt as though that might be true. His behavior was completely irrational. Even he couldn't deny it.

Audrey was first to regain her composure. "You object? Exactly what is it that you're objecting to, Marshall?"

"Your marriage to Dr. Wahler." He pointed his finger at the doctor. "I object to your marrying that man."

Dr. Wahler grinned. "Well, you're a bit out of order. This isn't a marriage ceremony, where one is asked to offer an objection."

"That's exactly my point. I don't want to wait until I have to object at your wedding ceremony." He turned toward Audrey. "I understand that you might feel sorry for the doctor. He's experienced the loss of his wife, and he has two little girls who need a mother. And I realize you care for them and enjoy teaching them, but you can have children of your own. Sympathy for a man isn't anything upon which to build a marriage."

Audrey appeared dumbstruck by his outburst. When she recovered, she said, "I can't believe . . . What are you thinking?"

Before Audrey could collect her thoughts and give him a proper response, the doctor burst into laughter. "This is because I mentioned a proposal, isn't it?" Once again Wahler's laughter filled the room, and he tapped Audrey's hand. "He thinks I've asked you to marry me."

Audrey clapped her hand over her mouth. From the look in her eyes, Marshall couldn't tell if she was attempting to withhold laughter, or anger, or if she was going to be sick. None of those choices appealed to him. Marshall stepped closer. He'd obviously made a fool of himself, but he didn't care. "Where I come from, a proposal is exactly that — an offer of marriage."

"Well, you'll have to agree there are other types of proposals, Marshall. My proposal to Audrey had nothing to do with marriage. I was merely seeking her assistance as a governess of sorts for my daughters — to aid in their future education and to teach them etiquette so that they will be prepared to enter boarding school in the future." Dr. Wahler pushed to his feet, a strange smile on his lips. "You need not suggest a duel, Mr. Graham. I have no plans to remarry — not now, nor in the future. Miss Cunningham is all yours. That is, if she'll have you." The doctor strode from the room, his laughter echoing after him.

CHAPTER 21

Audrey folded her arms at her waist and scowled at Marshall. She hoped her appearance left no question about her mood. He had managed to embarrass her in front of the doctor, and she didn't intend to brush aside his actions and let him think she approved of such behavior. "Exactly what were you thinking to burst in on my private talk with Dr. Wahler? You'd obviously drawn incorrect conclusions, and you'd obviously been eavesdropping on our conversation. Otherwise, you wouldn't have known about the doctor's proposal."

Marshall's brows dipped low over his chestnut brown eyes and formed a deep pucker above the bridge of his nose. "That's not exactly true. I heard him mention his proposal when you were talking in the parlor several days ago." He was obviously pleased with himself, for his thoughtful look disappeared into one that could only be interpreted as a challenge.

Audrey squared her shoulders in preparation. If he wanted to throw down the gauntlet, she'd pick it up. "You were eavesdropping or you wouldn't have heard my conversation earlier or the one just now." She rose to her feet and, with her arms still clasped across her waist, paced in front of the divan. "You jumped to conclusions about Dr. Wahler's proposal." She stopped pacing and eyed him with a steely look. "I can't believe that you would behave in such a foolish manner — and over something as commonplace as a teaching position. How you could conclude that Dr. Wahler was seeking my hand in marriage is beyond my comprehension."

Marshall drew closer. "I think you would understand my logic had you been viewing it from my perspective."

"You mean *hearing* it from your perspective. You were eavesdropping and listened to a private conversation. From that you drew an incorrect conclusion. I am indeed uncertain you possess the attributes —"

In three long strides, he covered the distance between them and swept her into his arms. "Please don't say anything more. Not until I tell you that it's because of my feelings for you that I sometimes act a fool in your presence. I'm in love with you, and I couldn't take a chance that you would agree to marry Dr. Wahler. If I embarrassed you, I'm sorry, but it doesn't change the fact that I love you."

Audrey stared at him, unable to think of one intelligent reply. Even if she had, her throat and mouth were as dry as cotton, and she couldn't have uttered a word had her life depended upon it.

Marshall chuckled. "I believe this is the first time I've seen you without anything to say. I know this all must come as somewhat of a shock to you, but I feared that I would lose you if I waited any longer."

Without another word, Marshall lowered his head and pressed a passionate kiss against her lips. Audrey's mind whirled. He had no way of knowing this was her very first kiss. He had no way of knowing that she had dreamed of this moment all of her life.

He pulled back abruptly. "What's wrong?"

Audrey shook her head. "Nothing . . . I mean . . ." She looked at him. Had she done something wrong? "Why do you ask?"

"You seem . . . well . . . do you not like to kiss? Have I been too forward?"

Audrey gave a giggle to cover up her embarrassment. "Yes, you are very forward,

Marshall Graham. As for whether or not I like to kiss — I would hardly know. This is my first experience."

Marshall's expression changed to one of wonder. "Truly?" He grinned. "Well, I'll be." For a moment he just stared at her, but then a frown formed. "What about my question? You might not have the experience of other kisses, but did you like this one?"

She shrugged. "Seemed rather short. I'm not sure I can really give you a proper assessment."

Laughing, Marshall pulled her close again. "I believe I can easily remedy that."

Audrey lost herself in his kiss and the warmth of his touch. She could smell the scent of the sea on him. It stirred something inside her, causing her to feel as if a flame had touched her heart and set fire to her entire body. Almost fearful, she pushed Marshall away and gasped for air.

"I'm sorry," he apologized. "I'm afraid I lost control and all sense of the moment. I believe I was just motivated by the good doctor. I feared not letting you know my feelings. I realize marriage is a big step — one that should never be entered into lightly."

"You're proposing?" she asked, her hand to her throat.

Marshall held her gaze for a moment and then smiled. "You didn't think I'd kiss you like that if I didn't have marriage in mind, did you?"

She shook her head and backed up a step. "I don't know. I can't honestly say that I had any rational thoughts when you were . . . when we were . . . kissing."

"So you enjoyed it?" He seemed quite pleased with himself.

"I felt like . . . well . . . I thought for a moment I'd stepped too close to the fireplace." She looked at the back of her gown just to be sure she'd not set herself on fire.

Marshall laughed and stepped toward her. Audrey took another step back and put up her hands to ward him off. "I think you should stay over there."

His dark eyes seemed to blaze with passion. "I think you should marry me."

Audrey felt her breathing pick up. She sidestepped the fireplace and found herself backed against the wall. Marshall ignored her fear and moved in like a hunter after his prey. Taking very gentle hold of her hands, he began to kiss her fingertips.

"I've found myself beset with you from the first day I arrived here," he said, moving from one finger to the next. "I wanted to run my hands through your hair. I wanted to tell you how beautiful you are."

Audrey found it impossible to speak or move. She found it impossible to do anything, in fact, but focus on breathing and standing. Her knees felt like jelly, and at any moment she was almost certain she'd faint.

"You are everything I've ever longed for in a mate. You aren't afraid to stand up to me." He moved to her left hand and began kissing those fingers. "I think there is great passion between us, and when I saw you with the good doctor, I knew I couldn't let you get away from me."

He finished with her fingers and pulled her toward himself. Audrey saw no reason to fight him. She was quite enthralled with the prospect of once again being in his arms.

"Audrey, I'll be good to you. I promise that I will love you like no one else could." He turned her in a circle as if they were dancing. "I will build you a beautiful home in the West."

"The West? But what of Aunt Thora? I can't leave her here. And there's Bridal Fair to consider."

He chuckled. "I would never leave dear Thora behind. She is welcome wherever we make our home. As for Bridal Fair, I believe you'll discover that Mr. Morley and the investors will be more than pleased to purchase the property. You have nothing to worry over, my love."

She leaned against him weakly and continued to savor the dreamlike pleasure she'd discovered within the warmth of Marshall's embrace. Somewhere in the distance the sound of shuffling feet attempted to break the spell, but she remained in Marshall's embrace until she heard a loud gasp.

"Miss Audrey!"

With a jerk, Audrey saw Irene came to a jolting halt in the parlor door. Mouth gaping open, Irene stood frozen in place.

Startled, Audrey took a backward step and immediately collided with the heavy library table. Had Marshall not caught her arm, she would have landed atop the offending piece of furniture. She started toward the girl, uncertain whether Irene had been struck dumb when she'd captured sight of Audrey in a man's arms or if something else had caused the maid's terrified appearance. Audrey continued forward and said loudly, "Do speak up, Irene. Whatever is wrong?"

Audrey's command stirred Irene to action, and she found her voice. "It's Miss Thora. She's collapsed in the kitchen. I can't get her to respond." She gasped for air. "Please come and help me."

Audrey raced from the room, leaving Irene and Marshall in her wake. Aunt Thora lay on the floor, her skin pale and ashen. "Aunt Thora! Can you hear me?" The moment Irene and Marshall entered the room, she turned to them. "Irene, get me a wet cloth for her forehead."

Marshall stooped down beside Audrey. "I'm going to move her to her bed. Irene can bring the cloth to you in there." As if she weighed no more than a feather, he scooped the old woman into his arms and carried her to the bedroom. Audrey hurried to maneuver around Marshall and pull back the bedcovers. Gently, he placed Aunt Thora on the crisp white sheet and then unlaced her shoes.

Irene rushed forward with several wet cloths and handed them to Audrey. Thora groaned as Audrey placed a damp cloth on her forehead and one across her eyes. Her fingers trembled as she hastened to unbutton the top of the older woman's black dress.

Only minutes had passed when Aunt Thora surprised them all by yanking the cloth from her eyes. "How do you expect me to see what's going on when you put that wet rag on my eyes?"

Marshall chuckled. "Well, I see you

haven't lost your sharp tongue, Miss Thora."

The woman's eyes grew large as she focused upon him and then realized where she was. "What's a *man* doing in here, Audrey?" She flitted her hand. "Scat. Get out of here. Men don't come into a lady's bedroom. The thought of it! Your mother was a Southern lady, Marshall Graham, and you should know better."

Marshall nudged Audrey. "She's obviously feeling better, don't you think?"

Thora attempted to slap Marshall with the wet rag. "I heard you, Marshall! There's nothing wrong with my hearing. Now, go on before I have to get up and take a broom to you."

Audrey grasped Marshall's arm as he turned to leave. "I think Dr. Wahler should examine her — just to be certain. I don't want another episode like this to happen. It's better to have him check her, don't you think?"

Marshall nodded and grinned. "I don't relish the idea of going after the doctor so soon after we've parted company, but I'll do as you ask." He leaned a little closer. "I'd do most anything for you, Audrey. You know that, don't you?"

Thora yanked the sheet and let it flutter to a rest beneath her chin. "What are you two whispering about? I keep telling you to git on out of this room. I'm thinking you're the one with a hearing problem, Marshall."

"I'm leaving, Miss Thora. You don't need to ask me again."

He winked at Audrey before he strode from the room. The front door clattered as he departed. Thora grabbed Audrey's hand. "You're in love with him, aren't you?" The old woman clutched Audrey's hand with a surprising strength. "No need to ask about him. He's been in love ever since he laid eyes on you."

Audrey grinned. "I do believe you're a romantic at heart, Aunt Thora. Let's just say that Marshall and I are interested in the possibility of a future together."

Thora raised her head off the pillow? "He declare himself yet?"

"If you mean has he told me he loves me, yes. And he has proposed marriage, but I didn't give him an answer. I need time to make such a big decision. It's so soon after Father's death that I don't trust my emotions just yet."

"Pray about it, but you better not wait too long. Isn't like you have a lot of other opportunities."

"Aunt Thora!" Audrey said, looking at her in shock.

"Well, at least he's God-fearin', and I'm sure the good Lord brought him here to help us deal with them Yankees."

Shaking her head, Audrey walked to the basin of water Irene had placed near the bed. "I believe you've done entirely too much thinking." Audrey dipped another cloth into the basin.

"I reckon this means you'll be forgettin' about me. Probably movin' me on to one of the old shacks on the property."

Audrey returned to the bed and shook her head. She didn't want to rebuke Aunt Thora — especially when she wasn't feeling well. However, when the time was right, Audrey would explain that her future wouldn't be planned without taking the older woman into consideration. There was no way Audrey would leave Aunt Thora to fend for herself.

Audrey reapplied the damp cloth to her head. "You need not worry about such things right now, Aunt Thora. I simply want you to rest until the doctor arrives."

Thora snatched the cloth from her forehead. "I don't need a doctor to tell me how I feel. I feel just fine, and I'm going back to the kitchen. I don't want folks makin' a fuss over me." Pushing Audrey's arm aside, she attempted to sit but immediately closed her eyes and fell back against the pillows. For a moment she said nothing, and Audrey thought maybe the older woman had fainted again.

"Aunt Thora?"

Without opening her eyes, Thora replied, "Maybe I should rest a little longer. But I don't need the doctor."

Audrey didn't argue, and moments later the old woman slipped into a peaceful sleep. While Irene returned to finish washing the supper dishes, Audrey sat by Thora's bedside, her thoughts returning to the earlier events. Her lips curved in an unexpected smile as she recalled Marshall's confrontation with the doctor. Though it had been embarrassing, she was deeply touched by the fact that he'd been willing to set aside pride and speak his heart. She wondered if many other men would do such a thing and decided the possibilities were likely quite slim. As Aunt Thora said — it wasn't like she had a lot of prospects. But Marshall was more than prospect enough. He was really all she had ever wanted in a man.

Her thoughts continued to linger upon the possibility of marriage when she heard the front door open and the sound of Marshall's voice. Although he escorted Dr. Wahler to the door of Aunt Thora's room, he didn't enter.

Aunt Thora roused and her eyes fluttered open at the doctor's greeting. "I told Audrey I don't need no doctor. I'll be just fine."

Dr. Wahler set his black leather bag on the bedside table and opened the clasp. "Why don't you let me be the judge of whether you need medical attention, Miss Thora? I'd like to put my medical training to good use."

Thora grumbled as she readjusted the sheet. "Well, if you put it that way, I suppose I can't refuse. A man should earn his keep."

"I'm most grateful, Miss Thora." He removed his stethoscope and placed the flared ebony disc against her chest while he listened through the ivory-tipped earpieces. When she opened her mouth to speak, he silenced her with an upraised hand.

Audrey remained close at hand throughout Thora's examination. When the doctor finished, she arched a brow. "Well? Is Aunt Thora as healthy as she tells us?"

After a fleeting glance at Audrey, the doctor returned his attention to Thora. He grasped her hand and gave a slight shake of his head. "I'm afraid your heart is giving out, Thora. You need to slow down and spend most of your time in bed. Rest is the best medicine for you. And before you give me any arguments, let me say that I know both Irene and Audrey are more than capable of handling things without you."

Wisps of white hair fanned the pillow as Thora shifted her head to the side. "So you're sayin' I'm not worth my salt? You think the work will get done without me — is that what you're sayin'?"

The doctor chuckled. "Not at all. But you do need to slow down. And getting excited isn't good for your heart. You need to remain calm." He gently patted her hand.

Thora yanked away as if she'd been seared by a hot iron. "I'm not a small child that needs to be coddled." She flitted her hand toward the door. "Go take care of someone who is in real need of a doctor."

If Thora had offended the doctor, he didn't let on. He bid them good-bye but was quick to tell Thora he'd return for a visit the next day. Her lips drooped in a frown, but she didn't object. Though Thora wouldn't admit the doctor was correct in his diagnosis, she'd obviously taken some of what he said to heart, for Audrey detected a hint of fear lurking in her eyes.

"Everything is going to be fine, Aunt Thora. Irene and I can manage. And if you're a good patient and rest, perhaps the doctor will permit you to come and sit in the kitchen and keep us company for a few hours next week."

Thora pointed at the Bible sitting on a table near the window. "I think it would help me to hear some Scripture. Do you have time to sit for a minute and read? I'm not certain I can manage to hold my Bible and read if I'm to remain flat in this bed."

Audrey smiled. The doctor hadn't said she had to remain flat in bed. And had the older woman asked, Audrey would have propped her pillows so that she could read. However, it was obvious Thora was frightened and wanted someone with her for a while longer. Whether she waved a shotgun or merely used her sharp tongue, Aunt Thora had always appeared confident and bold. But Audrey now realized the old woman wasn't completely fearless.

She picked up the Bible and sat down near the bed. "I have more than enough time to sit with you, Aunt Thora. Is there anything in particular that you'd like me to read?"

"I've always been fond of Psalms or Proverbs when I'm feeling a little anxious. Whatever you read will be just fine."

Audrey opened Thora's Bible to the book of Proverbs. After settling back in the chair, she began to read the third chapter and lingered over the fifth and sixth verses. " 'Trust in the Lord with all thine heart; and lean not unto thine own understanding. In all thy ways acknowledge him, and he shall direct thy paths.' "

"That's a hard one," Thora murmured. She picked at a loose string along the hem of her sheet. "I know God is a better judge of what's best for us, but trusting with your whole heart — that's a hard one for me." There was a slight twinkle in her eyes when she looked at Audrey. "I do my best to pray and ask God to guide me, but I'm not always so quick to give in if His answer don't meet up with what I think is best. After all these years, it seems I still haven't learned to completely trust Him."

"How do you know when it's what you want and when it's what the Lord wants?"

Thora shifted to her side. "Well, the best way I can explain it is that once I've prayed, I'll get a nudging deep inside that let's me know if I'm headed in the right direction or the wrong one. Usually the wrong direction is the one I'd like to take." She cackled and shook her head. "The good Lord has had a time trying to teach me, that's for sure. Probably why I'm still on this earth. There's just too much that still needs fixing."

Audrey didn't think that was true. Aunt

Thora might be feisty and determined, but she had a good heart. Still, maybe there was something to learning to lean on the Lord. She certainly didn't depend upon God to lead her in her own decisions. Maybe if she'd depend upon God, He'd show her if Marshall was a man she could trust — someone she could count on and grow old with. She stared at the open Bible. Was Marshall the man God intended for her? Maybe she should ask.

CHAPTER 22

As Audrey hastened into the kitchen the following morning, she wondered how long it might take before she received that inner nudge Aunt Thora had mentioned. After her one-way conversation with God last night, she was eager to receive His answer. She'd been careful to let God know she'd prefer a plan that included Marshall Graham but excluded Bridal Veil Island. If God didn't agree, she wasn't sure she'd be as eager to receive that inner nudge.

She glanced up when Irene returned from the henhouse with a basket of eggs. "Good morning, Irene. I trust you slept well."

"As good as I ever sleep what with Miss Thora and her snoring. I can hear her through the walls." She pointed to the basket. "Don't plan on eggs this morning. Hens aren't laying very well. Must be the colder weather. Either that or those little girls have returned and helped themselves."

Audrey chuckled. "I don't think the twins will try that again. Dr. Wahler let them know that raising baby chicks was not going to be a part of their future." She lifted a crock of cornmeal to the table. "I can mix up a batch of cornmeal griddle cakes. The men enjoy those."

"Especially Marshall?" Irene grinned, her eyes alight with mischief.

"What's that supposed to mean?" A blush of heat stole across Audrey's cheeks.

Irene giggled. "You know what it means. I saw you two in the parlor. I think love is such a grand thing." The girl's skirt billowed as she twirled across the kitchen before bumping her hip into the heavy oak cupboard. "Ouch!" After an angry glare at the wooden structure, Irene rubbed her side. "That hurt!"

"I'm certain it did, but perhaps you shouldn't attempt to dance in the kitchen. This room is too small for such a performance." Audrey smiled and shook her head. Irene could brighten any cloudy day, but she could also slow down the progression of work with her antics. Still, having her help had been a genuine blessing. And now, with Aunt Thora unable to work, Audrey would need Irene's assistance even more.

Not heeding Audrey's admonition and

obviously forgetting her injured hip, Irene did a half skip, half dance back across the kitchen. "Has Marshall asked you to marry him? He's very good-looking." Irene lifted several eggs from the basket. "And you're beautiful, as well," she hastily added. "A wedding would be a lovely diversion after all the sadness . . ." She clapped a hand over her mouth. "I'm sorry, I didn't mean . . ."

"It's quite all right, Irene. We have experienced our share of sadness lately; what with my father's death, all the problems and delays at the construction site, and now Thora's illness. However, I don't think there will be a wedding anytime soon."

The girl's smile faded. "Oh-h-h. So he didn't ask for your hand?"

If nothing else, the girl was persistent. "We've mentioned the possibility, but there's nothing definite."

"But he loves you, and you love him?" She danced from foot to foot like a child awaiting a special treat.

Though she realized Irene meant no harm with her questions, Audrey's muscles tightened. She wasn't certain how much she wanted to share at the moment. After all, she was awaiting that nudge from God before making any final decisions about her future. "We care for each other, and we are seeking God's direction for the future."

"Well, I think God is going to agree with your father. This is all working out just like your papa wanted." Irene picked up a knife and began to slice thick pieces of bacon.

Audrey stopped stirring the batter and stared at the girl. "Whatever do you mean?"

Irene hitched a shoulder. "I shouldn't tell you, but one day when I was dusting upstairs, I heard your papa and Marshall talking. It was before your papa got so terrible sick — back when he enjoyed company in his room." She hesitated. "You aren't going to get angry at me for eavesdropping, are you?"

Audrey sighed. She didn't want a commentary on her father's final illness. She wanted to hear about the conversation between her father and Marshall. "I'm not going to get angry, just get on with it and tell me, Irene. What did my father say?" She picked up the spoon and continued to stir.

"We-l-l-l." As if she feared that someone else might be listening to her admission, Irene drew close to Audrey's side. "Your papa told Marshall that he wanted him to look out for you. That he would be a perfect choice to help you. Your papa said he could die in peace if he knew you had Marshall to take care of you."

Audrey's jaw went slack and the mixing spoon clattered against the edge of the bowl. Irene started, and Audrey forced a faint smile as she picked up the spoon and forced herself to continue. For a fleeting moment, she felt as though she might be dreaming, but as Irene's comment slowly entered her consciousness, she knew this was real. Like autumn leaves in a strong breeze, questions flitted through Audrey's mind, yet she remained silent.

Taking Audrey's silence as a cue to continue, Irene set aside the slices of bacon. "I just find it astounding that your father could choose a husband for you and that you would fall in love with that very man. Honestly, how often do you think that would ever happen? There are lots of girls, especially the wealthy ones, who have to marry a man to increase the family fortune or name." Her lips puckered into a frown. "I hope Mr. Morley doesn't force June to marry someone she doesn't love. His daughter is such a sweet thing, and I know she could never refuse her father."

Audrey pointed to the skillet. "The bacon isn't going to fry itself, and the men will be late for work if we don't hurry."

After a brief look of confusion, Irene

giggled and placed the sliced bacon in the skillet. "Do you think Mr. Morley would force June into a marriage?"

"I truly don't know, Irene, but we need not worry over it right now. It will be years before June is of a marriageable age."

While Irene continued her aimless chatter, Audrey's thoughts returned to Marshall. Had his talk of marriage been nothing more than the fulfillment of a promise to her father? She couldn't imagine the two of them concocting such a scheme. Yet the entire tale was too farfetched to be a misunderstanding.

"Must be a real comfort to you, Audrey." Irene's lips curved in a sweet smile as she lifted the sizzling bacon from the skillet and dropped the slices onto a china platter.

Audrey wasn't certain if it was the heat from the skillet or Irene's voice that drew her from her thoughts. "What must be a comfort?"

"The fact that even on his deathbed your papa was making sure you'd be taken care of by a good man." Irene set the skillet back on the stove. The girl's gaze roamed toward the windows and the huge live oaks in the distance. "If the two of you marry, will Marshall become the owner of Bridal Fair?" A gleam of excitement shone in her eyes.

"Do you suppose Marshall will want to sell Bridal Fair to Mr. Morley for a lot of money? That's enough to make a man want to marry, don't you think?"

Audrey arched her brows. "Indeed, I suppose it is."

"Ohh, I didn't mean to imply you're not a woman that any man would be delighted to call his wife." The girl fumbled for words as she placed the last of the bacon into the hot skillet. "You're absolutely lovely, and you know how to take care of a house and operate this business."

A tidal wave of humiliation washed over Audrey. The mere idea that her father may have struck such an agreement with Marshall caused her stomach to lurch. "Why don't you take breakfast to Aunt Thora while I finish up in here."

"Are you sure? There's still a lot to get done before the men come downstairs."

"Yes, I'm sure. And please stay with her to see that she eats. Otherwise, she won't regain her strength."

Irene prepared Thora's plate and scuttled off toward the bedroom while Audrey's thoughts returned to Marshall and her father. She knew her father had convinced Marshall to come to Bridal Veil Island, but it had been to give her father an opportunity to explain the circumstances surrounding Wilbur Graham's death — hadn't it? That's what both Marshall and her father had said. And she had believed them! Irene was likely correct. There had to be something more to all of this. Was Marshall interested in gaining Bridal Fair and selling it for a tidy sum? After all, he'd mentioned selling it to the investors. The money would certainly prove an excellent resource to finance his new life in Colorado. That must be it. He'd seen her as an opportunity to finance his new life and had quickly accepted her father's offer.

Stop! The word slammed through her consciousness like a hammer striking iron and brought her rambling assumptions to a halt. Wasn't this what she'd done before? Jumped to incorrect conclusions about Marshall? And hadn't she regretted it?

She closed her eyes. Before she went any further with these outlandish thoughts, she needed to clear the air and speak with Marshall. Tell him she wanted nothing more than his honesty — that she wouldn't judge him for any agreements he'd made with her father. That final thought might not have been absolutely true, for she didn't like the idea that Marshall and her father had struck some sort of deal that included her. But if she wanted the truth, she needed to remain calm — and give Marshall an opportunity to defend himself.

Sounds of the men clattering down the stairs stirred her from further thoughts of her father, Marshall, or their secret plan. She needed to hurry if she was going to complete breakfast preparations and get the men off to work on time.

While she served breakfast, Audrey did her best to calm herself. She didn't want to appear strident when she spoke to Marshall. Although it probably wasn't actually the case, today it seemed as if the men were lingering over their coffee longer than usual, but as several of them slipped away from the table, she approached Marshall.

"If you have time, I'd like to speak with you."

He dropped his napkin on the table and nodded. "I need to get to the work site, but I can always spare a few minutes for you." His lips curved in a broad smile.

She nodded toward the parlor, and he followed close on her heels. She didn't mince words once they were away from the two remaining men. "It has come to my attention that you and my father may have entered into some sort of arrangement — one that included your marriage to me."

His smile broadened. "Indeed we did."

She gasped at his quick admission. Why, he seemed downright proud of what they'd done. "You aren't even going to attempt a denial?"

"No, why would I? Your father harbored a great deal of concern about your future, Audrey."

"And he asked you to take care of me?"

"He did. And I told him it would be my privilege, if you would agree to such an arrangement."

"I can't believe you would agree to such a thing." Her heartbeat increased until she thought it would thump its way right out of her chest. How dare he!

"I don't see why you're so upset. Your father loved you and was simply doing the best thing possible to provide for your future care. He wanted to provide for you in the best way possible."

"Provide for me? And what about you? Was he providing for you, as well?"

"What's that supposed to mean?"

"Trying to provide for me need not have included a marriage proposal. Are you looking out for me or for yourself, Marshall?"

He frowned and glanced toward the door. "This entire conversation makes no sense. Unfortunately, I need to get to work. We can talk this evening."

"If you consider your work more important than resolving this matter, you go right ahead." Audrey gathered her skirts and turned on her heel. So now discussing his marriage proposal was a waste of time. She rushed off before he could say anything further.

Marshall maintained a close watch on Audrey throughout the evening meal, but she wouldn't so much as glance in his direction. He had hoped to catch her eye and at least give her a look of assurance and signal her to meet him after supper.

Still holding out hope that they could talk, Marshall remained at the table after the other men went upstairs to their rooms or out to the front porch for a smoke. When Audrey finally stepped back into the dining room to retrieve the dirty dishes, he pushed away from the table. "I'd like to talk to you, Audrey."

Her eyes shone with anger when she looked in his direction. "There's nothing left to say. You've already admitted you took part in the scheme."

"Scheme? This isn't a scheme." He raked his fingers through his hair. "I granted a dying man his final request."

"Well, good for you!" She rushed to the

kitchen and left him sitting at the table. Moments later Irene shuffled into the dining room and began clearing the dishes. No doubt Audrey planned to avoid him. He strode into the kitchen and grasped her arms. "We need to finish our discussion, Audrey. Running away from me isn't going to resolve anything."

At that moment, Thora called to Audrey, "I need a drink of water." Audrey freed her arm from Marshall's hold, retrieved a glass from the shelf, and filled it with water.

"If you'll excuse me, Mr. Graham, Aunt Thora needs my attention. As you know, she's quite ill." She stopped and turned on her way to the bedroom. "However, I doubt she'll be making any sickbed requests that include marriage."

It was a morning nearly a week later before Marshall could finally corner Audrey. He took hold of her hand and all but dragged her from the back door to a nearby path. "We need to talk," he declared, leaving no room for her rejection.

"I'm very busy," she said. "You know that Aunt Thora is sick and that Irene and I are trying to manage on our own."

"Audrey, I know that very well. What I don't know is why you are mad at me. I've prayed and searched my heart, but I can see nothing that I've done to cause you such offense."

She looked at him for a moment. It was almost as if she was warring with herself. "I've already made that clear. Perhaps you simply do not understand."

The day was already getting warm and Marshall felt sweat trickle down his back. He motioned to the live oak where a swing hung. He knew Audrey liked this place and hoped that perhaps it would soften her anger toward him. "Let's take some shade."

Audrey allowed him to pull her along, but she acted as though it were a great hardship. "I have nothing more to say about this."

"You have a great deal more to say," Marshall declared. "I deserve an explanation."

"We have already been over this." Audrey pulled away, and Marshall allowed her to go. "You and my father conspired in secret about my future — my welfare and needs. You both should have considered what I wanted in life — you should have talked to me."

"I agree," Marshall said, nodding. "We were wrong not to consult you."

"I am not baggage to be handed off. I'm

fully capable of taking care of myself and Aunt Thora. And if you consider it fully, I think you'll realize that what you'd gain in the sale of Bridal Fair is hardly worth saddling yourself in a marriage of obligation."

Marshall found her words all the more confusing. "What do you mean — a marriage of obligation? I feel no obligation. If you feel obligation, then I'm truly baffled. I thought you had come to care for me."

Some of the hardened resolve left Audrey's expression. "I do care for you. I care enough not to live a charade. I care enough to keep you from making a mistake in honoring a dead man's request that you take on his spinster daughter."

"You aren't making any sense, Audrey. I made my feelings clear."

She smiled sadly. "Please. Let's just live in peace. The construction around here won't go on forever. Do your duty as you must, but say nothing more of marriage. I'm sorry that my father ever put such a responsibility on your shoulders."

Audrey headed up the path to the house, and Marshall started to go after her, but something stopped him. He had a nagging feeling from deep inside that he should let it drop.

"Give her time to realize the truth of your

love," a voice seemed to whisper in his mind.

He drew a deep breath. "But I don't want to give her time. Time might very well take her away from me." On the other hand, hadn't he already lost her in a sense? Maybe time was the only way to get her back.

CHAPTER 23

Marshall waited on the pier, his heart pounding as Captain Holloway maneuvered the *Bessie II* alongside the dock. Mr. Morley had been in Atlanta for three weeks for meetings with the investors. Although his original plan had been to return to Bridal Veil within ten days, he had wired Marshall stating he had been delayed. Ever since he'd received the wire, Marshall had been worried. Had the investors decided to replace him with another manager? Did they believe the rebuilding was taking too long? Would this project cause him to lose out on his plans for Colorado?

During the older man's absence, he'd done his best to remain focused on the construction and follow Mr. Morley's instructions. The investor had urged him to keep an eye on Ted Uptegrove and seek out any other information that could help them solve the question of who was responsible for the sabotage. Marshall had no idea how to investigate any further — he had suggested a private investigator, but Mr. Morley hadn't agreed. Other than the money clip and Ted Uptegrove's clandestine meetings in Biscayne, he continued to come up empty-handed.

The only thing Marshall had to report was that both Frank and Ted had become increasingly defiant since Mr. Morley's departure. They came and went at will, never seeking permission or telling Marshall where they were going. Even his admonitions that they must report their whereabouts to him went unheeded. Marshall wrestled with the possibility of firing Ted but worried that such action would cause Frank to stir further disruption among the men. And he couldn't fire Frank.

Mr. Morley clapped him on the shoulder. "It's good to be back, Marshall. I'm sorry I was gone so long, but much was accomplished. After learning the costs involved due to the explosion and rebuilding, the investors are adamant that the culprits be captured. Had the rebuilding not been so extensive and if the problems at the work site had ceased, they might have overlooked the incident, but that's not the case. However, I believe we've developed a plan!"

The older man's excitement was contagious. If they had a workable idea, he wanted to help. "I'm eager to hear what you've come up with."

"During supper this evening, I'm going to tell all of the foremen that the investors have decided to change the plans. That we are going to expand the clubhouse beyond anyone's expectations. New plans — false ones — were drawn while I was in Atlanta. Plans that indicate Bridal Veil is going to outshine any resort in the country."

Marshall frowned. "And how is that going to help us discover the criminals?"

"If there is intent to cause our investors financial difficulty by destroying or slowing our progress here on Bridal Veil, someone will want to steal the plans. If they simply want to outdo us, they'll want the plans, as well. However, the investors believe there may be several men in collusion to destroy those who invested in Bridal Veil." They continued along the path to the house. "I realize you may not understand the competitiveness that exists among wealthy men, but trust me, they can be your best friends one day and your enemies the next."

"So the Bridal Veil investors believe the Jekyl investors are involved?"

Marshall still thought Frank Baker was

the primary suspect, but it didn't sound as though anyone else agreed.

"We're not saying it's the men from Jekyl. But given the incidents that have occurred from the outset — the explosion and the continuing mishaps — we don't believe this is simply a group of hoodlums from the mainland." Mr. Morley tapped his suitcase. "We'll try this and hope it works."

Marshall nodded his agreement but couldn't help wondering what he would do if the plan didn't work. Since Boyd's death, his time at the island had been a test of both his faith and his patience. Audrey continued to maintain her distance, and Marshall wondered if he would ever have an opportunity to penetrate the invisible barrier she'd placed between them. Each night he prayed God would soften her attitude and give him an opportunity to explain, but so far his requests had gone unheeded, and God seemed only to encourage Marshall to wait.

As all of the men gathered at the supper table a short time later, Marshall watched for reaction among the foremen. Harry appeared annoyed by the idea of changes while Ted and Frank asked numerous questions, both of them eager to have a look at the plans.

"For now, Marshall needs to be the one to study the plans. It's more important he have a clear understanding of what's to be done. I'm certain his orders to each of you will be quite clear."

Frank reared back in his chair. "You saying we don't know how to read plans?"

Mr. Morley frowned. "I'm saying that I want Marshall to have time to go over the drawings — nothing more and nothing less. And if you have a problem with my decision, we can talk about it in private after dinner."

Frank didn't take Mr. Morley up on the offer. Instead, he pushed away from the table and went outdoors. Shortly thereafter, the rest of the foremen excused themselves.

Mr. Morley tipped his head to one side. "Now all we have to do is wait and see what happens. Frank and Ted appeared disturbed by the announcement, but it may mean nothing. Make certain the foremen see you take the plans to the work site tomorrow, and I'd suggest you leave them in the cabin you've been using as an office." He glanced toward the windows to see if anyone was within earshot. "I want the plans left there, and we'll stake out the cabin to see if anyone makes a move to either review or steal the drawings."

"I'm willing to give anything a try. I just want all of these problems to end." Marshall wasn't convinced the plan held much merit, but he did believe Mr. Morley and the other investors had far more experience when it came to planning such strategies.

"Let's take the drawings to the parlor and look at them. If anyone is watching, it will appear more realistic that we're reviewing them." Mr. Morley picked up his empty coffee cup. "Why don't you ask Audrey if she'll bring us more coffee while I get the drawings from my room."

Marshall didn't say that he'd count himself fortunate if Audrey would stay in the same room with him for more than two minutes. "I'll see if Irene is in the kitchen. I imagine Audrey wrote and told you Thora isn't well."

He nodded. "Yes. I arranged for a young woman from Biscayne to help Audrey and Irene, but I plan to speak with Audrey to see if she wants me to hire some additional help or if she'd rather wait. From her letter, I wasn't certain if Thora would be able to resume any of her duties or not."

Marshall detected a question in the tone of his voice. "I seriously doubt that Thora's future will include being able to assist Irene and Audrey anymore. I believe Audrey would feel at ease speaking to you about any needs they may have."

Instead of Irene, Audrey was in the kitchen when Marshall entered. "Mr. Morley asked if you or Irene might have time to brew another pot of coffee." Marshall carefully couched the question as a request from Mr. Morley, in case Audrey might ignore the appeal — or tell him she didn't have time to give him any special treatment.

Audrey stepped toward the sink. "Tell Mr. Morley that I'll bring a tray as soon as I've prepared the coffee."

His shoulder muscles tightened at her formal tone. "Yes, ma'am. I'll be certain to give your message to Mr. Morley." He turned on his heel and strode from the room, his jaw clenched as tight as a boxer's fist.

When he arrived at the parlor door, Mr. Morley was already at work spreading out the drawings on the library table. A look of expectation shone in his eyes. "I hope you've come with good news regarding the coffee."

Marshall nodded. "Yes. Audrey said she'd bring a tray in shortly." He crossed the room in four long strides and stood beside Mr. Morley.

"Here we have it," Mr. Morley said, tapping the drawing with his finger. "I believe anyone reviewing these would find the changes believable. We haven't altered the main portion of the clubhouse. Rather, we had the architect add two long additions to the building that will house more luxurious suites, as well as a glass-enclosed dining area. He's also noted all of the changes to more luxurious amenities and decor in the main building." Mr. Morley pointed to a notation that indicated orders had been placed for items that would rival the most lavish hotels in Europe.

Marshall stared at the drawings, not totally convinced by Mr. Morley's idea. "I still fear this may not work."

"I believe Frank is careless and greedy enough that he'll make some sort of move to get these drawings." Mr. Morley arched his brows. "If he's the kind of man we think he is, I doubt we'll have to wait long."

The following day Audrey managed to take some precious time away from the house and Aunt Thora to enjoy a visit with the Wahler twins at the beach. She had hoped it might clear her head and help her to refocus her heart. Audrey had just begun to relax when she spotted several men further down the beach. They were pulling a small boat toward a secluded marshy area not far from the shore. Where had they come from and what were they doing? Though occasional visitors came to the island, they didn't approach from this marshy area and they didn't hide their boats.

Sensing something amiss, she hurried toward the twins. "Come along, girls. I think we need to return home."

"Aw, not yet." Julie looked up to Audrey with a frown. "I want to find some more shells."

"Now! Come along. We need to get back to the house." She hadn't meant to sound strident, but fear had taken hold.

"I've got a lot of shells to take back," Josie declared.

"Gather them quickly." She tried not to seem as though she were watching anything in particular as she looked down the beach.

"I don't know why we have to go," Julie grumbled.

The hairs on Audrey's neck prickled to attention. What if those men heard them and approached? If they intended any harm, she'd never be able to protect the girls. Only Sadie and Dr. Wahler knew they'd come to the beach today. If the men had been out on the water and seen the three of them alone, they would appear easy prey, wouldn't they?

After hastily gathering the girls' treasures and tucking them inside the picnic basket, she folded the blanket and patted Josie's back, hoping to hurry her along the wooded path. Audrey's actions had little effect upon the girl, for she dawdled at every opportunity, stopping to bend down and examine first this rock and then another. The sound of brush crackled in the distance, and she hesitated before urging the girls forward.

"We still have a ways to go, and I need to get home to help Irene with supper." She didn't want to frighten the girls, but her pleas to hurry were meeting with little success. Once again, Josie spied a shiny pebble along the side of the path and stooped down to examine the prize.

She looked up at Audrey with pleading eyes. "Help me get it, Miss Audrey. It's beautiful."

Unable to resist, Audrey bent forward to pry the pebble from the hardened dirt. "I think we'll need to use a stick to loosen it, and there isn't —"

She held her breath and rose to a stand. Placing her index finger over her pursed lips, she signaled the girls to be quiet. Once again, she heard crackling brush, this time followed by the thud of heavy footsteps. Taking a backward step, she peered down the path, spotted a man in the distance, screamed, and dropped the picnic basket. Pushing the girls behind her skirts, Audrey shoved them back against the trees. Head bowed low, the man came toward them at a rapid pace.

Increasing to a trot, he raised his head and his features became distinguishable. "Marshall!" Audrey exhaled his name in a giant whoosh of relief and clasped a hand to her chest.

CHAPTER 24

"You scared the life out of me, Marshall!" The girls moved from behind Audrey's skirts as Marshall drew nearer.

"I'm sorry. It wasn't my intention to frighten you." He smiled at the girls. "To tell you the truth, I was surprised to see the three of you out here in the woods." The twins rushed forward and attacked him in unison, one taking to his left side and the other his right.

"We had a picnic and got some pretty shells. Wanna see?" Josie asked.

"Maybe later," Marshall declared.

Audrey went back for the picnic hamper, and Marshall whispered something to the girls. They quite happily danced down the path, glancing back over their shoulders. Audrey returned with their things and started after them.

"I'm surprised I caused you such a fright. You know these woods like the back of your hand," Marshall said as he stepped in beside her.

Audrey nodded. "Under usual circumstances, I wouldn't have startled at seeing someone out here, but something strange happened down at the beach." While continuing to keep an eye on the girls, she went on to explain what she'd observed only a short time earlier. "I don't know what those men were doing, and when I saw you —"

"You thought I was one of them."

"Exactly. And having the girls with me made it all the worse. I don't know what I would have done if someone threatened them harm while they were in my care."

Marshall grasped her elbow. "I'm truly sorry I added to your concern, but I have a feeling those men you saw are up to no good. I think they may somehow be involved with the problems at the work site. Mr. Morley has developed a plan that may reveal who's behind everything or what is going on, and we're hopeful it won't take long before we meet with success. Until we figure it out it's probably safer if you and the girls remain close to Bridal Fair. I don't think these men have plans to harm anyone, but if they thought they'd been seen and could be identified, who can say what might happen."

Audrey's arm shivered beneath his fingers. Maybe he shouldn't have told her. He didn't want her to startle at every shadowy image that crossed her path, but he was determined to keep her safe. Better to have her frightened than to have her wander into harm's way.

"You need not worry. I plan to be much more cautious about where I take the girls." Disappointment shone in her eyes. "I never thought I'd have reason to fear walking the beaches or wooded paths of Bridal Veil."

"I don't think you'll need to worry for long. If Mr. Morley's plan works, this will be settled in short order." When her lips curved in a slight smile, he decided she'd been encouraged by his remark. He inhaled a deep breath. This might not be the perfect time, but he needed to speak his heart and didn't know when they'd be alone again. "There are a couple of things I'd like to clear up between us, Audrey."

She peeked from beneath the brim of her hat. "Clear up?"

"Something I feel God would have me share with you, and I hope you'll hear me out."

"I can't imagine," she said softly.

There was no doubt she knew exactly what he was talking about. He detected a hint of reluctance in her tone, but he needed to state his case. "First of all, you need to know that I never promised your father I would marry you. I promised only that I would look after you. To die in peace, your father needed assurance you were going to be all right. To him, that also meant having a man around to help or protect you when needed."

"I don't —"

He held up his hand to stop her protest. "Let me finish. I know you may not think you need a man's help. I didn't set this plan in motion. It was your father's doing. I told him I didn't know if you'd permit me to help, but I would do my very best."

He stopped in the path and took her hands in his. Although they were much smaller than his own, he could feel their strength. With one finger, he lifted her chin and was struck by the vulnerability he discovered in her eyes. She was an intriguing mixture of meekness and defiance — perfect for him in every way.

"I love you, Audrey, and I'm asking that you give me a chance to prove my love for you. I don't want to marry you for any other reason than love, and if it takes forever . . . I guess I'll have to be patient and wait it out."

She tilted her head to the side, the brim nearly hiding the faint smile that curved her lips.

"Forever is a terribly long time."

He nodded. "I feel like it's been forever since you would even speak to me."

She grew quite serious. "You know I've come to care for you, but I won't build a life on promises you made to my father. If we are to build a future, it has to be formed from our love and from a belief that this is God's design for our lives. I know my father's motives were pure, but they weren't the basis for a strong marriage."

Marshall chuckled. "I keep repeating that I never promised your father I would marry you. Would you please erase that thought from your mind? The only promises I want to build our life upon are the ones I make to you — starting with this: I promise to love you forever." He lowered his head as he took her in his arms and captured her lips in a slow, lingering kiss. Lifting his head, he looked deep into her eyes. "Do you believe me?"

She remained in his arms, the softness of her body resting against his own. "I do."

"The next time you say those words to me, I hope it will be in front of a preacher."

The twins shouted in the distance, and

the embracing couple jumped apart as if they'd heard a gunshot. Audrey laughed and took hold of his arm. "I believe we'd best check on the girls."

"And I owe them each a piece of candy for permitting me time to talk with you."

Audrey let loose of his arm and turned toward him with a look of mock horror. "Marshall Graham! You bribed them?"

"I prefer to think of it as a reward for good behavior." He tipped his head back and chuckled, pleased when she joined in his laughter.

A little later they all gathered around the dining table. Even Audrey sat with her guests. Irene had been adamant that a hostess should dine at the table when she'd invited special guests, and Sadie had agreed. In fact, Sadie had insisted upon taking over Audrey's kitchen duties for the evening.

Audrey peered down the table and was struck with a pang of melancholy for the days when the dining chairs would have been filled by family members and valued friends who had come to partake in a festive meal and would then join her family in the parlor to be entertained with a musical performance or a poetry reading. Tonight the faces that peered back at her were boarders and acquaintances, not dear family friends — except for Marshall, of course, and the twins. They had become dear to her heart. Though the girls had wanted to sit next to Audrey, they'd lost the battle. With their hair neatly combed and their faces scrubbed clean by Sadie, they flanked their father at midtable.

Mr. Fenton craned his long neck around Jim Parks. "Glad to have such pretty young ladies with us this evening. You girls been studying with Miss Audrey today?"

Julie eyed him suspiciously, but Josie scooted to the edge of her seat for a better look at Mr. Fenton and his beaklike nose. "We studied nature today. It was lots of fun because we picked up shells." She turned her attention to her father. "I found a special one for you, Papa."

Julie pushed her lower lip into a pout. "I would have found you a good one, but Miss Audrey made us hurry from the beach like some monster was chasing us. We ran down the path, and I got scared when she screamed."

Josie poked her sister in the side. "She didn't scream. It was just a little yip like a puppy or something. Besides, she was okay when she saw it was Marshall."

Julie bobbed her head. "Um-hum. 'Specially when he put his arms around her and stole a kiss." The child wrapped her arms around her own shoulders, pursed her lips, and blew an imaginary kiss into the air.

The boarders' heads swiveled in unison to gawk at Audrey, their eyes awash with curiosity. In spite of the coolness of the room, she could feel the heat crawl up her neck and spread across her cheeks. Forcing a laugh, she said, "I do believe we have apple cobbler for dessert. I'll let Irene know we're ready." She pushed away from the table and hurried into the kitchen, hoping the conversation would change before she returned to the table.

Both Irene and Sadie attempted to shoo her back into the dining room, but Audrey refused and insisted upon helping with the dessert. When Audrey and Irene entered with the apple cobbler, all conversation shifted to the hearty servings topped with fresh cream that Sadie had whipped until it stood at attention.

Once the girls finished their dessert, Dr. Wahler pushed away from the table. "I know it's impolite to leave so soon, but the girls need their sleep, and I have a patient over at the workers' quarters that I promised to look in on this evening. I hope you'll overlook my bad manners." He didn't wait for a response before signaling to Sadie. His housekeeper gathered the girls' belongings and, amidst their protests, ushered them on their way.

Though Audrey didn't want to admit it, not even to herself, she was glad to bid the girls farewell. She figured the men would tease Marshall about the stolen kiss, and maybe a few would be bold enough to tease her, as well. If so, she'd stop their taunts with a frosty retort — if only she could think of one.

Before she could give the matter further thought, Mr. Morley tapped her on the shoulder. "If you have a minute or two, I'd like to speak with you in the parlor."

"Of course, but then I must help Irene with the dishes." She certainly hoped he didn't plan to mention Marshall's stolen kiss. Pleased that she'd thought to give herself a reason to escape in case he wanted to discuss inappropriate behavior among unmarried couples, she followed Mr. Morley into the other room.

After closing the doors, he gestured toward the chairs on the other side of the room. "Marshall tells me you had quite a scare today down on the beach. He told me about the men and the boat that you saw while there."

She nodded, her throat suddenly dry. Perhaps he simply wanted to reinforce Marshall's warning about going to the beach. "I've promised Marshall I'll stay close to the house."

"Good." He stared out the window into the darkened sky. No stars shone to light the night. Even the moon had hidden its face behind the clouds. "I believe there are those who want our plans ruined here at Bridal Veil."

She frowned, disliking the thought of danger visiting itself upon Bridal Fair's doorstep. "Surely there need not be any rivalry between Jekyl and Bridal Veil. There are enough wealthy Northerners to fill both resorts."

Besides, if competition for guests was the reason for this subterfuge, wouldn't these same men also target the new hotel in Biscayne? If her boarders got wind of this, she feared they'd want to arm themselves. It was bad enough when Aunt Thora had been wielding a shotgun; she didn't want men sitting around her dining room table wearing guns.

"You're absolutely correct. I'm sure both islands will have waiting lists long before the doors open." He glanced at the door and leaned a bit closer. "The thing is, I'm not sure this has anything to do with rivalry. The more I dig into the matter, the more I'm wondering if it has something to do with a personal grudge." He rubbed his jaw. "Problem is, I can't determine if this is aimed at me or at one of the other investors in our consortium. That makes it doubly hard to figure out why it's happening. Heaven knows there's not a member of the consortium who hasn't made an enemy or two. Could be any one of us."

"I don't know if I can be of any help, but I'll keep my ears open, and if I hear anything, you can be sure I'll let you or Marshall know."

"Thank you, Audrey. By the way, I seem to have misplaced my pocket watch. Have you or Irene seen anything of it while cleaning?"

"No, but I'll let Irene know you've misplaced it." She pushed up from the chair and strode toward the door.

As she reached for the handle, Mr. Morley said, "Marshall's a good man, Audrey. You can trust him — even if he does steal an occasional kiss."

Audrey glanced over her shoulder and grinned. "I'll remember that. Good night, Mr. Morley."

She hurried to the kitchen, surprised when

she didn't see Irene at the sink. Some of the dishes had been washed, but others remained stacked on the table. She heard conversation drifting from Thora's bedroom and she tiptoed to the doorway. The old woman lay in her bed smiling at Irene. "You be sure and remember everything I'm tellin' you. There's men that make good husbands, and there's those you'd never want putting their shoes alongside your bed. Make sure you find you a man who fears the Lord and loves the South — you can't go wrong if you do those two things."

Irene chuckled and agreed. "I'm sure you're right. I thought you asked me to come in and read the Bible to you. Instead, you've spent the last half hour telling me how to find a proper husband."

Thora pointed a wobbly finger in Irene's direction. "Finding a husband is important. I know it and so does the good Lord. He sent Audrey a good man in Mr. Graham — even if he does have some Northern blood — and He'll send you one, too. Now, get my Bible and commence to reading. Start with Proverbs. Lots of good lessons in there."

Audrey was surprised but pleased with Aunt Thora's comment. She smiled at the two women. They'd developed a love and understanding for each other that warmed her heart. Irene had certainly managed to soften Aunt Thora, or maybe it was just her illness that had softened her. Either way, they'd become friends. Audrey backed away from the door. She'd finish up the dishes and let the two of them enjoy some time together.

Chapter 25

The next morning the sun was slow to rise from the bank of heavy clouds hanging low on the horizon. During the early morning, the cold and warm fronts had joined together out in the Atlantic, and the mixture of the two had proved a strong deterrent to sunlight. Audrey hung a dish towel on a row of pegs her father had pounded into the wall near the sink. She traced her fingers across one of the wooden pegs, remembering how he'd hit his thumb while finishing the job. Forcing back the lump that started to rise in her throat, she lifted the worn cotton apron from around her neck and slung it over a peg before she walked into Thora's bedroom.

"You awake, Aunt Thora?"

"You ever gonna learn to knock on a door?" The old woman's raspy retort was half welcome, half reproach. Aunt Thora had always been a stickler about the knocking-on-doors rule, but Audrey had been more of a poke-your-head-in-and-announce-yourself kind of child, and she hadn't changed when she became an adult. With a gnarly finger, Thora gestured toward the window. "Open those drapes while you're in here." She gasped for another breath before she continued. "I need some sunlight in this room."

There wasn't any sun outside to brighten the room, but Audrey tied back the drapes as well as the sheer curtains that hung beneath the heavy damask. "That any better?" She arched over the bed and brushed a kiss on Thora's sunken cheek.

The old woman turned toward the window. "Not much, but anything's better than nothing." Her pale lips quivered in the attempt at a smile.

"I suppose that's true about most everything," Audrey said as she folded into the overstuffed chair that had been pulled along one side of the bed.

Wispy strands of Thora's white hair danced about as she shook her head. "It's not true about men. A woman shouldn't settle for just any pair of britches that comes strolling down the road." She tapped her knobby finger on the side of her head. "You need to use your noggin, and a lot of prayer helps, too. A smart woman will seek God in all things, but especially when she's getting ready to marry."

If Audrey didn't know better, she'd think Marshall had been talking to Aunt Thora, but that wasn't possible. Except for the doctor, Thora wouldn't let any unaccompanied man visit her bedroom — not even Reverend Nichols, the preacher from Biscayne. "Is that what you did, Aunt Thora? Wait for the man God sent you?"

"No. I forced the man God sent me to wait a long time before I'd marry him. Regretted it, too." Her eyelids drooped shut, and Audrey thought she'd likely fallen asleep. There was little doubt Aunt Thora was slipping. Dr. Wahler had warned she didn't have much longer for this world, and Thora's frail appearance was testament to the doctor's prediction. Audrey shifted in the chair, and Thora's eyes popped back open. "You leaving already? You just sat down."

"I thought you were sleeping, and I didn't want to disturb you."

"I was resting my eyes, not sleeping. Where was I?"

"You were telling me about forcing your husband to wait before you'd marry him."

"Oh yes. Well, Nathaniel — that's my

406

husband's name, Nathaniel Homer Lund — he'd been after me to marry him from the time I was eighteen years old. We met at a coming-out party for one of the Savannah debutantes. He was smitten with me. Even got my daddy's permission to call on me and started talkin' marriage after about six months. Land alive, when he proposed, I was beside myself. I didn't want nothing to do with marriage. Thought it would be too confining and keep me from the exciting things in life." She pointed to the water glass. "I told him so, too."

Audrey held the glass to Thora's lips and waited until she'd sipped the water. "And what did he say to that?" She put the glass back on the table and sat back down in the chair.

"He said he was gonna keep courting me till I gave in and married him." A raspy chuckle rumbled deep in her throat. "My Nathaniel sure was a determined fellow, and I'm mighty thankful for that." Once again she closed her eyes.

"You want to rest, Aunt Thora?"

"No, I don't want to rest. I'm telling you something important, girl. You need to listen to what I'm saying."

"I'm listening," Audrey said.

"My biggest regret in life is that I wasted

all those years I coulda been Nathaniel's wife. Being single didn't show me no adventure at all — not one thing that compared to my years of marriage. Turned out that marriage to Nathaniel fulfilled everything I ever hoped for. Well, most everything. We wanted children of our own, but we never could have any. Both of us was sad about that, but the good Lord put other children in our lives to love." She opened her eyes a little wider and reached for Audrey's hand. "You were always one of my favorites."

Audrey traced her finger across the tissue-thin skin of Thora's hand. "And I have always loved you, too." A knot of pain settled in Audrey's chest. She'd barely had time to absorb the death of her father. She wasn't prepared to lose Thora, too.

Thora lifted her hand from Audrey's and pointed to the window. "Them live oaks out there are anchored by roots that run deep into the ground so they can weather the storms that sometimes batter these islands — the roots hold them fast in the ground. Unlike those trees, God didn't give us roots to hold us in place. You know why that is, Audrey?"

"He wanted us to have our freedom?"

"That's true enough. He lets us make our own choices. And if we choose to place our trust and faith in Him, He'll be our anchor when we're flooded by the storms of life." She inhaled a raspy breath. "You need to remember that, Audrey. No matter what happens, your faith in God will carry you through. My life is proof of that. He's given me the strength to live without Nathaniel and taught me to accept the aggression of those Northerners. And thanks to you, the Lord even showed me I could live under the same roof with Yankees."

Audrey chuckled. The Lord had certainly had His hands full dealing with Thora, her shotgun, and the Yankees. "And you've done a fine job of it — at least once you accepted the fact that they were here to stay."

Moments later, a ray of sunlight broke through the clouds and stretched across the room, with the brightness coming to rest on Thora's pillow. Audrey jumped to her feet to pull the curtain, but Thora waved her back to her chair. "You jest remember to trust the Lord with your life and look to Him when you're makin' decisions. He'll guide you, if you let Him. That was my biggest downfall. I was always wantin' to tug against the pull of His hand when He wanted to lead me down the right path. Don't you do that, Audrey. You listen to your old aunt Thora. Maybe I wasn't right about the Yankees, but I'm right about this."

"Marshall asked me to marry him. I want to say yes, but I'm so afraid." She hadn't planned to tell Thora, but her tongue got ahead of her, and the words slipped out.

Thora chuckled. "Life wouldn't be no fun if there wasn't moments of frantic anticipation. You jest remember that the Lord will take your hand and lead you in the right direction — if you let Him. Marshall's a good man. You should go right ahead and say yes."

The old woman's eyes closed, and soon soft snores confirmed she'd truly faded into a deep sleep. Audrey remained in the chair, her thoughts swirling with Thora's words. She did need to increase her trust in God — and she needed to figure out exactly how she'd do that. *Ask and I'll increase your faith.* The words echoed in her mind like a distant drumbeat — over and over — until she finally bowed her head and silently asked God to increase her faith and provide her with the ability to trust Him in all things.

The mild scent of the river carried on a breeze that helped cool and refresh the men who were working at a feverish pace on the resort buildings. Although Frank continued with his lackadaisical attitude, at least he'd remained at the work site since Mr. Morley's return. Today, Marshall had assigned Frank and his men to the far end of the site, a short distance from the cabin being used as an office. After making his rounds to inspect the work and to answer questions, Marshall moved near the perimeter of the construction area. He stopped beneath the shade of a live oak and let the late afternoon breeze wash over him like cooling rain. Pushing his cap back on his head, he let his thoughts wander to Audrey, how he hoped he could win her heart, how he hoped she'd soon believe he could be trusted, and how he hoped she'd say yes to his marriage proposal. He was dwelling on that final thought when a flash of movement near the cabin captured his attention.

He shaded his eyes and strained for a better look. Someone was outside the office. Careful to keep his movements slow and easy, he lowered his cap. Shoving his hands into his pockets, he sauntered in the direction of the office, being careful not to stare at the cabin. He tipped his head only far enough to gain another glimpse, but the man had disappeared.

From this distance, there was no way to be certain whether the man had entered the cabin or if he'd discovered the door locked

411

and gone away. Marshall hadn't gone much further when one of the workers called his name. "Where you going, Mr. Graham? We supposed to go back to work or not?"

Marshall came to an immediate halt. "Of course you're supposed to go back to work. I need to check with someone about a shipment of supplies. I'll be back shortly." He increased his casual saunter to a long stride. Hopefully the exchange hadn't alerted anyone else to watch his movements.

He made his way to a thicket near the cabin and stooped down behind the prickly growth. Keeping his breathing shallow, he trained his eyes on the shack. The door was ajar. He placed his palm on his chest and tried to calm himself. He didn't want to make a wrong move and alert a possible intruder, but he didn't want to make a fool of himself, either. *Best to wait,* he thought. *Just stay quiet and watch.* Sweat rolled down his forehead and along the sides of his face as he kept out of sight in a crouched position. His legs cramped and he longed for a breeze to dry the perspiration burning his eyes.

Just when he'd come to the conclusion that he could no longer remain in the uncomfortable angles he'd forced upon his body, the office door inched open. The muscles along his back rippled with tension, and he instinctively doubled his large hands into tight fists. "Come on," he whispered. "Show yourself."

Marshall's murmured request was soon answered. Casting a glance first in one direction and then the other, a figure sidled along the edge of the door. Keeping his focus upon the emerging figure, Marshall clamped his lips together until his jaw ached. The man waited to be certain there was no one in sight and then revealed himself. Marshall's breath caught in his throat. It was the same man who had been talking with Ted Uptegrove in Biscayne.

Obviously, word of the fake change in plans had leaked, and someone was taking the bait. Head bowed, the stranger didn't waste any time getting away from the cabin. Using a tree for balance, Marshall unfolded his legs and pushed to an upright position. He didn't want to lose sight of the man, but his leg had gone to sleep, and when he stood, it nearly gave out.

Still hobbling, he pushed through the underbrush, unwilling to wait until he regained feeling in his leg. No doubt the man would double back around until he could pick up one of two paths: either the short one that led to the river or the longer one to the ocean. If he was going to capture sight of the intruder, Marshall needed to pick up his pace before the man selected which path he would take.

He stopped short when he arrived at the spot where the stranger would need to make a choice. "Where is he?" The only answer to Marshall's muttered question was the melodic chirp of buntings as they called to one another. He stopped and listened, straining his eyes in every direction. There! He caught a glimpse of movement. The stranger was taking the path leading to the ocean. No doubt the intruder had discovered there was less likelihood of being observed on the ocean side. With the construction site much closer to the river, he'd obviously decided that by skirting along the ocean side of Bridal Veil, he could come around the tip and back to the river, where he'd be far enough away to go undetected.

In all likelihood the stranger had hidden his boat near the same spot where Audrey had seen the men when she'd picnicked with the twins. Once he'd taken to the ocean path, the man slowed his pace, no doubt confident his venture had been successful. A sense of satisfaction swelled in Marshall's chest as he continued to follow at a distance. Once the stranger arrived at the beach, Marshall hunkered down in the undergrowth while doing his best to maintain a lookout. He expected the stranger to pull a boat out of hiding and head for the water. Instead, he remained near the shore. Without warning, another man appeared and closed the short distance between the two of them.

Marshall edged forward, hoping to gain a better view of the second man. What was going on, and who was this other man? It wasn't Ted Uptegrove or Frank Baker — possibly it was a worker from Jekyl Island. Marshall held his breath, expecting to see the lanky stranger pull paperwork from his jacket.

He didn't hear a thing before a forceful blow sent him face down into the brush and sand.

CHAPTER 26

The ocean lapped against the shore in a melodic rhythm that lulled Marshall in and out of consciousness, but as his senses alerted, he forced himself to take stock, to open his eyes, to summon his waning strength. How long had he been there? Hours? Days? He tried to push the haziness from his mind and recollect what had happened. Why he was lying near the beach. Why his body ached. Why his head throbbed.

A full array of stars shone from the heavens, and shafts of moonlight glistened on the sandy beach. His body was arced across a fallen tree limb, where he'd apparently fallen. While he'd remained in a lifeless sleep, the awkward curve of his body and the unforgiving timber had combined to punish his body. He groaned in a feeble attempt to move his limbs or persuade his muscles to flex.

"Please, Lord." The plea he whispered toward the starry heavens was slurred and muted, but God knew he needed help and knew he trusted help would come. *The Lord is my strength and my shield; my heart trusted in him, and I am helped.* Marshall silently repeated the words until he finally mustered the strength to push himself off the merciless piece of timber that had served as his resting place. Forcing all thought of pain from his mind, he pushed into a sitting position and leaned against the offending timber. Circling his arm to the back of his head, he touched the base of his skull. His fingers rested in a tacky glob of blood.

Beginning to recall what had happened, he reached into his pocket for his handkerchief. He'd been hiding on the beach, watching two strangers. He tried to calculate how much time had passed, but he had no idea of the time. It could be nine o'clock, or it could be midnight. Either way, he needed to get back to Bridal Fair and tend to the gash on his head. He patted the ground around him until his hand landed on a thick branch, and he pulled it close. Using the branch as a support, he forced himself up. He had to get back. *One step at a time,* he told himself as he forced one unsteady foot in front of the other. His head pounded in unrelenting objection to his movement.

He stopped several times and rested against live oaks as he slowly made his way back to Bridal Fair. Finally seeing light inside the windows of the mansion, he cast aside the branch he'd used as a crutch. Never before had he been so thankful to arrive anywhere. "Thank you, Lord," he said, nearing the front porch.

As he climbed the steps, he knew he shouldn't have cast aside the makeshift crutch. Grasping a pillar at the landing, he steadied himself before opening the front door. The toe of his shoe caught as he crossed the threshold, and he grabbed the doorjamb to steady himself. On wobbly legs, he moved toward the chattering voices in the kitchen.

"Why weren't you at supper?"

He'd been concentrating on forcing his feet to do as he bid and hadn't heard Audrey come into the dining room. His gait shifted in a reckless pattern as he continued unsteadily toward her. Not wanting to alarm her, he forced a grim smile. "Don't worry, I'm going to be all right."

She covered her mouth with the back of her hand and shook her head. "Worry?" Her eyebrows dipped low on her forehead, and her lips pressed into a scowl. "If I remember

418

correctly, it will take about ten hours of sleep for the effects of the alcohol to wear off. Where did you drink your supper?"

A combination of nausea and dizziness assailed Marshall. He didn't have the strength to argue with her. Once again, Audrey was jumping to conclusions. He jerked one of the dining room chairs away from the table and collapsed onto the tapestry-covered seat. "I need a doctor." His shoulders dropped forward, and he rested his head on the cool wood of the dining table.

"Oh, Marshall! You're injured." Audrey touched the back of his head, and he flinched. "Irene, go for Dr. Wahler — and hurry. Tell him Marshall's been injured, and he's bleeding. Run!"

He heard the panic in Audrey's voice and wondered if the gash was worse than he'd imagined.

"I'm going to get some wet towels and see what I can do before the doctor gets here. Don't move." Her tone was soothing and kind — now that she realized he wasn't drunk.

She didn't need to worry about his moving. Right now, he just wanted to rest his head and have the pain subside. He could hear Thora speaking to Audrey and heard the dripping of water as she wrung excess water from a towel.

Her footsteps were light as she approached him. "I'm going to dab lightly to clean off the wound, and then I'll put a clean wet towel in place. I'm not certain what else to do, but I'm sure Dr. Wahler will be here soon."

He bit his lower lip while she cleaned the area. When she finally announced she'd done all she could, he let his muscles relax. She placed a clean cloth on the injured area and gave him another damp towel to place on his forehead. The coolness of the towel spread across his brow and strengthened him. "Thank you. Perhaps you should have considered nursing as a profession." He held the cloth in place and slowly lifted his head. "Seems you've had more than your share to deal with."

She knelt down beside his chair. "Are you feeling some better? You gave me a terrible fright when you came in."

He forced a smile. "You thought I was drunk. After all we've talked about, I don't know how you could even imagine such a thing, Audrey." He didn't want to hurt her, yet she needed to realize that her behavior pained him. After all their talk of childhoods darkened by alcoholic fathers, how could she think he would imbibe?

"I jumped to conclusions again, and I owe you an apology. I don't know what I can say that will justify my outrageous behavior, but when I saw you staggering through the dining room, horrible memories of my father's drinking days returned in a flash. I spoke before thinking." She tipped her head closer. "I'm trying so hard to overcome my suspicious nature, Marshall, but I can't tell you that I'll ever change. Trust is difficult for me. Every time I think I can trust someone, the person does something that destroys the little bit of hope that I've had. I'm sure you can't understand. I'm not asking you to, but I do want you to know that I'm sorry for wrongfully accusing you."

Marshall looked deep into her eyes and saw pain and fear. "I do understand, Audrey. I've told you how it grieved me to watch my mother suffer over the same issues you're still suffering with — the broken promises, the fear of trust. I've felt them all myself, too. All I'm asking is a chance to prove myself. Don't judge me by other people or by your past. Instead, let me prove that you can trust me."

A tear rolled down her cheek. "No, Marshall. You've already proven yourself over and over. I'm the one who is at fault in this, and I'm begging for your forgiveness." She clutched his hand. "If you'll still have me, I'd be honored to marry you."

Mouth agape, he stared at her, unable to push words from his lips. His tongue simply wouldn't move. Had he heard her correctly, or had the blow to his head affected his hearing? By the time he regained his ability to speak, Irene came rushing into the room with her skirts flying.

She pointed her thumb over her shoulder and then bent forward to catch her breath. "The doctor's right behind me. And Mr. Morley, too."

She'd barely uttered the breathless report when Dr. Wahler and Victor Morley hurried into the house. Dr. Wahler immediately took charge. His leather medical bag landed on the table with a thump. "I'll check you as soon as I wash my hands. Irene, boil some water, please."

While the doctor washed his hands in the other room, Mr. Morley pulled another chair close. "Do you feel well enough to explain what happened?"

"My memory is pretty clear about what happened, but I sure don't know who's to blame for this gash on my head or the bruises on my side."

Dr. Wahler returned and ordered Marshall to place his head on the table. "Use your

422

arm to cushion your head and hold still while I work. I'm not sure if you're going to need some stitches in the wound or if it only needs to be cleaned and bandaged."

With his forehead cupped in the crook of his arm, Marshall described the incident he'd observed on the beach. Mr. Morley interrupted with several questions, and Marshall was glad for the diversion. It made him think about something other than the doctor probing the wound on his head.

Unfortunately, the doctor declared the gash would require several sutures in order to properly heal. Irene gasped and immediately departed while Audrey and Mr. Morley remained for the procedure. When he finished, the doctor placed a clean bandage over the sutures and instructed Audrey to watch for any seepage and replace the dressing as needed.

The doctor returned his instruments to the black leather bag. "I'll remove the stitches when you've properly healed, Marshall."

"Would you care for a cup of coffee, Dr. Wahler?"

Audrey glanced at the clock as she spoke, and the doctor followed her gaze. "The hour is getting late, but thank you for the offer. I think I'd better get home." He snapped the metal clasp on his bag and lifted it from the table. "Remember, if he has any problems with his vision or if he can't be roused in the morning, you must send someone to fetch me." The doctor spoke to Audrey as if Marshall weren't in the room.

Marshall cleared his throat. "If I'm not downstairs at my usual time in the morning, you should probably tell one of the other men to rouse me, Audrey."

The doctor chuckled. "I suppose that would be more appropriate." He picked up his hat and waved it in the air. "No need to come to the door. I can see myself out."

Marshall straightened in the chair and exhaled a groan. "Leaning over that table didn't help the pain in my side."

Victor frowned. "He struck you in the side, as well? You should have had the doctor look. You might have some broken ribs."

"I don't think anything is broken." He pushed to his feet and rubbed his side. "I think I would be more comfortable in the parlor."

"Maybe you should go to bed and get some rest. I don't want you involved in this any further. There's no telling how far those men will go. They'll be closely watching you now. I'll look for someone else that I can trust to keep his eyes and ears open." Mr.

Morley's brows furrowed. "It's probably best if we keep this incident to ourselves, for now. Marshall, do you have someone in mind that I could count on at this point?"

In two steps, Audrey was at Mr. Morley's side. "I can do it."

Both men turned toward her. Both had the same response. "No!"

"But I want to help."

"I am ordering you to stay out of this," Mr. Morley said. "It is far too dangerous. You see what has happened to Marshall. I don't even want to think about what those men would do to you."

"Those men will suspect anyone who shows allegiance to you, Mr. Morley, but they would never suspect me. I'm sure I could be of much more use to you than any man at the construction site. Besides, you know you can trust me, while you can't be absolutely certain about any of them."

Mr. Morley shook his head. "There is absolutely no way you will convince me that you should become involved in this, Audrey. You have heard my last word on this matter. You are to tend to Bridal Fair and the boarders — nothing more."

Marshall pressed his lips together and waited for her answer. It took far too long, but she finally agreed.

■ ■ ■ ■

The following morning, Audrey's heart fluttered with pleasure when she spotted Marshall coming down the stairs with the other boarders. Either he was putting on a good show for the men or he was feeling much better. She wasn't certain which, but she hoped it was the latter.

"What happened to your head, Marshall?" Harry Fenton asked, peering down the length of the table.

Marshall pulled out a chair and sat down across from Ted Uptegrove. "I took an unexpected fall and needed a few stitches. Nothing serious."

Ted glanced at Frank before he met Marshall's gaze. "Maybe you need to be more careful."

"Thanks for the advice. I plan to do exactly that." Marshall waited until all the men were seated. "Let's pray." He bowed his head and offered a prayer of thanks for their breakfast. The custom of praying before meals had passed to him upon Boyd's death. None of the others had shown interest in assuming a leadership role when it came to prayer.

Audrey lifted the platter of eggs from the

sideboard and handed it to Marshall. The fact that she hadn't seen him holding his side or taking extra care as he sat down gave her hope. She wanted to ask if he'd slept well, but such questioning would surely embarrass him — and her, if the men noted her display of concern and teased him.

Once the other men had filtered from the room and headed toward the front door, Audrey motioned Marshall into the kitchen. "How are you feeling this morning? I hope you slept well."

He stepped to one side, permitting Irene a clear path from the dining room to the sink. "My side is still a little sore, but nothing I can't manage. And my head didn't give me any problem unless I rolled onto my back."

"I better check the bandage to be certain it doesn't need to be changed. I don't want Dr. Wahler thinking I've been negligent in my duties. I don't want him to replace me with Irene or Aunt Thora." Audrey pulled a tall stool to the window, where she'd have better light.

"No need to worry. I won't let that happen." He settled on the stool.

Her stomach flipped when he looked up and gave her a wink. "It might be best if you remained at the house today and gave yourself additional time to heal."

"Why?" He reached for the bandage, and she pushed his hand away. "Have the stitches come out?"

"No. It looks fine, but it might be best if you didn't rush back to work right away."

He chuckled. "I promise I'll be careful, if that will make you feel better." After a quick glance, he leaned forward and stole a kiss.

Heat rushed to her cheeks like a fire raging through underbrush. She tapped his chest with her finger. "That isn't acceptable behavior."

"No? Then I'd better see that I perform in a more acceptable manner."

In one easy movement, he swept her into his arms and covered her lips with a tender kiss that deepened with warmth and intensity until her knees began to buckle. Had he not held her tight against his chest, she would have dropped to the floor.

"Marshall." His name escaped her lips in low murmur.

"Audrey! Marshall!" Irene stood in the doorway, mouth agape. "You better not let Aunt Thora see you." Irene jutted her chin toward the bedroom door, and the two of them jumped apart as if Aunt Thora's shotgun had blasted through the room.

Weeks ago, they had moved Thora's bed

near the windows to permit a view of the outdoors. From her new vantage point in the bedroom, she could also see a portion of the kitchen. Audrey and Marshall stood directly in her line of view.

Marshall grinned. "She must be asleep."

"I'm not asleep, and if I didn't approve, you'd already have a round of buckshot warmin' your backside, Marshall Graham."

"Aunt Thora! That's not very nice." Audrey covered her mouth to contain a squelch of laughter.

"Nobody ever accused me of being nice, but I am truthful."

Marshall peeked around the doorjamb. "Sounds like you're feeling better today, Miss Thora."

"Good enough to see you're stealing Audrey's heart. You best be careful with it or you'll rue the day you ever set foot on Georgia soil." She gave him a wink, but her voice lost some of its strength. "These girls have chores, and you're holdin' up their progress."

"I'm leaving. You have my word." Marshall motioned to Audrey to follow him. "She seems to be getting better, don't you think?" he asked as they stood by the front door.

"Some days are better than others, but Dr. Wahler doesn't hold out much hope for a recovery." She grasped Marshall's hand. "Please promise that if you begin to feel weak or have any other problems you'll come back to the house and rest."

He nodded his agreement and then left for the work site. Audrey gathered her cleaning supplies from the storage closet beneath the steps and hurried upstairs. She needed to pick up the soiled bedding and get it to Irene so she could begin the wash. Then she'd return to dust and sweep the rooms. They cleaned the rooms once a week. If the men wanted their rooms cleaned more often, they knew where to locate the supplies. So far, none of them had shown any interest in additional cleaning.

After Irene headed off to the washhouse, Audrey peeked in on Thora and was pleased to discover the old woman napping. Had she been awake, there would have been questions to answer, and she wanted to finish cleaning the rooms before undergoing Aunt Thora's quiz about her recent acceptance of Marshall's marriage proposal.

She completed the first two rooms before moving on to the third, all the while pondering last night's conversations and what had happened to Marshall. She shivered as she recalled Marshall staggering into the house. Why would anyone do such a thing to him?

Even Mr. Morley couldn't discern a clear motive for what had happened.

Broom in hand, she stepped into Ted Uptegrove's room and set to work. Each time she cleaned the rooms, Audrey was thankful they'd removed her grandmother's velvety Wilton carpets. The dirt and grime of the construction workers would have ruined the beautiful carpets in short order. Now, with only a small braided rug beside each bed, sweeping the wooden floors didn't take long. Bending sideways, she shoved the broom beneath the bed.

When the bristles hit against something hard, she tried again. Annoyed that Mr. Uptegrove had broken rule number twelve and stored some of his belongings under his bed, she dropped to her knees to investigate. With her head resting on the floor, she could see an object pushed against the baseboard near the center of the bed. It would be difficult to reach, but she flattened onto her stomach and stretched out until she could wrap two fingers around the object and pull it closer.

Drawing the object from beneath the bed, she gasped. A hammer — with a broken handle. She pressed her lips together and examined suspicious markings that dotted the head of the hammer. Markings that appeared to be flecks of blood.

CHAPTER 27

Throughout the night and next morning, Audrey gave much thought to the hammer that she'd tucked beneath a stack of blankets stored in an oversized trunk at the foot of her bed. She'd planned to speak with Mr. Morley, but it seemed there was never a good opportunity. He was either gone from the house or in the company of other boarders. And telling Marshall wasn't an option. Mr. Morley had given strict orders that Marshall remove himself from the investigation. She didn't want to do anything that would cause Marshall to go against his superior. In truth, Mr. Morley had been adamant that she distance herself from the investigation, as well. But given the circumstances, she thought he would be thankful for her help. And Marshall would, too — if everything turned out well.

When Dr. Wahler had arrived to examine Marshall's head early that morning, she'd inquired about the twins. "They're hoping you'll have time for a visit today."

Her mind raced with ideas. "Why don't I come by and get them after lunch? It's a beautiful day, and we can go for a walk."

"I'm sure they would enjoy some time in the fresh air. I'll tell Sadie to expect you."

Marshall had already told her to stay away from the beach, but she might be forced to disobey him this one time. And if the twins didn't tell, he'd never know.

Throughout the morning she'd formulated a plan. When they'd finished the lunch dishes, she peeked in on Aunt Thora and then returned to the kitchen. "Aunt Thora is sleeping. Would you like to come along with me and take the twins for a walk?"

Irene's brow puckered. "Do you think we should leave Thora alone?"

"She's been feeling some better these last few days, and she's sleeping now. I told her earlier that we might take the girls for a walk, and she said for us to go ahead. Besides, we won't be gone long. We'll go for a short stroll and then come back here, where they can play in the yard."

"Or the henhouse," Irene said with a grin. "Let me get my shawl and bonnet."

The twins were waiting on the front step of their cabin and Sadie was sitting on the narrow porch with her mending basket. "We thought you were never going to come and get us," Josie said as she jumped from the step. Brown curls bobbing, Julie followed and grabbed Audrey's hand, while Josie drew near to Irene.

Audrey greeted Sadie, and though she'd planned to visit with the woman for a few minutes, the girls were eager to depart. Sadie waved them on. "We can talk when you bring them home." She pointed her darning needle in the girls' direction. "You two mind your manners and do what Miss Audrey and Miss Irene say."

The twosome danced from foot to foot as they promised to behave. With Audrey and Julie in the lead, they took to the path. Audrey had been contemplating the route she wanted to take and knew where Marshall had been hiding when he'd been struck from behind. After finding the broken hammer, she wanted to investigate a bit further. Perhaps she'd see footprints or locate something else that would give her a little more evidence. She couldn't be positive that hammer had anything to do with the attack on Marshall, but it certainly was suspicious that Mr. Uptegrove had a broken hammer under his bed — and that it appeared to be spattered with blood.

"Let's turn down this way," she said, taking the path that would lead to the beach. Marshall had told her to stay away from the beach, but with Irene and both of the girls along, nothing would happen to them. After all, who would assault two adult women and two little girls who could shriek loud enough to pierce an eardrum?

"We going to the beach and find shells, Miss Audrey?" Julie's eyes twinkled with excitement.

"Just for a little while. We can't leave Aunt Thora alone for too long."

Josie hop-skipped to Audrey's other side. "But Marshall said we weren't s'pose to come to the beach anymore. Not unless he was with us."

"I don't think he'll mind, since Irene is with us, too." Audrey patted the girl's hair.

"Ohh." When Josie skipped back to grab Irene's hand, Audrey sighed with relief, thankful the child hadn't pursued the matter.

"Is that what Marshall said?" Irene called.

"It's fine, Irene. There are two of us plus the girls. There won't be any problem." She looked at Irene and was met by an icy stare. Irene wasn't going to prove as adventurous as Audrey had hoped. Well, that was fine. She'd place her in charge of the children

436

while she scoured the area.

When they neared the beach a short time later, Irene took the girls to look for shells while Audrey walked toward an area a short distance away that would have offered Marshall perfect protection. After pushing aside the low-lying branches, she was certain she'd located the exact spot. She stooped down near a thick limb. Leaves and debris were strewn and scattered, a sign that someone had been in the area not long ago. "I'm sure this must be where he fell," she murmured.

Training her eyes on the beach, she realized this would have been the ideal location for Marshall to watch whatever had transpired. It wasn't far and provided a good view. She could see every move Irene and the girls made as they walked on the beach, picking up shells and other treasures washed ashore by the tide. Turning away, she noted several broken branches behind Marshall's hiding place. Audrey crouched low, but as she attempted to move her foot and step into the area, she tripped on a hard object protruding from the underbrush. Her ankle twisted and she groaned.

Reaching down, she massaged the upper portion of the leather boot that covered her ankle. "I need to watch where I'm going," she muttered. She lifted her foot to see what had caused her to slip. At first glance, it appeared to be nothing more than a piece of tree branch, but upon closer examination, she realized exactly what she'd found. Her heart pounded with such fierceness she thought her chest would explode. She turned the piece of wood in her clammy palm. This was the rest of the handle, the other part of the hammer she'd found under Ted Uptegrove's bed. Her mouth was as dry as cotton when she stood and shoved the piece of wood into her pocket.

She took care as she placed weight on her foot. If she hobbled to the beach, there would be too many questions to answer. After several steps, she swiped the leaves and rubble from her skirt. Careful to avoid limping, she straightened her shawl, waving to the girls as she approached.

"I hope you've found some wonderful treasures to take home. We can walk a little farther down the beach, but then we'd best go back to Bridal Fair." When the girls objected, Audrey shook her head. "We can't leave Aunt Thora alone for any longer. We'll come back another day." Either her offer to return at some future date or the remembrance of Sadie's admonition curtailed any further argument from the girls. While the girls chattered about their shells, Audrey drew near to Irene. "I need you to take the girls back to the house while I stop at the construction site. There's something I need to discuss with Mr. Morley. It shouldn't take long."

"So you want me to take care of Thora's needs, mind the two girls, and cook the evening meal? Anything else I should do while you're off visiting with Mr. Morley?" Irene cocked her head at a defiant angle. Irene was usually a sweet girl, but there were times when her sweetness turned sour.

"I said I won't be long, and the most Aunt Thora will likely need is a drink of water. The girls can play in the yard. Tell them to stay in sight of the kitchen windows. They'll do as they're told. You can go into Biscayne next week and enjoy some time away from the island if you'd like."

Irene's features softened. "In that case, I suppose I can handle everything for a while, but you'd best be back before time to serve supper. Otherwise, you'll hear complaints from the men, as well as from me."

After kissing each of the girls on the cheek and promising to return home shortly, Audrey hurried toward the work area. Circling to the far side, she approached the cabin the men used as an office and tapped on the door. When there was no answer, she pushed open the door and stepped inside. A shaft of light reflected through a small window and slanted across the paper-strewn desk, but there was no sign of anyone. She retreated from the office and scanned the area for any sign of Mr. Morley or Marshall. Her presence here would be questioned, so she had hoped to avoid being seen, but Harry Fenton waved in her direction.

There was no reason to hide any longer. She waved in return and waited until he drew near. "Have you seen Mr. Morley or Marshall?"

"Nope. Not sure where they are."

Another worker standing nearby hitched a thumb over his shoulder. "Mr. Morley was over talking to Mr. Baker about an hour ago, but I don't know where they went. Never did see Marshall since we left the breakfast table."

After one final look, she thanked the men and headed toward Bridal Fair. Irene wouldn't be quick to forgive if Audrey didn't arrive back home as promised. Taking long strides, she entered a path on the far side of the construction area. Mossy veils hanging from the live oaks swayed in a gentle breeze as she wrapped her fingers around the hammer handle and withdrew it from her pocket. She clutched it tight in her hand. If only Mr. Morley had been at the work site. Lowering her head against the mounting breeze, she fixed her gaze on the dirt path.

Moments later, with a thump that took her breath away and sent the hammer handle flying, she came to an abrupt halt. Her breath caught as she looked into the face of Ted Uptegrove. "W-wwhat are you doing here?" She hadn't seen him step into her path.

His eyes darted to the wooden handle on the ground and then back at her. A flash of recognition shone in his eyes before he rushed to grab the incriminating piece of evidence. He knew she'd discovered the rest of the hammer in his room. Fear pounded in her ears like a beating drum and set off an inner alarm. In spite of her aching ankle, fright sent her racing toward home. Leaves and twigs crunched beneath her feet as they pounded the dry earth. She had to get home before he caught her. Her chest heaved, and her lungs contracted as they cried out for air. She opened her mouth and gasped, afraid to look over her shoulder, afraid to listen for his footsteps, afraid to slow down.

When she neared the back door of Bridal Fair, she slowed her pace and peeked behind her. There was no sign of Ted Uptegrove, but that didn't mean he wasn't nearby. She swallowed several gulps of air before attempting to slow her breathing.

"Audrey! What's wrong? Has something happened?" Dr. Wahler's brow puckered as he came down the steps.

"I was just hurrying home to check on Aunt Thora," she said. Right now she didn't want to talk to anybody except Marshall or Mr. Morley. Trying to explain to Dr. Wahler would be impossible.

"I just stopped by to check on Thora myself. Sadie said I should take the girls home with me so you wouldn't have to fuss with them any longer. Irene is giving them a cookie to sustain them on their way." He glanced back toward the kitchen. "Thora seems to be doing a little better. She's resting easy, but as I said, don't get your hopes up. I've seen lots of patients rally for a brief time."

"I understand. I do thank you for being so attentive to her. It means a great deal to me."

She longed to go inside, but the doctor continued to chat until the girls scurried outdoors, holding a cookie in each hand.

"Only one before supper," he said to them. "Thank you again for your help with the girls, Audrey, and don't hesitate to send for me if Thora takes a turn for the worse."

She stood at the steps as the doctor and his daughters waved their good-byes, then turned toward the porch. At the sound of men's voices, she swiveled around, her heart racing. Clutching the porch rail, she prepared to run inside. If necessary, she'd locate Aunt Thora's shotgun, but moments later, she sighed with relief when she caught sight of Marshall and Mr. Morley.

Clasping a hand to her bodice, she stepped forward to meet Marshall. "I'm so glad to see the two of you. Come inside. You're not going to believe what I have to tell you."

With their coffee cups in hand, the men sat at the table and listened as she told of her encounter with Ted Uptegrove. It wasn't until she'd completed the tale that she noticed the twitch in Marshall's jaw.

"Why didn't you wait until one of us came home? Why did you have to take matters into your own hands once again? I asked you not to go to the beach, yet you ignored me. And you took the twins and Irene along." Marshall's nostrils flared as he pressed his lips together in a hard line.

"I did make an attempt to speak with Mr. Morley, but he was never alone. I was worried about your injury and didn't want you to become upset. I took the girls along because I didn't think anyone would be foolish enough to bother two women with children."

When Marshall opened his mouth, Mr. Morley waved him to silence. "You can't be certain what these men would do if they feared being recognized, Audrey. And you and Irene would be no match for them. And those little girls . . ." His eyes glistened and he shook his head. "As a father, I can only imagine the pain it would cause Dr. Wahler if something should happen to them."

Audrey bowed her head, now ashamed she'd been so foolhardy. "I only hoped to help," she whispered.

Mr. Morley placed his hand atop her wrist. "I know. But please — leave this to us. You tend to Bridal Fair, and we'll take care of finding who's behind all of this."

When Ted didn't appear for supper that night, Mr. Morley settled his gaze upon Frank and nodded toward the empty chair. "Where's Ted this evening? Hope he hasn't taken ill."

Frank's eyes darkened, but he hiked his shoulder with a nonchalant shrug. "I sent him to Biscayne to check on some orders and told him to take several days and see if there might be any skilled workers arriving."

Mr. Morley raised his eyebrows. "You sent him? Since when are you in charge of such things?"

Frank shifted in his chair. "We'll need at least one more capable woodworker for all the detail work in the rooms. I heard there might be some men arriving from up north this week."

"Don't take it upon yourself to send anyone to Biscayne. You're not giving the orders around here, Frank. Am I clear?"

Frank's only response was a grunt, but Audrey was relieved to know Ted was off the island, for she was certain he was responsible for Marshall's injuries.

CHAPTER 28

For the past two nights sleep had eluded Audrey, and it seemed tonight would be no different. Tired of tossing about, she pushed aside the bedcovers and paced the short distance between bed and wall until she could no longer abide the tiny space. Slipping a wrapper over her nightgown, she tiptoed into the kitchen and out the back door. If she was going to pace, she wanted the full length of the wraparound porch rather than the short distance her bedroom provided. A full moon filtered its glow through the mossy trees, and a host of stars twinkled overhead.

"Such a beautiful night." Her words were a mere whisper as she circled and returned to the rear door for the second time, yet restlessness continued to nip at her heels. Dropping to one of the wicker chairs, she hunched forward and wrapped her arms around her waist. A shadowy figure crossed the path and then another. She squinted and leaned forward as the hairs along the back of her neck prickled to attention.

For a brief moment, she considered rushing down the steps to see if she could get a better view, but the warning from Mr. Morley and Marshall held her in check. She would go upstairs and awaken Marshall. Careful not to let the door bang behind her, Audrey hurried through the kitchen while uttering a prayer of thanks for the moonlight that shone through the lacy curtains. One of the steps creaked beneath her weight, and she stopped to listen. When no one stirred, she continued up the stairs. Her heart pounded as she lightly rapped on Marshall's door. At least the rooms Marshall and Mr. Morley occupied were far enough away from the other men that she doubted anyone else would hear her knocking.

She tapped again. "Marshall!" She hissed his name and tried once more. There wasn't time to stand in the hallway much longer, and she couldn't barge into his room. Glancing down the hall, she hurried to Mr. Morley's room and tapped on the door, quietly calling his name. When he didn't respond after several attempts, she returned to Marshall's door.

Her hand stopped in midair as a loud

crack echoed in the distance. Beads of perspiration dampened her hand, and a knot of fear settled in her stomach. Were her ears playing tricks on her or had she truly heard a gunshot? She couldn't take a chance "Marshall!" When he didn't answer, she turned the doorknob and peeked into the room. Slivers of moonlight danced through the curtains and onto the empty bed.

Her fear mounted as she returned to Mr. Morley's room, knocked, and then opened his door. She swallowed hard. He wasn't in his room, either. Her feet slipped on the carpeted stairs, and she frantically grabbed at the railing to steady herself.

"Remain calm or you won't be able to help them," she whispered to herself. The hushed admonition resonated in the nighttime stillness that accompanied her down the remaining steps. *What if one of them has been shot?* Her fingers trembled as she clutched the newel-post.

She'd done her best to follow Marshall and Mr. Morley's instructions. They'd said she should come to them with any further problems, but they hadn't said what she should do if they couldn't be found. She considered waking one of the other men, but how could she determine who was loyal to Mr. Morley and who was loyal to Ted Uptegrove? Uncertainty gripped her as she slipped back through the dining room and into the kitchen. She couldn't sit tight and do nothing. Her thoughts raced. Perhaps Dr. Wahler would help.

Marshall would likely disapprove of her leaving the house, yet something was amiss, and to stay idle wasn't an option — at least not to her. After fastening her skirt and slipping into her shoes, she wrapped a shawl tight around her shoulders and tied it in a knot. She considered retrieving Aunt Thora's shotgun, but if she came across danger, it would take her far too long to load the thing. Besides, she doubted she had the intestinal fortitude to shoot anyone, even if she could load the gun. Better to leave the weapon at home and seek Dr. Wahler's assistance. She'd already lost far too much time.

Careful to watch her step and keep her ears attuned to the night sounds, Audrey hastened along the path. Fear proved a powerful motivator: She made it to Dr. Wahler's cottage in record time. Her heart pounded as she knocked on the door and waited. Dancing from foot to foot, she muttered, "Hurry! Answer the door!" She'd lifted her hand to knock once more when the door swung open. "Dr. Wahler. I'm so happy you're here."

His eyebrows furrowed and his lips drooped into a frown. "Where else would I be at this time of night?"

"I-I-I don't know." His curt tone and abrupt question surprised her. She obviously hadn't wakened him, for he was still fully clothed. He could have been over at the workers' quarters tending to an ailing laborer, but she didn't think to mention that before he waved her inside.

"Has Thora's condition worsened?"

She grasped his arm. "No. Aunt Thora is sleeping soundly, but I do need your help."

His frown returned, but he gave her his full attention while she explained there had been two men prowling outside of Bridal Fair. She detailed the concerns of sabotage and that she'd heard a gunshot only a short time ago. "I discovered that both Marshall and Mr. Morley have left the house. I fear one of them has been shot."

"I didn't hear any gunshot, and I've been up reading. I think you're probably imagining things." His voice faltered. "And the men you saw may have been Marshall and Mr. Morley — have you considered that possibility? I wonder if these claims of sabotage are really true or if Marshall and

Victor are in on this together."

Audrey's eyebrows furrowed and her mouth dropped open. "What? Why would you even think such a thing? That makes no sense at all. Mr. Morley is eager for the project to reach completion. That's why he's remained here at Bridal Veil."

"This idea of a rivalry between the investors on Jekyl Island and Bridal Veil could be nothing more than a scheme to divert attention from the truth." Instead of gathering his hat and medical bag, he sat down. "I know you're not familiar with the ways of men when it comes to money and business — few women are — but before you jump to the conclusion that someone is shooting at Marshall and Mr. Morley, I think you need to evaluate all possibilities."

Forcing a feeble smile, Audrey did her best to overlook his patronizing tone. If she hadn't needed his help, she'd have told him she wasn't interested in his lesson on the frailties of men and money. "There isn't time for evaluation. We need to go and find them. What you're suggesting makes no sense." She stepped toward the door and grasped the metal door latch.

Dr. Wahler didn't flinch — he didn't move at all. "What I'm saying makes complete sense. Mr. Morley could have plans to burn down the hotel and collect the insurance money — or perhaps he and Marshall have developed a scheme. After all, Marshall did appear at Bridal Veil rather conveniently. You're a kind young lady who can't even imagine what men will do where money and power are concerned."

A twinge of doubt leaped into her consciousness, but Audrey immediately pushed it aside. Neither Marshall nor Mr. Morley would ever do such a thing. Dr. Wahler could think the worst of them, but she wouldn't entertain such thoughts.

"What's all the noise out here?" Sadie stood in the doorway, the twins following close behind in their cotton nightgowns.

"Nothing at all, Sadie. Miss Audrey and I were merely having a chat."

The older woman frowned, obviously skeptical of the doctor's explanation. "Kind of late for a visit."

The twins scampered around Sadie, both of them hoping to join the visit, but their father stood and waved them back. "Back to bed. Come on now, girls."

While the doctor and Sadie herded the girls back to bed, Audrey slipped out the front door. If the doctor wasn't going to help, she'd find someone who would.

CHAPTER 29

Keeping to the path, Audrey did her best to avoid stepping on branches or making any noise. Twice she'd squeezed the tip of her nose between thumb and forefinger to avoid a sneeze. The thought of alerting a lurking prowler sent a chill quivering through her body, and she instinctively pulled her shawl tight around her shoulders. She'd be safer with one of the men, but there wasn't time to determine whom she could trust. Maybe she should awaken Irene. She didn't possess the strength of a man, but she could be trusted.

Audrey's breath caught and goose bumps raced down her arms as she approached the house and spotted a figure scurry to the side of the porch and then disappear into a curtain of darkness. Had Ted returned to the island? Cautiously, she stepped from behind a live oak and continued toward the back of the house. She longed to know who had been near the house and why. She silently weighed her options. To go alone could prove disastrous, yet she didn't want to forgo an opportunity to identify the prowler. She knew it wouldn't take long to rouse Irene, but the activity might awaken Aunt Thora. If so, she'd be forced to give up any hope of pursuing the shadowy figure.

"Why did you leave?"

A hand grasped her arm, and Audrey wheeled around. She slapped one hand to her mouth to keep a scream from escaping her lips. When she finally recovered from the startling encounter, she lowered her hand to her side. "I didn't hear you approach." She squinted into the darkness to see if someone else was there.

"I was worried when I returned to the front room and discovered you'd left while I was with the twins. I had planned to escort you home." Shadows and moonlight emphasized Dr. Wahler's frown. "You shouldn't have left without me." Audrey attempted to free her arm from his grasp, but he tightened his hold. "You need to go inside and stay there. Take my advice, Audrey — don't venture outside again tonight. Is that clear?"

There was a menacing tone to his voice that caused a fresh wave of fear to wash over her. She had hoped to escape inside, but unless he loosened his hold, she'd remain his captive. "I want to know what's going on. There's obviously more to all of this than you're telling me." She'd been unable to control the tremble in her voice.

A slow smile spread across his face, and she knew he'd detected her fear. "There's no need to be distraught, Audrey. Soon everything will be settled, and your life can go back to the way it was before Victor Morley and his wealthy friends decided to compete with the Jekyl Island investors."

Her thoughts raced as she tried to digest exactly what he'd said. Undoubtedly Dr. Wahler knew more than he'd said — likely much more. Perhaps the Jekyl Island investors had a sinister plan in place — a plan that included the ruination of the resort on Bridal Veil. And if Dr. Wahler knew of the plan, he was a part of the sabotage that continued to plague progress on the development. How could a doctor be party to something that would place the lives of others in jeopardy? One thing was certain: Dr. Wahler wasn't at all what he appeared.

"How could you be party to something so despicable? You took an oath to save lives, yet you've been willing to do just the opposite. Knowing the pain you've caused others, I don't know how you're able to sleep at night." This time, it was anger rather than fear that caused the tremor in her voice.

"I don't want you to think I'm some sort of ogre. My involvement in all of this is meager. I am a doctor, nothing more and nothing less. Men with much greater power and influence have orchestrated this entire affair." When he dipped his head closer, she leaned her shoulders away from him. "You don't need to be afraid of me, Audrey. You've been good to me and to my children. They adore you, and I don't want to see you come to any harm. That's why I warned you to stay inside the house for the remainder of the night." She made another attempt to wrest her arm from his grasp, but he shook his head. "First, you must give me your word that you're going to go inside and stay there."

She tightened her jaw and glared at him. "I'm not going inside until I find out exactly what's going on."

"I suppose there's no harm in your knowing. It's too late for you to do anything that will alter the plan that's already been set in motion. There will be a fire at the clubhouse here on Bridal Veil."

She stared at him, her senses numbed by disbelief. *This must be some sort of dreadful joke.* Soon he would laugh and tell her he'd been teasing. She waited until she could no longer bear the silence.

"I can't believe that you can so casually accept the devastation that a fire will cause on this island. If you have no concern for the clubhouse — and it's obvious you don't — think of the possibilities a fire could create. What if it spreads to the workers' quarters? With a little wind, a fire could spread throughout the island and destroy plants and animals alike. Live oaks that have been on this island for hundreds of years could be burned to the ground. Men who have families could be injured or die. Have you no sense of compassion?"

With his free hand, he raked his fingers through his hair. "There needs to be an end to this entire affair. If Morley's investors hadn't been so determined to rebuild after the explosion, this fire wouldn't have been necessary."

Her anger mounted. "How dare you blame this on the fact that the investors rebuilt after the collapse. I have no doubt you were at least partially responsible for that disaster, as well."

He shook his head. "You may not believe me, but I had nothing to do with that incident. It wasn't until Morley moved ahead with rebuilding the hotel that I was presented with an offer I couldn't refuse. An offer that will provide me with the means to enrich my daughters' future and move far away from here. My part in this is minimal."

Audrey couldn't believe her ears. "*Minimal?* If you've decided to align with these men and do the devil's work, then don't blame others. Have the courage to own up to your vile choices, for you'll live with the consequences for the remainder of your life."

"My only consequence will be a tidy sum of money." He straightened his shoulders and exuded his usual air of confidence. "No one will know of the part I've played in any of this."

"*I* know. Do you believe I'll stand by and say nothing?" Once she'd uttered the challenge, she wanted to take it back. If he would idly stand by and see the island destroyed, no doubt he'd want to have her silenced — permanently.

He inhaled a deep breath, and then sighed. "It would be your word against mine. If you continue to harbor such an idea, I will simply state that you must have taken an accidental fall and hit your head, for I found you wandering near my house in the middle of the night in a delusional state."

She didn't know if others would believe his explanation, but some probably would. After all, he was a doctor and well respected. "Where are Mr. Morley and Marshall?"

He shrugged. "Who can say where they are? You're the one who told me they weren't in their rooms. It only helps that they are out roaming the island. Victor will be held responsible for the arson, and further thoughts of building a resort on this island will disappear. He's the driving force, the one with enthusiasm and influence for this project. The other investors will survive their losses and move on to some other idea once he is out of the way."

The doctor's words chilled her. This man who had appeared to be a kind and caring doctor and a devoted father to his daughters was a cold and calculating ogre who cared nothing about the welfare and reputation of others. "If you'll turn loose of my arm, I'll go inside."

"Audrey." The inflection in his voice and the tilt of his head told her that he'd not fall for such a ploy. "I'm afraid the time to trust you has passed. You asked to know what was going on, and I've told you. I can't possibly leave you alone now. We both know you would try to find Mr. Morley and Marshall. You'd feel honor bound to warn them, and

I can't have that."

"What do you plan to do with me?" Hoping to appear undaunted, she squared her shoulders and met his dark gaze.

"Though I dislike the thought, I believe I'll be forced to tie you up until all of this has come to a satisfying end." As if deciding where he should take her, he turned his head and peered toward a stand of trees in the distance.

If she was going to get away from him, it would have to be now. She had hoped to escape into the house, but he'd positioned himself to block her entry. With all the force she could muster, Audrey propelled the toe of her work shoe into the doctor's shin.

When the doctor dropped his hold on her wrist to grab his ankle, Audrey ran toward the wooded area. The moon guided her path, but it also gave the doctor a clear view of her whereabouts. She may have injured his shin, but it didn't stop him from racing after her. The sound of his footfalls pounded in her ears. With his long strides, she feared he would catch up before she entered the stand of trees. She dared not take time to look.

Inhaling deep breaths, she pumped her arms and propelled herself forward until she finally entered the shelter provided by the immense trees. Beneath the foliage, she could easily hide from Dr. Wahler. She'd grown up beneath this canopy of live oaks, but the doctor was a stranger to the area. He would never find her. Nestled and protected by the low-lying branches, she waited and prayed.

When she was certain the doctor had moved in the opposite direction, she furtively moved toward the workers' cottages. She couldn't return home — that's what the doctor would expect. And if God answered her prayer, she would soon locate Marshall or Mr. Morley.

Careful to remain off the path and hidden by the underbrush and trees, Audrey picked her way toward the old slave quarters, the hooting of an owl in the distance the only sound she heard. Gathering her courage, she peeked from behind the mossy veil of a live oak. A breeze stirred and shadows danced across the trail like nimble elves.

Satisfied she wasn't being followed, Audrey stepped from the security of the trees. A branch snapped and she whirled around. A shadowy figure appeared and filled the path behind her. She stood frozen in place while fear pumped through her veins like ice water.

CHAPTER 30

Marshall didn't move — not an inch. His legs ached from holding his position, but the rustling sounds not far from where he was hiding forced him to remain alert and still. He'd selected this spot with care. From this position he could remain on the ground, completely hidden from sight, yet still see the path with clarity, a genuine advantage should he need to move quickly. On at least two separate occasions he'd heard movement. Perhaps it was a small animal, but he didn't think so, for it would have moved along by now.

Victor and Captain Holloway, using a small skiff, had departed for the mainland some time ago. If all went according to plan, they would return with help from the authorities. If not, Marshall feared what might happen.

A figure stepped from the stand of trees that arched the path — a figure wearing a skirt. He sighed, annoyed yet not surprised to see Audrey in the distance. A squirrel darted in front of her and captured her attention as he stepped from his hiding place. She wheeled around, and he rushed forward, capturing her from behind. When she let out a scream, he covered her mouth.

"It's me — Marshall! Quit screaming or you'll alert everyone on the island."

She turned and collapsed against his chest. "Marshall! I was so frightened."

"Good. You ought to be. I thought I told you —"

"Yes. Yes. I know what you said, but you don't understand, and you have to hear me out." Her breathing came hard and fast as he attempted to calm her. She leaned away from his chest and looked into his eyes. "Dr. Wahler is a part of what has been happening at the construction site. He's chasing me at this very moment. That's why I screamed." She glanced over her shoulder. "I thought he'd caught up with me."

"I know all about Wahler. Mr. Morley learned that the doctor accepted a sum of money to help sabotage the clubhouse." Marshall shook his head. He couldn't see all the details of her face, but he knew she was scared. "Look, I —" He stopped.

The bushes rustled, and before either of

them could utter another word, Dr. Wahler appeared in front of them holding a weapon that glistened in the moonlight. He pointed the gun at Marshall's midsection. "I do believe I've had more night air than I care for. Now it's time to see that neither of you causes any further problems."

Marshall reached around Audrey's waist and tucked her behind him. "If you're smart, Doctor, I believe you'll give up this idea. The island is swarming with local authorities and members of the militia from Biscayne. By this time, I'm sure they've already taken all of your cohorts into custody." When the doctor didn't appear convinced, Marshall continued. "I doubt you want to make matters worse for yourself. If you don't care about yourself, think about your daughters."

The doctor's derisive laughter echoed in the stillness. "I am protected by a friend who is powerful and far-reaching. He won't let anything happen to me. As for my daughters, you need not concern yourself. I plan to be at their side within the next hour. We'll be gone from this dreadful island by morning, and our lives will be much richer."

"If the friend you speak of is Johnson Radliff, you should know that he is already being dealt with and can provide you with no help at all."

Audrey nudged Marshall. "Johnson Radliff? Is he one of the Jekyl Island investors?"

"He isn't any longer."

Audrey gasped as she tried to peek around Marshall's shoulder. "I'm confused. Have the investors in Jekyl Island been involved in this attempt to ruin the clubhouse on Bridal Veil?"

He shoved her back. "No. I understand Radliff attempted to convince them that another resort would be the downfall of their investment in Jekyl Island, but they didn't agree. In fact, they were pleased with the construction here and even encouraged the new hotel that's being constructed in Biscayne. They decided competition would be good for everyone. The Jekyl investors are not enemies of Bridal Veil Island. Mr. Radliff was acting solely on his own. His part in this was based upon an old grudge he holds against Mr. Morley, while Dr. Wahler's part was purely financial. Isn't that correct, Doctor?"

Dr. Wahler continued to point his weapon at Marshall. "If you think all this talk is going to change anything, you're sorely mistaken. You underestimate me if you think I believe your story about the authorities coming over from Biscayne. I'm intelligent

465

enough to know that you're simply trying to save yourselves. Unfortunately for you, it won't work."

The words had barely passed his lips when Stuart Griggs appeared behind Dr. Wahler. The doctor waved the architect forward. "I'll make it worth your while to help me. Get that piece of rope lying over there in the bushes and tie up these two." Dr. Wahler waved the gun in Marshall's direction.

"Unfortunately for you, Dr. Wahler, I'm loyal to Victor Morley." As the doctor started to turn, Stuart knocked the weapon from his hand. Hitting the ground with a thud, the pistol discharged. Audrey screamed as Marshall pulled her to the ground, while Mr. Griggs grabbed Dr. Wahler around the neck and secured him in a chokehold.

Suddenly the woods were alive with the sound of pounding feet and shouting men. Uniformed militia appeared, with Mr. Morley following close on their heels. In no time, they'd taken Dr. Wahler into custody.

Marshall helped Audrey to her feet and steadied her. She was trembling, and while a part of him wanted to offer comfort, another was furious that she'd once again endangered her life. Would the woman never learn? Maybe taking her to Colorado wouldn't be a wise decision. Just thinking of all the trouble she might get into gave Marshall a headache.

"This is all a mistake. I'm not the one responsible for anything that's happened on this island. Where are Baker and Uptegrove?" Dr. Wahler shouted.

An officer stood on either side of the doctor, holding his arms. "No need to worry about those two. They were both arrested at the work site, carrying cans filled with kerosene. We got there in the nick of time, or that place would have gone up in blazes." The officer nodded toward Mr. Morley. "We found Mr. Morley's pocket watch in Uptegrove's jacket. Apparently they planned to leave it at the site so that he'd be blamed for the arson."

Dr. Wahler's eyes shone with panic as he looked over his shoulder at Audrey. "Tell them I have small children who need my attention. I can't go to jail." When she didn't respond, he attempted to wrest his arm from the policeman. "Tell them, Audrey!"

The doctor's voice ricocheted in the stillness, and Marshall pulled Audrey close to him. "She can't help you, Dr. Wahler. You've made your choices, and now you and your daughters will suffer the consequences."

"But it's not fair that they must suffer."

The doctor turned his attention to Mr. Morley. "You have children; surely you'll show some compassion. Tell them this is Johnson Radliff's doing, not mine."

Mr. Morley shook his head. "I feel great compassion for your children, but your crime can't go unpunished. You were willing to harm others without any thought for their future or their families. It will be up to a judge and jury to decide your fate. Save your arguments for them."

The doctor settled his frantic eyes on Audrey. "Please tell Sadie to take the children back to Atlanta. Would you help her send word to their mother's cousin in Charleston? Sadie can't write and will need help with the letter."

Audrey bobbed her head. "Yes, of course. I'll help the girls in any way that I can."

Mr. Morley gestured to Marshall. "I'll accompany the authorities back to Biscayne and return in the morning. I trust that you'll see Audrey safely home after you stop by Dr. Wahler's to speak with Sadie."

"You can count on it," Marshall said.

After breakfast the following morning, Marshall entered the kitchen and drew close to Audrey. "I wonder if I could speak with you outside for a few minutes before I head off for work." Samson curled around Marshall's legs and purred.

"Our Samson has truly proved himself to be an excellent judge of character." She swiped her hands down the front of her apron and glanced toward the other room. "Give me a moment to tell Irene." A few minutes later she returned from the dining room. "I promised Irene that I wouldn't be gone for long."

"I understand. This will take only a few minutes." He walked her to the door and held it open. "Why don't we walk down to that live oak you love so much."

She grinned. "You want to push me on the swing?"

"That might be a possibility, but first I want to discuss your inability to follow instructions."

Her smile faded. "What do you mean?"

He grasped her hand and guided her toward the huge tree. "We were both very tired last night, so I didn't want to bring this up. But as I recall, I distinctly told you to remain in the house and not take matters into your own hands. Isn't that correct?"

"Yes, but you didn't tell me what I should do if you weren't in your room when I needed your help. And Mr. Morley was gone, as well. What else was I to do?" She looked at him as if that resolved the entire topic.

"Well, I certainly wouldn't have advised you to go risking your life in search of me."

She assumed a frustrated expression. "I went to Dr. Wahler, seeking help, but he tried to convince me that you and Mr. Morley were involved in a scheme to collect insurance money. That the two of you were the ones attempting to set fire to the clubhouse."

"And what did you say to that?"

Her eyes shimmered in the morning light. "I told him I knew you were an honorable man and innocent of any wrongdoing."

Some of his anger melted away. "I'm glad to hear you came to my defense. Perhaps I should thank you properly." He stopped in front of the swing and drew her into his arms, enjoying the warmth of her body next to his. Lowering his head, he slowly captured her lips in a sweet, prolonged kiss.

"I believe that's the very best thank-you gift I've ever received." A smile lingered on her lips.

"I'm glad you enjoyed it, but there's one more thing we need to resolve." He grasped her shoulders and looked deep into her eyes. "I promised your father that I would take care of you, and I intend to keep my word.

But, if you ever pull something like this again, I'm going to turn you over my knee and give you the paddling of your life. And that's a promise!"

Her mouth formed the shape of an O as she stared back at him in surprise. Marshall would have laughed had the moment not been so serious. He reached up and smoothed back her errant curls.

"I can't lose you, Audrey. You've come to mean entirely too much to me. If you won't heed reason and follow instruction from those who know more than you, how can I take you to Colorado?"

She assumed a very proper stance and nodded. "I can be most obedient."

Marshall laughed. "I have yet to see that, but I suppose you can endeavor to prove it to me."

To his surprise, she moved in to stand very close. Wrapping her arms around his neck, she pulled his head closer. "I promise you I'll be a most obedient wife. I'll even seal it with a kiss." She rose up on tiptoes, and Marshall touched his lips to hers. She kissed him most ardently and then pulled back with a grin.

"You learn quite quickly," he said, feeling rather breathless from her touch.

She threw him a sly grin and started back

toward the house. "I've always been a fast learner. I just hope you can keep up."

During lunch, Mr. Morley returned from Biscayne. After they'd finished the meal, he asked Marshall and Audrey to join him in the parlor. "I hope the two of you managed to get a little sleep last night."

Audrey smiled. "I slept much better knowing that those men were in jail. I still can't believe Dr. Wahler was involved. He seemed such a gentleman when he first arrived. And the girls — my heart broke when I went to the cottage this morning to pen a letter for Sadie. They're so young and have already suffered the loss of their mother. To now have their father taken from them seems too great a loss for little children to bear."

Mr. Morley nodded. "Indeed. I only wish the doctor would have considered his daughters before agreeing to close ranks with Radliff, Baker, and Uptegrove."

Marshall leaned forward. "And what about that money clip? Did you discover who that belonged to?"

"Frank Baker. It seems what we thought was an *R* or *P* was a damaged *B*. Frank admitted he'd admired Johnson Radliff's money clip, so Radliff gave Baker a money clip of his very own — an expensive gift to further entice Frank."

"I still don't understand why Johnson Radliff was so determined to ruin the resort here on Bridal Veil." Audrey scooted back into the cushions of the overstuffed chair.

"Unfortunately, it all ties back to me and an incident I wasn't aware of until all of these events unfolded last night." Mr. Morley leaned forward and rested his forearms across his thighs. "Years ago I learned of an opportunity to invest in a mining project out West. I spoke to several wealthy bankers and investors about the possibility of getting involved, but none had any interest. The opportunity faded away — or at least I thought it had." He inhaled a deep breath and slowly released it. "I've now learned that one of the investors I had talked to mentioned the idea to Benjamin Radliff, Johnson's father. Benjamin took it upon himself to heavily invest in the mining project. He lost everything, and took his life. I'd heard that Benjamin had died but had never known the details. In any event, Johnson held me responsible for his father's death and was determined to bring me to ruination."

Audrey slowly digested what Mr. Morley had revealed. "But how did Baker and Uptegrove become involved in all of this?"

473

"Frank had previously met Johnson Radliff through his uncle Thaddeus. Johnson played on the fact that Frank's uncle expected him to work as a laborer when he could have simply supported him. Frank's greed and emotions took hold, and he was willing to betray his own uncle. It was the same with Dr. Wahler — they were all interested in a monetary payoff. It seems they thought we wouldn't rebuild when the explosion and collapse occurred, but when I convinced the investors that we should continue, Mr. Radliff became even more incensed. Thinking I'd give up if we couldn't meet our construction deadlines, he then convinced Baker and Uptegrove to use every opportunity to impede progress — which they did."

"And when that didn't work, he decided to go even further and completely destroy the project and frame you, certain the other investors would then give up," Audrey said.

Mr. Morley nodded his agreement. "I'm sure the others would have withdrawn. To begin anew would have been more of a delay than most of them would have accepted. I'm thankful the plan was thwarted. Otherwise, all of our work to build this area into a luxurious resort would have been in vain."

Audrey looked back and forth between Marshall and Mr. Morley. "How did the militia appear at the very time when they were needed?"

Mr. Morley raked his fingers through his hair. "We have Captain Holloway to thank for that. When Frank sent Ted Uptegrove into Biscayne on the pretext of locating another woodworker, Captain Holloway happened into a pub along the waterfront for a bite to eat. He spotted Ted talking to Radliff. When he overheard the two of them making plans, he remained out of sight and overheard their entire scheme. Had it not been for Captain Holloway, they might have succeeded."

Audrey shook her head. "All of these men were driven by their greed, but Dr. Wahler's part in this has proved the most disheartening." The two men listened as Audrey revealed the remainder of what Dr. Wahler had divulged to her the night before.

Mr. Morley closed his eyes. "It's sad to realize how far men will go in order to settle grudges."

Marshall clasped his hands together. "And also sad to see how easily they will betray those who trust them in order to line their pockets. These men thought money and power would make them happy. Others, like my father, look to alcohol. I'm thankful I discovered the Lord was what I needed to fill the longing in my heart. We can only pray that they'll see what is truly needed before it's too late."

Mr. Morley leaned forward. "Now, do I understand correctly that there is to be a wedding?"

Audrey held up her hands. "There has only just been an engagement. Marshall tells me that he's much too busy to have a proper honeymoon, so we will wait until the completion of your resort."

Morley considered this for a moment. "Then I should probably bring in more workers. There are houses to complete along with the clubhouse. We want to have everything in order for the grand opening date of January twenty-first."

"Then we can set the wedding for the twenty-second," Marshall declared with a smile. "That's just a few months away. Will that give you time to make all of the arrangements?" he asked, looking to Audrey.

She grinned. "I believe it will, Mr. Graham."

"I hope you will allow me to help," Mr. Morley interjected. "I know that you are at a disadvantage with both your mother and father gone. If you wouldn't be offended, I would like very much to offer my support — at least for the financial side of this affair. I'd be most pleased if you would agree to hold the wedding at the clubhouse. I will furnish you with the finest wedding meal and give you a send-off to rival that of any society affair."

Audrey's eyes widened and Marshall chuckled. "I think she likes the idea."

"I'm . . . I don't . . . well, I don't know what to say." Audrey shook her head. "I'm quite amazed."

"It's settled then. I'll notify Mrs. Morley and Mattie. I'm certain they can make arrangements for Mattie to come and help you in this endeavor."

Marshall grinned and could see that this pleased Audrey very much. He got to his feet. "Well, I'd best get to work if we're going to get this finished by the twenty-first of January. I have a feeling I'll be very busy after that."

CHAPTER 31

January 22, 1888

Her wedding day dawned as beautiful as any day Audrey had ever known. She hurried to her bedroom window and gazed out on the grounds below. The live oaks were resplendent in their expanded and gnarled branches, dripping Spanish moss in the same bridal veil fashion Audrey's grandfather had once discovered. Soon, Audrey would be veiled in a similar manner. She would walk down the aisle and pledge her life to the man who held her heart.

With a sigh, she leaned back against the window and smiled at the dress form that even now held her wedding gown. The dress, a gift from the Morleys, had arrived with Mattie — her dear friend. The gown's foundation of crisp white satin had been overlaid in many areas with the finest of Belgian lace. The bodice of the dress, although modest in cut, was extravagantly trimmed with seed pearls and intricate weavings of ribbon and lace. Audrey couldn't help but finger the neckline one final time. This was a gown intended for a princess, not a former boardinghouse owner.

She smiled and glanced to where a framed daguerreotype of her grandmother and Aunt Thora graced her dresser. The dear old woman had given Audrey the keepsake shortly before her death. It touched her that Thora, cantankerous and difficult as she could be, had thought of Audrey in her final moments.

The picture showed the two women much younger and happier. It had been taken before the war had stolen their innocence.

"I wish you both could be here," Audrey said, picking up the frame. She had been surprised to see how much she favored her grandmother in appearance. Audrey couldn't help but wonder if she'd also gotten her determined will from the woman. The thought brought a smile to her face.

"Maybe I inherited just a bit of my stubborn determination from you, Aunt Thora. Even if we weren't related by blood, we were surely related by spirit."

A knock at the bedroom door tore her thoughts from the past. "Come in," Audrey called and replaced the photo on her dresser.

Mattie came in carrying a tray. "I thought I'd bring you a bit of something to eat, and then we'll start dressing you."

A morning wedding was the tradition in these parts, as well as along much of the eastern seaboard. In fact, there were places where it remained illegal to marry after sunset. Still, in the warmth of the South, morning weddings were preferred.

"I doubt I can eat," Audrey said, putting her hand to her stomach. "I already feel like there are hundreds of butterflies nesting here."

Mattie smiled. "I expected as much, but a little bit of food might settle them down." She pulled back the napkin to reveal biscuits, jam, butter, and tea.

Audrey sat down at Mattie's instructions and began to butter a piece of biscuit. Mattie, meanwhile, picked up the hairbrush and began to comb through Audrey's hair.

"Good luck with that task," Audrey said as Mattie continued to work. "I tossed and turned all night. I even tried to wear a cap, but it was no use."

"Not to worry," Mattie declared. "I've worked with worse. I'll have you looking every bit the beautiful bride in no time. It's quite an honor, you know."

"What is?" Audrey asked between bites of biscuit and jam.

"To be the first to marry at the resort. Quite an honor. I heard that there are already a dozen or more weddings planned for the weeks to come. Word is spreading about the island and the owners' plans for the future."

"It's hard to imagine," Audrey said, shaking her head. "I suppose it should matter to me that I'm leaving it all, but honestly . . . this was never home."

"But neither was Pittsburgh. You said so yourself many a time." Mattie went to the dresser for hairpins and returned with a handful.

Audrey considered her words as Mattie began pinning the curls into order. "I know you're right. Pittsburgh wasn't really where I wanted to remain, but neither is Bridal Veil Island. I'm glad that Marshall is of the same mind. I'm looking forward to our great adventure in the West."

"But won't you miss the memories?"

"The memories will come with me, silly." Audrey put the biscuit aside and wiped her fingers on the napkin. "Who knows, maybe I'll have Marshall plant me a live oak wherever we finally decide to call home."

Mattie continued working and soon had Audrey's hair arranged in a fashionable crown of curls. "You will certainly carry the memory of this day with you." She handed Audrey the mirror. "What do you think?"

Audrey studied her reflection and shook her head. "It hardly looks anything like the woman I know to be me." She sighed. "I wish Father could have been here to give me away. I miss his boisterous laugh and the way he could affirm me just by glancing my way."

"No doubt he will be watching from heaven," Mattie said. "Come. Enough daydreaming. We have a wedding to prepare for."

"I, Marshall, take you, Audrey, to be my wife, to have and to hold from this day forward. . . ."

Audrey scarcely heard anything else after the word *wife*. She had waited a very long time for this day to come. Now, standing in the glorious ballroom of the Bridal Veil Island Clubhouse, Audrey felt as though all of her dreams had come true. Her elegant gown looked like something out of Godey's, her veil of delicate Belgian lace had been remade from a piece her grandmother had once owned, and the flowers were the most beautiful white and pink camellias money could buy.

There remained a tinge of sadness that her father and Aunt Thora had gone on to heaven and couldn't share the day with her, but Audrey felt confident that they were, as Mattie had said, looking down upon her.

"You're not listening," Marshall whispered, nudging her.

Audrey looked up, rather alarmed. "What?"

Her reply came so loud that the guests burst into laughter. She turned to see many of the island investors and their families smiling in amusement at her. She felt her face grow hot and was thankful for the veil that hid her from view. She hadn't expected to have such a crowd for the exchange of her vows, but Mr. and Mrs. Morley had convinced her that since it was the very first wedding at the resort, she should openly welcome the investors. Besides, Mrs. Morley told her in confidence that they were very generous folks, and no doubt Audrey and Marshall would benefit nicely from their kindness. An overflowing table of gifts in the breakfast room was proof of that.

Audrey hadn't said yes for that reason, however, but for another. Mr. Morley had been a blessing to her family, and she would do just about anything to please him and help him in his endeavors. That included selling him the remaining property on Bridal Veil Island. In return, he had insisted that Audrey and Marshall, as well as their offspring, would always be welcome on the island. Inviting his investors to the wedding would benefit his revenue and future, and for that she was more than happy to give her assistance.

"Well?" Marshall asked. "Should we just call this off?"

Audrey squared her shoulders and looked at the minister. "He's always so impatient. I'm ready now." She turned back to her soon-to-be husband. "I, Audrey, take you, Marshall, to be my husband, to have and to hold. . . ."

An hour later, still dressed in her bridal finery, Audrey listened in wonder as Mr. Morley offered a toast to the wedding couple.

"I have known this young woman for quite some time. She has proven herself to be a blessing to my family, and so on this day I am glad to honor her. Marshall has also made himself quite the benefit to me — well, to many of us."

"Hear! Hear!" someone called from the

gathering of wedding guests. There were rumbles of approval from even more people.

Audrey smiled and nudged closer to Marshall. "I think they like you."

"*Hmm,* I'm afraid they're only agreeing to hurry along the toast. They're most likely half starved."

"Well, certainly not for long," Audrey whispered, glancing at the extravagant arrangement of foods. The finest dishes had been prepared to entice the investors to see exactly what could be accomplished on this little Georgia island.

There were perfectly roasted game hens, ducks in honeyed orange sauce, platters of quail eggs, and poached eggs with hollandaise sauce. Fruits of every kind had been carved, balled, sliced, and arranged in such fashionable centerpieces that it seemed almost criminal to eat them. Other platters contained cheeses and pastries of every sort, as well as a variety of baked quiches, minced pies, and of course a beautiful five-tier wedding cake that had been especially prepared by the new French baker.

"And so I wish for this wonderful couple the blessings of a lifetime. May God give you happiness and tranquillity. May He give you the desires of your heart."

The guests rose to their feet and lifted

their glasses to Audrey and Marshall in cheers of agreement. Audrey turned to her husband and smiled.

"Including Colorado," she murmured.

He grinned and leaned closer. "And many offspring."

Audrey pulled back rather quickly, unable to hide her surprise. She could feel her cheeks grow hot and quickly looked away.

"It would appear the blushing bride and her handsome groom have something to add," Morley said in a teasing tone.

Audrey wanted to crawl under the table, and to her horror, Marshall got to his feet and turned to her. "I do have something to say," he announced.

She forced herself to look at him with an expression of adoring surprise. She could only pray he would refrain from saying anything that might further embarrass her. He glanced at her momentarily before speaking.

"I would like to offer a prayer of thanksgiving for the food, and then . . . eat."

The suggestion was well received, and Audrey breathed a sigh of relief as Marshall gave a brief blessing and then quickly rejoined Audrey at the table. He winked and handed her a slice of melon.

"Wife."

She took the piece and smiled. "Husband."

An hour later, the couple managed to slip away. It wasn't in keeping with the traditions that Mrs. Morley had planned, but Audrey didn't care. She preferred to make her own traditions, and when Marshall suggested a waterside walk, Audrey quickly agreed.

The sun was nearly full in the sky, and the day continued in a radiant beauty that Audrey would always remember. Glad to have left the long train of her gown back at the resort, she maneuvered without much difficulty when they left the path and headed to the water's edge.

"Will you miss it?" he asked as the water lapped softly against the shoreline.

"Oh, there are things I will remember fondly," she replied. "The trees, the water, the slower pace of life."

He laughed. "Well, you certainly haven't had that these past months."

"No, perhaps not," she said, "but there is something about this island that beckons one to rest."

Marshall pulled her closer and resumed their stroll. He led her away from the water and back up through the forested path, under the tranquil canopy of her beloved live oaks. Audrey could not imagine being any happier than she was at that exact moment.

When they reached her childhood swing, Marshall assisted her to sit. "Won't you miss this?" he asked, giving her a gentle push.

Audrey held on to the old rope and closed her eyes against the rhythmic sway. "I will miss this, but then I thought it might be possible to have someone . . . someone who is capable of working with wood and rope . . . someone who perhaps is trained in construction of houses and such, build me a swing in Colorado." She opened her eyes and cast a quick glance over her shoulder to see Marshall laughing.

"You already have jobs figured out for me, eh?"

"Just one or two."

The swing slowed and after a few moments, Marshall took hold of the swing and halted it all together. He pulled Audrey up and into his arms and wrapped her delightfully close against him. She felt emboldened, despite the fact that it was broad daylight, and clasped her hands around his neck.

Without waiting for him to initiate, Audrey leaned up on her toes and pressed her lips to his. Marshall needed no urging. He lowered his head and deepened the kiss. Audrey could scarcely draw a breath, but she didn't care. A lifetime of sorrows were lost forever in that moment.

However, as Marshall tightened his hold, Audrey could feel every inch of the spoon busks in the center front of her corset. They dug in painfully against her tender flesh until she could no longer stand the pain. "Ouch!" she squealed in protest.

Marshall was so surprised he dropped his hold. "Did I do something wrong?"

"It's just this . . . well . . . I have . . ." She felt her cheeks again grow hot. Lowering her face she whispered, "It's my corset."

Marshall's roaring laugh was not at all what she had expected. Nor was his action of pulling her along the path.

"What are you doing? Where are we going?"

"Back to our room at the clubhouse."

"Our room?" She looked at him oddly as she hurried to keep up with his long strides.

"You don't intend to do something about your corset out here, do you?"

She stumbled at his words and would have fallen flat, but he pulled her close and lifted her into his arms.

"You are positively scandalous, Mr. Graham. Imagine if our guests knew what you'd just said. Imagine if they saw you doing this."

His voice came low and husky. "Imagine if they knew what else I was thinking of doing."

Audrey giggled. "It's four flights up to our room. Do you intend to carry me all the way?"

He glanced at the distant building and stopped midstep. "We couldn't get a room on the second floor? How about we just make our way back to Bridal Fair? After all, everyone else is at the party. The house will be empty, at least for a time, and I'd only have one flight to climb."

"You forgot about Samson. He will be there," Audrey said seriously. "My guardian is quite protective. He would hardly tolerate our not including him in our . . . celebration."

Marshall laughed, set her down gently, and swatted her playfully on the bustled back of her gown. "Then the resort will have to do. Get a move on, Mrs. Graham. Four flights are a lot of stairs to climb. We might well have to rest on the way. Perhaps we can make it by nightfall."

Audrey giggled again and took hold of his arm. "The length of the journey doesn't matter, so long as you are at my side."

"Funny, I was thinking the same thing about you."

She leaned her head against his shoulder and sighed as Marshall put his arm around her waist. "Imagine that."

AUTHOR'S NOTE

Dear Reader,

The idea for this independent series was born when a reader attended one of our book signings for the Broadmoor series set in the Thousand Islands. She'd stated that now that we had written about the Thousand Islands, we should consider a series set on one of the islands along the southeastern coast of the United States. She mentioned both St. Simons Island and Jekyll Island as possibilities. We tucked away the idea, and when the time came to develop another series, we decided the rich history along the southeastern coastline would provide another unique setting for us.

As in most of our books, there are fictional characters and settings, as well as authentic people and places. While Jekyll Island is an amazing resort in the southeast, we decided we would enjoy creating our own island, just as we had in the Broadmoor series.

Bridal Veil Island is fictional, as are Bridal Fair and the Argosy River. However, we do make many references to Jekyll Island, so we wanted to point out that because our books are set prior to 1929, you'll notice that the spelling appears as "Jekyl" Island rather than "Jekyll" Island. It wasn't until the summer of 1929, at the instigation of club members, that the Georgia legislature passed a resolution to correct the spelling of Jekyl by adding a second "l." The resolution noted that the island had been named by General Oglethorpe in honor of his friend, Sir Joseph Jekyll, and the correct spelling had been corrupted by omitting the last letter. Thereafter, Jekyll became the proper spelling for the island.

The city of Biscayne is also fictional, although loosely based upon Brunswick, Georgia. However, never doubt that the live oaks are very real and exceedingly breathtaking trees.

In the second book of the series, *To Love and To Cherish,* you'll discover President McKinley makes a visit to both Jekyl Island and to Bridal Veil. The president did visit Jekyl Island, and it was, of course, the highlight of the season for those wintering on the island. Names of some well-known wealthy industrialists and entrepreneurs of the time period are sprinkled throughout the series, but the characters we hope you will come to know and love are the fictional ones that we have developed in our imaginations.

If you'd like to learn more about Jekyll Island, please visit their Web site http://www.jekyllislandhistory.com/ and consider a visit in the future. You'll fall in love with yet another part of our beautiful country.

We hope you'll enjoy this new series.

~Tracie and Judy

ACKNOWLEDGMENTS

No book is written without the help and support of many people. The entire Bethany House staff constantly amazes me with their creative talents and ability to make each book shine. Special thanks to editors Sharon Asmus and Charlene Patterson for their encouragement and assistance. It is a genuine privilege to work with such talented editors as well as every member of the Bethany House family.

Thanks to Mary Greb-Hall, Lorna Seilstad, and Mary Kay Woodford for their prayers, critiques, expertise, and friendship.

Thanks to Gretchen Greminger, curator of the Jekyll Island Museum, for her speedy replies and helpful responses to my questions.

And special thanks to you, dear readers, for your e-mails and letters of encouragement, your expressions of kindness and love, your prayers, and your eagerness to read each book.

Above all, thanks and praise to our Lord Jesus Christ for the opportunity to live my dream and share the wonder of His love through story.

~Judy

ABOUT THE AUTHORS

Judith Miller is an award-winning author whose avid research and love for history are reflected in her bestselling novels. Judy makes her home in Topeka, Kansas.

Tracie Peterson is the bestselling, award-winning author of more than 80 novels. Tracie also teaches writing workshops at a variety of conferences on subjects such as inspirational romance and historical research. She and her family live in Belgrade, Montana.

For more information on Tracie and Judith's books, including behind-the-scenes details and photos from the BRIDAL VEIL ISLAND series, check out the Writes of Passage blog at *writespassage.blogspot.com*.